Ruth Hamilton is th *er to the Living, With* *of Sorrows, Billy Lon* *he September Starlings, A Crooked Mile,* *ne, The Bells of Scotland Road, The Dream Sellers, The Corner House, Miss Honoria West* and *Mulligan's Yard*. She became one of the most popular authors who recreate the lives of the north-west of England. Ruth Hamilton was born in Bolton and has spent most of her life in Lancashire. She now lives in Liverpool.

For more information on Ruth Hamilton and her books, see her website at:

www.ruth-hamilton.co.uk

Also by Ruth Hamilton

WITH LOVE FROM MA MAGUIRE
NEST OF SORROWS
BILLY LONDON'S GIRLS
SPINNING JENNY
THE SEPTEMBER STARLINGS
A CROOKED MILE
PARADISE LANE
THE BELLS OF SCOTLAND ROAD
THE DREAM SELLERS
THE CORNER HOUSE
MISS HONORIA WEST
MULLIGAN'S YARD

and published by Corgi Books

A WHISPER TO THE LIVING

Ruth Hamilton

CORGI BOOKS

A WHISPER TO THE LIVING
A CORGI BOOK : 0 552 13384 1

First published in Great Britain

PRINTING HISTORY
Corgi edition published 1989

11 13 15 17 19 20 18 16 14 12

Set in 10/11pt Imprint

Corgi Books are published by Transworld Publishers, 61-63 Uxbridge Road, London W5 5SA, a division of The Random House Group Ltd, in Australia by Random House Australia (Pty) Ltd, 20 Alfred Street, Milsons Point, Sydney, NSW 2061, Australia, in New Zealand by Random House New Zealand Ltd, 18 Poland Road, Glenfield, Auckland 10, New Zealand and in South Africa by Random House (Pty) Ltd, Endulini, 5a Jubilee Road, Parktown 2193, South Africa.

Printed and bound in Great Britain by Mackays of Chatham PLC, Chatham, Kent

In loving memory of my parents.

Also for Allison Williams, a true friend
who is sadly missed.

Acknowledgements

Many thanks to: My two sons who tolerate me while I write; Diane Pearson for her patience and encouragement; Lyn Andrews who made me carry on through thick and thin; Dr Sonia Goldrein for her help, support and advice; the *Bolton Evening News* and the *Liverpool Echo* for factual guidance; the people of Bolton and Liverpool, my two home towns; friends and colleagues in Kirkby, especially those at Millbridge, Millbrook, Northfield and Springfield Schools.

'The fall of a leaf is a whisper to the living.'

English proverb

Contents

Part One

The Fall of a Leaf . . .

Chapter One: Beginnings

On 28 January 1940, I was born dead.

My mother, Nancy Byrne, after suffering for forty-eight hours on a horsehair sofa under the stairs, placed me as gently as she could on the peg rug in front of a cold range, then collapsed on to the stone floor beside me.

Fortunately for both of us, the widow from next door had, with the help of her two sons, managed to clear a way through the nine-foot drifts of snow, thus enabling Dr Clarke to put in a somewhat tardy appearance. This had been one of the worst winters in living memory and Bolton had ground to a virtual halt.

My mother, small-boned, fragile – no more than five feet tall, had produced an oxygen-starved infant whose head, swollen and blackened from long imprisonment in the birth canal, seemed larger than its body. Mrs Hyatt from next door, before busying herself with paper, kindling and coal, hastily bundled the motionless girl-child into a blanket which she then stuffed into a cardboard box.

Tom and Freddie Hyatt, her strapping fourteen-year-old twins, were dispatched upstairs, from whence, with much cursing and clattering, they fetched my mother's bed. The infant remained ignored in its box, the doctor's main concern being for the state of Nancy Byrne's health, for the lower part of her body had lost all feeling.

It was therefore a very shocked Tom Hyatt who heard my first mewlings, who stared down into my makeshift coffin, his mouth agape, Adam's apple bobbing wildly as he tried to attract the doctor's attention.

I was snatched from the box and carried through to the scullery, where Dr Clarke cleared the obstructive matter from my throat, permitting me to express my anger at the incompetence with which I was surrounded.

I believe that my character was formed almost completely in those first few moments of life. My fear of small spaces, my attitude to authority, my tendency not to trust or depend, all these were born with that furious ear-splitting scream.

I was given to my mother, who smiled wanly and said, 'Eeh, she looks about six months old already.' To which Dr Clarke replied, 'Well, she must weigh at least eleven pounds – you're very lucky, both of you.'

My mother did not feel lucky. Firstly, she was in no two minds that my father had set his heart on a boy. Secondly, this infant did not look at all normal – in fact, it was ugly to the point of revulsion. And lastly, most importantly, would she, Nancy Byrne, ever walk again? From the waist down she had no sensation at all; it was as if she had been cut off at the middle.

I was a bitter disappointment to her. Had I been pretty, or even manageable, then I might have been forgiven for being female. But there I was, bald and blue-black about the face, screaming incessantly, a hideous reminder of the uselessness of her lower limbs.

She handed me to Mrs Hyatt. 'Here, you take her home, love. I can't cope with her while I'm this road. Give her a bottle or something.'

So I spent the first two or three weeks of my life at number 22, while, in the kitchen of number 20, my mother drank Mrs Hyatt's beef tea and concentrated on her toes.

Her two short white legs lay stiff and still on top of the army greatcoat that served as quilt for the bed and she stared at them for days on end with never a word for the nurse who came in daily or for Mrs Hyatt who fed her, washed her, emptied her bedpans.

Now that the thaw had set in, visitors began to arrive, aunts bearing black-market fruit and cigarettes, uncles with bottles of stout and words of encouragement. They visited me too, declared me to be a fine lass, but still my mother would have none of me.

By the middle of February, Nancy Bryne's self-hypnosis began to pay off. She moved first her toes, then her feet, after which happy event she set about the business of learning to walk again. This proved a painful process, because her spine had been damaged during confinement, but her determination was so great that she was fully mobile by the time I was two and a half weeks old.

She collected me from next door, carried me home in a hand-knitted shawl and, with her usual deliberation, began to know and love me. As she explained to me in later years, 'You see, lass, you can only do one thing at a time. The road as I looked at it, I had to get me legs back. If I'd have never got me legs back, I'd have given you away. Better a foster Mam with legs than a real Mam stuck in a bed or on a chair for the rest of her life. And I didn't want to be looking at you and blaming you for me legs, 'cos it weren't your fault. But human nature, aye, mine included, being what it is, I would have blamed you in a way. Anyroad, all's well that ends well as they say.'

My father, far from being disappointed, was delighted with his daughter. As a regular soldier fighting, as he put it, 'for King, country and a pair of bloody boots as 'll fit', he was home infrequently, but he lavished me with love, attention and such gifts as could be obtained during those war-torn years.

And it was a terrible war, both inside and outside our house. While German planes droned their nightly song overhead, my mother, who would go nowhere near the air-raid shelter in the back yard, would sit in the darkened kitchen clinging to me under the table, a rolled-up *Bolton Evening News* clutched tightly in her hand. When the all-clear sounded, she would creep out furtively, turn up the gas mantle and begin her own war on the cockroaches, battering them to pulp with the paper and crunching them into the flags with the wooden soles of her clogs.

Thus, having learned early on to count cockroach corpses, I was quite numerate by the time I began to attend nursery class at the age of three. Also, once my mother had recovered from her disappointment at my not being a boy, she determined to make the best of things and began the task of teaching me to read and write at a very early age. I was, as a result, precocious and very advanced in comparison to my classmates at All Saints nursery.

The mills were still turning out cotton in spite of the war and my mother returned to her work as a doffer and spinner just after my third birthday, abandoning me to the tender mercies of the Sisters of the Cross and Passion, who had little patience with a waif as maladjusted as I seemed to be. I had been baptised by Father Sheahan in Mrs Hyatt's scullery a few days after my birth, and was therefore designated Catholic, although my mother no longer practised her religion.

Until I was three, my world had been very small. It contained me, my mother, a father who visited occasionally, our immediate neighbours, an aunt or uncle who would drop by from time to time and the parish priest whom I hated with an unreasoning venom known only to small children. I disliked his long black cloak, which terrified me, especially when the wind shaped it into something unspeakable and nightmarish. I loathed his silly biretta which sat on his large head like, as my mother put it, a pea on a drum. Most particularly, I objected to his big red hands reaching down, patting me on the head, or, worse still, lifting my chin so that I had to look into his grey, lifeless face. The face shaped itself into a smile sometimes, a smile that never reached the eyes.

When my world was made larger, I noticed the same unamused eyes in the faces of the nuns and although I didn't recognise it yet, my quarrel with Catholicism had begun.

* * *

Miss Best was not a nun. She wore proper clothes and her legs showed. Also her eyes smiled, but not all the time. They were not smiling now. 'Annie Byrne, get into your cot. Now – this minute!'

'No.' I stamped my new red clog on to the polished floorboards. It was daft, going to bed every afternoon. I had never been to bed in the afternoon before. Bed was for night, not for daytimes. The cots were set out in rigid rows, canvas structures on folding metal frames, each with a pink or blue blanket. Under every pink or blue blanket lay a child, round eyes popping as they stared at me, the sole dissenter.

'Come on now, Annie, take off your clogs.' For answer I kicked out at her, narrowly missing a lisle-stockinged leg.

At that moment the door was thrown open and there stood Sister Agatha, headmistress, despot, monarch of all she surveyed. From her right hand there dangled a short leather whip which she was tapping gently against her thigh through the thick folds of her voluminous habit.

'What have we here?' Her Irish voice held none of the pleasant lilt common to most of my own immigrant uncles.

Miss Best all but curtseyed. 'Oh . . . Sister . . . it's just that little Annie doesn't like to lie down in the afternoon.'

After a bone-chilling silence, the nun spoke, her voice cracking with anger. 'Doesn't like? Doesn't like, is it? Well, we'll just have to see about that now, won't we? Get into that cot now, this instant, you bold girl.' I said nothing, but some devil in me made me drag my eyes from the whip, forced me to stare up at her, straight into those icy eyes.

'Did you hear what I said? You're not deaf as well as stupid, are you? Did you hear me, girl?'

'Yes.'

'Yes, what?'

Miss Best put a hand on my shoulder. 'Yes, Sister. You must say yes, Sister.'

'Yes, Sister,' I muttered through clenched teeth.

Sister Agatha drew Miss Best aside. Although my heart was pounding in my ears, I caught snatches of their whispered conversation.

'. . . very advanced, Sister . . . more like a six year old . . . doesn't need the sleep . . .'

'They must conform, Miss Best . . . grow up delinquent . . . mother lapsed . . . child too big for her boots . . .'

It looked to me as if Miss Best was getting into trouble and it was all my fault. Quietly, I slipped off my clogs and lay flat on the cot, pulling the blanket high over my head. The two women stopped talking. I knew they were staring at me, for I could feel the chill of the nun's eyes as they swept over my body.

This was my first remembered encounter with compromise. Many more were to follow, but this became, for me, a point of reference. For a long time afterwards, whenever I had to relinquish my principles in order to keep the peace, I would say I was 'doing my Best', for Miss Best was the one who taught me to make room for people, to consider others as well as myself.

Fortunately, I knew nothing of what lay in store for me. I would be 'doing my Best' for many years to come.

We war babies grew up quickly. Each day, we set off for school, gas masks swinging from our shoulders, stopping off at Connie's corner for a ha'porth of cocoa and sugar, scurrying into the playground to stand in regimented rows beneath the eagle eye of Sister Agatha, then lining up once more for our daily dose of cod liver oil and orange juice.

I became outwardly docile, realising quickly that I must have no opinion, voice no objection, because if I did, I would invoke the wrath of my elders and invite the alienation of my peers. Nevertheless, I established myself as pack leader, organising playtimes, inventing games of dragons, of princes and princesses in which I always played the chief role.

Just after my fourth birthday, I was moved into the infants' class because of my ability to read and write. I was heartbroken, not so much because I had been placed with a nun, for Sister Immaculata was near-human, the exception that proved the rule, but because I had to leave behind my beloved Miss Best. However, I settled quickly into the new routine, enjoying the challenge of learning, soaking up like a sponge everything that was on offer.

The sirens often sounded as we left our school. They were part of our lives and we never hurried when they began their raucous wailing. Even at three and four years of age we were responsible for ourselves, negotiating main roads, scurrying across trolley and tram tracks, making our own way home through mazes of terraced streets and cobbled entries.

I never went straight home, but stayed with Mrs Hyatt till my mother came back from the mill. But one afternoon, as I passed my own house on my way to Mrs Hyatt's, I noticed that our front door was open. I heard voices and muffled crying coming from within, so I sat on the step and listened. It had been my experience thus far that anything worth hearing would never be spoken in front of me.

So it happened that I learned of my father's death as I sat on a cold doorstep with nobody to comfort me. It was a chilly September afternoon in 1944. I stared up our sloping street towards Derby Road, remembering the times I'd watched my father running down faster and faster towards me, how, when he had reached me, he would pick me up high in the air, tossing me about, making me squeal and giggle. I recalled the smell of him, tobacco and beer, sometimes whisky.

I had always snatched the Glengarry from his head, cramming it down on to my own yellow curls as he sang 'A Gordon for Me'. He would never come again. Never. My Daddy was dead. My Daddy who always took me to the lions in the middle of Town, under the big clock.

No, he couldn't be dead, not my Daddy. He'd be there with the lions. It was a mistake. Grown-ups were always making mistakes.

As fast as my legs would carry me, I was up and away to the top of Ensign Street, down Derby Road towards the town. The sirens were screaming again, but I never heeded them, so intent was I on reaching my goal. Blindly I ran past the deserted market place and through Moor Lane, stopping only to catch my breath as I reached the Civic Buildings.

The Crescent was empty of people; no vehicle moved and though dusk had begun its descent, not a single lamp was lit as I climbed the Town Hall steps towards the lions. I sat, shivering on the stone slabs waiting for my father. Opposite, I could see the memorial to those who had lost their lives in the previous war, the war during which my parents had been born.

Somewhere, bombs were falling, but I was used to that; I had never lived in a world at peace. When the bombers had finished vomiting their contents on to Manchester, a thin, cold drizzle began to fall, wetting me through to the skin within minutes. A warden found me there sometime during that night, but I was not grateful to him, for even in my weakened state I fought to maintain my vigil.

'I'm waiting for my Dad,' I insisted.

'Nay, lass. Tha can't stop 'ere. Gerry'll be back, more than likely.' He picked me up and I hit him full in the face with a clenched fist. 'I'm stopping. I'm waiting for my Dad. They said he's dead, but he's not . . . , he's not. He always comes to the lions. Please let me stay, Mister . . .' But the man was already carrying me down the steps to a waiting policeman who shone a dimmed torch into our faces.

'I reckon she's bloodied tha nose, then, 'Arry.'

'Aye, she 'as that. But she's in a fair state, wet through an' all. Tha'll 'ave to tek 'er 'ome.'

'Where dost live, lass?' the policeman asked.

'I'm not telling you.'

'Oh, well then.' The policeman removed his helmet and scratched his head. 'Well, in that case, we'll 'ave to tek thee to t' Cottage 'Omes.'

The Cottage Homes? That was for children that nobody wanted, that had no mams and dads. Still, if I hadn't got a dad, I might as well go and live at the Cottage Homes. But then, if I did, I might never see my Mam again. And I did have a Dad. I did.

'Number 20, Ensign Street,' I muttered.

'And what's yer name?'

'Annie Byrne.'

'How old are you?'

'Four and a half and a bit.'

'By. Tha's a clever lass for four and a half and a bit. What are you doing stuck out 'ere with old 'Arry an' a couple o' pot lions?'

'I've told you once. I'm waiting for my Dad.'

'Right. Well where's yer dad comin' from?'

I thought hard before answering, 'Italy, I think.' The two men looked at one another over my head before Harry handed me to the policeman, whispering as he did so, 'They've told 'er 'e's dead.'

I stiffened in the policeman's arms. 'They haven't told me nothing. They never tell me nothing. But I heard them saying it.'

There was a lot of rain by this time and the policeman's muslin-draped torch gave little light, so I wasn't sure that I saw tears running down his face. He raised his head, craning his neck towards the sky. 'Sod you,' he shouted and his voice was high and strange. 'Sod you bloody bastards.'

Normally, I would have been fascinated by such interesting language, but by this time I was too tired, wet and worried to wonder anew about the anomalies of grown-ups and their rules, one law for them and another for me.

When we finally reached home, my mother was in a state of total hysteria, laughing and crying at the same time, clutching at my hands, slapping me for my naughtiness, then hugging me in her relief. I was shocked to the core when Mrs Hyatt got up from her chair, crossed the room with her waddling gait and hit my mother very hard across the face. I could not understand this at all.

But I was given little time to wonder, for they stripped me off and wrapped me in a warm blanket, then we sat, my mother and I, the policeman and Mrs Hyatt in the four chairs that surrounded the kitchen table.

My mother, after drawing several shuddering breaths, said, 'Annie, your Dad's not coming home any more.' The gaslight flickered and I stared at the spluttering mantle, trying to fix my attention on something – anything other than what was being said to me.

The policeman took my hand in his. 'Tha'rt a big, fine lass, Annie. Yer dad 'as died for 'is country. When yer older, you'll be proud of 'im.'

'Who killed him?' I asked, of nobody in particular.

'Why, the Nazis, luv – the Germans,' answered the bobby.

'The ones that dropped the bomb on Emmanuel Street and killed Rosie Turner?'

'Aye, lass.'

'The ones that dropped the bombs tonight?'

'That's it, Annie, They're the ones.'

A terrible anger rose in me, heaving in my throat like vomit. I fought for breath, pushing away the hands that reached for me. Something in my chest swelled and swelled until I felt I would burst. I had to do something bad, something really bad to let the anger out. Jumping up from the table so quickly that my chair fell away, I flew to the window and threw back the blackout.

Staring up into the rain-filled night sky, I screamed at the top of my voice, 'Sod you bloody bastards.' And my mother, who would normally have berated me for such gross misconduct, pulled me into her arms, pressing her tear-soaked face against mine.

'That's right, lass,' she sobbed. 'You tell 'em.'

Chapter Two: Neighbours

Apart from the war ending, two things of note happened during the sixth year of my life. Firstly, old Mr Higson from the end house, number 30, died on the outside lavatory. We children received this news with a mixture of sadness and revulsion, the former because he had been kind to us and the latter because we didn't think anyone should die with his trousers down.

The second event, which was not completely unconnected with the first, was that my mother started courting.

Mr Higson's youngest son, Eddie, who had been a prisoner of war for several years, was allowed out of the Infirmary to attend the funeral. Thin almost to the point of emaciation, he went with his older brothers to thank the neighbours for their kind thoughts and floral tributes. His appearance appalled and fascinated me. A cadaverous head was not improved by flesh of a yellowish shade which seemed to be stretched like parchment over forehead and chin, only to darken in great shrivelled hollows where cheeks should have been. His eyes were sunken too, small navy-blue dots set well back in circular craters of bone. The nose was prominent, wide-nostrilled and with a gristly bump near the top, while his lips were thin almost to the point of total absence, giving the mouth the appearance of a slit in the fold of some ageing newspaper. This whole death's head was crowned by an incongruously vigorous mop of crinkly dark hair, all flattened and shiny with grease.

Eddie Higson had never been married. My mother immediately pitied him for his poor condition and took to visiting him at the hospital to which he had had to return immediately after the burial of his father.

During these visits, for which my mother prettied herself up with powder and rouge, I was left with Mrs Hyatt who voiced her disapproval of the affair regularly – not to me, but to her two sons. Freddie, the elder by ten minutes or so, made little response to his mother's mutterings, while Tom, who always seemed to feel a degree of responsibility towards me, would whisper, 'Hush, Mam. Not in front of the lass.'

I was fond of Tom. He always brought me sticks of barley sugar on a Friday when he got his wages and sometimes, when I was daydreaming, I imagined that Tom might be my uncle. Not my Dad, nobody could replace my Dad, but Tom was the best uncle anybody might wish for.

I sat in Mrs Hyatt's rocker by the fire, sucking my stick of barley sugar. Mrs Hyatt took a rice pudding from the range oven and banged it down on to the table between the two men.

''E's got sly eyes. I never did like 'im. When yer dad were alive, 'e never liked 'im neither.'

'Listen, Ma,' drawled Freddie. 'Me Dad never liked nobody, specially when he got near the end. People with cancer isn't noted for their sense of humour.'

Mrs Hyatt clipped Freddie round the ear with the oven cloth. 'Bit of respect when you talk about yer dad. And it were nowt to do wi' cancer. It were to do with . . . well . . . with other things.' She cast a furtive glance in my direction, then mouthed a few silent words at Freddie and Tom.

'That was all just talk, Mam. Nothing was ever proved,' said Tom. 'And mind what you say. Little pigs have big ears.'

I reacted not at all, pretending to concentrate on the sticky sweet at I stared into the fire. Tom went on, his voice almost a whisper, 'Nancy Byrne has her own life to lead now. You can't go telling her who she must go out with and who she mustn't. And she knows nothing about . . . all that, I'm sure she doesn't. What's more, that tongue of yours will get you into trouble one of these days, mark my words. What you're saying about Ed . . . about you-know-who is nothing short of slander. Aye, you'll choke on that tongue, you will.'

Mrs Hyatt bristled visibly, her back straightening, her head moving slightly from side to side as she spoke. 'Slander, you say? Slander? Why do you think he joined up so bloody quick, eh? 'E's no flaming 'ero, I can tell you. And who's to speak up now? Aye, answer me that one – if you can. With 'alf Emmanuel Street flattened and them as was involved cold in their graves? Oh aye, it's all forgotten now, isn't it? But I've not forgot, the dirty evil bast. . .'

'Be quiet, Mother.' Tom stood and raised his hand. 'Hush your noise. Give the man the benefit of the doubt.'

'And what about 'er?' Mrs Hyatt jerked a thumb in my direction.

'I'll watch out for her,' answered Tom.

'Aye, well. You'd best grow eyes in t' back of your 'ead, then.' With this final remark, Mrs Hyatt grabbed her coat from its peg and, picking up a tall white jug from the dresser, announced her intention to go to the outdoor licence for a drop of stout.

A few minutes after her departure, Freddie went out to the air-raid shelter – which he now used as a pigeon house – to tend his prize birds, leaving Tom and me as sole occupants of the kitchen.

I gazed into the fire once more, wondering yet again if I could trust my instincts and place my faith in Tom. Most grown-ups got mad if you asked questions. Those who didn't get mad treated you as if you were soft in the head or something. But Tom never got mad with me. Would he now? There was only one way to find out. Without turning my head, I asked, 'Is he a bad man, Tom?' The clock ticked noisily.

'I don't know, Annie.' This was promising. Adults were usually so positive, so sure of their ground – an admission of indecision could be a step in the right direction.

'What did he do?' I asked carefully.

He came slowly round the table, then squatted down on his haunches in front of me. 'Annie, love – I can't answer your questions. But I will say this to you. If anything ever worries you – anything at all – you come straight to me. Right?'

'Right.'

'You know I was there when you were born. If it hadn't been for me . . . well, never mind all that now. You're almost a little sister to me, Annie. If anything ever happens to you . . . if anybody . . . well, you just come straight to your Uncle Tom.'

'I will.'

'No matter what?'

'No matter what, Tom.'

Footsteps in the narrow lobby made him rise to his feet. My mother, flushed and smiling, burst into the room, her eyes sparkling as she cried, 'He's coming home Friday, Tom. Ooh, I can't believe it. He's near ten stone again – he was only seven and a half when he got back. I'm that excited – we must have a party. And guess what, Annie?'

I stared at my radiant mother as she threw her handbag down on to the table and ripped off a white cotton glove to reveal a narrow gold band with a small shining stone set into its centre. 'Your Mam's engaged – you're going to have a new Dad, Eddie's going to be your Dad. Isn't that great news?'

I looked from Tom to my mother, then back to Tom.

'Well? Have you nothing to say, Annie?' she cried.

My hands were shaking as I rose to my feet and I gripped the fireguard tightly as I positioned myself next to Tom, leaving the table as a barrier between us and her.

'He will not be my Dad,' I heard myself say. My mother, seeming to deflate visibly, sank down on to one of the ladder-backed kitchen chairs.

'No, I know he won't be your real Dad, but he'll be your new Dad.'

'NO. NO. HE WON'T.' I stamped my foot on the hearthrug. 'You are choosing him, Mam. I'm not. If I wanted a new Dad, then I'd choose my own. And I don't want one, anyway. Especially him. He's ugly and . . . and . . .' I groped for words, then Mrs Hyatt's statement, after echoing in my head for a split second, fell out of my mouth. 'He's got sly eyes,' I announced.

The silence that followed was nearly deafening. My mother looked almost pleadingly at Tom, but he turned his back to reach a pipe from the rack to the side of the range.

'What can I do with her, Tom?' For answer, he shrugged his shoulders.

'She can't run my life for me. I'm too young to be . . . well, you know, to be without a husband. I need to settle down again and I know he's right for me. And I might not get another chance, being as I've got An . . . being as I'm not on me own.'

Tom stuffed tobacco into the bowl of his pipe before turning to face her. 'It's a bit soon for the lass, Nancy. Billy's not that long gone, maybe the child needs to serve out her mourning.' The implication that Nancy herself was not mourning did not miss its mark.

'You can't mourn forever, Tom,' she said quietly. 'And kids gets over things quicker than what we do. She'll get used to him.'

Tom stared at my mother for some time before answering, 'If you say so.' Whereupon he turned to light a spill at the fire.

'You don't like him, do you, Tom?'

'I've no feelings either way, Nancy. You know him better than I do, though I daresay there's folks round here as have known him longer. Anyway, what should you care about the opinions of a lad not yet twenty?' He applied the spill to his pipe, puffed for several seconds then swung round to face her once more.

My mother turned her gaze on me. 'You coming home then, Annie?'

I kicked at the rug with the toe of my clog.

Tom nudged me gently. 'Get on home then, lass.'

I made up my mind there and then that should my mother become Mrs Eddie Higson, then I would move in with Tom, Freddie and Mrs Hyatt. It seemed a simple enough solution. If my mother loved Mr Higson more than she loved me, then I would go and live among people who really cared for me.

It had not yet occurred to me that I would not be allowed to put this plan into action. But, having found Tom, the one adult in whom I could place a measure of trust, I went home if not happy then at least comforted, believing I had discovered some if not all of the answers.

Chapter Three: My Immortal Soul

Like many ugly babies, I had developed into an acceptably attractive child. Although I outstripped my peers by a good couple of inches in height, a fact that often made me a target for Sister Agatha's wrath (since I was the most visible victim in my class), I was blessed with an abundance of soft yellow curls and wide-spaced green eyes. Other assets included two sets of fine strong limbs that made me an adequate competitor in games involving either sex and a respected adversary when it came to combat of any kind.

Of course, like most females, I was not satisfied with my appearance. My mouth was too big for my face, my nose silly, small and freckled, my knees were lumpy, making the long calves appear thin, while my elbows always protruded at odd angles from the few skimpy dresses I owned.

Nevertheless, I was reasonably at peace with myself, having established my leadership at school, having learned to live with, if not to like, the various compromises required by the adults who dominated my life.

My mother was fond of me; of that I was fairly sure. During the long years of war we had shared a bed, shared our hiding place under the solid squareness of the kitchen table, we had divided equally between us our odd meals of dried egg and blackened potato. We had also pooled our fears, my mother often turning to me with her worries, making me far older than my years.

Our dependence was mutual; often I played the role of comforter when she returned from long fruitless hours of queuing for food or when, in the dark hours, she would turn to me in her loneliness, her tears wetting my pillow as well as her own. For her part, she nursed me through those black days after my father's death, never once leaving my side until I had wrung myself dry of grief. 'We must stick together now, Annie,' she would say. 'You're all I've got and I m all you've got.'

I began to plan our future, seeing it mapped out before me with all the clear simplicity of a five-year-old mind. 'I'll never leave you, Mam. When I'm fifteen, I shall be a hairdresser and we'll get a shop. You won't have to work in the mill any more and I shall keep your hair pretty for you.' And she would smile her sweet sad smile, looking all the while into the flickering flames of our ill-fed fire, wondering, probably, about her own future.

She was only twenty-seven when my father died, a beautiful, tiny woman with Titian curls, grey-green eyes and the sort of walk that made men turn and stare when she passed by. I knew that my mother was pretty, but I never thought of her as young or marriageable. We had had a Daddy, my Daddy. Never in my wildest imaginings did I think that she might want, or need, to replace him.

So when she turned to Eddie Higson, she turned away from me, threw away all my carefully thought out plans, dismissed me almost, from her thoughts, from her heart and from her life. She stopped loving me, stopped caring about me. And no amount of cajoling or bribery on her part or on his could alter my very set opinion.

I became louder, more boisterous at school, seeking trouble, accepting my punishments almost gladly, because I was no longer lovable and deserved to be punished. My teachers, alarmed at this change in me, sent for my mother.

'She has gone wild, Mrs Byrne. We have all tried.' Sister Agatha raised her eyes ceilingward, her hands rattling the large rosary that hung from her waist, because she held no whip at this moment. She never held the whip when a parent visited. 'We in the convent have offered umpteen decades to implore our Blessed Lady to intervene.' She turned her steely gaze on me. 'But nothing at all seems to be setting this . . . this poor child back on to the right path.'

My mother squirmed in her chair, putting me in mind of Willy Walford from the Cottage Homes, an orphan boy who came for his lessons with his head shaved against the nits. He was a squirmer, was Willy Walford. And here was my mother carrying on the same way, the only difference being that she was bigger and had a full head of hair.

I knew I was getting angry. My mother might not love me any more, but I didn't want old Sister Nasty Knickers (as we called her on the sly) making my own Mam squirm like somebody from the orphanage. I fixed my gaze on the statue of the Immaculate Conception with the blue-glassed night light burning at its feet.

'Have you anything to say for yourself, Annie Byrne?'

I shifted my eyes towards the black-robed figure which, silhouetted against the window, looked like a grim monster from hell.

'No,' I replied, my voice clear and high.

'No, what?'

'No, Sister.'

The nun came round the desk and stood in front of me and my mother and although this left but a few inches of space between her and us, I determinedly held my ground, though my mother did scrape her chair back a fraction, which made me even more angry and impatient.

'Did you or did you not write those . . . foul words on Sister Immaculata's blackboard?' There was a long silence.

'Answer the Sister, Annie.' I felt very annoyed with my mother. Although her accent was never strong and her speech was virtually free of the usual Bolton colloquialisms, here she was, trying to talk dead posh just because we were in old Nasty Knickers' office. My mother was afraid of Sister Agatha! Well, so was I, but I wasn't going to let it show.

'Yes. I wrote them.'

Sister Agatha's lip curled into a snarl. 'Then I suggest

you learn to spell, girl. The undergarment you mentioned in your scribblings begins with a K. And my name, young lady, is Sister Agatha.'

My mother's face was bright crimson by this time. No doubt she had already been informed that I had inscribed on the blackboard 'Sister nasty nickers is a wicked old wich.' It had only been for a dare anyway. Peter Bates had promised me his biggest, silverest bolly-bearing if I'd do it. And I'd done it, while Peter Bates had not, as yet, fulfilled his side of the bargain. I would deal with him later. Even if he did have irons on the soles of his clogs, while I had only rubbers on mine, I'd deal with him. I knew where to kick the boys to make it hurt.

'Come on now, girl. Do your catechism,' Sister Agatha was now saying. 'Show your Mammy that we've taught you something, at least. Who made you?'

'God made me.'

'Why did God make you?'

'God made me to know Him, love Him and serve Him in this world and to be happy with Him forever in the next.' I paused for breath.

'And have you any idea at all of what that means, Annie Byrne? It means that you are to be a good girl for the sake of your immortal soul.'

My immortal soul was something I had not yet managed to come to grips with. Sister Immaculata had drawn an immortal soul on the blackboard only last week. It was like a balloon. When it was full of grace, it was round and coloured in with bright pink chalk. When it was empty, it sagged and had no colour at all. Except, of course, for the black spots of sin covering it like an attack of measles. And there again, you only got the measles if the sins were venial. Should your misdemeanours be mortal, then the soul would surely be black right through to the core – black, deflated and totally without shine.

Of the location of my immortal soul I was unsure. Perhaps it was in my chest where I got the bad feelings when I was angry; perhaps that swelling, choking sensation I got was my immortal soul erupting and letting all the grace drain away. But I wasn't sure. Sometimes I knew that my soul was in my belly where I often suffered pain after a bout of naughtiness. The whole thing was a terrible worry and I tried not to dwell on it too frequently.

'And you will be making your First Confession soon, Annie Byrne. After which you will receive the most Blessed Sacrament of all, the Body and Blood of Jesus Christ.'

I felt sick. I had no notion of cannibalism and therefore no opinion on the subject, but this did not sound quite right to me. I looked pleadingly towards my mother, who was no help at all. She just sat there staring at her shoes, her face grim and still crimson.

Sister Agatha tutted her annoyance then, warming to her subject, went on in a shrill tone, 'My goodness, child, have you not a grateful bone in your body? Jesus Christ suffered for you, died for you . . .'

I didn't hear the rest, because here was something I could latch on to, something I appreciated and understood. Jesus Christ was a hero. He had died for me. Well, my Dad had done the same; he was a hero too, he had died for me, for all of us, in fact. Why, he'd even died for old Nasty Knickers, though I felt sure she didn't deserve it. My Dad had died so that the Nazis would stop bombing the mills and our houses. They were hopeless shots, Nazis. Four or five times they'd had a go at Trinity Street Station and missed. And they didn't just miss a bit, they missed by miles.

'Are you listening to me, Annie Byrne? Would you look at that now, Mrs Byrne. She's away daydreaming while we're here, the both of us, concerned with the survival of her immortal soul.'

My mother nudged me none too gently with her elbow. 'Whatever are you thinking about, Annie?'

'Nazis,' I replied, looking straight at Sister Agatha. Perhaps my original half-formed idea had been to elaborate, to tell Sister Agatha that I now understood the theory of martyrdom, that I was beginning to appreciate the fact of Jesus's sacrifice. But something held me back and that single word, dropped into the room from the mouth of a five year old, seemed to have almost as devastating an effect as another bomb on Emmanuel Street. Sister Agatha nearly sat down on the edge of her desk as she groped for support, her right fist clenched tightly over her left breast, while my mother's chin dropped, her gaping mouth allowing her a vacant and rather idiotic appearance.

'Did . . . you . . . hear . . . that, Mrs Byrne?' gasped Sister Agatha. 'This child is wicked . . . wicked, I tell you!'

I waited for my mother to speak, hopefully in my defence, but no answer came, though her tongue moved in her mouth as if she were trying to shape her thoughts.

Sister Agatha began to pace back and forth across the room, throwing her arms wide then crossing them over her chest, looking for all the world like an ugly black crow trying to get off the ground. 'She called me a Nazi . . . a Nazi – you heard her, Mrs Byrne.'

She marched towards me, her claw-like hand pointing towards my face, the extended index finger stopping about an inch from the end of my nose. I looked straight at her, didn't flinch, made no move away from her and I could see plainly that my boldness was not appreciated.

'You will go, Annie Byrne, into the corridor. There you will say a decade of the Holy Rosary before the Sacred Heart. You will not stand, you will kneel and you will have no cushion for your knees.'

Knowing I had done something bad, but having no real concept of what my sin had been, I toyed with the idea of standing my ground. Had my mother not been there, had I not been a witness to her lack of sympathy for me, I probably would have chosen to remain and take a whipping. But knowing that my mother would neither support nor defend me, I took one last look at her mortified expression before creeping out into the corridor to stare at the effigy in the corner.

It was a statue of a long-haired man in a red cloak, patience and suffering etched deeply into its face. One hand lay across its chest where a heart dripping vivid red blood sat on a plain white undergarment. This was the Christ who had died for me. This was the Christ whose Body and Blood I would have to receive. I still felt sick.

I touched an icy bare foot, tracing the toenails with the end of my finger. Well, this was definitely not body and blood. I scraped away a bit of the flesh-coloured paint to reveal chalky white plaster underneath. Then, kneeling on the cold marble floor, I took the beads from my pocket and began to count my way through the Our Fathers, the Hail Marys and the Glory Bes. My knees hurt. On the end of my rosary, another Christ figure dangled, this time crucified and made of base metal and I swung this item about a bit to relieve the monotony.

I knew I didn't believe in what I was doing, in what I was saying. None of it made any sense. I shut my eyes tight and fought to believe, reaching down inside myself, trying to locate my immortal soul, hoping that it would inflate and fill with grace as I prayed. Nothing happened. I shuffled about the floor, trying to ease the agony in my knees.

When I opened my eyes and gazed once more at the dripping heart, my stomach heaved and I vomited noisily on to the clean black and white floor before sliding down into unconsciousness. They found me there eventually, cleaned me up, put me into a nursery cot and gave me sips of water and a cool cloth for my head.

From that day on, Sister Agatha ignored me almost completely. She never seemed to look directly at me again, avoiding me whenever possible, delegating my punishments to beings lesser than herself. Occasionally, I caught her looking at me sideways, but as soon as I met her eye she would turn away quickly, leaving in the space between us an atmosphere I did not yet recognise as shame.

My contempt for her grew then lessened as other, more pressing, events pushed her from my mind. She was, after all, a person of no importance.

Chapter Four: Changes

'See what Eddie's got for you, Annie. Come on, hurry up.'

I pretended not to hear, whipping my newly chalked top into further frenzy until it skidded to a halt among the cobbles at the pavement's edge. Sheila Davies, my best friend for the moment, straightened from her task of marking out a hopscotch on the flagstones. 'Yer Mam's shouting, Annie.'

I picked up my top and sauntered over to Sheila.

'Why don't you go and see what she wants?' she asked. 'I think you're right daft not playing with all them things he's bought you.'

She was right, I supposed. There I was with a veritable treasure trove – a scooter, a skipping rope set in varnished wooden handles with ball-bearings for smooth turning, a dolls' house with curtains and smart furniture, all ignored out in the air-raid shelter. I couldn't explain, not even to Sheila, why I wouldn't play with the things. In truth, I found it difficult – indeed impossible – to explain to myself why I couldn't, or wouldn't take advantage of Eddie Higson's generosity.

'Get in here now, Annie!' The tone of my mother's voice precluded the possibility of any further attempts to ignore her.

On entering our kitchen, I found Eddie Higson sitting, as usual, in the big rocker, my father's rocker. This was placed to the left of the range and sideways on to the window, a position chosen by my father because the light enabled him to read his *Bolton Evening News* until dusk forced us to use the gas.

I resented Eddie's presence in my Dad's chair, resented

his presence in our house, the way he would put his feet up on the fireguard while my mother fetched him pint pots of thick, stewed tea and wedges of window pie. I had always loved window pie; it had been my favourite, made specially for me and only for me. Now I refused it, just as I refused to share anything with this man who had invaded my house, stolen my mother and spoiled my life.

But this time, it was not going to be easy, for Eddie Higson held in his lap a beautiful ball of blue-grey fur, a tiny scrap of feline life that mewed and clawed gently at the man's fingers.

'It's a little cat, Annie,' he announced, his small deepset eyes narrowed in anticipation. Did he think I was daft or something? I'd seen cats before. My heart went out to the little creature. I longed to pick it up, stroke it and love it, make it my very own. It would love me in return, I knew it would.

'It's a Persian,' said my mother. 'Eddie's paid a bob or two for that, I can tell you.'

I knew what was expected of me. I knew what I wanted to do – I wanted to do the very thing that was required of me, to take the kitten, express my gratitude and forge the link that both he and my mother were waiting for – depending on, almost.

I wandered to the dresser and picked up my copy of *Robinson Crusoe*, the one my father had bought for me during his last leave.

'Well?' enquired my mother. 'Aren't you going to thank Eddie for getting you such a pretty little cat? Smokey, he's called.'

I flicked through the pages of my brightly illustrated children's version, then snapped the book shut loudly. 'I don't want a cat,' I said, carefully avoiding looking at Smokey whom I wanted in that moment more than I'd ever wanted anything before in my life.

'Bloody hell,' cursed Higson. 'There's no pleasing some folk. What does she want, then?' he enquired of my mother who simply raised her arms in a gesture of despair.

'What do you want, then?' he asked of me.

I placed my book back on the dresser. 'Nothing,' I replied.

'She bloody hates me, Nancy,' he shouted, furious now. He hurled the kitten to the floor and I steeled myself not to flinch as its little body hit the peg rug. My breathing quickened and became shallow as that familiar feeling of anger and confusion rose in me, overwhelming me almost, filling my chest to bursting point. I had always known instinctively that this was a cruel and vicious man, but now the living (or dying) evidence lay at our feet, mewling piteously before the fire. I also knew that had I accepted the cat, his fate would have eventually been similar, for Higson would have used the animal to get at me sooner or later. I was full of hatred for Higson, full of contempt for my mother, who was stupid, so stupid not to see through this terrible man.

She ran now and picked up the kitten, cradling it in her arms as she screamed at me. 'Now look what you've done, Annie. Poor little thing.' Obviously, she was blind as well as stupid. I took a slow and deliberate breath. 'I didn't do it, Mam. He did.' I pointed an accusing finger at Eddie Higson. 'He is a bad man,' I announced. 'And I don't want him in my house.'

Higson crossed the room in two strides and hit me full across the face with the flat of his hand. This was the first time he had hit me, but I knew, with an unwavering certainty, that it would not be the last, that should my mother marry this man, then I would suffer for a long time to come.

'Don't touch her,' screamed my mother. 'Don't you ever hit her, Eddie.'

Although my face smarted from the blow, I stood my ground as he glowered before me. 'Don't hit me again,' I said quietly, simply repeating my mother's words and staring full into his small, deep-sunken eyes.

I never found out what happened to the little cat, but I

wept bitter tears for him in the privacy of the air-raid shelter. When my tears were dried, I took the scooter and the skipping rope down the back street and flung them on to the Emmanuel Street bombsite. The dolls' house followed suit, but it looked incongruous sitting among the dust and rubble of ruined homes, so I picked up a half-brick and destroyed it as efficiently as the German bombers had wiped out the real houses that once stood there.

At the end of my destructiveness, I felt exhausted but victorious. One battle at a time. If I won enough skirmishes, I would surely win the war.

The real war broke out, of course, after the wedding. Considering our improverished state (since Eddie Higson was still unfit for work) and taking into account the post-war shortages, it was a lavish affair. The reception was to be held in my grandfather's house, which was a large one, in the centre of a high terrace on Vista Street at the top of Daubhill. The street was aptly named, because from my grandfather's house you could see for miles across the moors surrounding Bolton. We had even had a grand view of Manchester as it burned after one massive raid, three or four sets of cousins pressed against the upstairs windows marvelling at the orange brightness of the night sky.

The wedding took place at All Saints in August 1946. The church was filled to bursting with aunts, uncles, cousins and friends of my mother from the mill. Higson seemed to have no friends. His two brothers and their wives and offspring were in evidence, but apart from them, he had few supporters.

My mother had decided against bridesmaids, knowing full well that I would be, at best, an unwilling participant and that my absence from such an entourage would attract comment and cause embarrassment.

In fact, I did not really attend the service, escaping early on to a small side pew next to a confessional box, where I busied myself studying a spider that was carefully constructing a web across a corner of the door. This was Saturday. By Wednesday night the web would be in ruins when the first sinner would cross the confessional threshold at seven o'clock.

I wore a silly pink satin frock with smocking on the bodice and a wide sash that kept coming loose and trailing on the floor. On my feet I had black patent ankle-strap shoes which had cost, so I had been informed, an arm, a leg and a cartload of coupons.

My mother was dressed in powder blue crepe and wore a hat with a small open-weave veil. She looked pretty, but rather like a fragile china doll with her painted rose-bud lips and pink-rouged cheeks.

Higson looked clean, at least, though rather uncomfortable in his greenish-grey suit with the wilting carnation hanging from a button hole. But then, I thought, no self-respecting flower would survive long in such unsavoury company. His hair, usually crinkly and springy, was plastered flat to his head with a liberal application of grease. There were some improvements – even I had to admit that, because he didn't really look like something off a pirate's flag now. The face was rounder and fuller, the skin a more acceptable colour. But nothing would ever improve that nose, nasty black bristles poking out of the nostrils, the whole thing hooked like the beak of some flesh-eating bird. He was, in my opinion, a very ugly man.

I would not smile for the photographs. My mother, gritting her teeth and trying to hang on to her patience on this happy day, rubbed at my scuffed shoes with her wisp of a handkerchief and told me to smile, for goodness sake. There was nothing to smile about, so I carried on frowning and dragging my toes in the dust.

As most of my relations, including my mother's father, were Irish, a small ceilidh band had been engaged and my grandfather's large front room had been emptied for the dancing.

I had just one interesting cousin called Eileen. Her father, Paddy Foley, had deserted Eileen and her mother two years previously, so I had, of late, come to identify with the fatherless girl. Her mother, Nellie, was my mother's sister, though they did not look alike. Nellie was tall, thin as a reed and dark-haired, with the pale skin so often found in those of Irish descent. My mother, prettier by far than Nellie, had a softer, gentler look about her.

Eileen herself was plain to the point of ugliness, with straight mousy hair and strange eyes that darted about constantly as if she were frantically searching for something.

We took ourselves off to the top of the house, right up to the attic, away from all the fiddling, shouting and stamping of feet. We sat side by side on an old army trunk, our heels dangling and bumping gently against its side. She stared at me with all the wisdom of a ten year old, those odd, quick eyes seeming to pierce through my skull right to the very centre of my thoughts.

'You don't like 'im, do you?' She put an arm around my shoulders. Unaccustomed, of late, to such empathy, I allowed a few tears of self-pity to run down my face and she dried them, none too gently, with the rough-ribbed cuff of her grey cardigan.

'Me Mam says as 'ow you'll get used to 'im, like,' she went on. 'You'll be better off than what we are at any road – once he can get work. At our 'ouse we've seen nowt but bread and drip for a week now. See.' She opened a brown paper bag. 'I've fetched loads of butties up and a bottle of stout – we can 'ave our own party.'

'No!' I made up my mind quickly as an idea flashed across my brain with all the sudden brilliance of a streak of fork-lightning. 'Save my half, Eileen. I'm running away.'

Expressing no surprise, as Eileen had ceased to feel surprise at a very early age, she merely asked, with great calm, 'Where to, like?'

I thought about this for some seconds. 'Well, I'd go next door, but they'd only find me straight off and drag me back. I think I'll go to . . . to . . . Blackpool. That's it, I'll go to Blackpool.'

She stared down at her white blancoed canvas shoes. 'Where will you live?' she asked. This was getting a bit complicated for me.

'I'll find somewhere. I can sleep on the pier or in a tram shelter. And . . .' I began to warm to my subject. 'And I'll get food off people on the sands – bits of picnics and that.'

Eileen shook her head wisely. 'They'll only bring you back. They always do – I've been fetched back four times now – mind, I never got as far as Blackpool, but it makes no difference. They'll always get you in the end, Annie. Then you'll get a right good 'iding off yer Mam. Nay. You'll have to go 'ome with them and make the best of it.'

She was right, of course. They did always get you in the end. I sighed deeply, trying to imagine what life was going to hold in store for me. I had already been banished from my mother's bed, was already forced to sleep cold and alone in the small front bedroom.

And I'd have to eat with him, sit with him in the kitchen every evening. There was no privacy in the house, no bathroom. If you wanted a wash, you used the tin dish in the slopstone. If you wanted a warm wash, then you heated water on the range or on one of the two gas rings in the scullery. Weekly baths took place in front of the kitchen fire in the metal tub from the back yard. Which was all very well when there was just me and my mother. But now, with a stranger in the house, how would we manage?

I sobbed my unhappiness into my fingers, squeezing the tears in my palms until they ran right up to the elbows. It was the unfairness of it all that frustrated me. Grown-ups could do exactly as they pleased. We just had to fit in, were forced to fit in. We had to wait until we, in turn, became adults before we could have any choice at all in things that really mattered.

'Don't take on, Annie,' whispered Eileen. 'Don't let them know 'ow you feel. Just carry on going t' school and do your booklearnin'. I've 'eard as 'ow you're clever at school. They can't take that away from you now, can they? You'll likely get a scholarship when you're eleven – oh aye, you'll pass for t' grammar alright. Then you can be what you want, do what you want.'

'What can I be, Eileen?' I gripped her hand tightly.

'Ooh, anythin'. Well, nearly anythin'.'

I thought about this for a few minutes, my sobs beginning to subside.

'Could I be a teacher, Eileen?'

'I reckon as 'ow you could, yes.'

'Then I could tell people what to do instead of them telling me. Only I'd be a nice teacher like Miss Best with legs. I could never be a nun. I don't like nuns.'

Eileen, a not too frequent attender at St Gregory's, which was also under the tender auspices of the Passionists, agreed with me wholeheartedly. She sat, tugging at her hair, twisting it about her fingers. Perhaps she thought if she twisted it for long enough it would go curly.

'I'm goin' to work in a shop,' she announced. 'A food shop. If they don't pay me proper I can always pinch enough to eat.' She grabbed a sandwich from the bag and swallowed it in two bites. For a moment or two I forgot my own troubles and thought about poor Eileen.

Auntie Nellie worked full time in the mill, yet there was never enough to eat, seldom any coal for the fire. Most of the time, Eileen did not go to school, simply because she had little to wear. For days on end, her mother would lock her in, telling her that the house was being watched and should Eileen ever open the door, let alone step outside, then she, Auntie Nellie, would surely be informed by her spies.

This poor ten-year-old child was, therefore, left without food to eat, without fire to warm her, while her mother, who did not always come home as soon as the working day had ended, spent her wages in the Swan or the Black Bull, returning only once her purse was empty and her belly full of ale. Surely my life, even with Eddie Higson in it, could not be as terrible as Eileen's?

'Do you get frightened when you're shut in?' I asked.

She nodded quickly.

'Shall I come sometimes and put a bit of bread or maybe an Eccles cake through the letterbox?'

Now she was shaking her head vehemently. 'No. They'll only find out. Whatever you do, they always find out.'

'But it's not fair,' I cried. 'You should go to school like me and you shouldn't be locked in on your own all day with no dinner.'

She put a finger to her lips. 'Shush. Nobody knows, 'cepting you. If me Grandad ever found out, he'd flay me Mam, you know he would. Then me Mam would go for me – aye, she would that – and where would that get me, eh?'

'But it's not fair!' I shouted again.

She looked at me wisely, shaking her head as if exasperated at me for expecting it to be fair.

We sat together for a long time until the room grew chill, two girl children separated by four years, connected by the strangeness of our lives, she with the crazy mother, I with the horrible so-called stepfather. Yet we drew strength from each other as we sat there waiting, waiting for our day to come. It would be a long wait, we knew that. It would reach beyond this room, this house, this day and into dimensions as yet uncharted. But our strength, joint and separate, lay in our youthfulness, in our unspoken hope that we would be survivors.

Thus began my journey into my mother's second marriage, my pathway into a hell I could never have imagined. So fierce was the heat in my particular hell that when, some three years after this wedding day, I learned that Eileen and her mother had perished in their gas-filled scullery, I felt not only pity and grief, but something approaching envy too.

Eileen had not survived. I was condemned to live.

Chapter Five: Moving On

Our house in Ensign Street was a slum. Although my mother did her best, scrubbing floors, blackleading the grate two or three times a week, making sure her doorstep and the two or three square feet of flags outside the front door were donkeystoned daily, she was fighting a losing battle.

We were constantly overrun by vermin; in the night the kitchen and scullery floors would become blanketed in silverfish and cockroaches, while mice and even rats put in regular appearances around the meatsafe and under the slopstone.

It was a poorly built two up two downer, with a sloping scullery attached at the back and a brick air-raid shelter in the yard. The roof leaked with monotonous frequency and the bedroom walls were decorated with a variety of moulds, some wet and green, some white and furry.

Facilities were, to say the least, primitive. At the bottom of the back yard was a tippler toilet consisting merely of a wide earthenware pipe which protruded from the flagged floor, the seat being a crude circle of badly splintered wood with a hole in the middle. There was no flushing mechanism. A suspended bucket in the pipe simply emptied itself into the open drain below once the contents became heavy enough to make it tilt.

Next to the lavatory was a midden, a low wall over which debris and decaying food were thrown. Two or three times a month, the cart would rumble up the back street and men with rags wrapped around their mouths and noses would shovel the putrid contents of middens on to the open lorry, thereby disturbing the rats' nests, causing the creatures to panic and move once more towards our homes in search of food.

Yet there was a predictability about life in Ensign Street, a monotony that made us feel secure in spite of our unclean environment.

Because most of the women worked on weekdays, washing was done on Saturdays. Each household had its own posstub and posser and the pounding of wood on metal, the swish of garments in water, the scrubbing of sheet against washboard, these sounds were our dawn chorus at the beginning of each weekend. Should it rain, then these activities must take place in the sculleries and tempers were always frayed on inclement Saturdays, for no-one, not even the most hardened of heathens, would dare face the contempt of her neighbours by washing on a Sunday, however bright the weather.

Once the clothes had been rinsed and forced through the rollers of the wringer, they were hung across the back street to dry, row upon row, three or four lines to every house and woe betide any child found playing round the backs on washdays. Inside the kitchens were pulley lines where the wash was hung to air once brought in or, in the event of rain, clothes would be transferred straight from mangle to pulley, thus forcing the residents to live in a steam-filled atmosphere for the whole day.

The rentman came on Saturdays too, when he knew that the women would all be about their washing and could not, therefore, hide from him. He had a small moustache like Hitler and a large black book to write in, but he was a pleasant enough man and always gave me a mint imperial or an Uncle Joe's mintball.

On Tuesday evenings, the clubman arrived, collecting our pennies for the Providence cheques with which we bought most of our clothing. He had bright red hair, a tooth missing at the front and he did bird imitations. At least, he used to, though once Eddie Higson moved in with us the Provvy man never stopped again, but just took his money and left quickly. I was pleased in a way. It made me realise that I was not the only one who disliked Higson.

Wednesday night was insurance night. Like most poor people, we set aside a few coppers each week so that we would not be buried as paupers.

Lamp Eel came on Friday evenings, the sad carthorse dragging its load up the back street while his master, who always wore a trilby hat with a flower stuck to the brim, called in a high voice, 'Lamp eel, lamp eel, come on Missus, bring out your dead . . . lamp eel. . .', and we would rush out of our houses to inspect whatever was on offer this week. Lamp Eel, whose original function had been to deliver oil for lamps, sold just about everything from donkeystone to sets of china, though where he got the stuff during the shortages nobody seemed to know. His cart was wonderful to behold and to hear, for it shone like a million jewels and jingled magnificently as pans and bottles clattered together whenever his cartwheel hit a rut between cobbles.

So although my mother had married a man I despised, I took comfort from the familiarity of my surroundings, drew solace from the continuing routine, reassuring myself that nothing had really changed, that life was still, more or less, the same. I knew every flagstone, every crack, every cobble that paved my walk to and from school. I was even allowed to the shops now and had made friends with the keepers, enjoying a chat in the fruit store or the Co-op, pretending to be grown-up as I commented on the price of a gas mantle, the cost of a tape of Aspros or a packet of Fennings Cooling Powders. The Co-op was my favourite place, because I loved the smells, loved to watch the staff as they deftly shovelled up potatoes or scooped precious sugar into blue bags. I would breathe in the odour of ground coffee, the scent of hanging bacon, the perfume of the earth that clung in wet lumps to potatoes and carrots. If there was a heaven and if there were smells in heaven, I knew it would be just like the Co-op.

But for recreation, the bombsite was my favourite place, because again I could play shops, resting an old door on two piles of bricks for a counter, grinding up brick dust to 'sell' as sugar, using small stones for fruit and sweets. I had never seen a field except from a distance, had never needed a field, for I had, right on my doorstep, a real adventure playground. Of course, the bombsite was forbidden territory, a fact that made it all the more attractive to us and we never minded the trouble we got into for playing there.

Tom Hyatt remained my dearest friend. He was twenty now and a very great age this seemed to me. He had become a qualified tradesman, a painter and decorator and he brought me sweets every Friday when he got his wages. As soon as Lamp Eel had been and gone, I would rush next door to visit and collect my bounty, sitting in the big rocker with dolly mixtures and halfpenny spanishes while Tom told tales of the great houses beyond the moors where he was working. During the first few months of my mother's marriage, Tom often asked, 'Are you alright?' and I would nod, not wanting to worry him.

There were some beatings, just a few, but my mother and Eddie Higson ignored me for the most part. I was left more and more to my own devices and although this neglect did not make me exactly happy, at least I was free to do much as I pleased.

So when I discovered that we were moving, that Eddie Higson had found a job of sorts, that we would be leaving the street and Tom and the bombsite – and yes, even my school suddenly became attractive when I thought of moving to another – I felt as if my world had been completely shattered.

Higson was out. I faced my mother across the kitchen table where she was rolling out pastry, arms covered to the elbows in flour. This time, I was fully determined to dig in my heels and get my own way. They couldn't do this to me. Hadn't they done enough already?

'You and him can go if you want, but I'm going nowhere. I'm stopping here and that's that.'

She wrapped the pastry round the rolling pin and transferred it to a blue-rimmed enamel dish.

'Ah, so you're stopping, are you? And who'll pay your rent and do your dinner? What about your washing and who'll drag you out of bed every morning for school, eh?'

'I don't know and I don't care.'

'Well then, I suggest you start knowing and caring pretty damn quick. We are moving up Long Moor and that's flat. Now stop being so daft and pass me that pan of mince off the range.'

I banged the large iron pan hard on to the table, causing utensils to rattle and fly about. My mother pushed a lock of hair from her face, leaving a smudge of flour on the end of her nose and I studied this as she spoke.

'Eeh, it's a lovely house, Annie. Wait till you see it, just you wait. It's got a back-boiler and a bathroom – well, a sort of bathroom, just like a big cupboard off the front bedroom. And we're getting the electric in – proper lights and a cooker.' She paused in her labours to look at me. 'Listen, Annie. Your Grandad has give us the deposit – some money, like, to put down. Now that's a secret and you mustn't tell nobody, even your cousin Eileen, for Grandad can't do it for everybody and we don't want to cause no fights. Can't you see what this means, love? We're to have a mort-gage, a proper mort-gage instead of a rent book. It'll be our house, not the landlord's. Won't you try to see I'm doing what's best?'

It was hopeless. I'd have been as well off talking to the wall, yet still I went on. 'But it's not what I want, is it? Nobody ever asks me about anything in this house. I just get told what to do – not asked – told. And if I don't do it then I'm in trouble.' I stopped for a second to draw breath. 'You went and married him and I have to live with him. I can't choose, I never get the chance to choose. Now you say I've got to leave my own house, my Dad's house, and go piking off to live where you want to live. Well, it's not fair. I don't want to live up Long Moor with electric and a bathroom.'

'Do you want to stop here with rats and cockroaches, then? Is that what you want, to stop in a filthy slum the rest of your life?' She was waving the rolling pin in the air now. 'Now you listen to me, our Annie. Six sisters I've got and every last one of them married to some no-good lump of an Irishman, every one of them up to their eyes in muck and kids they can't feed. Well, I never married an Irishman, because apart from your Grandad they are the scum of the earth. Your Dad was a fine man, a Gordon Highlander and he would have looked after us if he'd lived, oh aye, your Dad would have done right by us.'

She must have seen my lip quiver, because she continued in a quieter tone, 'But he didn't live, Annie. Get that into your head, will you? And now he's dead, Eddie has took us on, both of us, and he'll do his best now he's on the mend. Oh, Annie . . .' She came round the table and took my hand in hers. 'All I've ever wanted is me own front door, me own bit of garden with a few daffs and marigolds. It's got a bit of garden at the front, you know. And there's fields nearby where you can play and the tram stops right outside the door to take you to school.'

I wrenched my hand away. 'You go then. You go and catch the tram, because I'm stopping here. I shall move in with Mrs Hyatt and Tom and Freddie. Tom'll look after me.'

My mother sighed deeply before saying 'Tom won't be there, love.' My fists clenched into tight balls as I asked, 'What do you mean?'

'Tom's off to America soon, lass. He's away to seek his fortune and I can't say that I'm surprised . . . Annie . . . where are you going. . .?'

But I was already off and down the lobby, into the street and hammering on Mrs Hyatt's door. A startled Mrs Hyatt peered through the window, then I had to wait, hopping from foot to foot until she finally let me in.

'Is Tom there?' I gasped.

'Aye, he's just sat down for his tea. I . . .'

I flew past her and into the kitchen. Tom paused with a forkful of food in his hand as he saw me standing breathless in the doorway.

'Whatever's the matter with you, Annie? You look like you've seen a ghost . . .'

I swallowed hard. 'Is it true?'

'Is what true?'

'That you're going to America?'

'By the hell.' His fork dropped with a clatter and he pushed his chair back from the table. Looking past me, he spoke to his mother. 'See? I told Nancy not to tell her. I told her I wanted to do it in me own time and in me own way.' He looked straight at me now. 'Yes, it is true, Annie. I'm going, sooner or later.'

'Why? Why, Tom?' My voice was full of pleading as I choked back the tears. How many more people would I lose? Did I have to lose everyone I loved?

'I'm going for a better life, Annie. There's more chances over there, I'll get a good job, better training . . . oh heck, how do I explain all this to a child?'

Mrs Hyatt came to stand beside me, her aproned bulk filling the small space between dresser and table. She placed a fat, heavy arm around my shoulder, but looked at Tom as she said, 'Nay, Tom. This is no child. This one were never a child, God love 'er.' Then to me she said, 'I'll still be 'ere, you know. And Freddie. We'll look out for you – you've only to bang on the wall.'

'But Tom said he'd always be here, Mrs Hyatt,' I sobbed. 'He said he'd always look after me . . . and he tells lies, just like all grown-ups.'

It seemed to me that this was the last straw, the final betrayal. My Dad gone, my Mam's affections and attentions directed elsewhere, now Tom was going . . . I would be alone. Utterly, completely, totally alone, no adult on my side, nobody to turn to for comfort or love. Even Tom, my Tom, whom I had begun to trust, was deserting me.

'Is it far to America?' I gulped between tears. 'Can I get

there on the tram or a trolley-bus?' But I knew the answer before it came and confirmation arrived in the form of a choking sound from Mrs Hyatt, who turned away quickly towards the dresser. But she was not laughing at me. There was no laughter in those sagging shoulders.

'No, Annie,' said Tom. 'It takes a good few days on a ship to get there.'

I ran to him, flinging my arms about his neck and he drew me gently into his lap. 'Take me with you, Tom. I'll be a good girl, I promise. Just take me with you – please.'

Mrs Hyatt, who was weeping openly now, her wide back shaking with sobs, said, 'You're not the only one as'll miss 'im, Annie. Nay, 'e'll be very sadly missed, will our Tom.' Then she went through to the scullery, clattering the pots and pans to drown the sound of her sobbing.

'You'd want your Mam, Annie,' said Tom gently. 'You know you can't leave your Mam. She'll be needing you one of these days when you're a bigger girl.'

'She doesn't need me, Tom. She's got him.'

'But you love your Mam, don't you?'

What a daft question this was. Even the best of adults seemed to ask daft questions. Of course I loved my Mam. But did she love me? If she had loved me, would she have needed that dreadful Eddie Higson, would she have married a man like that? And would we be moving up Long Moor if she loved me?

'Yes, I love my Mam, Tom,' I answered, almost wearily.

'And if you ever need anybody to help you, or just somebody to turn to, Freddie and my Ma will be here to see to you.'

Obviously, Tom didn't know anything about the proposed move. Briefly, I wondered whether or not I'd get into trouble for telling the Hyatts our business, for Mrs Hyatt was, in my mother's book at least, a busybody and a gossip. But I couldn't keep it to myself, so, throwing caution to the winds, I blurted out, 'We're moving, Tom.

Up Long Moor. They're making me go with them. But if you'd stop here instead of going to America, then I could get back and see you and . . .'

Mrs Hyatt bustled into the kitchen, drying first her eyes, then her hands on a corner of the capacious apron. 'Long Moor, you say? When?'

'I don't know, Mrs Hyatt. Soon, I think.'

'Well!' She lowered her bulk into a chair. 'Well, I'll go to the foot of our stairs! What have I always said, Tom? What have I always said? Ideas above 'er station, that one. By! Next news, she'll be 'avin' tea parties wi' bone-china cups and lace doyleys. I'd not be at all surprised if she stopped talkin' to the likes of us.'

'Shut up, Mam. Before you go too far again.'

But Mrs Hyatt was not going to shut up, not for anyone. She was on her high horse and she'd probably stop there till she fell off, or got kicked off – and Tom was too gentle a man to go hard on his mother.

'Buying a house then, is it, Annie?' she asked, her tone sweetening.

'Yes. My Mam says we are to have a mort-gage.' Instead of a rent book, my mother had said. Perhaps it was bigger than a rent book, or a different colour. Though it sounded more like an exotic fruit to me.

'Well, we'll just have to see 'ow your Mam goes about paying her mort-gage while she's married to that soft bugger. Oh, 'e doesn't fool me, Tom. Like I said before, 'e's no bleeding 'ero, comin' back snivelling from a prison camp after sittin' it out for four bloody years. I'll bet 'e built no escape tunnels. Only reason 'e joined up was over that lass . . .'

'Watch what you're saying, Mam.'

'Anyroad, Nancy'll have to work all the hours God sends for 'er fancy ideas. 'Cos there's no road as 'e'll pay for much. And shortage o' money's not the only thing she'll be worrying about . . .'

'Nancy knows nothing about all that, Mam. And neither

do you if the truth were but told.'

'Don't talk to me about truth, Tom Hyatt. Are you going to eat this or not?' When Tom made no reply, she snatched his plate from the table, then, jabbing the air with Tom's fork as if to emphasise every word, she said, 'The truth is dead, Tom, dead and can't speak up for itself. And 'e seems to me to be the right type to . . .' she faltered, placing the fork on the plate. 'Alright, Tom. 'Ave it your own way. Maybe I am wrong, maybe I've said too much in front of this one.' She gestured towards me. 'But I do know this – something about you-know-who is not quite right. And I can't 'elp 'aving me say. Speak as I find, I do.'

She wobbled into the scullery and we heard her, as she scraped Tom's dinner into the slops bucket, muttering not quite to herself 'there's no smoke without fire' and 'a wrong un if ever I saw one'.

Tom took my chin in his fingers and gently turned my face towards his. 'Look, lass. I'm sorry if it looks like I'm letting you down, but I'll be back some day with all kinds of tales to tell you – and presents for you too. Oh yes, I'll bring back some fine presents for my little Annie. You're a sensible girl, got a good head on them shoulders. Now listen to me. Just you stick up for yourself, do what you think's right and do your best at school. I shall write to you every week from Philadelphia – for that's the name of the town I'll be bound for – and you can write to me. How does that sound? You'll have a pen pal in America.'

I knew I was beaten. I had no way of preventing Tom from going to America, no way of changing my mother's mind about moving to the other end of the town.

When I got down from Tom's knee and crossed the room towards the door, I was aware that I was letting him go there and then, for he had already left me, was making plans for a new start away from me. He didn't love me, couldn't love me. Perhaps I really was not lovable, perhaps nobody would ever love me enough to stay with me.

Within the space of two years I had lost the three people who had been most important to me. With my father, I had had no choice, but with my mother and Tom, I felt I had made a conscious decision to let go.

But that decision was just an invention of mind, a pride-saving piece of my imagination. Because, in truth, I had had no choice in any of these matters.

I was forced to admit to myself, however grudgingly, that Long Moor Lane was a great improvement on Ensign Street. Although the rooms at the back of the house had flagged floors, there was a proper kitchen instead of a scullery. This large, single-storeyed square was attached to the rear living room and its unplastered brick walls were painted in a light shiny green colour.

My mother was proud of her new kitchen, especially after she had replaced the low slopstone with a proper porcelain sink and had purchased a kitchenette, a tall cupboard, green to match the walls and with many compartments and drawers fitted into it. She also bought a real cooker which she tended with loving care, forever polishing and cleaning its various surfaces, while in truth she still depended greatly on the living-room range, though she would never have admitted her distrust in the new-fangled gadgetry with which she was filling our home.

For many months she would not switch on the new electric lights unless she had a cloth in her hand to protect herself against the unknown. For a while, she even wore wellington boots for such occasions, having heard or read somewhere that rubber soles 'stopped it going through you'. She adhered rigidly to the use of her flat irons until Eddie Higson proved, by plugging in the new iron to the ceiling light fixture and surviving, that she might try an easier way of pressing the clothes.

Our living-room range was another novelty, being constructed of a beige ceramic material that required no leading and having a raised area of tiles set on to the floor in front of it. In the recesses to each side of the chimney were floor-to-ceiling cupboards in which we stored crockery and such linens as we owned, thus making redundant the large mirrored dresser that had always dominated our Ensign Street kitchen.

There was no lobby in this house, just a small square vestibule leading straight into the front room, which had a wooden floor, a source of great pride in my mother's book. This room also had cupboards in the recesses, but while the living-room cupboards were panelled in wood and strictly utilitarian, these were ornate by comparison, their upper portions being glazed and leaded. Into these compartments went my mother's few treasures, bits of cut glass, framed photographs, a plaster saint or two and a set of white demi-tasse coffee cups, a wedding present for which she had never found a use. A square of moss-green secondhand carpet was acquired and my mother spent many hours varnishing and polishing the surrounding floorboards.

But outside, there was still the midden and the tippler lavatory and no amount of fancy cupboards and instant lighting could compensate, in my mother's mind, for these two festering sores. So when Eddie Higson's window round became reality, when he had finally purchased bucket, leathers and goodwill, my mother began to save with a grim determination known only to the victims of true deprivation. We were forced to eat strange meals, soups thick with lentils and barley, meat and potato pies with the emphasis strictly on the potato, scones without raisins, jam butties without margarine. The closest Eddie Higson and I ever got to camaraderie was then, as we stared blankly at one another across a table that held these odd offerings.

I had never had many clothes, but now I began to look shabby and down-at-heel, was forced to curl up my toes so that weekday clogs and Sunday best would last a few months longer. She stopped smoking too, which meant that her temper became less than even and I learned to keep my distance at certain times, like after meals when she most craved a Woodbine. Eddie Higson took to rolling his own, using bits of paper and a strange machine like a miniature mangle, often including the contents of discarded dog-ends he had picked up in the street, occasionally treating himself to an ounce of fresh tobacco.

To give him his due, he worked hard during those first few months at Long Moor Lane and, after reading several borrowed tomes on the subject of plumbing, he undertook, with the help of his brother, the installation of our new bathroom.

He divided the back bedroom into two equal parts, put in new windows, then fixed a bath, a washbasin and a flushing toilet into one of the two new rooms, leaving the other half as a small third bedroom. The cupboard which had incorporated the old bath became a walk-in wardrobe where my mother, who must have felt like the Queen Bee (being the first on the block to have a proper bathroom) hung her sparse trousseau.

The second bedroom, up another flight of stairs, was an attic room with a three-sided sloping window set into the roof. This was my room, my very own domain with an interesting view up and down the road and plenty of space for my bed and the newly acquired tallboy and dressing table.

The houses across the way were smart corporation dwellings, their occupants mere tenants, so my mother, a home owner, was on no more than nodding terms with them. Although she still worked in the mill, still came home with her hair full of fluff and the soles of her shoes encrusted with tiny steel rings, she declared herself to be up-and-coming now and announced that she would, in future, be voting Tory.

My attic window enabled me to see over the rooftops to the moors that surround Bolton like a huge green dish. My mother had told me that Bolton was so named because it sat in a dip between moors and that it had therefore been named, originally, Bowl Town.

Now that we lived on one of the moors, albeit on a main road, the air was cleaner, clearer and fresher than in the centre of town where the trapped dampness was so valuable to millowners whose spinning factories depended on a wet atmosphere.

As a town-dweller, I did not, as yet, find myself attracted to the greenness beyond the roofs. Like any seven year old, I required playmates, the company of my peers, so I came down from my tower to explore my new surroundings, venturing a little further each day into the unknown.

It was time to establish my territory.

Chapter Six: Encounters

My first encounter with other children came, of course, when I began to attend St Stephen's school. This was five tram stops up the road towards Harwood, though most of the trams were buses now and not so much fun, so I often saved my penny fare by walking the distance to and from school.

Standards at All Saints must have been high, because within a week I was in and out of first-year juniors and put to work with the eight year olds.

I loved the school right from the start. All the teachers had legs; no more flapping habits and rattling rosaries to disturb my peace of mind.

There was a priest though, because the school was attached to a church – in fact, the church itself was an infants' classroom, the altar and the first few pews being partitioned off during school days, while the rest of the benches were piled around the walls, ready to be brought out for Sundays and Holy Days of Obligation.

The priest was Father Cavanagh. He was fat and bald and wore a long black cloak with a clasp of metal chains at the throat. I didn't like him, but then I had never expected that I would. Priests, like nuns, were odd, legless animals from whom I expected neither kindness nor sympathy. This one, like most of them, asked a lot of questions. His voice was high and silly, the Irish brogue so thick that until I got used to him, he would have to repeat himself several times before I understood him. But he was, at least, a patient man and he spoke to me slowly, mouthing his words as if addressing an idiot or a deaf-mute.

'You'll be making your First Communion then soon, Annie?'

'Yes, Father.'

'And your family will be along to the Mass for to see you take the Blessed Sacrament?'

'I don't know, Father.'

He patted my head. Priests always did that and I hated it, it made me feel like a dog at its master's feet. He turned to my teacher, Miss O'Gara. 'They never come to the church, you know. I'll have to be paying them a visit, I'm thinking.' He looked back at me. 'You know, Annie, once you've made your Communion, you'll have to come to the Mass every Sunday or 'twill be a mortal sin?'

I nodded. This was familiar territory; we were back to the immortal soul business again.

'And you must come regularly to Confession to prepare yourself for the Blessed Sacrament.'

'Yes, Father.' He patted my head once more.

'Is your Mammy a Catholic then, Annie?'

'I think so, Father.'

'And your Daddy?'

'I haven't got one, he was killed in Italy when I was four.'

The priest took a step away from me, a puzzled expression appearing on his wide face. 'Ah well, 'tis sorry I am to be hearing that, child. But tell me now, is there not a man living at your house just now?'

'Yes, Father. Eddie Higson.'

Father Cavanagh glanced quickly at Miss O'Gara. 'Is he your stepdaddy then, Annie?' he enquired of me.

'No. He is not my stepdaddy, Father.'

Father Cavanagh removed his biretta and passed a fat hand over his bald pate. Miss O'Gara stepped forward and whispered something into the priest's ear.

I heard his sigh of relief before he spoke. 'Ah. So they are married. Well thanks be to God for that at any rate. Now, Annie. If your Mammy has married Mr . . . Mr Higson, then he is now your stepfather both in the eyes of the law and by the rules of your faith. Are you understanding me?'

This I would not pretend to accept. It was bad enough

having him pat me on the head all the time and listening to his stupid questions, but this was going too far.

'No. He is not my stepfather,' I said quietly. 'My Daddy was my father and I don't want a stepfather.'

Father Cavanagh tutted his dismay, then shaking a finger at me he said, 'You know your Commandments, do you not?'

'Yes Father.'

'And is not the fourth "honour thy father and thy mother"?'

'Yes, Father.'

'Then surely you must honour Mr Higson, for he is looking after you as a father would, caring for you, is he not? It will be a mortal sin for you not to honour your stepfather, Annie.'

My stomach turned over. Whatever I did, wherever I went, there were adults tying me in knots, confusing me to the point of madness. And the worst offenders were these priests and nuns with their laws about this and that, telling me what I must think, what I must believe, how I must act – even who I must be.

But I kept cool, nodding my assent. My lips had formed no lie, but that nod, with its mute falsehood, laid yet another stain on my immortal soul which was by now, I felt sure, so pitted with black holes that it might have been used to drain cabbage.

I took my place next to Josie Cullen who was eight and nearly as tall as I was. We did not sit together by choice, but simply because we were both cn the same page of the sum book and sum books were always one between two. Yet in spite of the fact that our proximity to each other had been forced upon us, we were fast becoming friends.

Josie and I were termed tomboys because neither of us wore ribbons or hairslides, nor did we play sedately like the other girls. We were frequently dispatched to the washroom after playtimes, for we seemed to attract dirt, gathering it about our persons like a pair of magnets collecting filings. The boys liked us, respected us almost, as we were not averse to a bout of rough and tumble and while Josie was conker champion of St Stephen's, I excelled at marbles, cleaning out the boys' stock of glass alleys and bolly-bearings with a frequency that alarmed them and won their admiration.

Josie nudged me. 'Take no notice of 'im. 'E's a soft old sod.'

I gaped at Josie. She had already made her First Confession and Communion. She would have to tell Father Cavanagh in the confessional that she had called him a soft old sod. I voiced my concern in a whisper.

'Don't be so daft,' she hissed back. 'For a kick-off, I can always disguise me voice. Or I can go down to St Patrick's and tell some other soft sod as I've called this soft sod a soft sod.'

This was terrible. Now I had two immortal souls to worry about – mine and Josie's! 'You can't call a priest a soft s . . . a name like that, Josie. It's a sin. You'll go to hell!'

'Oh shut up, Annie. You're beginning to sound like a bloody soft sod yourself . . .'

Although I was worried by all this, I felt elated somehow. I suddenly knew that it wasn't just me, that I wasn't the only one who entertained bad thoughts about people, important people too, like priests. But I would never have dared to voice my contempt as Josie just had. Whenever I got bad thoughts, whenever my temper rose, I became overwhelmed by guilt, weighed down by the knowledge that I was heading for certain damnation. But if Josie felt any guilt, she never showed it.

She chewed now on the end of her pencil. 'What's eight eights?' she asked.

'Sixty-four.'

'How do you do that, Annie?'

'Do what?'

'Sixty-four just like that, without having to go back to one eight is eight.'

'I don't know.'
'You must know.'
'Well I don't.'
'See? I told you you were a soft sod.' Furtively, she passed a sticky square of chocolate across the desk and I pushed it into my mouth before Miss O'Gara could spot it.
'Want another?'
'No. Save it for playtime. Where did you get it, anyway?'
'Paper shop.' She copied down another sum. 'I nicked it. It's dead easy at Warburton's. Anyroad, there's never any toffee coupons at our 'ouse.'
I almost choked. I was eating stolen chocolate. Thou shalt not steal, that was number seven on the list of Commandments. Josie's soul must be as black as hell itself. Mine too, since I was sharing her spoils. Or would the stains be brown? Chocolate was brown . . .
'Annie Byrne. Have you finished those sums?'
'No, Miss.'
'Then get on with your work and stop daydreaming.'
I got on with my work.

Eddie Higson blamed me for a lot of things. Firstly there was the atmosphere in the house, which was not good as I spoke to him seldom, going for days on end without even looking in his direction. Then there was the fact that I would not, even when I did deign to speak to him, call him Dad. When I spoke of him, he always got his full title and this angered him greatly whenever it happened within his hearing. He blamed me for shouting too much, singing too much, being too quiet. He blamed me for the cost of living and most of all for being alive, for being another man's child.
As time went by and it began to appear that my mother would have no more babies, he apportioned this problem to me also, saying loudly and often that I had 'ruined' my mother by being born such a huge great lump. Of this I took little notice, because I was impressed by none of

Higson's opinions and was determined to minimise his influence on my life.

But I was afraid of his quick, blind rages, tense in his presence and I took to absenting myself from the house for hours at a stretch, taking refuge in Josie Cullen's chaotic but happy household.

The Cullens lived in a corporation house in Ince Avenue at the back of the library. There were so many Cullens that they were forced to eat in relays, the littlest ones often being sent to sit on the stairs with a bowl on their knees and one spoon between two or three.

Mrs Cullen put me in mind of Mrs Hyatt from Ensign Street, being of similar build and nature. Although her house was already filled to bursting, she always found space, time and a wedge of bread and dripping for me. 'There y' are, lass. Get outside o' that, it'll stick to yer ribs. Now, our Josie, get that wash in to soak. And where's our Allan? ALLAN!' she would scream through the ever-open door, 'Get thisen in 'ere while I mend yer pants.'

Mrs Cullen would then turn to survey her rumbustious troop. 'Right now, Ellen, get down that corner shop and ask fer five o' spuds on tick. Be nice. Smile at the woman for God's sake. Martin, get that knitting needle off our Tony, 'e'll 'ave 'is bloody eye out like a lolly on a stick in a minute. An' get that bloody cat out o' the cupboard, Cathy. Yes, I know she's lookin' where to 'ave 'er kittens – find 'er a box in the front room an' a couple of old *Evening News*es. Now. 'Oo's took the bloody lid off me bloody kettle? Annie love, go an' 'ave a look round t' back garden will yer? An' while yer about it, see if you can catch sight o' me fryin' pan. Only they've been playin' 'ouse again, so you'll likely find a cup or two while yer at it . . .'

I loved every minute I spent in that smelly, untidy house. There was nowhere to sit, scarcely an inch of room to even stand in, but at the centre of it all was Mrs Cullen, her great belly heaving with laughter as often as not, calmly dealing with each crisis as it arose, spreading her love and generosity equally amongst all-comers.

When I would go home, always reluctantly, I could not help comparing my mother with Mrs Cullen. Long hours in the mill were taking their toll and it was plain that my mother was not a happy woman, for her face, once rounded and well-fleshed, was becoming sunken and seemed to be acquiring new and deeper lines with each passing day. Even her Titian hair was losing its vibrance, while her shoulders became rounder, as if they were carrying a great invisible weight.

Higson, on the other hand, appeared to be thriving on good food and fresh air and had regained most, if not all the strength he had lost while in the prison camp. But however many windows he cleaned, however many spools my mother doffed, however many frames she tended, there was never enough money in the house.

Furthermore, now that men had returned from the war and had recovered from wounds of body and mind, they were reclaiming their jobs and my mother was forced to agree, with reluctance, that she would eventually take an evening shift at the mill. This bitter pill was sweetened by the offer of promotion to supervisor in charge of two rooms and as this meant an increase in rate, her money would not be noticeably reduced.

The elevation in her status should have cheered her and improved the atmosphere at home, at least between her and him, but still the long silences continued. I knew that my mother was very unhappy and I understood enough to realise that Eddie Higson was responsible for her state of mind. This was one thing for which I could not blame myself, because I was being as good as I knew how to be, was keeping out of 'his' way as frequently as possible, spending my time at the Cullens' or in my attic room.

But for many months now, I had not heard my mother laugh, had seldom seen her smile. The marriage had been a mistake. Even at my tender age, I could sense this. Yet I derived no satisfaction from having been proved right.

Chapter Seven: Communion

Father Cavanagh persuaded them both to attend my First Communion and they looked so embarrassed and out of place, never having been inside St Stephen's before, that I rather wished the priest had kept his nose out of our business. I wore a long dress of creamy-white satin, a veil with a stiff crown of artificial flowers and new white shoes. In my hands I carried a nosegay of mimosa and gypsy grass, together with a white missal and a rosary that my father had had blessed by Pope Pius XII himself.

The priest placed the bread on my extended tongue while an altar boy held a solid gold plate under my chin in case of crumbs. Should the body of Jesus Christ crumble, then it must crumble only on to precious metal.

I blessed myself, trying to feel solemn and dignified and waited for the wafer to melt, for I had been forbidden to chew. It stuck to the roof of my dry mouth and I hoped that Jesus wouldn't mind too much when I edged it away with my tongue, for this thin consecrated biscuit now embodied Christ, who had died for me.

I felt empty of grace and of breakfast, as we were forbidden to eat or drink before Communion. We new communicants, eight boys and seven girls, went obediently back to our families while Father Cavanagh droned his solemn way through the rest of the Mass.

Then it was over. Now I would have to be very, very good, for every misdemeanour I committed would have to be relayed through the black grille of the confessional and right into Father Cavanagh's ever-inquisitive ear. If sins were left untold and if the Blessed Sacrament was allowed, therefore, to descend into a stomach full of sin, then this would be a sacrilege, for which crime there would be no absolution.

Yet I felt nothing at this, my first communion with Jesus Christ. What I had expected to feel, what I should feel, I didn't know, but I was sure that I should not feel so . . . so ordinary, that Jesus should be filling me with grace and happiness, that I should be inviting Him, welcoming Him into my heart and soul. And when I returned to my pew and saw Eddie Higson sitting next to my mother, my loathing for him hit me with renewed force and I fell to my knees to make yet another act of contrition. 'Lord I am not worthy that Thou shouldst enter under my roof; say but the word and my soul shall be healed. O my God, I am sorry and beg pardon for all my sins . . .'

After the Mass, there was a party in one of the classrooms and we were given a breakfast of sorts, sandwiches, biscuits and orange juice. My mother and Higson stood awkwardly to one side, while the rest of the parents, obviously regular churchgoers, grouped themselves about the room, exclaiming over what a lovely Mass it had been and didn't their Mary look sweet in the white frock and wasn't Jimmy quite the little man in his new suit.

Father Cavanagh, when he entered the room, made a bee-line for my mother. As consecrated shepherd of this particular flock, it was his bounden duty to round up the stray sheep first. The priest beckoned me to follow, which I did with reluctance as the food was disappearing fast and I hadn't had much.

'Well now,' he was saying. ''Tis lovely to see the pair of you here, so it is. And you'll be after setting a good example for little Annie here now, won't you?'

My mother nodded while Eddie Higson stifled a yawn – he was not used to being out of bed so early on a Sunday.

'And will you be attending the Mass in the future then Mr . . . er . . . Higson?'

'Depends on the weather. I sometimes do a few houses on a Sunday if the week's been bad.'

'You work on a Sunday? On God's holy day? Mercy in heaven, isn't that a sin now?'

Higson shrugged. 'Well, you work on a Sunday, don't you? I reckon Sunday's about your busiest day. And if we all did what you're suggesting, they'd have to shut all the hospitals for a start, wouldn't they? So do we just leave people to die being as it's Sunday?'

'Ah well now, that's a different matter altogether, for hospital work is essential and as for my work, well . . .'

Eddie Higson interrupted loudly. 'So's window cleaning if it pays my bills.'

The two men glared at one another for a few seconds, then Father Cavanagh turned to my mother.

'Will yourself be bringing Annie to the Mass then, Mrs . . . er . . . Higson?'

'I'll try, Father.'

'Yes, yes, you do that. And isn't it time you made your Easter Duties? I have not seen you at Communion, Mrs Higson.'

'I'll bear it in mind, Father.'

'Aye, you do that now, and God bless you.'

The priest moved on to speak to the other parents and Eddie Higson grabbed me by the arm and dragged me out of the classroom. My mother followed at a slower pace crying, 'But she's not had her party, Eddie . . .'

'Bugger her party. We're getting out of here.'

Then, at the far end of the corridor, I spotted two familiar figures making their way towards us. With a great cry of joy, I wrenched my arm free and began to run, coronet and veil slipping unheeded to the floor.

'Aw, we missed it, luv.' Mrs Hyatt enfolded me in her large heavy arms then Tom pulled me away from her, lifting me up, swinging me into the air just as my father had used to do.

'You've not gone to America, then,' I said happily.

'Not yet, Annie.'

'But you're still going?'

'Aye, he's still going,' said Mrs Hyatt before moving on to greet my mother.

'Are you alright, Annie?' Tom whispered.

'Yes, I'm alright.'

'Is he . . . good to you?'

I looked over my shoulder at Eddie Higson who was standing a little way apart from my mother and Mrs Hyatt. 'I don't take any notice of him,' I said. 'I just keep out of his road.'

'He doesn't hit you or anything?'

I shrugged. 'Not much. When are you going anyway?'

'Next week.'

This news dropped like a stone into my stomach and I had to swallow deeply before I could say, 'I wish you wouldn't, Tom.'

'Tell you what, Annie. You wait for me and I'll come back and marry you when I've made me fortune. How does that sound?'

'Daft,' I said, but I knew I was blushing.

My mother and Mrs Hyatt joined us now.

'Will you come and have a cup of tea with us then, Florrie – and Tom, of course. And I've a scone or two and a bit of window pie left – come on back with us.'

'Aye, we will that,' answered Mrs Hyatt. 'And I'm sorry we missed your Communion, Annie, but it's a fair stretch from Ensign Street up here – more ways than one, eh, Nancy?'

The walk back down Long Moor Lane was uncomfortable, for neither Tom nor Mrs Hyatt spoke to Eddie Higson after the initial greeting. My mother and he walked in front while I skipped along behind, one hand in Mrs Hyatt's, the other in Tom's.

They were, of course, very impressed with the house – or at least, Mrs Hyatt was. Tom had little to say on the subject, but his mother oohed and ahed over every detail, especially when it came to the bathroom and the walk-in wardrobe.

Eddie Higson, after drinking just one cup of tea, went out to collect money from his customers. In truth, I felt, he went to get away from Mrs Hyatt who, apart from casting the odd furtive glance in his direction, had ignored him almost completely.

When there remained just the four of us, Mrs Hyatt, more relaxed now, said to my mother, 'By, tha looks a bit weary, lass.'

'Yes, well, it's tiring at the mill. I'm starting evening shift soon, so it should be a bit easier.'

Mrs Hyatt stirred her second cup of tea slowly. 'And who'll be looking after 'er while yer out?' she asked.

'Oh, Eddie'll see to her.'

'Will 'e now?'

I felt Tom's leg brush past mine as he kicked his mother's shoe under the table. My mother, bristling slightly, spoke up. 'He's quite capable of seeing to the child, Florrie. Fact is, Annie can very near take care of herself.'

'Aye, 'appen she might 'ave to an' all from what I've 'eard.'

In the silence that followed, you might have heard a feather, let alone a pin drop. My mother rose with exaggerated quietness, taking with her the teapot as a signal that the Hyatts were no longer welcome, then she said softly, 'That, Florrie Hyatt, was all talk and you know it. And if you've come all the way from Ensign Street to cause bloody trouble, you can just damn well get back where you belong.'

Tom, leaning an elbow on the table, put a hand to his forehead. 'Cut it out, Ma. I've told you before and I'll say it again – no good can come of this.'

But Mrs Hyatt, her colour heightening, jumped up from the table as fast as her bulk would allow. 'Leopards doesn't change their spots, Nancy Byrne – ooh, I'm forgettin' meself, aren't I? Nancy 'Igson, I mean. What can't speak can't lie an' them as is dead don't get up and talk for theirselves, do they?' Her face was darkening to a purplish hue.

'They don't need to. You do all the talking for them. Who the hell do you think you are, anyway, Florrie Hyatt? Mouthpiece of Bolton? Why don't you get under the clock in the Town Centre, maybe they'll give you a loud-hailer.'

''E did things. You know 'e did.'

'I know nothing, Florrie and neither do you.'

Tom looked anxiously at me, then waved an arm towards the door, asking me, with a raised eyebrow, to step outside with him, but I shook my head. I was not going to miss this. For once, I might learn something about Eddie Higson.

Mrs Hyatt continued. 'I know 'e were wild and evil, that's what I know. 'E were a bad lad and bad lads becomes bad men.'

My mother slammed the teapot back on to the table, causing cups and spoons to rattle. 'Do you want me to get the law on you, Florrie Hyatt? Is that what you want, a big scandal? Because I will, you know, I shall get a solicitor. And if Eddie knew what you were saying . . .'

'Why, what 'ave I said?'

'That he's a bad lot.'

'Prove me wrong, then.'

'Oh no, you prove you're right. I know enough about the law to know the onus is on you. Innocent till proved otherwise, Florrie Hyatt. You just remember that. Whatever happened all those years ago – if anything ever did happen – was before I ever lived in Ensign Street and if you hadn't kept your great mouth flapping it would have died a death by now. Eddie's a good man. He works hard, he's got the house nice – what more proof do you want?'

Tom looked quickly at me. 'There's a time and a place for this sort of thing. Have neither of you any consideration for this child? And you listen to me, Mam, once and for all. A lot of lads sow wild oats but turn out decent. So shut up, will you?'

This was, by now, totally beyond my comprehension. As far as I could work out (and it wasn't very far) Eddie Higson might have done something bad and then again, he might not. Whatever he might have done had made Mrs Hyatt go a funny colour and Tom said it was something to do with sewing. I had never seen Eddie Higson sewing. It was always my Mam who did the mending and stitching and sewing on of buttons.

Whatever it was all about, Tom and his mother were leaving and I might never see Tom again. As my mother and I stood in the doorway watching them walk away, I felt the tears of self-pity pricking my eyelids. I had not enjoyed my First Communion day one little bit.

Swiftly, I pulled myself away from my mother and ran down the road, the long satin skirt lifted high and bunched carelessly in my two clenched fists.

'You won't forget me, Tom?'

He looked down at me, his own eyes suspiciously wet. 'No, I'll never, ever forget you, Annie.'

'And you'll write to me?'

'That I will. Soon as I get there.'

Mrs Hyatt bent to give me a kiss and whispered in my ear, 'Remember, lass, any bother at all an' tha comes fer me an' Freddie. Okay?'

'Okay.'

I sighed deeply as they walked away. Grown-ups were such a puzzle to me, telling half a tale, warning you about things you couldn't understand.

But I was to understand only too soon what they had meant, what they had been trying to guard me against. I was eight years old and teetering on the brink of a nightmare that was to last for many years to come, a bad dream from which I would not wake until I had gained considerably in age and experience.

For a while at least, forgiving Tom and Mrs Hyatt would not be easy, for they might have protected me if they had tried harder. But they were, after all, no blood kin to me and I was no responsibility of theirs.

Forgiving my mother would, strangely, be easier, because I would have to care for and protect her from the evil in our midst.

But I would never, as long as I lived, forgive Eddie Higson for what was about to happen to me.

Mrs Cullen was having a clearout.

This was something she did two or three times a year and it was carried out with a precision that fell a long way short of the military. The idea was, as she put it, to 'shift all th' upstairs muck to downstairs an' all t' downstairs muck out ter t' back o' the 'ouse, then kick it about till it disappears'.

We lined up on the stairs like a chain-gang, playing a game of pass the parcel with objects of varying size, shape and incredibility. We handled torn sheets, rag rugs, jerries without handles, half-sets of false teeth, corsets with the whalebone whipping free about our ears, toothless combs, bits of lino and oilcloth and several dozen back copies of the *Bolton Evening News*, some turning yellow with age.

Once this lot was piled into the narrow hallway, there was scarcely room for Mrs Cullen to make her descent past all the children who had gathered on, around and under the mound of debris.

'Now,' she announced, her huge breasts heaving with exertion. 'Tha mun get this lot out the back, then we mun mek a start on t' front room. Allan, put them corsets down. No, yer can't keep 'em. What the 'ell are you plannin' on doin' with 'em anyroad – makin' a rabbit 'utch? No, Josie, you are not 'angin' on to that jerry for growin' daffs in, yer don't know where it's been. Or, more ter t' point, yer do know where it's been. An' Martin – put them false teeth down – hey, not on yer Dad's chair this time! Where's our Josie gone wi' that jerry? Annie – put that bloody kettle on, lass, I'm fair clemmed . . .'

On this particular Thursday night, we had started on the front room, which was the worst room in the house, having been given over to the children as a place to play, leaving only the large kitchen as true living space for this huge family. The front room was so bad that even opening the door to get in required careful planning and Lizzie, being the smallest of those old enough to walk, was pushed through a tiny gap in order to remove the main obstacles from behind the door, thus enabling the rest of us to enter the room.

Once inside, we met a total and glorious chaos. There were large matted tangles of wool and string, three-wheeled skates, wooden crates with pram wheels and lengths of rope attached and what seemed to be about a hundred cardboard boxes in various sizes and states of decay. Although nothing was intact, everybody had a good reason for wanting to keep some of it.

Allan wanted the boxes as he was a compulsive collector and needed 'things to keep things in'. He also had grandiose ideas for the crates on wheels and insisted that he could get the skates mended by an old farrier up Breightmet who had taken to skate-mending now that horses had become fewer and farther between.

But Mrs Cullen was ruthless in her insistence. Everything must go into the back garden where it would join last year's mouldering and rusting heaps of prams and broken furniture.

We had just begun to transfer the last of the rubbish into the hallway, when a sharp rapping at the door made us pause, a sudden and miraculous silence falling over the whole ensemble as we pondered. Would it be rent, water or gas? Had they come to turn us off, turn us out or was it just the bum bailey? The latter would have come as no surprise and little threat, for few bills had been paid and there was nothing worth the bailiff's trouble to carry away, the few sticks of furniture that had survived the seven children being too scarred and battered to be of any value whatsoever.

Mrs Cullen paused, a finger to her pursed lips, then she

whispered, 'Tha'd best open t' door, Annie. Say yer not family, at least that's the truth. Tell 'em to come back tomorrer – wi' a pick-axe an' a police escort.' Josie giggled and Mrs Cullen clipped her gently round the ear. 'Shut up, our Josie. It might even be the flamin' priest an' I can do wi'out 'im 'Oly Maryin' all over me back kitchen an' me in t' middle o' me clearout.'

I crept surreptitiously down the hall and opened the door just a crack.

'Can you come back tomorrow?' I whispered through the gap, trying not to giggle as Josie's stifled snorts of laughter reached my ears.

'No, I can't come back tomorrow. Get out here now.'

I must have stiffened visibly because Mrs Cullen came forward, negotiating her way carefully around the pile of rubbish.

''Oo is it, luv?'

I opened the door to reveal Eddie Higson standing on the step, a Woodbine making his lip curl even further into the snarl that usually occupied his face when he looked at me.

'Get yourself home,' he snapped. 'It's way past your bedtime.'

I stood my ground. 'I'm helping Mrs Cullen,' I said, trying to keep my voice steady, trying to keep the fear out of it, trying, most of all, not to lose face in front of Josie – I didn't want her to know how much I feared this man who was supposed to be my stepfather.

Eddie Higson swept a contemptuous eye past me towards Mrs Cullen and her brood, bringing his gaze to rest finally on the vast mound of debris at our feet.

'I reckon Mrs Cullen's got enough helpers of her own. She doesn't need you. Anyroad, happen she should get the council to shift that lot.'

Mrs Cullen drew herself up to her full five foot two, arms clasped beneath the pendulous bosom. 'My 'usband will see to all this when 'e gets in from the ropewalk. You go, Annie luv.'

'Aye,' Eddie Higson said, pulling the cigarette from his mouth and grinding it underfoot on the step. 'Come on. Get yourself out of this midden before you catch something.'

Mrs Cullen's body seemed to swell with anger as she stumbled closer to the door. 'This is no midden, Eddie Higson.'

'Oh aye?' he drawled. 'Well, you could have fooled me, for I've seen less on a corporation tip than what you've got here.'

Mrs Cullen was at the door now and she faced him, her complexion reddening as her anger rose. 'Aye, well, 'appen you spend a lot o' time up at corporation tips. Most people usually manages ter find their own level, their own place, like. I see you've found yours. So get back ter t' tip where you belong. Only don't tek Annie wi' you. She don't belong on no tip.'

'That's why I'm taking her home. Out of this bloody tip. You want to watch yourself, Mrs Cullen. You'll be having the Health round next and getting yourself fumigated.'

'Fumigated? It's your bloody gob wants fumigatin'. We may not 'ave t' poshest bathroom up Long Moor, but at least we 'ave an 'appy 'ome, one as your Annie's glad to run to. Poor little waif can't get away from 'er own 'ouse quick enough, seems ter me.'

Eddie Higson was shouting now as he said, 'You slovenly old bitch, you. She'll not be coming here no more, I'll see to that. And her mother will too when I tell her what a state this place is in. Get here now, you,' he screamed at me.

'No. No, I'm not coming,' I cried, the tears beginning to flow down my face and into my throat, choking me so that I had to fight for breath.

'Get here now or I'm coming in for you.'

Mrs Cullen pushed me behind her then stood in the doorway, her legs spread wide. 'You'll 'ave ter get past me first. An' I'm not lettin' you in my 'ouse wi'out a fight, you bad-mouthed bugger, you. Come on then. Try it. Just you try to get in. Don't forget, my George'll be 'ere in a minute. 'E'll sort you. You'll be climbin' no bloody ladders fer a week or two if 'e gets 'is 'ands round that scrawny little neck o' yours.'

I could hear Mrs Cullen breathing heavily in the silence that followed and I held my own breath, fighting back the sobs.

'Are you coming or not?'

'No,' I managed to gasp.

'I'll beat the bloody living daylights out of you, lady,' he yelled. 'You'll have to come out of that pig-sty sooner or later and I'll be waiting.'

Mrs Cullen, after slamming the door in his twisted face, turned to look at us, leaning heavily against the stair rail for a few seconds before speaking to me. 'Now don't tek on, lass. You can double up wi' our girls tonight – till yer Mam gets back off 'er evenin' shift at anyroad. Likely she'll come and collect you once it's all sorted. Don't worry, 'e'll calm down, it'll all be forgot, you'll see.

'Now come on, you lot. Get this muck shifted before your dad gets back an' breaks 'is neck over it. I'm goin' to warm a drop o' milk fer Annie. Lizzie, see if yer can find a clean cup. Martin, get in that meatsafe see if there's a bit o' brandy left. Bring 'er through to the kitchen, Josie. Come on now, come on . . .'

My mother did not come for me at the end of her shift. I spent the night at Josie's house and it was not comfortable, for there was little room in the bed which contained four of us, two at the top, two at the bottom, like sardines in a tin.

Things were not made easier by Lizzie who wet the bed and everyone in it, which I later discovered to be a regular occurrence. For the whole of the next day at school I reeked of drying urine, a smell I recognised now as that which usually surrounded Josie, Lizzie and most of the rest of the family. I was also covered in spots, tiny red bites bequeathed to me by all the other creatures that occupied Josie's bedroom.

When I reached home that afternoon, Eddie Higson had not yet returned from his round. My mother was at the living-room range, her back towards me as I entered the room and she seemed, at first, to have little to say. When she turned to face me, I understood why she was so quiet, because her cheeks were bruised, her lower lip swollen to twice its normal size and one of her eyes was closed and surrounded in purplish black flesh.

She had received my beating. Because of my disobedience, because of my cowardice, my poor little mother had been beaten half to death by a man who must surely be crazed to inflict such wounds on his wife.

I ran to her and she flinched as I flung my arms about her waist. It was obvious that her body, too, was hurt.

Easing herself gently away from me, she pressed me into a chair. 'Annie, love. Things is hard enough without you making this kind of trouble. Why didn't you come home when you were told?'

I hesitated before replying, 'Because he was nasty to Mrs Cullen, Mam. He called her a slovenly old bi . . . well, a bad name. He showed me up in front of my friends.'

'Friends? Friends, love? Can't you smell yourself? They're mucky folk, Annie. You shouldn't be mixing with mucky folk. Oh, I wish I'd come and fetched you home after my shift, but I couldn't – not like this. You'd be best stopping away from the Cullens in future.'

'I like them,' I said stubbornly, yet immediately torn between wanting to agree with my poor hurt mother and wanting to defend those who had been good to me.

'You should have come home when he first came for you.'

'I don't want to come home with him. I don't like being here with him. Why can't you be here? Why can't you work days like you used to?'

'Because I can't, love. It's as simple as that.'

Flinching visibly, she lowered herself into a squatting

position in front of me. 'Now, listen, Annie. You're a big girl. I fell downstairs last night – you understand? I fell down the stairs. Now I've got a letter here from . . . er . . . from Dr Pritchard. I want you to go down to Millhouse mill and give it in to Ernie Bradshaw. Nobody else. If Ernie's not there, you bring this letter back. Can you remember that?'

I nodded and she went on. 'Only I can't go into work looking like this now, can I? I'd likely frighten the mill cat to death – let alone me mates if they saw me like this. So after tea, when the hooter's gone off, you get your coat on and go down Folds Road. You catch the 45 and get off at the stop after the bend. Go up Millhouse Lane till you get to the mill – you can't miss it, it's about the same size as Buckingham Palace. Ask for Ernie Bradshaw, second floor. And remember, that letter's for him and only for him.'

She rose painfully and took a step back. 'While you're there, Annie, have a good look round. And I mean a good look – you see what it's like in there, take it all in. Because except for today, I don't want you ever setting foot inside a mill again.' She reached out her hands in an imploring gesture. 'You've got chances, Annie. Chances I never had. Things are going to change, specially for women, you mark my words. Well, I want you to take them chances.' Her hands closed into tight, gripping fists. 'Take them, use them opportunities. Because I'll never rest in me grave if I know you're a spinner or a doffer.'

'You're . . . you're not going to die, are you, Mam?'

Her face stretched into as much of a smile as the damaged tissue would allow. 'No, lass. I'm not shuffling off just yet, not till you're a doctor or a lawyer or . . .'

'An Indian chief,' I said, finishing off the rhyme.

'You're going to be something great, Annie. I've always known it, right from the start when you brought yourself to life. There's something in you, something I can't put me finger on, so you'd best put your own finger on it, love.

Because the choices are there for you; they weren't there for me – it was the mill at fourteen and I've never known any other life. But you will, oh aye, you will.'

She placed my meal on the table in front of me. 'Remember, Annie. I fell downstairs.'

'I'll kill him, Mam,' I said quietly.

As she turned from me, I thought I heard her say, 'You'll have to get in the queue for that.' But I wasn't sure.

Chapter Eight: The Killing

It was an experience I would never forget.

Now that the trams and trolleys were gone, I had finally got used to the new buses, but this time I was going in the wrong direction, down the moor rather than up, travelling back towards Town and, it seemed, backwards through the century too.

The further down the road I got, the untidier the area became until, at the bottom of Folds Road where I alighted from the bus, it seemed that I was back in Ensign Street, for the tiny Victorian terraces ran in deep rows to the left and to the right of me as I walked down Millhouse Lane. Each street seemed so like Ensign Street, so neglected and small and squalid, that I began to appreciate my mother's ambition to move up the moor.

Had I really lived in a house as small as these were? Had I really played in those narrow, cobbled backs with open middens so close and never noticed the smell?

Our own midden up Long Moor Lane was now a coal shed, while the building that had once housed the tippler was used to store tools and Eddie Higson's buckets and leathers. Oh yes, we had come a long way up in the world, but what price were we paying? And would I have to tell in confession that my mother had taken my beating and that I wanted Eddie Higson dead?

I stopped at the mill gates as I pondered, realising after a few minutes that, yes, I would indeed rather live in Ensign Street without him than up Long Moor with him. Perhaps we could leave him and go back? But no, even after the beating, she would never leave her new bathroom. And, of course, as a Catholic, she could not abandon her husband no matter what he did to her.

I clutched in my hand the envelope that held a sheet of lies, a tissue of total fabrication that would protect Eddie Higson. Shouldn't I tell somebody the truth? Instinctively, I knew that in order to protect my mother, I could never, ever tell anyone about what had happened in the house. Someone had to look after her. It would have to be me. And how many more times would she have to 'fall downstairs'? Was that the price she would have to pay for her bathroom and electric light? And what would he do to me once she went back on evening shifts? Would he beat me too? Would I need a note to say I'd fallen down the stairs?

It was all too much to worry about, so I snapped out of my trance; if I stood here much longer, I'd be home late and I didn't want to have my mother worrying. And I needed to get back to make sure he didn't beat her again, because if he did, I would surely be there to find a way of hurting or even killing him.

Six flagged steps led up to a side door and I pushed this open to find before me another flight of stone stairs which I climbed until they turned to yet another flight. Up and up I went until I found a huge door with a large white number two painted on to it. This I had to push hard, for it was very heavy and had a spring to keep it shut.

I stepped through that doorway and into a hell on earth that almost knocked me back out again. The noise was incredible. Row upon row of frames filled the room. The workers, sandwiched between the machines, obviously got as little consideration here as they did at home, where the mill-owning landlords packed them into hovels, dozens to the acre.

Each spinning-frame was covered in what appeared to be a million moving parts, rattling and clanging, spools filling with cotton, filling so quickly that the women had to run to keep pace with the work.

I watched them for a few moments, fascinated by their

deftness as they doffed the full spools and replaced them immediately with empty ones, each time feeding the cotton through a maze of metal rings. Even from the doorway, I could see the sweat pouring from the women's faces, could make out vast damp patches on their clothing as they moved swiftly up and down the frames.

The air was wet and heavy; the temperature in the room must have been hotter than the hottest days I could remember, days when tar melted and pavements became too fierce for thin soles, let alone bare feet. This was where my little mother had spent her life since she was but six years older than I was now. I felt my own sweat pricking my eyes as it ran down from my hair; after one minute I was wet to the skin, clothes sticking to my back, palms slick with moisture.

A man came forward and dragged me back out on to the cool landing where the sudden quiet was almost deafening.

'What do you want here then, little lass?'

'I'm looking for Mr Bradshaw, my Mam's boss.'

'That's me.' Bright blue eyes twinkled and he brushed a hand through his light brown hair. 'It isn't every day a bonny lass comes up here and asks for me. I think my luck must be changing. Now, what's it all about?'

'It's about my Mam.'

'Eeh well. You're Nancy's lass aren't you? I can see the resemblance now. I wondered where our Nancy was tonight. Nothing up, I hope?'

I handed him the note and he tore at the envelope swiftly. It was not from the doctor at all – I recognised my own mother's writing.

Ernie Bradshaw leaned against the wall before speaking again. 'Tell her the job's safe. I just hope she is, that's all. And you can tell her . . . well, tell her Ernie sends his best. How is she?'

'She's hurt.'

'I know that. What's your name now – Annie, isn't it?'

I nodded.

'Well, Annie, you tell your Mam as Ernie will be up to see her. Tell her that if . . . if he's in, then she must leave a sign. Now, let me think a minute.' He paced about the landing, all the while stroking his chin and I thought what a nice man he seemed, friendly-looking, easy to talk to.

'I know,' he said suddenly, turning in mid-stride. 'Tell her if he's in she must leave a small stone on the front doorstep. Now, can you remember that?' This man seemed to know and understand my attitude to Eddie Higson, otherwise he would not be confiding in me now. Was he a friend and not just a boss to my mother?

'Yes, I can remember that, Mr Bradshaw.'

'Call me Ernie. Everybody else does. Now, can you keep this secret?'

'Yes, I can, I'm good at secrets.'

'You won't tell your Dad?'

'He's not my Dad. I tell him nothing.'

'Aye, so I've heard.' He grinned at me. 'I'm very . . . fond of your Mam, Annie. If anything ever . . . well, if anybody ever hurt her. . .'

'She fell downstairs, Ernie.'

'Aye.' He waved the note. 'So it says here. And I'm a monkey's uncle.'

So it looked as if my mother had confided in this man, had told him that she was unhappy with Eddie Higson, that all was not well up Long Moor Lane. Well, I wasn't surprised; this was a man you might take to, confide in and trust.

'Give her . . . my love, will you, Annie?' He pressed a half-crown into my hand. 'And that's for you, for being such a bonny lass. Don't forget now. The boss sends his love.'

'Oh thankyou, Ernie, I've never had a whole half-crown before.'

'You deserve it, love. Now get off home and see you look after that Mam of yours. Ta-ra now.'

'Ta-ra, Ernie.'

Once outside, I looked back at the building, craning my neck to see the top of the stack where thick smoke was belching forth into the sky. She had been right. I would never want to set foot in there again. Except for one reason. I'd like to see more of Ernie Bradshaw.

I got the chance to see him again, not just once, but many times. The first few visits he paid us were during the school holidays and the three of us spent long afternoons laughing and joking in the kitchen.

On the third occasion I was sent out to play and to keep an eye out for Eddie Higson in case he got home early; when I came back into the house my mother, whose face was healing nicely, looked flushed and happy and she had changed her dress.

'Where's Ernie?' I asked innocently.

'Oh he's . . . in the bathroom. He won't be a minute.'

'I wish we could swap Eddie Higson for Ernie,' I whispered.

'Keep your thoughts to yourself, Annie . . .'

My mother's affair with Ernie Bradshaw was beautiful. During those summer months she blossomed into her old self again, began laughing and singing 'Burlington Bertie' like she had used to, wore cheap, pretty clothes and make-up, bought some bright clip-on earrings and coloured beads.

She was quiet when Eddie Higson was around though, and so was I, because I knew too much to say or do anything that might puncture the frail bubble that was her happiness.

I learned to knock at the door before entering if there was no stone on the step, learned to watch in the back street for the familiar sight of Higson's ladder as it bobbed its way home on his shoulder, learned to live with my sins by framing my confessions carefully and rehearsing my piece each time before chanting my list of errors through the grille.

Ernie and my mother spent many afternoons together and although I was often excluded, they sometimes took me out to the Jolly Brows and once to Southport on a charabanc. What the neighbours must have thought I never knew; certainly my mother was not aware, in her bliss, of anything beyond the fact that she was infatuated with this man, that she had to be with him at every opportunity. But I knew in my bones that we were living on a knife's edge, that sooner or later Eddie Higson would find out and we would all suffer as a consequence. But it was no use; when I voiced my fears, she simply refused to hear me.

Once she returned to her evening shifts, my mother made arrangements for me to sleep at Rita Entwistle's house, nominally to keep Rita company as she, too, was an only child, but really to keep me away from Eddie Higson. Rita's mother and my mother worked together and although Rita was never a really close friend, she was, at least, clean and generous with her toys.

My friendship with Josie remained close and constant and I visited the Cullens whenever I could, was still happier in their house than I was anywhere else.

I was also receiving regular letters and parcels from Tom in Philadelphia, so my life, apart from the great worry about my mother and Ernie, continued on an even keel for several months.

When my mother began to get fat, I took little notice. Some people were fat, some were thin; nobody bothered much about shapes and sizes in those days. It was Mrs Cullen who inadvertently told me the reason for my mother's increased girth. We were sitting out at the back of the house enjoying a sunny September afternoon. Around us were piles of 'clear-outs' among which the little kids played while we elders – Josie, Allan and I – sat drinking dandelion and burdock with Mrs Cullen.

'What dost want then, a brother or a sister?' Oh no, not again. Surely there were not going to be eight Cullens? I noticed that she was not looking at Josie or at Allan as she spoke.

'Are you talking to me, Mrs Cullen?'

'I am that, lass. Did you think I were askin' our Josie? Don't you think I've done my share then? Nay, I'm 'avin' no more. I'm even thinkin' o' sendin' George off ter Siberia ter mek sure.' Her great belly shook with laughter. 'But it's time you got a little playmate, isn't it? Eeh, I can see yer now, pushin' yer pram round Long Moor. Aye, it's not before time. 'Ow old are you now?'

'Eight and a half,' I answered, hoping I didn't sound too stunned.

'Big gap, that. Still, never mind, eh?' She was staring hard at me now. 'Eeh lass – didn't you know, 'aven't they told you?'

I shook my head.

'Well then, tek no notice o' me, I could be wrong. It's just I've 'ad so many meself I recognise t' symptoms, if yer get me meanin'. She might just be puttin' a bit o' weight on, luv.'

I was trying to organise my thoughts. A brother or sister, a baby in the house, how did I feel about that? I concluded that my feelings were mixed. With a new baby about, Eddie Higson would be pleased and would perhaps take even less notice of me – that would be a good thing. But a baby would take my mother's attention too, leaving her with less time for me. And what about poor Ernie? She wouldn't be able to have a lie down with him in the afternoons any more, not with a baby to feed and change. Perhaps Ernie would go elsewhere now and we would both miss him.

'By the way, Annie,' said Josie. 'We're moving, you know.'

Oh no, not again! Mrs Cullen laughed at the expression on my face.

'We're movin' across the road from you, Annie,' she giggled. 'You'll be able ter stick yer 'ead out o' t' winders an' yell across at us.'

Thank goodness for that, at least. 'We've got a swap for a four bedroomed,' said Allan. 'Though I think the real reason is the council wants to get at this lot and clean it up.'

Mrs Cullen roared with laughter. 'Aye. 'Appen they'll move us every time as t' garden gets full!'

'When are you moving?' I asked, just for something to say, something to take my mind off the possible changes at home.

'Couple o' weeks,' answered Mrs Cullen. 'Now you get off 'ome an' see is yer Mam needin' you. If she's the way I think she is, she'll be needin' all the 'elp she can get. Oh, before you go – come 'ere a minute.' I bent down so that she could whisper in my ear. 'Tell 'er to go careful wi' that Ernie feller. Don't worry, I won't say nothin' ter nobody. I saw 'em together in Town last week an' once before at your door. Tell er . . .' Her voice dropped even lower. 'Tell 'er 'e's wed wi' three kids of 'is own.'

I fled homeward, my face burning with shame. I'd begun to pick things up at school, dirty words about what men and women did together, stories of bad women who would 'go' with anybody, even married men. Although I wasn't yet fully aware of what it all meant, I didn't want my Mam to be a bad woman.

When I opened the front door, all was quiet, yet the air seemed to crackle with an atmosphere, a bad feeling that soaked out of the living room, through the front room and right into the vestibule. I opened this second door quietly and stood rigid, waiting for I knew not what.

'You filthy bitch.' His voice was ominously quiet. 'Trying to pass it off as mine, were you?' I flinched as I heard flesh strike flesh. 'I'm sterile, you dirty piece. Sterile, do you hear me? My chances of fathering a child are about a million to one, they told me that in the hospital.'

He hit her again and I heard her moan of pain before she

spoke between gasps. 'But . . . there is a slight . . . chance of you . . . isn't there? And there's been . . . nobody . . . nobody.'

'Tell that to the cat, you stupid bag. How often have you let me at you lately, eh? And do you think I'm blind, with your new frocks and your earrings, walking round like a bloody tart? That is not my kid. Whose is it? I'll beat it out of you, I will, I will . . .'

Now the sounds were different. This time it was not flesh on flesh, but something solid hitting something soft. I didn't know what to do, where to turn. For what seemed like hours I remained riveted to the spot, sweat and tears pouring down my face. He was speaking again as he kicked her.

'I used to say she'd ruined you, didn't I? Well that was just a joke, you see, just a joke. I'm not joking now though, oh no . . .'

Suddenly galvanised, I shot through the house and into the living room. My mother lay at his feet in front of the range as he drove his foot again and again into her belly which she was trying to shield with very bloody arms. So involved was he in his task that he did not notice me as I crept behind him and brought the rolling-pin crashing on to the back of his skull.

He went down like a stone and I raised my hand to strike again, would have finished him off there and then, but my mother, raising herself slightly said, 'No, Annie. Get the doctor. He's killed my baby.' I noticed then that the rug beneath her was soaked bright red, that her skirt was sodden with blood, that more blood was pouring down between her thighs.

Instinctively, I grabbed some towels from the pulley line and packed them as tightly as I could between her legs, then I flew out of the house, not to the doctor's, but back to Mrs Cullen. She would know what to do. Mrs Cullen always knew what to do. Within minutes, Allan had been despatched for the doctor, Josie put in charge of the household, while Mrs Cullen and I ran, as fast as her bulk would permit, back to our house.

There was no sign of Eddie Higson. Obviously, I had not hit him hard enough, I thought viciously as I looked down at my mother whose lifeblood seemed to be covering the living-room floor.

'Get down to the prefabs, Annie,' said Mrs Cullen. 'They've got them fancy fridges, ask for ice. Go on, 'urry up.'

I picked up a bucket and ran down the backs until I reached the prefabs where I disturbed half a dozen residents with my screaming. They piled the ice into my bucket and, not thinking to thank them, I sped back home. But I was too late, for my mother was already being lifted into the ambulance. Mrs Cullen held me back, because I was all for getting in the vehicle too and I heard myself screaming my mother's name as the driver slammed the door and shot off at great speed.

'Is she dead?' I moaned.

'Nay, lass. She'll be alright in a day or two. Are you stoppin' at Entwistle's tonight?' I shook my head. 'No. Rita's down with the chicken pox. I'll have to stop . . .' Oh no, I couldn't bear it. 'I'll have to stop here.'

'Did 'e beat 'er up, luv?'

'Yes,' I answered flatly. 'But she'll say she fell downstairs.'

Mrs Cullen shook her head. 'That's what they always say. There must be more folk fallin' down t' bloody stairs than there is folk walkin' up 'em. Now listen, Annie. Like as not that bugger's gone off down the pub for the night. 'E'll be terrified o' what 'e's done, you see. With any luck, 'e'll not be back till late. If you get worried about yer Mam, I'll send George down the Infirmary, see 'ow she is. You know where I am. If you need me, just come down. You stop 'ere, see if the doctor brings any news. 'E's a nice feller is Dr Pritchard, go an' see 'im a bit later on. Are you alright now?'

I nodded, unable to speak. Mrs Cullen wobbled away, turning as she reached the edge of the pavement. 'Don't you worry now. Come round later if you like.'

I was frantic after she'd gone, driven almost out of my mind, pacing about the house like a caged animal, couldn't sit down, couldn't stand in one place for two seconds at a time. What should I do? What could I do? Panic flowed over me in waves, a blind, unreasoning feeling that was not really connected with what had happened, because my mind would not, just now, fix on any of it. This was fear in its purest sense, for I could not discover its real source. Yes, my mother was hurt, yes, I feared for her life – somewhere inside me I knew all that. But it was as if I were facing a tiger, a wild beast with an unpredictable nature that might pounce at any time and I ran from this invisible animal, room to room, storey to storey, until dusk fell and I knew that this house could no longer contain me.

The doctor's wife opened the door to my hammerings and looked at me as if I were something the cat had dragged to her doorstep.

'Yes? Can I help you?'

'I want the doctor, Dr Pritchard . . .'

'There is no surgery just now, I'm afraid, but if you'd like to come back in, say, fifteen minutes . . .'

'I want to see him now. It's an . . . an emergency.'

She looked me up and down again as if assessing my worth, her cool eye somehow making me feel better, because I was used to this type, had got used to this type at All Saints. She might have legs, but this one was a real nun if ever I saw one and I could deal with nuns any day of the week – yes, even now. She ushered me through to the waiting room.

Dr Pritchard was a kind and gentle man with a far-seeing eye and a respect for humanity that was unusual in a man of his calling. He treated everyone with equal respect, always bent a willing ear, always had a smile and a jelly-baby for a child, even during rationing.

He joined me on the brown leather waiting bench.

'Hello, Anne. Now, you'll want to know about your Mummy, won't you?'

I nodded and he took my hand in his.

'Well, dear, I have telephoned just now to the hospital and she is in no danger whatsoever. They are managing to replace the blood she has lost and apart from being a little tired and bruised, she is doing fine, just fine.'

This was another thing I loved about this dear man. He always explained things like what made your blood clot when your leg bled and why you should never scratch your chicken pox.

'What about the baby?' I asked quietly.

He paused before replying, 'The baby is gone, I'm afraid, Anne.'

It was then that the tears came and I leaned heavily against this man as I wept, clinging to his tweed jacket as my tears poured down the front of his clean white shirt. He leaned back and pressed a button on the wall. His wife appeared in the doorway after a few seconds and he spoke briskly to her. 'Warm tea, Edna – warm, not hot and with two teaspoons of sugar.' He dried my eyes on his capacious handkerchief and instructed me to blow my nose into the same. She stood in the doorway, an expression of disdain tightening her already bitter features.

'Tea, Edna.' She slammed the door behind her as she disappeared.

'Are you feeling better now, Anne?' He always called me Anne. I liked that.

'A bit, Doctor.'

'Crying's good medicine, you know. Better than all the stuff in the chemist shop. It's like – let me see now. You know how the sky goes black and the air hangs heavy before a summer storm?' I nodded. 'And then after the thunder and the rain there's a lovely clean feel to everything? Well crying can be like that. It clears the brain.'

'Is she hurting, Doctor?'

'No. They have put her to sleep. When she wakes up she will be all mended.'

'But with no baby.'

'That's right, dear. We could not save the baby.'

Oh God, how I hated that Eddie Higson. How would I face him now after all this? How could I live with a murderer? My mother was alive, but he had killed her baby, I knew that. My knowledge of anatomy was limited, but I was sure he had killed my unborn brother or sister.

'What's sterile, Doctor?' He sat bolt upright and stared at me before attempting to answer this one.

'It means . . . well . . . bearing no fruit. Or, in the case of an animal or a person, it means bearing no young ones, no babies.'

She entered then with the tea, thrusting the china cup and saucer into his hands as if she would as soon approach a snake as come near me. After she had left without a word for either of us, Dr Pritchard asked, 'Why were you asking about the word "sterile" Anne?'

Instinctively, I was on my guard. 'Oh, it's something I heard at school. I knew it was to do with . . . well . . . babies and all that, but I wasn't sure what it meant.'

'Ah.' He leaned back once more and studied me as I sipped my tea.

'Tell me, Anne,' he asked after several seconds. 'How did your mother come to be so hurt?'

I stiffened. What should I say? If I told the truth, would Eddie Higson be locked up? And would that be what my mother would want? I decided to go cautiously. 'I wasn't there when it happened, Doctor. I think she fell down the stairs.'

The doctor sighed loudly. 'Yes. That's what she said, too, so I suppose she must have fallen downstairs, mustn't she?'

He looked meaningfully at me and I answered meekly, 'Yes, Doctor.'

He took the cup from my hand and led me through the

hallway to the front door. 'Come and see me again, Anne. And don't worry, your Mummy is in very capable hands.'

I felt better now. The panic had left me; something about this warm and gentle man had calmed and soothed me. I had only to get through the next few days and my Mam would be home again.

I let myself into the darkening house and crept into the kitchen to make a bit of toast at the grill. Now I would have to look after myself, but as for him – well, he could go to the devil for his dinner. If the worst came to the worst, I at least had friends, could eat with Josie or Rita. He had nowhere to go and that was what he deserved.

When he staggered in at about eleven o'clock, I was on the sofa in the back living room, still fully dressed and with my mother's coat over me for warmth. Although I had been asleep, I woke the instant he entered the house, pulling the coat over my head, feeling, as an ostrich must, that if my face were invisible then he might not see me at all. I heard him switch on the light, then go through to the kitchen. He was making something to eat; I could hear the kitchenette compartments opening and closing, the sound of bread being cut on the board, the click of the cheese-dish lid.

He sat then at the table, not three feet away from me and I listened to the disgusting noise he always made when he ate.

What would he do to me? I knew he would never let me get away with it; I had hit him over the head with the rolling-pin and he was not one to forgive and forget. Also, I could smell the beer on him; the fumes permeated the room, soaked through my mother's coat and into my nostrils with a sickening intensity. Eddie Higson did not hold his drink well. I shivered as I awaited my fate.

I was suddenly blinded when, in one movement he crossed the small space between us and whipped the coat from me, throwing it across the room and almost into the grate where lay bloodstained towels and the twisted wreck that used to be my mother's best rug.

'Get up,' he growled. 'And where's your mother?'

I looked up into his hideous face. 'She's in the hospital.'

He threw back his head and laughed. 'Aye and that's where you'll be and all if you ever pull a trick like that again.' He pointed to the back of his head.

'She's . . . she's lost her baby, the doctor says.'

'Good. And what else did the doctor say? Does he know how she lost the kid?' He seemed frightened and I made him wait for a few seconds before answering, 'No. She told them she fell downstairs – again.' I did not manage to keep the venom from my tone.

'Get up when I tell you! From now on, you do exactly as I tell you – you hear me?'

I made no reply, but got up and stood by the sofa. He grabbed my arm tightly. 'You do whatever I say. Otherwise, I'll kill the bloody pair of you – you and your filthy mother. Because she'll pay for this, by Christ she will. And so will you. You knew all about it, didn't you? Well so do I now, 'cos a chap in the Star put me right tonight. I know the rat's name, rank and number now and his number's very near up, I can tell you. Ernie bloody Bradshaw, eh? I'll twist his sodding neck round for him; he won't know whether he's coming or bloody going by the time I've done with him.'

'He's bigger than you,' I ventured.

'Is he now?' His tone was sarcastic. 'And I've got brothers, so he can be as big as he likes. Now get up them stairs you and into that bath. You're as black as the ace of spades.'

I fled while the going was good. How was I going to warn Ernie? I would have to get to him tomorrow somehow and tell him that Eddie Higson was after him. What if I couldn't? I had no money for busfares, no money for anything and I wasn't going to ask Higson for money. I would have to walk, yes, that's what I'd do. School was still out, this being the September wakes week, so tomorrow I would go to the hospital to see my mother and, on my way back, I would wait at Millhouse mill for the evening shift to come on, then I could tell Ernie to keep his wits about him in case Eddie Higson carried out his threat.

The water was not very warm as the fire had gone out, so I had no intention of lingering in the bath. I scrubbed myself clean, wondering all the while how my mother was and whether or not I would get to Ernie in time.

Higson pushed open the bathroom door and stood leering at me. There was no lock on this door as Higson had declared himself averse to locks; had not his own father perished while bolted into the back-yard tippler?

The look on his face was horrible as he approached me, his eyes glazed, his mouth open in a weird and nasty grin. He bent down, picked up the sponge and began to wash me, the smell of stale beer on his breath making me heave almost.

Then he made me stand, lifting me up by the armpits. Muttering words I could not hear, he soaped my chest then my legs, his hands forcing my thighs to part so that he could touch me in a place I had never imagined to be touchable except by myself when washing or drying. So this was to be my punishment. I stood perfectly still while his fingers probed my body, wishing that he would beat me instead. Anything, anything at all would be better than this.

His voice thick now, he asked, 'Do you love me?'

God, the man must have been drunk. Could anybody love a man who did this? He thrust his other hand into his pocket and began to move it quickly, then, after a few seconds of frantic activity, he sighed and knelt down on the floor at the side of the bath.

But my punishment was still not complete, for now he jumped up and grabbed me so tightly by the hair that I felt some of the roots snap away.

'You tell anybody – anybody about this, I'll kill the both of you – understand?'

I nodded mutely, my head moving just a fraction in his cruel grip.

'I'm going to teach you a thing or two – right?'

Again, I nodded.

'And you'll learn to enjoy our little lessons. Yes, you and I are going to get to know one another really well.'

He released me and I fell down into the water as he left the room, slamming the door behind him.

Fiercely I scrubbed my body in the icy water while red-hot tears of shame coursed down my cheeks. I did not understand what had just happened to me, but I feared it and hated it. And who could I tell? How could I find words to frame this terrible act that had been perpetrated against me? How would I prevent it from happening again?

I did know one thing though. Tomorrow I would run away to someone who would care for me, someone who would understand. Ernie Bradshaw would have to take care of himself. Until my mother got out of hospital, I must disappear, get to the other side of Bolton, as far away from here as I possibly could.

The rest could take care of themselves. I was put into this world to survive and survive I would.

Chapter Nine: On the Run

The next morning, I was up by 5.30, creeping about the house like a burglar in my efforts not to waken him. My body still hurt, partly because I had scrubbed myself so hard with the loofah after the assault, but mostly because of the attack itself which had left me bleeding slightly through the night.

Quietly, I opened the bottom-right-hand drawer of the kitchenette where he kept his money, silver in a spinning-ring tin from the mill, copper in a larger wooden cigar box. I would not ask; I would simply take because by this afternoon I would be beyond his reach and among others who loathed and despised him.

I took a shilling's worth of copper for busfares and then emptied the whole of the silver tin into my schoolbag. From the kitchenette cabinet, I picked up the remaining bread and cheese, then, pausing only to collect my mac with the hood, I left the house by the back door, having decided that I was less likely to be seen from the backs. Even at this early hour there were people about, colliers in particular, who often faced a long ride or even a long walk before their working day could start.

I walked all the way to the centre of Bolton, keeping to the backs except when I reached Crowley Brow, a large bend in the road that was, in fact, a bridge over a very steep drop where water sometimes ran and I stared down for a few minutes into the dried-up bed before continuing on my way.

Everything around me seemed so normal. How could the world carry on like this, as if nothing had happened? Birds sang, early buses began to run, the sky was lightening in a promising way. And I was the one out of step, the one with the beaten-up mother and the dead brother or sister. I was the one who must live with a monster. Nobody cared. I tried to concentrate on not walking on the cracks. 'Stand on a nick, you'll marry a brick and the ghosties 'll come to your wedding,' chanted my mind as I went along. But it didn't work. Nothing could rid me of this crawling flesh where I could still feel the filth of his hands on me.

When I reached the middle of town, I walked to the cenotaph and paused before the statue of a mother holding a dead or dying son in her arms. In a few weeks, I would be laying my father's cross here, just as I had done every year, a plain white wood cross with a red flower at its centre. At home, I had a scroll from the king, to commemorate Sergeant William Byrne, Gordon Highlander, 'who gave his life to save mankind from tyranny. May his sacrifice help to bring the peace and freedom for which he died.' But where was my peace, my freedom? Where was my mother's peace? Had my father died just so that we might be handed to another kind of tyranny – oh, there were no bombs this time, but war was war, however small the scale.

And that other hero, Jesus Christ – where was He now with His forgiveness and His goodness and His 'Suffer little children to come unto me'? Suffer little children was damn right, for I was suffering, suffering beyond all measure. I was eight years old and on the verge of believing that there was no sense in life because life hurt, and that there was less sense in death, especially sacrificial death, which was futile as it solved no problems for those of us who must continue alive.

I stopped for a cup of tea and a piece of toast at an early café on Deansgate. The woman looked at me suspiciously, for it was only seven o'clock. 'You're about early, love.'

'I'm meeting my auntie,' I lied easily, yet amazed at my presence of mind. 'We're getting the train for Blackpool.'

'Ooh, lovely. Wish I was coming with you – here have a bit of marmalade with that . . .'

I ate mechanically, like a machine that must be oiled and fuelled, pushing the food down my tightened throat, scalding my mouth with the hot sweet tea. When I had finished, I sat in the café for a while. It was still a bit soon to call on people, whatever the reason, so I crossed over past St Patrick's and on to the railway bridge by Trinity Street Station. Had I been in a better frame, I would have enjoyed this, because I loved to stand looking down on a train as it pulled in, loved to be enfolded in that cloud of steam and smoke, was a budding train fanatic were the truth known, being in possession of a list of engines longer than most of the boys', though I usually collected my numbers at a smaller station, having been forbidden by my mother to venture too frequently into the centre of Town.

I caught the 39 up Deane Road and walked through as this would kill yet more time and once again I was amazed at the size of the houses, at the proximity of the rows and, most of all, I was shocked by the stench of poverty. But when I reached Ensign Street I found, to my horror, that the houses were mostly empty, windows broken or boarded over. Our own house was not occupied and it was plain that the Hyatts too were gone.

I ran across to number 17 and hammered on the door. Surely by half-past nine there should be somebody about in Wakes Week – only a few colliers and busdrivers and the like worked in Wakes Week. A head appeared at an open upstairs window. 'Annie!'

'Hello, Mrs Maguire. I'm looking for the Hyatts.'

She pushed her head through the gap. 'They got put in James Street, lass. The bombs made these houses unsafe, you see. We'll be going ourselves soon. Do you want to come in?'

'No, thanks. I'll get to James Street.'

She paused fractionally before speaking again. 'She'll not be there, love. They'll be up at All Saints – wait there till I come down then I can talk to you proper . . .'

But I didn't wait. As soon as she closed the window, I ran off towards Derby Road and across to the church, arriving just in time to see Freddie and a lot of other men, all dressed in black, lifting a coffin through the church gates. I stopped in my tracks, thunderstruck. Who was dead? And where was Mrs Hyatt? She'd be inside the church, wouldn't she? I walked forward slowly and spoke to a weeping woman who made little sense at first.

She bowed her head as the coffin passed her and I did the same.

'Salt of the earth, salt of the earth,' said the woman before blowing her nose into her handkerchief.

'It's Mrs Mort, isn't it?' I asked. She looked down at me. 'Oh, Annie, hello love. Fancy you coming all this way. Mind you, we were all neighbours, weren't we? She'll be missed, will Florrie. Pity Tom's not here, but still, I doubt he's heard yet . . .'

I leaned against the railing for support, toast and tea rising in my gorge and I swallowed hard to stop myself from vomiting. Mrs Hyatt dead? Where would I go now? And why could I feel no real grief for this lovely lady who was dead? 'How . . . I mean, what happened?' I managed.

'Heart attack, love. Out like a light, she went. Are you coming in for the service?' I shook my head. She followed the cortège into the church and I stood in the street, my head buzzing with exhaustion and the strangeness of it all. The one person who might have understood was being buried this very day. I looked up at the sky. Somebody up there, in that heaven of Sister Immaculata's, had it all wrong. Or was I being punished yet again? But now, I must find somewhere else to go, somewhere to stay for a while. My Grandad's? No, he would send or even take me home tonight. I could never tell him that I didn't want to go home and why, because I could not find the words for his ears and even if I could, he would make a fuss and Eddie Higson would kill my mother and me.

Aunts and uncles fell, of course, into the same category. I would have to find somewhere to be alone, absolutely alone until my mother got out of the hospital. And, strangely, my desire to visit her had gone, because my body was dirty now, had been dirtied by Eddie Higson's vile hands and I could not, as yet, countenance the idea of seeing my mother. She was alright. Dr Pritchard had said she was alright. So now, I must play for time, keep away from Higson, think things through.

I bought a bottle of lemon pop, two candles and a box of matches from Connie's Corner, then walked down the Ensign Street backs until I came to our old house. The gate swung open easily and I stepped into the tiny yard, just avoiding the corpse of a large rat that lay to the left of the empty midden.

The air-raid shelter was unbelievably dark, yet I took a strange comfort from the blackness, was glad that I could now concentrate my thoughts without fear of disturbance or distraction. But however long I thought, whichever course my mind took, it was always circular in that it brought me back to the same point. I could not, would never be able to, tell anyone about what Eddie Higson had done to me and to my mother. He was evil, truly evil and if I were to seek help, then he would surely finish off both of us.

And so the air-raid shelter became my home. I carefully rationed out my bread and cheese, anxious to save Eddie Higson's money for a real emergency. But as night closed in, I became chilled to the bone and, huddled in my corner, I decided that I must have a blanket. This would be my goal for tomorrow – to acquire more food and some kind of warm covering for the nights. I slept little, merely dozing in the cramped cold, easing myself from one uncomfortable position to another, all the time tense and on my guard in case he came and found me.

The next day I stole three flannelette sheets from the backs in James Street and a blanket from a line behind Cannon Street. My second night was, therefore, warmer but no more comfortable.

After that, I never went out again. I had run out of food, drink and candles, but an apathy had descended upon me, my head hurt and was burning and I coughed almost incessantly. On about the fourth day, I knew I was dying and I didn't care too much about it, even if my immortal soul was black from stealing. My head was filled with words and pictures all jumbled together and I slipped from time to time into blissful unconsciousness, only to be wakened by the coughing and the rasping noise of my own breathing.

They found me and took me to the Infirmary, though I remembered nothing of my journey there. I had something called pneumonia and had Mrs Maguire not recognised my name in the *Bolton Evening News*, had she not remembered seeing me in the street, had she not instigated the search of the area, I might never have been discovered.

My mother visited me in my ward and, as I got better, I went to see her in the other ward. Eddie Higson never came near, though I understood that he had been the one who had reported me missing. I told my mother nothing. In fact, once my illness was over, I began to wonder if I had imagined Eddie Higson's attack on me, for I had had some strange nightmares in my delirium.

My mother was allowed home before I was and she came to visit me each day, once bringing flowers from Mrs Cullen and Josie, another time a doll from Rita and her parents. The police questioned me, but I gave them no answers. I was dismissed with a telling off for being such a naughty girl and, towards the end of October, I returned home.

He was there when my mother brought me in.

'How are you, Annie?' he asked, pretending to be pleasant.

I stared at him and knew it had been no dream. Gripping my mother's hand, I said, loudly and clearly, 'You can go to hell.'

My mother's hand clutched mine tightly, but Higson merely chuckled, saying 'I see she's back to normal, then.'

He turned to the sports page and carried on reading. And I knew there and then that whatever he did to me, I could overcome it. There was no way he could hurt me any more than he already had and I intended to emerge victorious. How little I knew!

Chapter Ten: New Pastures

It happened again, of course. I was not always able to sleep at Rita's house and he got to me whenever he could, each time putting me through the same sick ritual, though it varied slightly as the years went by and he began to collect and scrutinise my underwear, looking for the tell-tale sign of menstruation, waiting, as he put it, for me to ripen.

By the time I was ten years old, I knew about sex, knew what Eddie Higson was planning for me, yet I managed to live with it, taking each day as it came, accepting, as children tend to accept, that things were far from right but that I could do nothing to alter or improve my situation.

My mother withered again; of Ernie Bradshaw I saw and heard no more except I knew that he had left the mill. Whether or not he got his beating, I ceased to care. But now I felt sure that I could never tell my mother about what was happening between Higson and me.

'You tell her, you tell anybody and next time I do you proper, ready or not – understand?' I never answered him, just sat or stood wherever he put me and let it happen, whatever he did, I just let it happen.

When I passed my scholarship, he said I could not go to St Mary's but, for once, my mother put her foot down and got a grant for my uniform, a nasty set of brown and yellow clothing that was all several sizes too big so that I would get my wear out of it. The hat was a monstrosity, a wide-brimmed brown velour with a yellow band and a badge in the front. Even the knickers were brown and long in the leg while the coat looked like something rejected from army stock.

We stood, my mother and I in front of her big mirror and she oohed and ahed over my appearance, her eyes glistening with pride and unshed tears.

I felt nothing except revulsion as I looked at the sight of myself in the mirror, was aware of little except the soreness of my tiny breasts and the pain between my thighs.

'You must work hard,' my mother was saying now. 'Work hard and get them exams you do at sixteen, then you can stop on and do the others when you're eighteen.'

My eyes met hers in the glass. 'I'd rather go to boarding school,' I said. 'I want to get away from him.'

'You can't, Annie. Anyroad, he never hits you now, does he? I mean, we've had no trouble since . . . well . . . since I lost the baby.'

'Since he murdered your baby.'

'Now, Annie love . . .'

'Don't defend him, don't you dare. He's a murderer and a wicked man.'

'We've all got our faults, Annie. Look at me and how daft I was over that Ernie Bradshaw. I just pushed your Dad too far, that's all . . .'

'HE IS NOT MY DAD. My father is dead and that . . . animal is nobody's father. He is not fit to be a father . . .'

'Alright, Annie. Now get that lot off while I sew the nametapes on. Will I put one on your vest as well?'

'No!' I did not want to take off my vest, could not allow my mother to see the bruises. It was getting so hard, this business of protecting her.

Just then Higson entered the room and I paused in the act of removing the gymslip, allowed it to fall once more around my calves so that I remained fully clothed.

'What's this then?' he snarled. 'Bloody fancy-dress parade?'

'I'm just getting her ready for her new school, Eddie.'

He threw himself on to the bed and lay there staring at the two of us, a wicked smile distorting his face. 'I don't see why she needs all that fancy booklearning,' he said. 'All she'll do is finish up wed and then what good will her education be?'

I turned slowly to face him. I knew I would suffer later, yet still I had to say it. 'My education will keep me out of the mill. It will also make sure I don't finish up married to a window cleaner.'

He raised himself to a sitting position. 'You'll be lucky if anybody marries you.'

'Oh, I'll find somebody, don't you worry. And I'll make sure he's a big man who can fight my battles.'

He blanched and I knew he was worried in case I came out with it all there and then in front of my mother. I decided to keep him worried.

Gathering all my strength, I forced myself to sit at the foot of the bed and, keeping my tone light, I went on, 'You see, there are people in this world I just don't like. You know the sort – they say things and do things that hurt. Well, when I'm old enough to have a boyfriend I'll give him a list and say "get them for me". That'll be good, won't it?'

He jumped up and stormed out of the room without a word.

'Ooh, Annie, you shouldn't upset him like that!'

'Upset him? I wouldn't dream of it, Mam.'

St Mary's was a Catholic Grammar School for girls. It sat on top of a mound between Daubhill and Deane Road and it turned out young ladies of varying abilities, many reaching Oxford or Cambridge, some becoming adequate seamstresses and housekeepers, others going on to be teachers, a few, a very few, entering the Passionist convent after several years' constant indoctrination and brain-washing.

Although this was, for me, a golden opportunity in educational terms, I felt like a little child again, especially on my first day when I travelled on the 39 with girls twice my size, sixth formers who, although they wore the same uniform, carried it with panache, with flair – a tilt of the hat, a tightening of the belt to emphasise a true womanly shape.

There were six hundred girls in the school, most on scholarships, some fee-paying. Once again, I was back with the Passionist nuns, though many of the staff were lay teachers. The atmosphere in the school bordered on the sinister, was holy and serious enough to allow fear into the hardest breast among the ninety-odd new starters. Corridors were dark and occupied by a collection of plaster saints dotted around to remind us of the real reason for our being here. First and foremost, we were to become holy; education was secondary and incidental compared to this prime and vital objective.

The Headmistress was a Mother St Vincent, four feet two of solid dynamite and with a tongue that lashed like a whipcord. There were rules, rules and more rules. Never run in the corridors, say grace before eating even a sweet, speak to a teacher each time you meet one in a corridor (the staff must have been exhausted after a day's answering of a thousand greetings) keep your gym shorts long – to test the length, assume a kneeling position and measure no more than four inches from hem to floor – and so on.

Each morning we lined up before Mother and sang Latin dirges after which we prayed, then listened for at least ten minutes to a lecture on behaviour and deportment before marching to the sound of an ill-played piano to our various and wide-spread destinations.

As a first-year, I was destined for St Gertrude's building, which was separated from the main school by a garden through which we were forbidden to walk, being forced instead to take a circuitous route past the tennis courts. During that year I spent much of my time sneezing because I was, more often than not, drenched through to the skin by that famous Bolton rain as I passed, with monotonous regularity, from building to building. Each time we changed buildings, we changed shoes, 'indoors' for inside and 'outdoors' for out. Uniform inspections were carried out after Mass Register (we had to account for our Sundays too) each Monday and scorn was poured on any poor girl who had lost the brown gloves or whose shoes were of inferior quality.

Nevertheless, I settled to my various tasks, took to French, Latin and English Language and Literature like a duck to water, coped, just about, with maths and hated history right from the start. Sister Olivia, who had a severe speech impediment which caused her to spit as she spoke, was our history teacher. We mocked her with the usual viciousness of youth and those of us who sat on the first four rows talked of bringing in umbrellas (brown, of course) to protect ourselves from Sister's leaky mouth. I felt sorry for her, but this pity of mine did not endear me to her subject which I dismissed as pointless, as everybody was dead and I could not see the virtue in learning lists of battles and treaties that nobody had respected anyway. I knew enough about Chamberlain now to realise that bits of paper promising peace were a waste of ink.

The science facilities were poor, as science was not quite ladylike or pretty and was definitely not holy. But we still managed to create a fair amount of mayhem with a couple of bunsen burners, one or two pipettes and the odd sheep's eye or earthworm.

My chief regret was that Josie Cullen had failed to gain a place and was destined, therefore, for another school – St Anne's, which was a secondary modern and churned out mill-fodder or, at best, waitresses and shopgirls. Josie was clever – I knew that – and I was annoyed with her for not trying. But, in Josie's book, St Mary's girls were a 'right soft lot' and she was determined to be a 'hard case' and earning by the age of fifteen.

For my own part, I began to excel, particularly in

English and French, in which subjects I came out top of the class on most occasions. My essays were often read out to the whole school, an honour I learned to accept without blushes. When it came time to produce the school magazine, I wrote almost all the first-year contributions, selling my pieces to the other girls for pocket money.

In my second year, a shocking thing happened, a thing that caused me to pull myself up and assess my situation anew. Sheila Davies, my friend from those hopscotch and skipping-rope days, who had also gained a place at St Mary's, died of kidney failure. The school choir sang her requiem and I sat staring at the small light-wood coffin in All Saints Church, my heart and mind filled with grief and sadness. She had been so alive, so vibrant. Now she was gone, gone forever. What if this were to happen to me? If I were struck down in this way, then I would not be given the chance to work out how to make sure Eddie Higson got his just deserts in this world.

As the coffin was carried out past us, I made my decision. Surely here, in this holy place, I could get help? Surely a priest, a man of God would come to my aid and rescue me?

But I would not speak to Father Sheahan of this parish, or to Father Cavanagh from my own; better, in this case, the devil I did not know.

After much deliberation, I chose St Patrick's, as it was far enough away from both the churches I knew so well, yet near enough for me to reach for tuppence on the number 45.

I sat in St Patrick's the very next evening, waiting until every sinner had passed through the confessional, making sure that I would be the last. I wanted to know that no believer lingered to listen to what I must say once I got inside the box.

It was a pretty church, stone-built and with beautiful stained-glass pictures in the arched windows. I gazed at the Stations of the Cross, vivid portrayals of Christ's suffering that lined the walls of this and every Catholic church. The scent of incense lingered in the peaceful air. For a few moments, I began to understand why people came here, because the tranquillity was somehow hypnotic and comforting. Then, at last, it was my turn. I genuflected as I left my pew, hesitating for just a second or two before entering the confessional.

I closed the door quietly behind me and knelt on the deliberately uncomfortable plank near the floor, making the Sign of the Cross on my forehead, chest and shoulders before beginning. 'Bless me, Father, for I have sinned. It is three weeks since my last confession.' The priest, a dark shape at the other side of the grille, yawned audibly. I was, after all, the last of a very long queue of penitents. 'Tell me your sins, child.'

'I have taken the name of the Lord in vain twice – I said God when I was angry.'

'Anything else?'

'I laughed at Sister Olivia because she was spitting when she talked and she can't help it.'

'We must not mock the afflicted, child. Go on.'

'I tell lies. I honestly can't remember them, Father, but I do tell fibs. I stole a sixpence from a girl at school, but I put it back in her desk the next day.'

'Good girl. Anything more?'

'I listened to dirty talk at school, but I didn't join in.' I hesitated. I had to do it now. It was now or never . . .

'Go on, my child.'

Seconds passed. I could feel the sweat dripping down my forehead, running along the bridge of my nose and I wiped my face with the sleeve of my blazer. He sounded kind and gentle like Dr Pritchard. Perhaps God was real after all, perhaps He had sent me here so that He might perform one of His miracles. I found myself praying, really praying, begging for God to intercede on my behalf, to show me the way, to show this hidden priest the way . . .

'What is troubling you?' asked the tired, pleasant voice.

'I . . . I do not honour my . . . stepfather and I can't honour him. Ever.'

'Oh, I see. And why is that now?'

I paused, then passed a piece of paper under the grille. 'That is my name and address, Father. I am not of your parish, but I want your help.'

The shadow behind the partition picked up the paper then straightened in its seat.

'In what way can I help you . . . er . . . Anne?'

I cleared my throat before continuing, 'The man who is married to my mother has been . . . well . . . doing things to me for about four years. I want it stopped.'

A brief silence followed. 'What sort of things, Anne?'

'Dirty things.'

'You'll have to be more specific.'

I swallowed hard. 'He touches me where he shouldn't. He says if I tell anyone, then he'll kill me and my mother. He already murdered my mother's baby before it was born. My mother was in hospital because he'd kicked her half to death.'

'What do you want me to do, child?'

I thought about this. 'I want you to make him stop. I don't know how, but you must. Perhaps you could . . . well . . . talk to him, tell him he'll go to hell and all that if he doesn't leave me alone. But you have to come in the evening and during the week, when my mother will not be there.'

I heard the priest shuffling about behind the grille as he prayed almost under his breath.

'Anne. Are you telling me the truth?'

'Yes!' It had never occurred to me that I might not be believed.

'You said yourself not a minute ago that you tell lies, child.'

'I do not lie in the confessional, Father.'

'And you have heard . . . dirty talk at school?'

'Yes, but that's nothing to do with this.'

'I have to be sure, Anne, for it is another person's sin you are telling me. And I have to admit to you, child, that I am at a loss. I have never had to deal with this kind of thing before. I will pray. We must both pray. Now, make an act of contrition.'

'Oh my God, I am sorry and beg pardon . . .' What the hell was I doing here? What kind of a fool was I? I knew Eddie Higson had a grudging respect for, even a fear of the church in spite of his bold words to Father Cavanagh, but could this man really do anything for me? Still, I had tried. From now on I would have to try everything – everything, that was, except telling my mother directly. Because soon, I would reach the age when Eddie Higson would do the really bad thing to me, the thing he had been promising for so long now. Against that, at least, I must protect myself.

The next assault took place the following evening. This time Higson wanted me to touch him, was on the point of opening his trousers when I managed to escape, naked and screaming, down the stairs and out into the back yard. He stood shaking in the doorway as I screamed my fury into the night sky. 'Come in, Annie. I won't do it again, I promise.'

'I don't believe you!'

'Stop shouting. Come in or they'll have you locked up as a mad woman.'

'Touch me again and I'll scream.'

'Alright then, come in.'

I rushed past him and through the house up to my attic room where I swiftly put on my nightie. All kinds of plans were running through my head. Perhaps I could loosen the rungs on his ladder so that he would fall to his death in the street, whereupon I could go and smash his dead face with the heel of my shoe and wipe him out of my mind forever. Or I could push him under a bus or put poison in his tea – he'd never notice the taste, he always drank it black and stewed. But I didn't know where to get poison, hadn't the strength to loosen his rungs, wasn't big enough, yet, to push the bastard under a bus.

He didn't come near me again that week and I decided that screaming had not been a bad idea.

Father Keegan, from St Patrick's, arrived on the Friday evening. He shut himself in the living room with Higson and I crept down, terrified, to listen at the door.

'Your daughter confessed to me earlier in the week, Mr . . . er . . .'

'Higson. She's my stepdaughter.'

'Ah, yes.' There followed a long pause.

'What did she tell you, then?'

'That, I am not at liberty to divulge, Mr Higson. The confession is a confidential matter between God, priest and sinner. You, as a Catholic, must surely know that.'

Higson cleared his throat and when he spoke again, his voice was high in pitch. 'Then why are you here?'

'To tell you that your stepdaughter is unhappy in this house, to ask you, beg you to . . . make her life easier.'

'In what way?'

'I think we both know what I'm talking about, Mr Higson.'

I heard the shovel in the scuttle as Higson fed the fire, probably to give himself time to think. He spoke again, his voice more confident now. 'She's a fanciful lass, is our Annie, very – what's the word now – talented, yes that's it. She's forever making up stories and writing them down. She even wins prizes for some of them.' His tone was wheedling now. 'So, you see, sometimes she doesn't know where her imagination's taking her. She does imagine things, you know. Her head's crammed full of nonsense – I put it down to her age; she's at that funny age, you see . . .'

'I'm not too sure of that, Mr Higson. She strikes me as a very level-headed young person. And I feel sure that she would not bring her imagination with her into the confessional.'

Higson coughed again. 'What are you going to do about it, then?'

'There is nothing I can do. My hands are tied by the laws of my faith. I only wish there were something I could do.'

'Then bugger off.'

He couldn't help me, he couldn't! I pressed a fist to my mouth to stop myself from crying out.

Father Keegan was saying now, 'I may be a priest, Mr Higson, but I am also a man. I tell you now that if the child ever comes to me again with her tales or imaginings – whatever you choose to call them – then I will quite simply take it upon myself to beat the living daylights out of you.'

'And break your own sodding commandments?'

'I too have a Father Confessor, Mr Higson. My soul is easily cleansed. Is yours?'

I heard a chair fall back as somebody stood up.

'So you'll give me a hiding? You and whose bloody army?'

'I and God's army, Mr Higson.'

'Try it then. Go on, you soft bugger with your big girl's frock on – try it, I dare you. Come on, man, get your fists up.'

There followed a crack like a pistol shot, a thud as a body hit the floor, then complete silence for several seconds.

I was just about to enter the room when the priest emerged, biretta in hand, tears coursing down his cheeks.

'Tell me to go for the police, Anne. I cannot break my promises as a priest, but you can ask me, outside the confessional, to intervene on your behalf. Please, Anne . . .'

'We can't get help, Father. He would kill me and my mother. I suppose it was stupid of me to expect him to listen to you.'

The priest squatted down in front of me. 'Anne, there must be a way.'

'There is no way, Father. I dare not even tell my mother what is happening.'

'Shall I tell her?'

'No!' I cried vehemently.

He rose and placed a hand on my head and this time I was not like a dog at its master's feet, for I could almost feel the goodness of this man flowing into me as he intoned 'in nomine Patris . . .' over me, his voice broken by sobs.

After he had left, I ran out and sat on the wall. Go for the police? As if I could! For a start, would a bobby believe me, a bit of a kid, while a grown man denied everything? And I couldn't imagine myself walking into the police station and saying all this to a man in uniform.

I knew now that there was absolutely no help for me. Everything I did in the future must come from within myself. What I could do, I didn't know, but I was sure that I must carry on protecting myself and my mother in the only way I knew how, by keeping silent.

When, after several days had elapsed, Higson recovered from the priest's blow to chin and pride, he renewed his assaults on me, threatening now to gag me if I screamed. He did not, for the time being at least, try to make me touch his vile body. But he told me, in no uncertain terms, that should I wander again into the parish of St Patrick, then he would surely cut my throat.

Again, I must bide my time.

Chapter Eleven: Losing Faith

School became my place of refuge, somewhere I could do well in the eyes of my peers while not faring too badly in the opinions of my teachers. Although the emphasis was very much on religion, a subject that was taught for at least forty minutes a day, we got the opportunity to explore languages and English literature, in which spheres I rapidly developed strong interest.

Home was another matter altogether. Apart from my usual problem, my mother, always tired from the mill, usually exhausted with worry about finances, was too engrossed in her own daily routine to spend much time with me. But she would occasionally pause on her way out to the evening shift to say, 'Do your homework, Annie. Work hard, I want to see you do well.'

And I was doing well, in spite of, or perhaps even because of my home life. The most difficult thing, at first, was that because I knew I was not, could not be normal, that I was the only person in the world with such a terrible secret to hide, I found myself acting all the time. After a while, the acting came naturally and 'putting on a face' became a pleasure to me. Being cheerful, appearing happy, boisterous and very much a leader made me popular with the other girls and so, after a while, I became two people almost – one for school and one for home.

My acting talent did not go unnoticed and even during my first two years at the school I was involved in several productions, playing minor roles two or three times a year. The Cullens, who had moved into a four-bedroomed house opposite us, came to see me play one of Cromwell's soldiers in *When Did You Last See Your Father?* This was an absolute scream, because they filled the front row and their main aim in life seemed to be to make me laugh. Apart from that, they had all helped me learn my lines, so when it came to 'Ho there, a pike – prick me this dog's hide' all seven of them chanted it with me while Mrs Cullen ran up and down the row, boxing ears. My mother came to see me act whenever she could get the time off or when we did a Saturday matinee. When we performed *Assorted Scenes from Shakespeare*, she wept over my Juliet and so did I because I froze partway and lost my lines. But I really did have some wonderful times at school, which compensated in no small way for the agony I still suffered at home. Rita Entwistle often had other friends to stay now, so between the hours of five and ten I was completely at his mercy. He struck at irregular intervals too, making it difficult for me to plan my homework and I often sat up well into the night studying and writing essays. But I was getting stronger and more aware all the time. I would have my own back, I knew it in my bones.

Though life at school had its pleasant side, it was by no means a bed of roses. One of the bigger showdowns came one Monday morning as Sister St Thomas, our class teacher, was calling out the Mass register.

'Anne Byrne. I see that you have not been attending Mass these last three weeks.'

I rose to my feet. We had been trained to stand when addressed by a teacher. 'That's right, Sister.'

'Why not? Is there some illness in the house, or some other reason why you have not attended?'

'No, Sister.'

'Then why have you not been to church? Missing Mass, as we all know, is a sin of omission and is not venial, but mortal. Why have you suddenly started collecting mortal sins, Anne Byrne?'

I looked around at my classmates whose eyes were fixed on me.

'I . . . do not believe in mortal sin, Sister.'

Sister St Thomas' pen fell to the floor and a girl rushed forward to retrieve it.

'You do not believe? You do not . . . well then, I suppose that if you don't believe in it, then it cannot exist.'

'I did not say that it does not exist, Sister. I simply stated that I do not believe in it.'

The nun raised her eyes to heaven. 'Then you must make an act of faith, Anne. You must make yourself believe.'

'I can't, Sister.' I was speaking the truth, voicing my truth, my thoughts, yet it was as if I were listening to somebody else. But I was weary, too weary for lies, too tired, just then, to carry on acting. For once, I had lowered the barricade and was indulging myself by this foolishness. Was I seeking attention, begging for help, looking for punishment? All my life I had, it seemed, been a rebel. But now, at thirteen. I was becoming restless, moody, unpredictable. Sometimes, I was not in control, not in charge of myself. Here I was, in a classroom full of Catholics, defying a teaching nun, decrying the Faith, attempting, feebly and stupidly, to shake the very foundation on which the school was built.

There was a ripple of movement in the room and Sister St Thomas gripped the edge of her desk as she asked, 'Why not? Why cannot you make yourself believe like the rest of us can?'

'Because it doesn't make any sense,' I answered loudly and clearly. Had I really said that? And why couldn't I hold my silly tongue? Perhaps the unthinkable was actually happening – perhaps I was going out of my mind.

The nun got to her feet. 'Come along with me now. The rest of you will study the notes we made yesterday on the gifts of the Holy Ghost. There will be no talking while I am out of the room.'

I was hauled before Mother St Vincent, whose head barely reached my shoulder, so she sat me down while she paced the room, her tiny hands clasped over her flat chest.

Now, here was a woman to fear. No one ever defied Mother. Yet I was strangely calm and detached as she delivered a long and vitriolic lecture, a sermon that would normally have made my ears burn and my head bow in shame. My answers to her quickly fired questions came, at first, in monosyllables, then suddenly, inexplicably, I didn't care any more, didn't give two hoots what she did or said. She was just a woman, a very small woman who knew nothing about things that really mattered, who had escaped with others of her kind to the safety of the convent where, untouchable, unhurtable, she could pray and teach a bit of advanced Latin, the odd smattering of Greek. She never scrubbed a floor or donkeystoned a step, seldom deigned to speak to the lower members of her order, those silent shadows who flitted about in large grey aprons, shoulders bowed from carrying heavy buckets, hands cracked by scalding water and carbolic soap. Deliberately, I met her steady gaze as she spoke.

'So what you are saying then is, at the end of the day, that you are not a Catholic.'

'I think I am not a Catholic, Mother.'

'And yet here you are, taking advantage of a Catholic education in an excellent Catholic school.'

'There are other non-Catholics in the school,' I pointed out. 'We have three in our class alone . . .' Was I never going to shut up?

'Those girls attend with special permission because their parents admire our standards. They have not had the same benefits as you, have never been baptised, were never given the opportunity to choose the right path to heaven . . .'

'I believe that there is no right path, Mother.'

'And how old are you, to be so sure of what you believe?'

'Thirteen.'

'And you, at thirteen, know better than the rest of us who were put here to teach you?'

'There are other religions, Mother. I will find the one that is right for me one day.'

She continued to look me straight in the eye without having to stoop, though I was seated while she still stood. 'Do you go to Confession?'

'Not any more, Mother.'

'Then we shall pray for you.'

'Thankyou.'

Her lips pressed themselves tightly together before she spoke again. 'Are you being sarcastic, Anne Byrne?'

'No, Mother, there's nothing wrong with praying. It's just that it's not only for Catholics – praying's for everybody.'

We stared at one another for several seconds, our combat silent though continuing. Then her expression changed and I knew that she was no longer angry with me. But I had not won, if indeed victory was my goal, because I could scarcely bear to face the sorrow and pain that showed so plainly in her eyes.

Mother retired to the window where she stared out silently on to St Mary's Road. She sighed deeply several times, her hands clutching now at the massive rosary that hung from her fragile waist. After a few moments of contemplation, she turned to face me once more. 'You are far too clever for your own good, Anne Byrne. That is the only conclusion I can reach.'

'No, Mother,' I said quietly. 'I am not clever enough yet to work out what I do and don't believe in. I have read a lot of books and will read a lot more. I am sure that I will sort it out once I get older.'

She reached out her hands in an imploring gesture. 'But Anne, can't you see what you are doing? Better a Protestant than a lapsed Catholic. Better no chance at all than one thrown back into the face of the Lord.'

I suddenly realised that this was the first time I had ever been granted the privilege of a proper, intelligent conversation with a nun. I was being treated as a human being rather than as a stray lamb and I decided that I respected this woman and that she, in her turn, held a grudging respect for me. This was no tyrant, no despot. Mother S Vincent and I had something in common, something that showed at last. We were both actors, each playing her part, each doing what was necessary in order to survive. How could I fear and loathe someone so vulnerable? How could I despise her for living in a convent when I too sought shelter from my own grim realities?

She stared at me now, her eyes full of questions, her quick glance seeming to assess the answers before they came.

'Somebody, or something, has shaken your Faith, my dear. Could you tell me who or what it was?'

I gave no reply and I could see, from the great intelligence in her face, that she expected no answer to such a question, at least, not from a thirteen-year-old girl. But she had done me the very great honour of asking it.

'My faith may come back, Mother,' I said, wanting to comfort this little woman whose reputation for viciousness had now been completely disproved, in my book at least.

'I understand, Anne, that you missed your Confirmation when the Bishop visited your parish three years ago. Why was that now?'

'I was ill in bed with tonsillitis, Mother. I've had tonsillitis off and on ever since I caught pneumonia about five years ago.'

'Ah yes, yes indeed. I know we've sent extra work home for you when you've been afflicted. That's a terrible disease, is it not? I had it myself for years until they removed the tonsils and the adenoids.'

She approached me now, standing just inches away from me as she asked, 'Will your Faith come back in time for your Confirmation by the Bishop next year?'

'I don't know: I wish I did know.'

'Pray for yourself, Anne. Something about you disturbs me. We will offer a Novena in the convent. You may go now. God bless you, my dear.'

'And may He bless you also, Mother. Thankyou for being so understanding.'

'Well now,' she said, smiling at me and deliberately thickening her brogue, 'isn't me bark worse than me bite?'

'I would say so, Mother – but do I tell the others?'

She threw back her tiny head and laughed. 'Ah no, that would be going too far. When you're my size, you need a card or two up your sleeve.'

My heart went out to her. The words were on the tip of my tongue, just waiting to leap out and please her – 'yes, Mother, I'll get confirmed . . .' but I held them back. It was easy to know other people, easy to work out what they wanted and required of me. But there was one person I didn't know at all, one person whose moods and attitudes altered, it seemed, every time the wind changed. Would I ever get to know Annie Byrne?

All during that night, I thought of Mother and her questions, tossing and turning in my bed, my mind a turmoil of jumbled thought. What had shaken my faith was the faith itself with its frigidity, its cold, clear-cut attitude to mankind. And yet within that faith there were real people, good, generous and intelligent men and women like Father Keegan and our Mother St Vincent. They must be the exception that proved the rule; they must, in spite of their cleverness, be misguided.

It seemed to me that most Catholic leaders could see only good or bad, black or white, everything cut and dried, rules to adhere to, laws that must never be questioned.

Catholicism left no room for moderation, no space for compromise. It required blind acceptance and stupidity; as far as I could see, it precluded intelligence and I could not understand how it captured people of integrity, people like Mother St Vincent. No matter how hard I might be pushed, persuaded, cajoled, I could not allow a bishop to lay his sanctified hand upon my unbelieving head. God, Whoever He was, created not just pretty flowers, charming animals, pleasant people. He also produced items like Eddie Higson. God made mistakes. And because the Faith commanded me to believe in God's perfection and omnipotence, I could not allow myself to embrace it.

I lay in my bed watching the sun rise over the moors. Another day was dawning. Perhaps this day would hold the answer, the answer to the main question. Who was Annie Byrne?

Chapter Twelve: Fighting Back

The learning process had been clearly defined for me; listen to a teacher, take notes, copy down the bibliography, read the books on the list, write more notes, produce the essay. So, although I had no teacher for this unscheduled subject, I set about the task of learning about myself in the same mechanical way, turning the pages of memory, re-creating my own history and writing it down in a carefully coded shorthand that no one but myself would ever decipher. And at last I understood Sister Olivia's mutterings about the importance of background, about a country without a history being like a man with no memory. My past was suddenly important to me.

Although I did not yet recognise or understand it, I was inventing my own therapy, defeating depression by allowing my anger to pour outwards on to paper, exorcising frustration through the painting of bold word-pictures. It was like talking to some invisible person and the writing of my short memoirs became an obsession almost.

I recognised early on in my research that people, like ants, lived in colonies, were interdependent and that I, a very small worker, could only know and judge myself by discovering how others saw me. While assessing their attitudes to me, I found myself in turn judging them and I soon had a large ring-file filled with studies of the various characters who had touched my life thus far.

'What are you up to, Annie?' My mother's voice floated from the bottom of the attic stairs. She seldom came up here; this was my domain and I was therefore responsible for keeping it in order.

'I'm writing, Mother.'

'For school?'

'Yes,' I lied, glancing down at the 'shorthand' notes I was currently compiling on the subject of Edna Pritchard, wife of our doctor, mother to my friend Simon.

'As long as you haven't got your head stuck in one of them daft library books again . . .'

Yes, my bibliography was indeed strange. At first, the historical novels had been an escape for me. They provided easy reading, were repetitive, predictable – history was history no matter how fancy the embroidery, the dead remained dead no matter what. But the books were teaching me things, things I might never have come across in the normal course of my life. Normal. Now there was a word to conjure with, a concept difficult to define. Was there anything 'normal' about my life? And how 'normal' were other people's lives?

Through the borrowed books, I had stumbled, quite by accident at first, on certain clues that might equip me for . . . for what? I faced it squarely before writing the word in my complicated code. Revenge. And because that was what I wanted, because that was where all this self-discovery and soul-searching was leading, I wondered sometimes if I were a good or even a nice person. I would not be confirmed, I could not be a proper Catholic or even a watered-down Christian. I was out of step, out of place . . .

'Just make sure you get that homework finished, that's all.'

'I will. Hasn't Angela arrived yet?'

'No, love. I'll leave the door on the latch so's she can let herself in. Eddie'll be late – he's gone up to his brother's. And don't be stopping up all night talking to Whatsername. I want you coming out top of the class again . . .'

My mother. So vulnerable, so transparent, so easy to write down. Her wants were simple. She needed me to be what she might have become had she not remained stuck in the mill all her working life. She was honest, good, caring, hardworking and very naive. Already she looked up to me because I was 'getting an education'. Yet this did not prevent her from laying down her law whenever she had time and opportunity, for beneath that façade of gentleness there lurked an iron will, a determination so grim that I would never have dared to bring home a book with bad marks in it. About once a month she would scrutinise my homework and although she did not understand some of the contents, she was swift to pounce on anything less than a seven out of ten. 'You're not trying, Annie . . .' She seldom raised her voice when she accused me. It would have been easier if she had shouted, but she would say the words in a sad and quiet voice that cut right through me. All her eggs were in one basket; had my brother or sister been allowed to live, then she might have depended less on me, on my success. But I was her reason for living; on account of me she slaved night after night in that filthy mill. I owed everything to her and was acutely aware of it.

Because of my mother, I was edging my way towards a solution that might protect both of us, was growing up quickly, speeding up the process by learning, observing, absorbing anything and everything that might serve my purpose. Although revenge was what I desired, protection for my mother and for myself was what I needed. She, most particularly, must not be hurt any more.

The books she complained about had taught me much. From them, I had learned about rape, had discovered what incest meant. Not that it would be incest – even if he did ever manage it – but it would be damned near, him being married to my mother. The burning question throughout had been – had I brought all this on myself? Had I pushed Eddie Higson into such a pattern of behaviour by treating him with so much disdain right from the start? But no, an echo from the past, already noted somewhere in the diaries, prompted me to know otherwise. Florrie Hyatt from Ensign Street, dead and buried these five years, spoke out loudly and clearly – ''e joined up on account o' that lass' and 'a bad bugger if ever I saw one'. What did you know, Mrs Hyatt? And how much did Tom know? Should I ask across so many miles of ocean?

Also, was my mother weak for sweeping such warnings under the carpet? Or was she simply afraid to be alone, was she insecure, dependent on marriage? Perhaps for my mother a bad marriage was preferable to none at all. But surely she didn't know, couldn't know what he was doing to me. I was too important to her. If she had known, or suspected, then she would definitely have tackled him and it was the fear of such a confrontation that had prevented me from telling her. Twice he had beaten her, once almost to death . . .

I flicked through the pages as I waited for Angela Marsh, my next piece of research, to arrive. On the first sheet was my Dad – or as much of him as I could remember, six foot four in his socks, a fine strong man with a wickedly loud laugh and a bristly chin. Then Tom, Freddie, Mrs Hyatt, Sheila Davies . . . and Eddie Higson. Even on the page, he made me shiver as I conjured up in my mind's eye the image of his face leering over me while he bent to touch my body. Oh God, how I hated the hooked nose, those mean thin lips, the stink of his breath, that corrugated black hair, the small deep-set blue eyes. I heard myself screaming aloud and this sound brought me back to reality, making me grip the edge of the table. Had anyone heard? Had my mother left for the mill, was Angela in the house yet?

No one came. I buried my face in my hands for a few seconds, forcing myself to breathe slowly and evenly. Control was the key; sometimes, I seemed less controlled now, at thirteen, than I had been at eight or nine. My body was changing – that was obvious, especially to him and to me. I now measured five feet and five inches in height, wore a size six shoe, had a definite waist and small breasts and a great deal of physical strength. So now he depended on blackmail, approached me more warily and less frequently, because even wits as dim as his could not fail to recognise that I was acquiring the bodily power with which I might, one day, overcome him.

Intellectually, I was streets ahead of him and it was on my intellect that I was depending totally.

But my emotional development was another matter altogether and I feared my feelings, was terrified that one day they might get out of hand, that I might commit murder or, worse still, run to my mother, turn for help to the law, scream out in the street and tell the whole world of Eddie Higson's crime.

I thought, not for the first time, about the police. I'd watched them in the streets many a time, chasing lads for fighting and scrumping apples, or telling folk the time and how to get to Affetside, checking up at night to see if doors were secure. They seemed ordinary somehow, just men dressed up, nothing unusual. How could I find the words for such ordinary men and what would happen anyway? Prison for him, shame for my mother and me. And to achieve even that, it would need to be a good day, a day when I was coping well, when I was fluent and confident with strangers. On a bad day, I might not even be believed . . . No. The police were well out of this; I could not turn to them. Instead, I wrote pages and pages, full accounts, searched my memory for the tiniest of details. This was my sole outlet. Perhaps one day, somewhere in the distant future and after my mother was dead, I would set this tale in another time, dress it up, have it published . . .

'You there, Anne?' I pushed the diaries into a drawer and went to open my bedroom door. Angela Marsh began her ungainly ascent of the attic stairs. Angela, at fourteen, was a fee-paying non-Catholic who had not moved up at the end of last year because she had failed her terminals. She was therefore in a class with younger girls and she treated us, on the whole, with a degree of contempt because she was experienced. Most good Catholic girls of thirteen were not interested in Angela Marsh's experiences. But I was not a good Catholic girl and Angela's knowledge, which she seemed only too willing to impart for a small fee, might prove very useful to me.

She stood in the doorway breathing hard. 'That's a lot of bloody stairs,' she grumbled.

'Never mind – see, I've got lemonade and cakes.'

Her eyes glistened with greed as she sat down on my bed and I handed her a glass and a plate which she accepted without thanks. She was a plump girl with large breasts, dark red hair and white skin. With her mouth full of cake, she spoke. 'Don't forget – you do my French homework for a whole month.'

I nodded mutely. She flicked a few crumbs from her ample bosom. 'Right,' she said. 'So you've got yourself a boyfriend and you want to know all about it?'

'Yes.' I hesitated. 'I don't want to . . . get into any trouble. I know this may sound silly, Angela, but I . . . er . . . want to know how far to go. You seem so clever about these things, but I'm just so ignorant. How far do you go?'

She grinned lewdly. 'Well, I've never done it. You know what I mean?'

I smiled at her encouragingly and she went on, 'I don't let them . . . you know . . . put it in me. I've got periods now – have you?'

'No.'

'Well, you might get away with it then. But I daren't – my mother would kill me if I got pregnant. So I just . . . well . . . let them touch me and sometimes I touch them.'

I had to go warily now. 'How do you stop . . . it . . . happening?'

She shook her head slowly. 'I've had a few near misses, I can tell you. It's not easy because sometimes . . . well . . . girls want to do it too, you know. I mean, it's only natural. But you see, it's a case of not driving them too far, hold them back a bit . . .'

'What do you mean?'

She swept a superior look in my direction. 'Christ, you don't know much, do you? And you're supposed to be the clever one?' She giggled and crossed her fat legs, one hand straying to her face to pick at a large ugly spot at the side of her nose. 'Look, for a start I make sure there's other people there – like in the back row at the pictures or behind a house with a light in the window. If he gets me on the floor or up against a wall, I usually . . . well . . . you know . . .'

'No, I don't know, Angela. And if you're not going to tell me, then you'll be doing your own French homework.'

She stared at me for a while and I thought she was going to get up and walk out. Then, because even she, the hard case of the class, could feel embarrassment, she came across the room to where I sat in my chair by the window and, in a whisper, she explained to me how she used her body to please the boys without actually allowing copulation to occur.

'Satisfied?' she asked, her cheeks scarlet as she stepped away from me.

I turned to look out of the window and asked, as casually as I could, 'What would you do if someone tried to force himself on you, tried to make you do it?'

I heard the bed creak as she threw her large frame on to it. 'That's what nearly happened to me a few weeks ago with Steve. He's older than me – nearly nineteen. It's the older ones you've got to watch. And you see, with boys, once they get excited . . . you know . . . swell up, they sometimes don't know what they're doing. I'd let him . . . well . . . unfasten my bra and once he got my blouse off, he just went crazy.' I could hear the pride in her voice. 'It's with me being so big. Anyway, the next thing I knew, he was pulling his trousers down. Christ, I was terrified . . .'

'So what did you do?' I turned to face her. 'What did you do, Angela?'

'I kicked him in the balls!' She began to roll about the bed, her body convulsed with almost hysterical laughter. I waited for a few moments.

'And that stopped it?'

'Stopped it? Stopped it?' she howled. 'I reckon it stopped him for a week or two.' She calmed down gradually. 'Since then, I've stuck to boys my own age, ones that have never done it. Don't go with anybody older, Anne. They're the ones that get you into trouble, they're the ones that force you. Once they've done it, they want to do it again and they're not satisfied with the other stuff. Has your boyfriend ever done it with anyone else?'

'I don't think so.'

'Who is he?'

'You wouldn't know him.'

'Ah – frightened to tell me his name in case I take him off you?'

'No.' There was, of course, no boyfriend. And now I had heard all I needed to know, I was no longer interested in the company of this very boring girl. 'I think you'd better go now, Angela. After all, I've your homework to do as well as my own.'

'Please yourself.' She flounced out of the house with an unattractive pout of her small lips and I watched her as she walked down the road, wide hips jerking from side to side, chest thrust out, sturdy legs mincing along, ankles swaying slightly as she balanced her weight on the cubed heels of her black plastic shoes. Yes, Angela had been quite useful.

After she had disappeared, I came out of the house and went to sit for a while on the library wall. This had always been the unofficial meeting place for us – the Cullens, myself and, when he could escape, Simon Pritchard. Here we had all gathered as children to play 'walk the wall, close your eyes, if you fall, mud in your eyes' and 'salt, pepper, mustard' on the steps. Here we had met to swap comics, to play marbles on the pavement, to exclaim over ladybirds and hairy caterpillars trapped in matchboxes – with air-holes of course.

Simon joined me after a short while, his eyes darting

constantly towards the house on the next corner in case his mother should be peeping from a side window. Edna Pritchard was a spy and I had written her down as such. She was a mean, hard-faced woman and I pitied Simon for having to live with such a mother, one who twitched at her lace curtains all the while, one who watched, it seemed, everyone who passed along Long Moor Lane. She didn't like me. Because she didn't like me, the same devil that had prompted me to defy the nuns often came to the fore in her presence, made me go out of my way to greet her in the shops, to open doors with a flourish, to offer assistance with her loaded baskets. I suppose Simon's mother amused me in a way. His father, Dr Pritchard, was a different kettle of fish altogether, lovable, warm, dependable, humorous. So while I pitied Simon for his mother, I could only envy him for having such a fine father, one I might have chosen for myself had I been granted but half a chance.

'What's up, Simon?' I asked, looking into the pale thin face. He ran a hand through his hair. 'Homework. Bloody homework,' he muttered.

'Don't talk to me about it, Simon. At least you're not getting persecuted for not being confirmed. Just be grateful you're at a non-Catholic school. They're all praying for me up there – rows and rows of little nuns in long black frocks – all praying for Annie Byrne's immortal soul. You can't move for praying nuns. I'd rather meet a praying mantis than a praying nun, any day of the week. Come on, cheer up – it can't be as bad as all that.'

He grinned widely, his whole face changing as he began to chuckle. 'You're having me on again, Anne . . .'

'I'm not – honest. Cross me heart, hope to die, cut me throat an' spit in me eye. It's murder. The headmistress is being nice to me. I'm under her wing and I don't fit because she only comes up to my knees. It's a very sinister situation, because Mother is never nice to anybody. Some of the girls are jealous of me because I'm getting preferential brainwashing in her office. On top of that, the parish priest keeps coming to our house, trying to get me to go to confirmation class with all the ten year olds. I daren't answer the door. Even my mother's a bit on their side, though she never sets foot in a church. I feel persecuted. Homework's nothing compared to that.'

'Oh heck. What are you going to do about it then?'

I shuffled along the wall and whispered in his ear, 'My mother's confirmation name is Winifrede. Don't tell anyone – it's a closely guarded family secret.'

'Winifrede?' he yelled before guffawing loudly.

'Shush. Can you imagine it? I suppose I could go through with it and choose a glorious name like Gorgonzola or Heliotrope . . .'

'Or Rumpelstiltskin . . .'

'But it has to be a saint's name. And saints are so good and so boring that it's difficult to pick one out. I think Saint Peter's about the best because he was a terrible sinner. Then there's always poor old doubting Thomas. I could be Thomasina or Petra . . .'

'Or Petrol-ina or even Paraffin-ina . . .' He laughed so much that he fell backwards off the wall and into a rhododendron bush. I dragged him out and back on to the wall, was just beginning to dust him off when his father's battered Morris stopped at the edge of the pavement and Dr Pritchard stepped out to join in.

'What's all this?' he smiled.

'Your son fell off the wall, Doctor. A couple of years ago that would have cost him two marbles or this week's *Beano* . . .'

'Oh Dad . . . Dad . . .' gasped Simon. 'She's thinking of calling herself Gorgonzola or Petunia . . .'

'I never mentioned petunias . . .'

'Ah. Changing your name, then?' Dr Pritchard joined us on the wall.

I tried to sober up a little. 'It's . . . it's for confirmation. I'm meant to get confirmed and choose another name . . .'

'You already have a perfectly good name.'

'I know, Doctor. But I'm supposed to choose a second one, one I'll never use . . .'

'Just as well,' chuckled Simon.

I gave him what I imagined to be a withering glance, then turned back to his father. 'Simon and I were just discussing the possibilities. But I shan't need a name because I'm not getting confirmed. Do you think that's wrong of me, refusing to be confirmed when everybody seems to want me to go through with it?'

'Especially the black widows . . .'

'Praying mantis, Simon.' I kicked him gently on the shin. 'Am I being terrible, Doctor?'

The tall man folded his arms across his chest. 'Depends on the reason. Are you just being awkward or are you genuinely against confirmation?'

I thought about this for a while. 'I'm not against it. I just don't want it for me, that's all. On the other hand, I might be acting difficult. It's hard to say.'

'Yes . . . yes. I expect you find it easy to understand what you know and impossible to understand what you feel . . .'

'That's it, Doctor! That's it exactly.'

'There, you see? Another perfect diagnosis. What would the neighbourhood do without me? You are suffering from adolescence, my dear. This is a condition from which you will, unfortunately, recover sooner or later. It's the worst of times and the best of times . . .'

'You're stealing from Dickens again, Dad.'

'I know, Simon.' He shook his head in mock weariness. 'It's so difficult to be original all the time – even for someone as brilliant as I am.'

He was so lovely to be with, amusing, comfortable and comforting.

'How's it going with you, Simon?' he was asking now.

Simon's head dropped a little. 'So-so, Dad,' he mumbled.

Dr Pritchard ruffled his son's hair and I, as witness to this affectionate gesture, suddenly felt jealous.

'Another case of acute adolescence, eh?' said the doctor. 'Maybe I should work on a cure? Yes, it's a funny old age, is thirteen. Neither man nor boy, neither fish nor fowl . . . though some of you can be pretty foul at times.' He looked at his watch. 'Come along then, son. We mustn't keep your mother waiting, must we? And I've a surgery to run.' He paused. 'The good thing about being thirteen is that you can sit on the library wall . . .'

'And the bad thing,' grumbled Simon, 'is that while you're sitting on the wall, you're not doing your homework.' He looked genuinely troubled and I realised, not for the first time, that Simon was having a problem keeping up at school. And I couldn't offer to help, because that would make Simon and Dr Pritchard think I was some kind of big-head, better than the doctor's son, a real clever-clogs. As for Simon's mother – well, she'd made it plain enough that she couldn't stand the sight of me. Anyway if Dr Pritchard was so gifted, why couldn't he help his own son? Furthermore, I'd enough troubles of my own at the moment, hanging around here or at the Cullens' house to keep out of Higson's way, doing my own homework in fits and starts on the bus, in the dinner hour, in the middle of the night or at tea-time before my mother left for the mill. And when I wasn't doing homework, I was working on the other thing, writing my story, doing research, planning a solution, trying to overcome the sudden bursts of nervous energy that often hit me without warning.

'Are you going home now, Anne?' Dr Pritchard was asking.

'I'll sit here for a while.'

He looked at Simon. 'Go and start Genevieve – no choke.' He tossed the keys into Simon's hand. 'I'll let you drive her home.' Home was only fifty yards away. 'But don't move till I'm a passenger.'

Simon ran round the car and jumped into the driver's seat.

Dr Pritchard turned to me. 'Why do you spend so much time sitting here in the evenings, Anne?'

I shrugged my shoulders lightly. 'I don't always sit here. Sometimes I visit the Cullens or other friends.'

'But you're here quite often – I've seen you.'

'I'm not doing any harm. It's a free country isn't it? No curfew?' My hackles were rising again. 'I like to watch the world go by – is there anything wrong with that?' How dare he? At least I didn't hide myself behind lace curtains, at least I was an observer rather than a spy . . .

'No. There's nothing wrong with that, Anne. It's just that you seem . . . very tense?'

I jumped down from the wall. 'I'm alright, Doctor. Are you ordering me to go home?'

He cleared his throat. 'There are some odd characters about, Anne. You're growing up now, becoming quite an attractive young lady. Some men are not trustworthy – not beyond dragging a young girl off into the bushes or into a car.'

'I can stick up for myself, thank you.'

'That's what they all say – until it's too late.'

He was only trying to be kind, only trying to warn and protect me. Yet I was suddenly angry with him for preaching to me about a subject already so dangerously familiar. Briefly, I wondered how he would react were I to tell him right here and now in the street, tell him that my particular nightmare would not leap from a car or from behind a bush, but would and already did pounce on me in my own house.

'Be careful, Anne,' he was saying now.

I boiled over, erupted with all the fury of a long-dormant volcano, words spilling like white-hot lava, pouring out in torrents to engulf the innocent, missing the guilty by miles. 'Stop telling me what to do! All of you keep telling me . . . nuns, priests, now the flaming doctor . . . have none of you anything better to do? Go to church, get confirmed, do your homework, don't sit on walls. How old will I have to be to make the tiniest decision for myself? I'll sit where I bloody well want – they can twitch all the curtains in the lane and I'll sit here! I'll sit here till midnight if I want to – I'll sit here till tomorrow . . .'

His hand was on my arm now and, in spite of my fury, I noticed the hurt in his eyes. Oh, to hell with him! Why shouldn't he feel pain, why did it always have to be me, just me?

'Calm down, Anne – please . . .'

'Why don't you get in that car and look after your own, Doctor? Why don't you take Simon home and give a hand with his homework? I don't see why you should worry your head over me – I'm just Annie Byrne from across the road, on a bloody scholarship, not fit company for Mrs Pritchard's son . . .'

'Who said so?'

'She doesn't need to say it, does she? I can tell from the way she looks at me, as if she wished I'd crawl back under my stone . . .' Tears pricked my lids and I knew that my anger was about to be drowned.

'And I don't like to hear you swearing. It doesn't suit you, Anne.'

Why wouldn't he fight back, give me something to sharpen my teeth on, give me a good reason not to cry? I'd had enough, more than enough of patience, understanding, condescension.

'You swear, Doctor. I've heard you on Sundays when you're fixing the car. But I'm not supposed to because I'm a girl and only thirteen, is that it? What can you expect of somebody so low-born? I'm one of the servant classes, remember that. Twenty years ago, I'd have gone straight from school at fourteen into the mill or into service. Why – I might even have swept your floors for you, Doctor.' This was my mother speaking. These were her words, drummed into me when I didn't come up to scratch at school. 'I can only be what I am. Education will not make a lady of me.' The tears were a hair's-breadth away now and my voice was rising in pitch, beginning to crack.

'You sound very bitter,' he said quietly.

'Perhaps I am.'

'Don't be bitter. Please, don't be bitter, love.'

I must apologise, I must! Not only had this man never done me any harm, he had always been someone to respect, to revere almost. Why take it out on him?

'I'm sorry, Dr Pritchard.'

'It's quite alright dear – I do understand and I'm not just being kind and platitudinous – look it up in the dictionary when you get home, eh? What you're going through is something that can be explained. All girls go through these changes, these moody and difficult times. You're fortunate in a way, because you can express yourself.' He turned to look into his car where Simon sat waiting patiently, then, almost to himself he said, 'And yet the more intelligent ones often suffer more acutely.' He stared at me for a few seconds then took a step towards the pavement's edge. 'Come and have a chat with me sometime soon. Remember Anne – you're not alone.' As the car hopped away with Simon at the wheel, I heard my mind's voice saying, 'Oh yes I am, Dr Pritchard.' If only he knew!

I stayed near the wall for a while, drying my few tears furtively with the cuff of my cardigan. When at last I regained a degree of composure, I began the short walk home. I watched the 45 as it dropped its passengers, noting that Higson was among them. He walked along on the other side, pausing by the pillar box to light a Woodbine.

From the opposite direction a black shape loomed large, its girth seeming to increase as it passed the ironmonger's, the chip shop, the Co-op on the corner. The cloaked figure crossed the small side street, waddled past the shop on our corner and along the block till it reached our house where it came face to face with Eddie Higson. I leaned on a gatepost and watched this encounter between priest and sinner. They had both seen me; there was no escape. After taking a deep breath, I crossed the road and joined them.

'Father Cavanagh wants a word,' snapped Higson.

I walked between the two men, opened the front door and led the way through to the living room. It was customary to offer food and drink to a visiting priest. Father Cavanagh in particular was obviously used to over-indulging in both – the size of his stomach demonstrated his fondness for food, while his nose, which shone like a rampant flame in the centre of his yellowing face, spoke volumes about the state of his liver. The fire was dying. I made no move towards the kitchen for refreshments and we stood, the three of us, in an awkward semi-circle with our backs to the range.

Higson cleared his throat. He'd probably had a pint or two and I could see that he was not in the best of moods. 'What can we do for you then, Father?'

The priest removed his biretta. ''Tis about the confirmation I'm here. Annie should be attending classes on a Thursday to prepare herself.'

'Aye, well – that's nowt to do with me. I reckon I'll go up for a bath.' Higson turned to leave.

'Sure, 'tis indeed your business, Mr Higson, as well as mine and the girl's. Are ye not interested in this child becoming a member of the Faith, the one true Faith?'

Higson turned on his way to the door. 'You'd best talk to her mam about that. Remember, she's not my kid.'

'She's your stepdaughter, Mr Higson . . .' The priest's voice tailed away as he found himself addressing a closing door. He now turned to me. 'You won't come, then?'

'No.'

He eased his large frame into the fireside rocker. 'Why not? Why won't you come to the classes?'

'Because I'm not going to be confirmed.'

His eyes flashed cold anger. 'If you'd been confirmed when you ought to have been – four years ago . . .'

'Then I would have had no choice. As it was, I was ill in bed. And it wouldn't have meant anything if I'd had no choice, would it? Now, I'm old enough to choose and I am choosing.'

'But your Mammy wants you confirmed,' he said, his tone wheedling. 'Honour thy father and thy mother. You're but a child yet, only thirteen years old. How can you expect to be allowed to make choices? Think of your Mammy now . . .'

Blackmail. How used I was to that! But no, I'd had enough and would not allow any more of it.

Higson suddenly re-entered the room and I almost laughed aloud when I noticed the sheepish look on his face. He was afraid, frightened to death that I might tell this black-robed ignoramus what my 'stepfather' was doing to me. After all, hadn't I told a priest once before?

'I think you'd better leave, Father,' he said. 'You'll get nowhere with her once she's made her mind up.'

The priest struggled out of the rocker and stood swaying at the edge of the rug. I suddenly realised that he was drunk, that he was probably often drunk, that he depended on whisky to get him through ordeals like this one. A strange mixture of pity and contempt flooded into me as I stared at the large bumbling fool who granted absolution, administered sacraments, represented the gateway to salvation.

'And you allow her to make up her own mind?' he shouted.

'What do you want me to do?' Higson yelled back, his confidence restored. 'Drag her up to the church by the hair and chain her to a pew? If she says she's not coming then she's not coming and that's that.' He folded his arms and stood, feet slightly apart, obviously enjoying every minute of his own Dutch courage.

'You're supporting her then, in this sin, Mr Higson?'

'He's not supporting me, Father. I don't need supporters.' Especially him. I needed him like I needed a broken neck.

I turned to the priest. 'I think it would be best if you left, Father.'

Yes, he had better go. I didn't want two rows in one

evening – my one-sided argument with Dr Pritchard had been enough. I was relatively safe now. My mother would be back in less than an hour, so I didn't need the priest to hang around and preserve me.

''Tis small wonder she has never honoured her step-father, Mr Higson. You are not fit to have in your care the soul of a young girl, especially a young Catholic girl. Are you ever to Mass these days? Ever to Confession or Holy Communion?'

For answer, Higson opened the door wide. When the priest made no move, he shouted, 'Get out and don't come back. Just leave her alone, will you? Come on you old drunk before I kick your backside out of here.'

Father Cavanagh pointed a finger, none too steadily in Higson's direction. 'You are excommunicated,' he pronounced.

'Excommunicated?' Higson threw back his head and laughed. 'Listen lad, I quit – bloody years ago, I can tell you. Get back to your whisky bottle and your rosary beads.'

The priest, speechless and purple in the face, stumbled out of the room. Higson followed him, slammed the front door, then came back into the living room. He was shaking. In spite of his brave words, he feared the Church. Like all Catholics, he had been indoctrinated from infancy and even now, he half expected a bolt of lightning.

'Bloody cheek!' he joined me in front of the range, his hands reaching out for the little warmth that came from the dying fire.

'Get that fire seen to and make some tea,' he snapped.

I stared at him levelly, forcing myself to meet the deep-set and bloodshot gaze. Knowing that I was inviting yet more trouble, I stood my ground. 'Do it yourself,' I said quietly. 'I'm not your servant.'

He pulled me roughly towards him, forcing my body against his and I struggled in vain to free myself. When would I learn to keep my big mouth shut?

'You're asking for it, you are,' he whispered, his spittle wetting my face. 'And you're going to get it. Know what I mean?' Yes, I knew what he meant. And no, there wasn't time for him to start on me just now.

'Are you going to do the fire?'

I nodded.

'And make the tea?'

'Just let me go.' He stank of beer, sweat, tobacco and bad teeth.

He released me so suddenly that I fell back against the range oven, banging my head on the mantel shelf. Whether it was the sharp pain, or simply a culmination of all that had happened that evening, I didn't know, but something in me snapped and I flew at him, my hands clawing at his face then beating against his chest. Someone was screaming, sobbing, cursing and only when his hand came over my mouth did I realise that these sounds had been coming from me. His breathing was laboured now and he had to struggle to hold me still.

'Listen, you little bitch,' he gasped. 'I've told you before and I'll tell you again – you do exactly as I say. If you don't, then I'll get your mother and you, the bloody pair. Understand?'

I tasted salt. Something warm and thick was dripping from my mouth. He howled like a wolf and sprang back, but even then my teeth maintained a bulldog grip on his finger until he brought up the other hand and sent me reeling across the room with a single flat blow. I caught sight of myself in the flower-bordered mirror, saw blood on my face and ran to the kitchen to swill his filth down the sink. My stomach heaved and I vomited noisily into the white porcelain, my hands gripping the edge to stop me sliding to the floor. I must hold on, had to keep sane. This was not the way, could not be the way. I was behaving like an animal, a wild beast – no. Animals did not carry on like this – they had order, a kind of discipline in their lives. What was happening to me? Where was my order, my discipline?

Some time later he came through to the kitchen, the stink of Dettol, with which he had no doubt bathed his hand, mixing with all the other scents that clung to his malodorous person.

'Try that again and I'll kill you,' he announced, his voice dangerously quiet.

Kill me, I wanted to say. *Kill me and you'll hang*. But this was not the time. Today had been a disaster and yet, out of this series of storms a plan was forming, spreading its tiny roots in my brain. Although I was uncertain of the details and felt very unsure of the outcome, the seeds were sown and I knew I would have to be not just cool, but icy cold to carry it out. So I shovelled coal and made the tea while he nursed his damaged finger.

When my mother came in, she commiserated with him about his poor hand, said that people should be sued for leaving nails sticking out of window frames. My, it was a mess and no mistake – if she didn't know different, she'd swear he'd been bitten by a mad dog. As she knelt at his side to apply a bandage, he looked at me over her bent head, a smile of triumph playing over his ugly, weathered features.

My skull ached where it had hit the mantelpiece and I was tired to the bones of all these charades. Yet I summoned up the energy to feel annoyed at the sight of my mother kneeling at his feet, the soles of her shoes crusted with steel rings, her hair dotted with cotton, the back of her work frock still damp from her labour.

'I hope you're well insured,' I said to Higson. 'You can get lockjaw from a rusty nail – there's no cure. It's a horrible death too.'

'Ooh, Annie.' My mother glanced up from her task. 'What an awful thing to say.'

'Well – I'm only being practical. It stands to reason – anybody who climbs ladders for a living should be well insured. It's just common sense, that's all. He might break his neck, mightn't he? I'm off to bed now.'

She got up off the floor wearily. 'Just you wait there, our Annie. Is that alright, Eddie? Not too tight?' He grunted and she turned to lean against the table as she spoke to me. 'All I ask, Annie, is for some peace when I get home from the job. Going on about him getting lockjaw and breaking his neck – it's not very nice, is it? Can't you have a bit of respect?'

'People have to earn respect,' I said, as calmly as I could.

'Have you two been arguing? Have you? Can't I even go to work now without worrying about you giving cheek, Annie? What's got into you these days, eh?'

'Ask him. He's your husband, supposed to be the man of the house . . .'

'Annie!'

'Oh leave me alone, Mother. Just leave me alone!' I stamped out of the room and slammed the door behind me.

'Let her go, Nancy,' I heard him say. 'Bloody priest's been down again mithering her – she's got a right bee in her bonnet over it.'

'She still won't get confirmed then?'

'Nay. She as good as threw the drunken old bum out of the house.'

'Oh Eddie – she didn't . . .'

'Just let it go, woman. For goodness sake – can't you see she's at a funny age . . .?'

Yes, he'd said that before, hadn't he?

I switched on my light and looked across into the Cullens' front room. Martin was standing in front of the fireplace staring into the mirror. He did that a lot these days. The single bare bulb in the centre of the parlour (as Mrs Cullen called it) shone down on Martin, making his hair a lighter red than it really was. He was a strange lad, the odd one out in that large family. Although he was Josie's twin, the two of them were like chalk and cheese. While Josie continued open and voluble, Martin seemed very reticent at times, as if he, like me, were planning something, a secret he could not share.

I took the diaries from the drawer and added the notes about Angela, who had confirmed what I already suspected. The plan unfolded as I wrote and I scribbled furiously in spite of my aching head. It was dangerous, but wasn't my situation already fraught with danger? This would simply accelerate matters, take me off the knife's edge, put me in charge. If I lost my gamble, then at least I would go down fighting instead of remaining as I was now, a sitting duck for him to take pot shots at whenever he pleased.

To ensure that I would not weaken, I forced myself to go back yet again through these notebooks, reaffirming that I was right, that these things had really happened to me, that none of it was my fault. I must fuel my anger, feed my resolve, make sure that I would not relent at the last moment.

Oh Mam, Mam . . . what would you say if you could read all this now? What did you think of me all those years ago when I told you I hated him, that he made me shiver, that his eyes were sly? Did you care? I bet you thought I was an odd little thing because of all I'd been through, losing my Daddy and all. Then that stray bomb had been enough to frighten any small lass and make her wary . . .

I pushed the book away and stared blindly through the window. Yes, she probably thought I'd been shell-shocked for a long time, because the blast had been deafening, terrifying. We had sat there under the table for hours until a warden, his feet crunching on splintered glass, had dragged us out. We were the lucky ones, we residents of Ensign Street, because half the next road had been blown to kingdom come. For weeks after that, I had searched for Rosie Turner, not believing, not wanting to accept. Then gradually, Rosie had faded, slipped away out of focus, leaving just a vapour-trail of memory. Now that too was gone and I could not even imagine what she had looked like.

Everyone had said that I was an unusual child, 'highly-strung' according to my mother's family, 'precocious' in Sister Agatha's book. My mother probably never expected me to react to Eddie Higson in a normal way, because I had not led a normal life. Few war babies had enjoyed a normal life.

I left the table, switched off my light and went to lie on the bed. Yes, I would do it – I would, I really would! Remember, I told myself. Remember the first beating . . .

We got back to the house on the wedding night. For reasons I could not fully understand, I shut myself in the small front bedroom with a pair of scissors and painstakingly cut to ribbons the awful pink dress I had been forced to wear. He beat me that night and my mother did not succeed in stopping him. So, on the night of my mother's wedding, I received the first of many such beatings, beatings I would never forget, would not allow myself to forget. Because my mother did not approve of his hitting me, he always got me on my own after that first time. I could not fail to notice how his face changed as he hit me, those small piggy eyes glazing over, the mouth wet, wide and panting.

I groaned and turned over, forcing myself to recall line for line what was written. I must face up to the past before I could organise the future.

Christmas 1946. My mother out shopping. Higson bending over me. Faded colours in the peg rug, hand-made on winter evenings from strips of clipped-up skirts and coats. A shine on the range, black-leaded earlier that day. Festoons on the ceiling, an orange lantern in the doorway. On the dresser a small Christmas tree with arms like bottle brushes. Smells. Pie, yeasty bread, mince tarts. Cherry Blossom polish on the boot that rolled me over towards the heat. A bitter taste in my mouth, vomit laced with hatred. Sounds. A hiss as an air-pocket exploded from the fire's red depth. Breathing. Panting. Gasping. He was dying. Only a dying man would make such noises.

Following him. Standing in the doorway as he leaned over the slopstone, his back towards me, legs apart, one hand moving in front of him. A splash, then a groan as he reached over to seek support from the wall . . .

Remember Tom. 'Are you alright, Annie?'

'Yes.' I could never tell Tom about the beatings, could not let him know how naughty I was. Just as I couldn't tell my mother. Why? Why couldn't I say, *Mam, he hits me when you're out* . . .? Because she might side with him, might agree that I deserved my punishments. There was always a reason for the beatings. I'd been playing on the bombsite, giving cheek, answering back . . . always a reason. But what had triggered him? He was alright at first, just ignored me. This question I could never answer.

Don't sleep, not yet, not now. Allow the anger, feel the pain. Where were you, Mam, all those times when I needed you, when it first began in Ensign Street? At the mill? Shopping? Passing the time of day with a neighbour, a friend? Shall I blame you, my mother?

The move to Long Moor. The baths. Soap bubbles, lather on my chest, calloused hands caressing my body. A huge finger, topped by a black-rimmed nail, forcing, pushing, tearing . . . no!

Sweat bathed my head, ran in small rivers down towards the pillow. There is me, just me. But my memory is clear, my anger deep, my body strong. He will never know my fear, my sweat, my tears. No one to help. No one to trust. Just me, only me. I am Annie Byrne. Annie Byrne is a thirteen-year-old girl with a secret. Holy Mary, Mother of God, where are you? Sleep is coming. My thoughts are disjointed, I am wandering lonely as a cloud, Mr Wordsworth. Too tired to get up and take off my clothes. Tomorrow, I shall be all creased. Like his face, tramlines on the forehead, white in ugly brown skin. A shallow forehead. No brains. Shallow. A pool of water, a pool of blood. Soon there will be blood. Every month, my blood. Whose blood, Annie? Whose blood? Wake up, that's it, wake up! Whose blood, Annie?

I stumbled out of bed and tore off my clothes, flinging them carelessly on to the chair, groping in the dark for my nightdress. Strange, I thought, how a plan could be finalised in a dream. It was complete. Before my blood came, I would have his. Or die trying. The proverbial worm was about to turn.

The dreams were bad that night. I was hitting out at everybody, screaming at Dr Pritchard and Simon, setting fire to Edna Pritchard's lace curtains, yelling at my mother, calling her a traitor. He eluded me completely. Always there was a long corridor between me and him. He stood far away, yet near enough for me to see the leer, the Woodbine smoke curling from a corner of his lip. I walked, but could not run. They reached out from doorways trying to stop me and although I eliminated them one by one, my mother, the doctor, Father Cavanagh, I still could not reach the right one, the one at the end with the ladder on his shoulder. Obscenities poured from my lips, echoing, bouncing off close walls.

I woke sobbing in the miserly light of dawn, my pillow saturated with tears, the dream shattering into fragments for which I groped desperately, trying to piece them all together before true consciousness would deny me access.

Remember . . .

Chapter Thirteen: The Worst of Times

There was a gap at the end of the bath, a space between end panel and wall where the wooden maiden sometimes stood with towels airing on its rails. With my eye, I measured the gap, then I climbed, fully clothed, into the empty tub as I ran through this final rehearsal of my piece. The mechanics might prove easy in comparison to the real acting I would have to do, the smiling, the sigh of pretended pleasure, the encouraging flutter of eyelashes.

I was not old enough for this. Female survivors in the books had been mature. Young ones always fell prey to Vikings, Romans, Cromwell's soldiers. Those who escaped were women of experience, twenty, thirty years old. But I had learned from them, hadn't I? Hadn't their small triumphs become mine? The books were fiction, I knew that. Yet writers must get their ideas from somewhere, from some central store of actuality and fact. I must believe, I must be prepared.

It would happen right here on the bath mat, black and yellow with a penguin woven into the middle. That awful big thing would be pushed inside me, would tear me apart on the penguin rug. Afterwards, he would have to kill me, because once it had happened, I would not be able to remain silent. Already I felt half-crazy some of the time, my nerves stretched like tight wires, my whole body tense and waiting. Rape would make me crack, I knew it.

So now, I must become the aggressor, because if I continued to do nothing, then it might not even be rape. Sometimes, in the newspapers, it was not rape because the woman didn't say no. My word against his – he would never risk that, because he knew I had ten words for every one of his. And I wasn't a woman, I was just a girl, he'd go to prison with enough proof. Yes, he would kill me. Then he would sneak out of the house and get what they called an alibi, probably from his brothers. It would be murder by person or persons unknown. I could not allow myself to become a file in the police station, a file never closed.

Joannie Walker. I'd never met her, never known her, but her name was burnt into my brain by my mother and the *Bolton Evening News*. Joannie Walker had disappeared in 1948 when she was seven years old. She was used as an example to all of us, don't talk to strangers, don't get into a car or a lorry. Her body had not been found and the file remained forever open. Well, I had never talked to strangers, had never got into a car. I smiled grimly as I climbed out of the bath, my assessment complete. No, Mam. I don't talk to strangers, but it happens all the same in your lovely bathroom with your delightful husband. The thing you don't talk about because it isn't quite nice – it's already happening to your daughter. Dear me, what a terrible world. Isn't fish an awful price these days and shall I put the kettle on?

No! NO! She did love me, she couldn't know, mustn't know . . .

Tonight. It had to be tonight or I might snap completely, lose my nerve and forget all my carefully made preparations. Now, while I was on my guard, I could and would orchestrate the whole thing. What if it didn't work? What if he got me? No . . . better now, while I was keyed up for it. What if I killed him? They'd put me away – not quite in prison, I probably wasn't old enough for that. But they'd put me away, wouldn't they?

Oh stop what-iffing, Annie Byrne! No alternatives. Just you. Just you and him, you or him, one winner, one loser.

It was Thursday. My mother left early on Thursdays to work out her two rooms' timesheets for the foreman. I went down to see her before she left, looking at her as if for the last time.

'What are you staring at, Annie? Is my face dirty or something?'

'No. I was just thinking how pretty you are.'

'Me? Don't talk so soft. Mind you, I was alright in my day, I can tell you.'

'You're still alright, It's just that your face is a bit thinner than it was. How old are you?'

'As if you don't know! Anyroad, never ask a woman her age. She'll usually lie through her teeth even if they're not her own. If she doesn't lie, you still can't trust her, because a woman who'll tell her age can never keep a secret.'

'You're only thirty-six . . .'

'Aye. Going on ninety.'

She tied her mill apron round her waist, a large pocket divided into two sections by a single vertical seam. This was where she kept the spools when doffing, in this pocket she smuggled home empty tubes for firewood. I watched her as she dragged a careless comb through soft Titian waves, kept my eyes on her every movement while she found her bag and purse, changed slippers for work shoes, drew on the dark blue cotton-spotted coat.

'Are you alright, Annie? You're standing there like cheese at fourpence. Is there something you want to tell me?'

I stared at her and knew in that moment that I would never be able to tell her. Even if I ignored Higson's threat to harm her, I could not destroy this little woman because I loved her too much. That it would destroy her I did not doubt. The idea of it, the thought of it, would tear her apart. And I knew her, better than he ever would. I recognised her power, knew her temper and her determination, saw the steel behind the softness, realised that a mighty though untutored brain nested beneath those gentle curls, behind the smoke-grey eyes. Yes, if I were to tell her now, or ever, she would take off the coat, pick up the meat knife and wait. Small she might be, cowardly she was not. The consequences would finish her. It was my battle and I would fight it alone.

'No. I've nothing to tell you. I thought I might go for a walk, freshen my brain up a bit.'

'Good idea. But make sure you . . .'

'I know. Finish my homework.'

'And don't backchat Eddie. You're getting just a bit big for your boots, you are. I don't know.' She shook her head. 'Give them a bit of education and they know it all.'

'Would you marry him again, Mother?'

'What a bloody daft question and me nearly late for the bus! The answer to that is for me to know and for you to wonder about . . .'

'You wouldn't.'

She tapped the side of her nose. 'Keep it out, Annie. There's things you just don't ask about. He could be better, could be worse. And so could you. I'm off. Make sure the kettle's boiled for him.'

After she had left, I felt lonelier than I had ever been in my life. Even the ticking of the mantel clock seemed slow and I found myself wishing that he would hurry up, come home, get this thing started and done with as quickly as possible. I sat still as a stone at the table, hardly daring to breathe as I heard the gate squeak. I listened to the scrape of his ladder as he dragged it up the yard, heard him walking slowly, so unbearably slowly, towards the back door. Sputum rattled in his chest and I felt myself flinch as he spat another of his vile messes on to the flags outside.

His brow was raised in surprise when he found me sitting in the living room. His meal was in the range oven and I got it for him, watching his eyes widen in further astonishment as I set the dish in his place. I usually left him to collect his own meal when my mother was out and I hoped, desperately, that my behaviour was not too uncharacteristic. Still, in for a penny, in for a pound – the old saying flashed across my mind as I hung the cloth on the oven door.

'Stew again?' he asked as he removed the pan lid from the plate.

'Thursday's always stew. Payday tomorrow.' I tried to

smile, but my face, numb and stiff, did not quite obey me.

He ate noisily like a pig at a trough, slurping the food, chewing small lumps of meat with his mouth wide open. He was revolting.

The spoon clattered into the dish. 'Talking to me now, are you? What's brought this on?'

'Just trying to be civil. Nothing wrong with that, is there?'

I walked carefully across to the mirror and began to brush my hair. This, according to the books, usually got them going. I gripped the brush tightly so that my hand would not shake and tossed the waist-length hair over my shoulder, stroking it in what I imagined to be a sensuous way.

'Somebody been looking at you, then? Some daft lad got his eye on you? I've told you before – if I find you with anybody . . . who is he?'

'Nobody. Not that I'm aware of anyway.'

'Keep away from the lads. Do you hear me? You do as I say.'

'There are no boys. That's the truth.'

I heard him scrape back his chair. 'Taking an interest in yourself, aren't you? What's all this in aid of?'

I turned and placed the brush on the edge of the table. My voice trembled slightly as I spoke. 'It's dirty – my hair, it needs a wash. I'll just go up and see to it.' Again, I half-managed a tight smile.

'Aye, well. Happen I'll come up and rinse it out for you. It doesn't do to go leaving soap in your hair – you might get nits.' He licked his lips salaciously. 'I'll be up in a minute to give you a hand.'

Halfway up the stairs my right knee suddenly buckled and I saved myself by gripping hard on the cast-iron handrail. I was breathing fast, too fast and my head swam. I managed the last few steps with difficulty, stumbled into the bathroom, turned on the taps and crumbled a violet-scented cube into the water. For a few moments I sat on the rim of the bath, forcing myself to calm down and breathe at a proper rate. After removing my clothes, I took a last look at myself in the glass over the washbasin. Whatever happened in these next minutes, I would never be the same person as I was now. If he didn't come up after all my preparations, my will would crumble. If he raped me, then I would probably not live to look at my own face again. I tried to say farewell to the white shape in the mirror, but I couldn't quite do it. Because if I won . . . oh God, how could I win against a grown man? What the hell had I been thinking of? This was crazy . . . mad . . .

A creak on the stairs, then a heavier footfall. He is coming. Remember the plan, pull yourself together. I am in the bath. My hands are shaking as I reach into the space at the end. The poker is heavy, iron with a solid brass handle. I place the poker in the bath, not quite under my body but out of sight on the side nearest the wall. Bits of ash and coaldust float on the surface. Do something! I reach for a sponge and squeeze violet-scented water over my body. If I survive this day, I shall always hate the smell of violets.

The door is opening. He walks across the room and sits on the edge of the lavatory seat, his eyes glued to my breasts. The end of the poker digs into my calf. But this is better than leaving it in the space, better than hoping for the chance to kneel, reach over and grab it. What if he drags me out of the bath right away? This time, he intends to do it, all of it, because he has received my unspoken message. I soap my body slowly, following the plan's minutest detail.

He is coming towards me now. He kicks off his shoes, tears away trousers, shirt, pants. The muscles on his arms are like great ropes, his chest is broad and covered in ugly black hair. I try to smile, try not to look at that horrible threatening thing that sticks out in front of him, blue-veined and swollen.

'Get up. On your knees,' he says hoarsely. I obey cautiously, anxious not to disturb the poker. Now! I grope for a towel, one eye closed. 'Just a minute.' I try to make the pain sound real. 'I've got soap in my eye.' Behind the large yellow towel, I reach down for the poker. Yes, his eyes are closed as he caresses himself. Thank goodness for this man's predictability! The other hand comes down to touch my hair. Suddenly I am cold, cold and angry. Nothing to lose now. He is guiding my face towards . . . A corner of the towel is in the bath. It is easy, so easy. The fool keeps his eyes closed as I swiftly drop the towel and drive the tip of the poker between his outspread thighs. All my strength goes into this action, one hand on the handle, the other halfway down the blackened metal shaft. There is no need for, no chance of a second blow . . .

I stood at the side of the bath, watching as he began to drown. He had jack-knifed forwards, face down in the water while I scrambled sideways to avoid his falling body. There were bubbles above his head and I stood as if fascinated by the patterns they made as they broke the water's surface. I climbed over his legs which lay crumpled on the penguin mat, reached down and pulled out the plug. No, I would not commit murder. No, I would not ruin my life, have myself marked as a criminal. He was not worth that, not worth anything.

Now I shook, trembled so violently that my teeth, chattering hard and uncontrollably, bit into my tongue several times. Without drying myself, I pulled on my clothes as quickly as numb fingers would allow, then, still shivering, I wrapped a towel around my frozen shoulders. There were fewer bubbles now and his face was still immersed in the last of the water. Steeling myself, I bent over, took two handfuls of wet crinkled hair and heaved him out of the bath and on to the floor. Vomit and bathwater spewed from his mouth and over the linoleum. Like a robot I carried on with my task, fetching and carrying, wrapping the contents of his stomach in wads of newspapers, carrying these bundles downstairs and throwing them to a sizzling death in the depths of the fire. I took the long-handled string mop and cleaned the bathroom floor, shifting the dead weight of his inert body so that I might reach all the water and mess. The automaton I had become lifted his clothes from the lavatory seat and, holding them at arms' length, carried them across the landing and dropped them on to the bedside rug. Finally, I fetched the poker and dug it deep into the fire, turning over the blackened newspapers, piling coal on top of the evidence.

I huddled over the fire for a long time, my ears straining for the sound of movement from upstairs. When, after an hour or more, I had heard nothing, I crept back up the stairs and stood in the bathroom doorway. His eyes were open, his mouth twisted in agony. My knees began to shake again, so I grabbed the doorframe to steady myself as I addressed him. 'You'd better get up, hadn't you?'

'Help . . . me,' he groaned.

'No!' Then my voice dropped to a whisper. 'You'll have a bit of explaining to do now, won't you?'

His face was white with shock and his body, usually tanned, seemed to be turning blue with cold.

'Listen, you,' I went on, determinedly fortifying myself with words. 'What you've been doing to me these last few years is not right. I'm thirteen now and I know what you've been up to right from the start. I've read about creatures like you – you're dirty, dirty filthy scum. Pity the Germans didn't finish you off – they'd have been doing the world a good turn for once. But I'll do it. If this kind of thing carries on, I'll get you.'

He cried out in pain as he tried to move and I took a firmer grip on the jamb to stop myself from falling. 'I swear on my own father's death that you will pay, Eddie Higson. I might even tell my mother what you are, because I'd rather be dead and I'm sure she would too if she realised what she's been living with all these years. Anyway, you're in no position to carry out your threats just now, are you? Take this as a warning, Higson. I could kill you right now and nobody would blame me. But I won't because I can't be bothered. As long as you realise I'm capable of it – understand? Touch me again and I'll kill you. Touch me again and you'll never be able to sleep, because you'll know that one night I'll come after you – with a big sharp knife.'

I closed the door and left him there naked and frozen halfway to death already. I had to negotiate the attic stairs on hands and knees because my body was suddenly disobedient, impossible to manage. Sugar for shock. I crawled into my room and reached up for the bottle of pop on the bedside table, my hand trembling so violently that I could scarcely unscrew the cap. I poured the liquid down my burning throat, my head filled by the sound of the glass bottle as it rattled against my teeth.

The door shook on its hinges when I pushed myself against it, forcing my spine to straighten while I fought to control the involuntary violence of nerve and muscle. The bottle slid from uncertain fingers, contents spilling as it travelled across brown and beige lino towards the long fringe of my bed-cover, a reject from the mill, woven in Bolton sheds out of cotton spun by my mother, or someone like her . . . He was dragging himself across the lower landing. We'd got the quilts two for the price of one. And some towels. Yes, I remembered the towels, four green, two blue . . . Someone moaned in the room beneath mine, moaned then howled like a stricken animal. And some flannelette sheets, pink with the hems not done properly.

Instinct made me crawl, in the end, on to my bed where I immediately lost consciousness. There was no bridge between wakefulness and sleep, no more thinking time, because I simply collapsed into a welcoming darkness, remaining motionless and without dreams until morning.

I woke with a start at about seven o'clock. The house was silent. All the horror of the previous evening flooded into my mind and I staggered across the room to stare at the colourless face in the tallboy mirror. Had I really done all that? I looked round. The floor was stained with orange pop, the bottle lay between door and bed. And yes, something more, a new pain, a grinding discomfort . . .

'Annie? Annie?'

I cleared my throat. 'Yes?'

'You'd best come down, love. There's been a bit of an accident . . .'

I took off my crumpled clothes as quickly as I could, pulled on a nightie and my dressing gown, then went carefully down the two flights of stairs.

My mother was sitting at the table, a cup of tea in her hand. She poured a cup for me and I sat down opposite her. My hand shook as I guided the tea to my parched lips.

'Annie? Annie, love? Whatever's the matter?'

The room swam. 'My . . . my period,' I managed, before falling into her arms as she rushed to my side. She helped me on to the sofa.

'Dear God in heaven,' she muttered. 'What a to-do, eh? He's in hospital – fell off his ladder yesterday, caught himself in an awkward place. And as for you, lass – well, you look like a boiled sheet . . .'

She covered me with the blue work coat and began to rub some life into my hands. 'I had to get the ambulance to him . . . looks like you should have gone and all. Will I get the doctor?'

I shook my head. 'No. But I need a couple of Aspros.'

I watched her as she bustled about making more hot tea for me, filling a hot water bottle, fetching aspirin and yet more tea.

She perched on the edge of the sofa. 'You'll be alright, lass.'

'Yes, I know.'

Then I was sobbing, crying my heart out into that beautiful hair as she rocked me in her arms. She was crying too and her body felt so small, so frail as I hung on to her, my mother, my own lovely tiny mother.

'Oh my poor lass, my little girl,' she whispered between her own sobs. 'It's alright, love. I know all about it, I know . . . I know.'

Oh Mam, Mam. You don't know. God forbid that you ever must.

Chapter Fourteen: The Best of Times

He was in hospital for weeks. According to my mother, who visited him regularly, his injuries had required surgery and he remained in considerable pain for a long time. Strangely, this knowledge gave me no satisfaction and I began to realise that revenge was not really what I wanted. My prime concern was for my own safety and for my mother's wellbeing and I knew that there was still much to fear if and when his recovery became complete. But I managed, for some of the time, to block my mind of such worries, to postpone them at least, because there was little to be achieved by wearing myself down even further.

The window round was temporarily taken over by a friend of Higson's, a drinking companion from the Star. So although this man took his share, we were not too badly off as there was just the pair of us to feed during this period.

I mended slowly and needed several days off school; my mother put this lethargy down to my age, said that starting periods was worse for some girls than for others and that I was one of the unfortunate few. I was sent to see Dr Pritchard who, after peering into my eyes, declared that I was not anaemic, that I was a disgustingly healthy specimen and if all his patients were like me he'd be out of a job in ten minutes flat.

'Still getting the blind rages?' he asked with a twinkle in his eyes.

'Not so often now. I . . . well . . . cry for nothing and laugh at stupid things – things that aren't really funny . . .'

'Hmm.' He leaned back in his chair. 'Hormones. They're a bugger, you know.'

I lifted my chin in pretended defiance. 'Yes, they're a bugger, Doctor.'

He laughed heartily at this and I noticed once again what a handsome man he was, especially when he laughed and made crinkles at the corners of those gentle blue eyes. He ran a hand through the untamable mid-brown hair and I realised that Simon had inherited the straight thick eyebrows from his father, whose own forehead was usually completely hidden as he never seemed to plaster his hair back with Brylcreem. It was a strong face too with features that were clearly defined, especially the square jaw which had a slight cleft not quite in the centre.

'And what makes you cry?' he asked now.

'Books, mostly – stories about people. And Beethoven on the wireless.' For a reason I could not explain, I felt able to tell this man anything. Well, not quite everything, but I did not mind him knowing me.

'Yes,' he said, 'Beethoven can hurt a lot. He was a great big bear with a sore head, that man. Bad enough having all that music rattling round in your skull without going deaf as well. Sometimes, I think only people who've led a tortured life can write good music – or good books, come to that.' He looked me up and down. 'You need a holiday,' he announced.

'I've never had one.'

'I know that. But you need one all the same.' He pondered for a few seconds. 'How about a quick day trip to Blackpool with Simon and me? Time I had a day off too, come to think of it.'

I stared down at my shoes. Mrs Pritchard wouldn't like it. Mrs Pritchard wouldn't allow it.

As if reading my thoughts, he said casually, 'Just the three of us?'

I found myself grinning at him. 'Can I be cheeky, Doctor?'

'Have you ever been anything else?'

'Well, there's somebody else who needs a day out just as

much as I do. Please could we take my mother too? Make it a Saturday or a Sunday – he's still in hospital, so she could go.'

'Hmm. Of course your mother can go with us.' He paused. 'I take it that "he" is your stepfather?'

'Yes. But I . . . don't call him my stepfather.'

'You don't like him.' This was a statement rather than a question, but I answered all the same – 'No, I don't.'

He rose and walked to the window. With his back towards me he spoke, almost to himself, 'Not easy living with somebody you don't like. Strange thing, a family. A bit like workmates, I suppose. You just have to get on with the situation whether you're suited or not.'

'You can change your job, Doctor . . .'

He turned round, seemed almost surprised to see me, as if he'd been about to lose himself in deep thought somewhere.

'That's right, Anne. But you can't change your family, can you? Would you if you could?'

'Not my mother.'

'But you'd change him?'

'I'd swap him tomorrow for a . . . a jar of tadpoles. In fact, I'd pay somebody to shift him.'

'Does he beat you?' The ground was becoming dangerous, yet I still answered, 'Not any more.'

He leaned on the window sill, hands thrust into his trouser pockets where I heard coins jingling. He was daft with money, was Dr Pritchard, never kept a wallet, stuffed it into any old pocket, often left a heap of coins out by his car when he'd been messing about with hub caps and wheel nuts. Yet whenever we found this treasure, we always, always gave it back to him. Even when we'd found a whitey one day – a whole five pounds – we'd taken it to him straight away . . .

'What does he do then, Anne, to make you dislike him so?'

I shrugged my shoulders as lightly as I could. 'He eats with his mouth wide open, slurps his tea at a distance of about three feet from the cup, snores like a stuck pig . . . shouts, loses his temper . . .'

'Hits your mother?'

'Once or twice he has, yes.'

'I thought so.' He came back to sit at his desk. 'The important thing is not to let yourself hate him. Hatred makes people bitter and negative, eats away their personality, destroys creativity – hatred is a waste of energy.' He leaned back in his chair and stared at me. 'My advice to you is that you must ignore him as much as possible. He won't go away, but at least you won't notice him so much. And we'll have a lovely day in Blackpool while he's nursing his . . . wounds.' He smiled wryly. 'How did that happen, by the way? I didn't see him – come to think of it, I don't think he's ever been to the surgery – he went straight to casualty in an ambulance, didn't he?'

'Yes.'

After a short pause, he asked again, 'How did it happen?'

I looked as steadily as I could into the calm blue eyes. 'He fell off his ladder.'

'Strange place to get hurt falling off a ladder. Your mother says he must have landed very awkwardly to sustain such a severe injury.'

'Yes. Yes, he must have landed awkwardly.'

I could no longer meet the constant gaze and I began to fiddle about with the buttons of my cardigan as if getting ready to leave. He knew something, I could sense it. The pores on my arms opened and I felt tiny hairs prickling as they stood on end. I was aware of his eyes on me, knew he was probing my soul for the answer to an unspoken question. He was clever, yes. But could he read minds?

'What's troubling you, Anne? What is it really?'

Oh to have someone like him for a father! 'Nothing I can put words to, Doctor. Probably just hormones or whatever you call them.'

'Sure?'

I finally managed to look him in the eye. 'Positive.'

Please God, it was all over now. Surely Higson would not dare, not again. Or would he? And if I did tell this lovely kind man what had happened, what would I achieve? There'd be no home for me because I'd be put somewhere safe, or, if they locked him up, no window-cleaning money for my mother, no way to pay the rates or the mortgage . . .

'Some day you will tell me, Anne.'

I shifted in the chair. 'I'd better be going, Doctor. The waiting room's pretty full out there . . .'

'I always have time for you, my dear.'

Kindness. These days I could scarcely bear it without tears threatening. And suddenly, I longed to run round the desk and hug him, to have some good, clean contact with a man who might have been my father had the fates been good to me. But I let the moment pass and rose hurriedly to leave.

'Saturday morning, then – nine o'clock sharp,' he said. 'I'll let you know if I have any trouble getting a colleague to stand in for me, but I think it will be alright. We'll pick you up.'

'Thanks, Doctor.'

I sped home to give my mother the news, expecting her to be as delighted as I was at the prospect of a day out.

'You what?' She threw the oven cloth on to the table, her grey eyes wide with surprise and shock. 'What the hell are you up to now, Annie?'

'Nothing. I'm up to nothing. He just said I needed a change for the good of my health and I asked if you could come too. What's wrong with that? What's wrong with a day at Blackpool?'

She lowered herself into a chair, her eyes still glued to my face. 'What's wrong? Well, if you don't know, then I wonder if it's worth my while telling you!' She picked up the cloth and began to fold it this way and that as she chose her words. 'Look, Annie. They're a different class – a different type of folk to us . . .'

'That's true. Dr Pritchard always votes Labour . . .'

'He never does!'

'She votes Tory, of course, so they cancel one another out. Simon says it's funny on voting days. They have this agreement not to go because it's a waste of time with them voting opposite, then they both sneak out and vote. Of course they smile secret smiles afterwards, thinking they've outdone one another . . .'

'Eeh well. You'd think he'd vote Tory, him being educated.'

'That's where you're wrong, Mother. And I thought you were the one who wanted to do away with class. You've always told me that if I got an education I could be anything, mix with anybody. I'm just an early starter, that's all. And I'm starting mixing now and you're coming with me.'

'It's not the same, Annie love. They're born to it.'

'Born to what?'

She bit her bottom lip before whispering, 'Money. They're born to money.'

'Rubbish, Mam! She was, perhaps. But he works hard for his wages, you know that. He's a worker the same as you.'

'Aye. And he's a walking flaming dictionary as well. I wouldn't know what to say to him, Annie, honest I wouldn't.'

'Now who's being daft? There's no need for you to be lost for words – ever. Who goes round all the chippies begging crossword pages out of the wrappings? Who's read all of Jane Austen, most of Charles Dickens and half the blinking *Canterbury Tales*?'

'Mucky book that – what I could understand of it . . .'

'I'll get you a translation – a modern version – for Christmas. If you'll come to Blackpool.'

She got up and began to set the table, reaching plates from the wall-cupboard and cutlery from a drawer in the small sideboard. 'I'll think about it.' She clattered a cup into its saucer.

'No you won't. You're coming.'

'Who says so?'

'I say so! Just for once, let me be the boss, eh?'

'Just for once? You've always been a wayward little devil . . .'

'Yes, but I nearly always do what you say. Nearly . . .'

'Aye. And how near's nearly?'

I decided to try another tack. 'Right then, have it your own way, Mother. Dr Pritchard and Simon will be here at nine o'clock on Saturday. What do I tell them? She can't come, she's got a previous appointment with the Prime Minister, just popped out to number ten for a chat? Or shall I say you're not well, then he'll fly in with his box of tricks and prescribe a day in Blackpool? Of course, I could tell the truth and say you won't go because you're not good enough for them.' I paused and watched a sparkle arriving in the quick grey eyes.

'Honest to God!' she exclaimed. 'What did I do to deserve you, eh? What harm have I done in this world? I've done my best, worked my fingers down to the bone . . .'

'Made sure you got an education,' I mimicked.

'Shut up, you cheeky young minx, you! By God, you'll make one hell of a politician, you will. I reckon you could make the bloody birds fly backwards. Whatever shall I wear?'

'Clothes, Mother.'

'And what about my hair?'

'There's nothing wrong with your hair. Put a scarf on anyway – Blackpool's a windy place . . .'

'See?' she said to the sideboard. 'See? She's got an answer for everything, this one has.' She looked back at me. 'And you know I'm frightened of cars. Especially his. Every week, there's half a dozen men pushing him home.'

'Yes, well – don't make any rude remarks about his car. He's very attached to it.'

'So I've noticed. He operates on it every Sunday just to keep it alive. It should have had the last rites years ago, that thing. I reckon it's held together with faith, hope and plasticine.'

'Mother. Are you a coward?'

'No. But I'm no Amelia Whatsername either.'

'Nobody's asking you to fly the Atlantic – or even the English Channel. All you've got to do is sit in a car, smile, get to Blackpool and enjoy yourself.'

'With the doctor?'

'With the doctor.'

She reached into the range oven and brought out a pie, crusty-gold and steaming through the herringbone pattern across the top.

'Smells good,' I remarked.

'Oh that's right, butter me up. Go and get the spuds and carrots out of the kitchen. They're drained and in the steamer. And I'm blinking well drained too!' she called as I disappeared.

I smiled to myself as I collected the vegetables, listening while she grumbled – for my benefit, of course. 'Sit in a car and smile all the way to Blackpool? That's if we ever get there in that boneshaker.' Bang, bang – that would be the salt and pepper arriving on the table. 'I don't even like Blackpool that much.' Bang, bang – sugar bowl and milk jug. 'And I've nothing to wear.' Bang – probably the pie knife.

I re-entered with the vegetable dishes. 'Did you say something, Mother?'

'Yes. I'm talking to the fire-back. I might as well, mightn't I? You'll probably sail through life getting your own road, you. Remember how you flattened Sister Agatha when you weren't the size of two pennorth of chips? Then you went and got round that Mother Thingy at St Mary's and you with no intention of getting confirmed. Now you think you're getting round me as well, don't you? I should tell you where to get off, it would do you some good. Anyroad, how come the doctor invites you out? What about the rest of his patients?'

'Well, he'd need about six buses, wouldn't he?'

'So why choose you?'

I grinned. 'Because I'm special.'

'Aye. Special and damned cheeky.'

'He knows I'm cheeky – he said so today.'

'Not a bad judge then. Oh well, happen I'll go if the rain holds off.'

The rain held off. After greeting our benefactors rather stiffly and properly, my mother clambered into the front passenger seat where she sat bolt upright while Simon and I stifled our giggles in the back. Fortunately, the engine was quite noisy and we were able to hold a whispered conversation in comparative peace.

'Your mother looks terrified.'

'She is.'

'Mine's furious. She's probably taking it out on the furniture, costing us a fortune in Johnson's Lavender . . .'

'Oh. Does she know you're with us – with me and my mother?'

'I didn't mention it and I don't suppose Dad did. They . . . er . . . don't talk much. She knows we're going to Blackpool, though.'

'Oh dear. Did she want to come?'

He shook his head slowly. 'You must be joking. Blackpool's common – it's where street people go. You'd never catch my mother in Blackpool. She tolerates Southport on the odd occasion, but that's just because the shopping's good.'

'What are you two whispering and giggling about?' called Dr Pritchard as he negotiated a left turn while my mother, white as a ghost, clung to the door and to the edge of her seat.

I struggled with my laughter. 'Oh we're just . . . passing the time of day. Isn't it a lovely car, Mother? Genevieve, she's called.'

'Yes. Lovely,' she muttered between clenched teeth and I dug Simon in the ribs to stop him exploding.

To be fair, Dr Pritchard's driving was sufficiently distinctive to strike fear into the heart of the most seasoned traveller. My mother, who had never been in a car before, was quite shocked when our driver repeatedly gazed round to indicate buildings of architectural merit, when he took his hands from the wheel to illustrate a point, when he seemed to be colour-blind with regard to traffic lights. Even I, who had made several journeys in cars belonging to the parents of classmates, was rather unnerved each time he cursed after one of his many near misses.

'Bloody fools,' he grumbled. 'Weekend drivers, you see. They come out like a rash on Saturdays and Sundays.' He put his head out of the window to yell at a rag and bone man, 'Oi – pull over. I'm a doctor on urgent business.' The poor ragman heaved his pony and cart on to the pavement while we jerked forward, gears grinding and wheels screaming.

At last, my mother could contain herself no longer and I sat back to enjoy what would surely follow.

'Dr Pritchard?'

'Yes, Mrs Higson?'

I gripped Simon's hand tightly; I dared not look at him properly, but from the corner of my eye I could see that he was stuffing a handkerchief into his mouth.

'You drive like a maniac, Doctor. I feel as though we're in the hands of a raving lunatic!'

'What?' We ground to a shuddering halt next to a fence. Everyone bounced forwards and back again with a spine-jarring abruptness. Simon and I, who could contain our mirth no longer, climbed out of the car and pretended to become engrossed in the wild flowers at the roadside. But we stayed very close to Genevieve – we would not miss this for the world.

'Does she realise what she's taking on?' whispered Simon.

'I'll bet five bob on my mother any day of the week.'

We spat on our palms, then shook hands to seal the bargain.

My mother's voice came strident and clear through the car's open windows. 'It's a wonder we're not all dead! Four sets of red traffic lights you went through in Preston.'

'Three. And they were amber.'

'Four, Doctor. I can count, you know.'

'Ah yes. But can you drive?'

'No. I can't do major surgery either, but I like to be damned sure that the bloke with the knife is flaming qualified!'

'I am qualified.'

'Ah yes. As a doctor or as a driver?'

I looked at Simon. 'Fifteen-love to my mother.'

'Mrs Higson, I drive every day of the week . . .'

'Do you now? Pity they did away with the bloke with the red flag then, isn't it? Though I daresay you'd have run him over in five minutes.'

'Now, let's be sensible . . .'

'How many notches on your gun so far, eh? It's a wonder they don't clear the roads when they know you're coming. How did you manage to miss that poor old lady a couple of miles back – error of judgement, was it? I reckon she's gone home now to have her heart attack in peace . . .'

Simon sighed heavily. 'Thirty–love,' he admitted grudgingly. Words poured from my mother's mouth in a seemingly endless stream and I smiled as I remembered how she'd worried about what she would say to the doctor. That she was enjoying this scene was obvious, but I found myself hoping that things would not get out of hand . . .

'Mrs Higson. Would you like to walk the rest of the way?' A nudge in my ribs said thirty–fifteen.

'Walk? Walk? I'd rather flaming well crawl than put my life in your hands for another yard!'

There followed a very brief pause, then both doors opened and my mother and Dr Pritchard spilled simultaneously and untidily out of the car.

'Come on, Annie!' she cried. 'We'll find a bus home.'

'Oh Mother – be reasonable . . .'

'Reasonable? Me? Tell him to be reasonable.' Her face glowed and I caught sight of the beauty she had once been. She turned the full force of her not inconsiderable temper on him now. 'I don't know about Pritchard, this here's Dr Jekyll! Put him behind a steering wheel and he changes into a monster!' While she, my darling Mam, had turned into a human being, feelings on show, little body bristling with energy, her eyes wide with passions that were usually well hidden. Had she ever been like this with Higson? Oh no, never a cross word there, seldom a sign of life in her at home. What a transformation! But here she was with a real man, a normal man, a person who allowed her to express herself, someone who had dragged her into the light where she could be seen as she really was, a powerful and rather splendid woman. I bit my lower lip. She had been like this with my father. Although I remembered little of their relationship, I knew I was catching sight of it now. It was healthy, beautiful, yet disturbing, because I realised now how much she had lost, how much she had failed to regain in her second marriage.

Dr Pritchard walked round the back of the car and came to stand next to Simon and me. 'Anne is not walking,' he pronounced. 'She has had some medical problems of late and I insist that she rides in the car.'

My mother drew herself up to her full height, straightening her spine and raising her chin as she spoke. 'Medical problems? Huh! She will have bloody medical problems once you've wrapped her round a lamp post two or three times. She'll be six months in hospital the road you're driving!'

The tall man took a step towards this very tiny but very angry woman. He looked down at her for several seconds then suddenly, he threw back his head and laughed. Dr Pritchard was endowed with one of those laughs that come straight from the belly, a laugh that could not be ignored or denied. It was more infectious than 'flu in hot weather and soon Simon and I were rolling about in the long grass, doubled up with the pain of trying not to laugh at my mother's expression, crippled by the agony of not being able to echo the doctor's merriment. Then we heard a loud scream and we turned to see if she had resorted to violence, but the scream was just the beginning of her own laughter and there they were, the pair of them, doubled up over Genevieve's bonnet and howling like a couple of banshees. Several motorists slowed down to view the spectacle and Dr Pritchard straightened up to wave them on with a very Shakespearian flourish. And suddenly I forgot to laugh because the moment was too precious. I stood very still and watched, drank in the sight and the sound of my mother's joy, for I had not witnessed such an event for years.

When we finally got back into the car, she was mopping happy tears from her cheeks and Simon pressed two half-crowns into my hand. I tossed one back to him. 'Easy money, Simon – too easy. She was never going to lose.'

We didn't reach Blackpool until after eleven, because Dr Pritchard travelled the rest of the distance like a tranquillised snail and this unprecedented phenomenon caused even more glee in the back of the car. But by the time we got there, the doctor was calling my mother Nancy and she wasn't calling him anything – not maniac, not Doctor, but not David either, though she had been invited to use his Christian name.

Blackpool itself was not a revelation – we'd all been there at some time or other. But what Blackpool did to us, together and separately, was very revealing. We decided to walk the Golden Mile, but didn't quite manage it, because we stopped to gaze at just about every shop and sideshow. My mother had ten minutes with Gypsy Rose Lee who told her that she had a marvellous future full of travel and money. Dr Pritchard advised a second opinion, so she double-checked with Gypsy Marina May two blocks away and was warned about tall strangers, the number seven and Fridays.

We ate all the things that were bad for us and thoroughly enjoyed them – fish and chips with vinegar dripping newsprint on to our fingers, candy floss, toffee apples, rock, black peas in thick cracked cups. We all had hats. I got the inevitable Kiss Me Quick, Simon had an Indian headdress, my mother sported a blue-and-white-striped cardboard boater while Dr Pritchard, not to be outdone, bought an enormous Stetson with 'Fast Shooter' emblazoned on the band. He was like a big kid. He was first in the cage for the tower, first on the caterpillar, dodgems, big wheel. It seemed that he needed to pack everything into this one day and I found myself wondering how a man with such a pronounced sense of fun managed to cope with his grim-faced wife and that never ending queue of ailing patients.

I also discovered that I was hoping that everyone who saw us in the street would think we were a family, mother, father, brother and sister, a proper family having a day out together.

As evening threatened to end our brief holiday, we walked to the front and sat on a bench facing the sea. We were all exhausted and the almost hypnotic sight of the advancing tide lulled us into temporary silence. On the horizon, the sun was slipping away to make another day somewhere else, to warm another patch of earth's scattered soil. It left in its wake a trail of glorious colours from orange through aquamarine to violet, all beautifully patterned with a lacework of tiny mackerel clouds.

Dr Pritchard was the first to speak. 'Of such visions dreams are made. Isn't that right, Simon?'

Simon glanced sideways at me then muttered quietly, 'He's going to make us play the dream game. He always did this when I was a kid – even got my mother to join in.'

I continued to stare at the sea, feeling that somehow there were only the four of us left in the world, that we had slipped through into an alternative dimension where we could remain untouched and untouchable. My troubles, everybody's troubles were of the past, from another time and place. This was contentment; this was all I ever wanted.

'My dream,' continued the doctor, 'is of a world without pain. Of course, I don't want people to live forever, but I'd like life to be full of joy and empty of war and argument. We should all die in our beds at three score and ten, no doctors, no nurses, no hospitals . . .'

'And no job for you,' said my mother.

'And no interruptions!' After a pause, he went on, 'Every night it would rain enough for us to drink and grow food. The days would all be sunny and full of fun. Silly dream for a grown man, isn't it?'

I didn't think it was silly at all, not now, in this magic place.

'What would you be in a world without doctors?' my mother asked.

'Oh, a mechanic, definitely. I'd have rows and rows of Genevieves to work on and at weekends I'd be a racing driver.'

'That accounts for it,' she answered. 'And you'd soon need a doctor, wouldn't you?'

'Nancy,' he sighed. 'Have you no soul? Your daughter has, I think. What's your dream, Anne?'

I closed my eyes. 'Well, if I can't stay here forever, I suppose I want a lot of children. I'd hate to have just one on its own. In my dream there is no religion and no politics, nothing to fight about. Everybody is equal. There are definitely no nuns and priests, no popes and kings. But the main thing is that my father comes back. I don't see any sense in the way he and the others died, you see. It's all politics and religion. They got rid of the Nazis and now we're getting White Russians and Red Russians – it's ridiculous. So. My dream is just as silly as yours, Doctor. I want the Jews to have peace, the Russians to stop being greedy, the Americans to stop piling up those awful bombs, people to stop hurting one another. Above all else, I want my mother to be happy.'

'I am happy, Annie.'

Yes, she was. In that moment when I opened my eyes after speaking my dream, I saw that her face was glowing with some light that came from within, that she looked about twenty years old. And I knew that I had spoken her idea of Utopia as well as my own.

Simon's dream was an odd one, I thought. I knew he was good at drawing, but when he said that he wanted to paint a picture as good and as meaningful as the *Mona Lisa*, I was taken aback somewhat. Surely he would be a doctor like his father? Wasn't that what usually happened – or was I being as naive as my mother sometimes seemed to be? I sighed sadly as I recalled Simon's homework problems. The rolling tide and the magnificent sky would not put everything right. Simon's talent lay in his hands rather than in his head – he was creative, probably talented, but not intellectual.

My mother took a lot of persuading, but she finally succumbed when the three of us threatened to put her over the rail and into the sea.

'I just want our Annie to do well. Course, I'd like a few other things, little things, but they're not important.'

'They are important, Nancy. All dreams and ambitions are important.' Dr Pritchard reached over and touched her arm. 'You have to tell. We've all done it, we've all made fools of ourselves – it's a matter of honour.'

'Oh well,' she sighed. 'If it's a matter of honour . . . I'd like for her to be a lawyer or maybe a teacher. And I want her to have a happy marriage and some nice children . . .'

'What about yourself, Nancy? What do you want for yourself?'

She paused momentarily. 'If anybody laughs, I'll belt them!'

'We won't laugh, Mother – honestly.'

She took a deep breath. 'A green frock with a matching stole.'

I stared at her in amazement. 'Mother! Whatever would you do with a green frock and a matching stole?'

'I'd go ballroom dancing with some of the girls from the mill. Yes, I think I'd like to learn dancing. It's good for you, you know.'

Dr Pritchard stretched long legs and crossed his ankles. 'A green dress. Yes, that would suit you very nicely, Nancy.' It was obvious that the man was moved, because he turned away as he spoke, his voice gruff and slightly choked.

I felt a huge lump in my throat. She'd never had anything, not for herself. It had all been for the house or for me, yet she never complained about being deprived. And all she wanted now was a dance frock. Yet I knew, felt certain that had she been educated, she would have outstripped us all. I would get a paper round and buy the dress for her. But what would be the use of that? He'd never allow her to go dancing on a Saturday night. And she'd already refused to let me deliver papers. It was something I would remember for the rest of my life, this simple desire for a green frock.

When we reached home that night, I felt that we each knew and valued the others a little better or at least, differently, though Simon was to remain something of an enigma for many years to come. Even when we'd played the dream game, he had held something back. Simon would be holding back forever, but I didn't know that then.

There was no going back to that enchanted time, that small island of contentment in 1953 when I learned so much about my mother, about myself – and about others too, when friendships were cemented between me and Simon, between my mother and Bertha Cullen, when we were free to choose where we went and what we did. And that was a strange alliance too, between my mother and Bertha Cullen, the one so houseproud and exacting, the other seemingly slapdash and fancy-free. But these two women were big of heart and they embraced each other's good points and bad, seemed to complement one another perfectly. The bond between Nancy and Bertha was thoroughly forged that year and Higson never managed to sever it. My mother owed her life to Mrs Cullen and her family – but for them, she might not have survived when her unborn child was beaten out of her, but this was never mentioned between the two women as far as I knew.

We picnicked on the Jolly Brows twice, Mrs Cullen and most of her brood, my mother and I, eating wedges of Hovis and cheese out of waxy bread-wrappings, drinking fizzy lemonade from shared enamel cups. Martin always stayed separate from the rest of us, tagging along with his rusty bike, then snatching his sandwiches before walking away hurriedly. I tried to speak to him several times, but he blushed and mumbled unintelligibly, so I learned to keep my distance from him.

Higson limped home in September. He spoke seldom, simply sat staring for endless hours into the fire, though when he looked at me with those sunken sharp eyes, I knew he was taking his revenge gleefully by refusing to go back on the round for several months, thus forcing my mother to take a morning job cleaning at the Star. For many weeks I watched her shabby little figure disappearing down the road each morning before I left for school, witnessed her exhaustion as she prepared to go out again in the evening for the five o'clock to nine shift. This was my fault. I had dealt him a blow from which, it seemed, he would never allow his wife to recover.

It was Bertha Cullen who set him to rights on Christmas morning when she arrived with my gift. He sat huddled over a roaring fire while my mother and I prepared the dinner. There was seldom any Christmas spirit in the house and this year the absence of festive cheer was even more marked than usual because of the silent figure near the hearth. He hadn't even stirred himself to go out to his brother's house this time and the living room felt chilled in spite of the blazing fire, as if Scrooge himself was sitting in our midst to dampen our pleasure. Perhaps we sensed the atmosphere more acutely because of the brief weeks of freedom we had enjoyed, because we had learned what life was like without him.

I was peeling carrots when Bertha rushed in unannounced as usual and I heard him spit into the coals when my mother and I exchanged seasonal greetings with our visitor. Bertha had a truly amazing capacity for ignoring Eddie Higson altogether, but on this occasion she decided to speak to him. With a broad smile on her face she approached his chair. 'Well then, Eddie – I 'ear as 'ow yer've been given th'all clear fer t' New Year.'

'You what?' He looked up at her.

'Well, I've a friend as works at t' Royal Infirmary, like. She says yer right now – yer can go back ter work in January.'

He shifted uncomfortably in his seat. 'Happen I might,' he said.

My mother's face brightened perceptibly. 'That means I'll be able to give up at the Star!' she cried.

'The money's handy,' muttered Higson.

Mrs Cullen cast a sideways glance in his direction. She had never had much to say to him since the night of the clearout and now she directed her attention towards my mother. 'Never mind t' bloody brass, Nancy. Tha's fair wore out wi' workin'. Now as 'e's right, tha mun stick ter th' evenin' shift an' bugger the Star.' She puffed out her already enormous chest. 'My George might not be up ter much, but 'e's never made me work over the odds. Pace yerself, lass.'

Higson picked up the poker and looked briefly but meaningfully at me before using it to stoke the fire. He seemed shrivelled somehow, as if the 'accident', of which he had never spoken to me, had almost finished him physically and mentally. But no, the anger was still there. I could sense it as he smashed the poker into the coals, could see it in the small sly eyes that sometimes seemed to spit venom in my direction. Had I stopped him? Or had I simply postponed the inevitable . . .?

'Come on, Annie. Open Bertha's present,' my mother was saying now.

'Our Martin chose it,' beamed Mrs Cullen. ''E said as 'ow yer'd like it.' It was a single strand of pearls. 'They're not real, like. Only our Martin said as they'll suit you a treat. 'Ey Nancy – I reckon 'e's got 'is eye on your Annie . . .' The poker clattered noisily into the grate.

'Thankyou, Mrs Cullen,' I said.

'Aye well. You deserve nice things, lass. Allers got yer 'ead stuck in a book – yer want ter get out an' enjoy yerself sometimes.'

'She's got to study, Bertha,' said my mother. And Mrs Cullen who, although she did not understand it, now appreciated my mother's need for me to succeed, picked up the large box of crackers I had bought for her family to share, made her goodbyes and beckoned me to follow her to the front door.

''Ey Annie, luv,' she whispered.

'What?'

'I made it up.'

'Made what up?'

'About 'avin' a friend at th' Infirmary. Only I reckon 'e's sat on 'is laurels fer long enough, that bugger.' She began to giggle like a girl. 'Ooh, what am I sayin'? Pity they didn't cut 'is bloody laurels off altogether, eh?'

'Behave yourself, Mrs Cullen.'

''Ey, don't you start laughin' an' all. It were 'is laurels as were the problem – am I right? Does 'e still 'ave ter sit on one o' them rubber rings what you blow up wi' a bike pump?'

'No!'

She wiped her eyes. 'No, listen. I'm bein' dead serious now. I've reckoned 'is number, I 'ave. T' longer as 'e sits there doin' nowt, t' less likely 'e is fer t' get back on t' round. That bloody mate of 'is 'll be buyin' it off 'im next news if we don't do summat. But 'e'll go back now, mark my words.'

And he did. But this proved to be a mixed blessing, because although my mother was able to give up her morning job, he seemed to grow stronger with every passing month and I noticed, gradually, that he was watching me again. But he made no moves in my direction and I managed to stay out of his way most of the time, studying with friends, visiting the Cullens, taking advantage of the fact that I was now old enough to make my own decisions about when I must arrive home and when I must go to bed.

Another year sped by, another Christmas, another birthday – my fifteenth. For eighteen months, he and I had spoken scarcely a word to one another and my mother had by now given up her attempts to enforce an armistice between us. Her own relationship with him was obviously strained and there was little speech or laughter in the house except when he was absent from it. I continued to grow and by the summer of 1955 I was five feet seven inches tall, weighed a good nine stones and was very strong. And he continued to watch, never coming near me, seldom speaking to anyone but watching, always watching.

I threw myself into my work, because I had just twelve months until my GCE examinations; now, there was no time for sitting on walls, little contact with others except fellow students, few opportunities for fun or relaxation. The term drew towards its close. Mother St Vincent remained concerned about me, but she had long since given up on the idea of my confirmation. The 'little chats', which we both enjoyed thoroughly, carried on and she was pushing me gently towards Oxbridge. My mother had been proved right yet again, because the 1950s had indeed opened new doors for the working classes and for women. But although I had decided that I would not leave the North, I did not enlighten the little nun about my intentions. Law and medicine were both available in Liverpool or Manchester and I would go no further from home. To leave my mother alone with him after all her sacrifice would be a crime for which I would never be able to forgive myself. Yet I kept my counsel and agreed with everything the headmistress said.

We spilled out of school on the last day of our fourth year, made our goodbyes, promised to meet sometime during the holidays and went our separate and widespread ways – Leigh, Farnworth, Westhoughton, Affetside, Bolton. The lucky ones would be going away for holidays, perhaps abroad or to Scotland. I had been offered a holiday in Maria Hourigan's caravan, but I could not go. Nothing in this world would entice me away from home, for I would never trust him alone with my mother. He feared me, had good reason to fear me. But without my constant vigilance, he would surely make her pay for what I had done to him. And my mother had already paid enough for me.

As I rode home on the 45, I found myself noticing, as if for the first time, how the world around me had changed during my short life. In the streets I saw girls who no longer looked like younger versions of their mothers, girls with a style of their own – the princess line was slowly making its exit and wide colourful skirts with waspie waists were taking its place. By the side of these girls walked lads with long slicked-back hair, drainpipe trousers, bright socks, deep-soled shoes and knee-length jackets. I realised that something of a revolution had been taking place while I wasn't looking, that young people were demanding attention, seeking a slot of their own in society, snatching a place for themselves, a place that had never been offered or even imagined by adults. They had their own spokesmen too – James Dean, Bill Haley and a new star called Elvis. The music and the words of the Fifties screamed rebellion and I was beginning to notice it.

Everything was changing. Even grown-ups seemed

crazy during this decade, entering the throw-away society with enthusiasm as if attempting to deny that there had ever been war, shortages, rationing. Plastic-coated coffee tables with fly-away edges began to appear in the sitting rooms of the nouveau riche, while in thousands of homes a large glass eye called television sat in a corner, often discreetly hidden behind tiny doors. Someone called Fairfield Osborn was warning us that we were using up the world's resources too fast, but nobody heeded him. It was an age of madness, an era of excitement and carelessness. I wondered who they were, these people with money to throw about, because they certainly didn't live in our road. My mother still ran a household on five pounds a week, paid coal and electricity bills, fed three people and managed a mortage with that paltry sum.

The bus stopped and I got off opposite the library. Martin Cullen, who seemed to have found his tongue when he acquired his first Teddy Boy suit, yelled a greeting across the road and I waved at him. Yes, everything was indeed changing. Now was the time for me to speak out, to join the rebels in my own way. But no, there she was at the gate waiting for me, her hair made fiery by the rays of an afternoon sun. I threw my satchel into our small patch of garden and lifted the tiny woman off her feet, pretending to be happy to have six whole weeks off school. One day, I promised myself, she would be comfortable and my education would buy her peace of mind and provide a passport out of the mill. For now, I must continue to act my part, must keep her as happy as I could manage. This was not the best of our times, but the best was yet to come.

Part Two

. . . is a Whisper to the Living

Chapter One: Martin and Simon

On 13 July 1955 Ruth Ellis was hanged for murder. The campaign for the abolition of capital punishment was reinforced by this terrible occurrence and for weeks after the event the newspapers argued the issue. Annie Byrne sat in the reading room of Long Moor Lane Library and wondered anew about man's inhumanity. How far had Ruth Ellis been driven? For how many months or years had she suffered before committing this so-called premeditated crime?

Annie replaced the paper in the rack and picked up her book. They would let you have just one book at a time, so she had been reading a novel each day during the first part of her summer holidays, losing herself in pages of the historical romances which had become something of an addiction now. Every morning she would stand at the library gates waiting for the staff to arrive, an impatient foot tapping the ground if the door remained closed one minute after ten o'clock. On Saturdays, she always chose an extra-thick book to get her through till Monday morning. This was escapism and she knew it. It was exactly what she needed. In a world that hanged desperate women, that forbade blacks and whites to travel together on the same bus, a world that had recently sent six million Jews to a filthy and unspeakable end, one needed to escape before madness set in. There was so much to run from now, because everybody's life seemed to hang by a thread, a slender strand that might so easily be snapped by another Hiroshima. So Annie divided her time into three parts, housework, study and reading. The first left room for thought and she got through it hurriedly in order to engage her mind elsewhere, in a place where she might ignore the Bomb, forget man's current cruelties by reliving those of the past, deny, by burying herself in the intricacies of algebra and Latin, that she might become the next Ruth Ellis.

She stepped out into the sunlight and stood for a moment on the top step to watch her particular bit of the world go by. Did any of these people worry about the atom bomb? Would any one of them care if they knew that in their midst there resided a potential Ruth Ellis, a girl almost grown to womanhood, a young female who might easily commit a premeditated murder any day now? Twice she had struck down her stepfather, twice she had allowed him to remain alive. The next time he might not be so lucky and Annie Byrne could well end up in prison or, if the event should be postponed until she reached her majority, then the gallows would be used again.

From Bryant's corner shop a figure emerged, jaunty and carefree in Edwardian suit, thick-soled shoes and bright orange socks. He called across the road, 'Ho there, a pike – prick me this dog's hide,' thereby identifying himself as a Cullen, harkening back to the time when the seven of them had tried to ruin her performance in a school play. Not that she hadn't recognised him in the first place – anybody who walked about looking like that was seeking attention.

He called again. 'Oy – Freckles – go blind with all that reading, you will.'

She turned to go back into the library, but in a trice he was by her side, a wide grin stretched over his own freckled face, the oily quiffed hair stained a darker auburn by liberal applications of grease.

'D' you like me hair?' he asked, turning his head so that she could see the slick folds at the back. 'It's called a DA – that stands for duck's arse.'

'Thankyou, Martin. I always wanted to know that.'

'Anyroad, you shouldn't be reading. You should be helping yer mam.'

'Oh. Why?' Cool green eyes swept over him.

'Well . . . because you should, that's all. All girls help their mams.'

'And boys – aren't they supposed to help in the house too? Or is there some special dispensation that gets them out of it?'

He shuffled uncomfortably. She just wasn't the same any more, was she? She used to be great fun, did Annie Byrne, always up to mischief. Why, Annie and his twin sister Josie used to be the best pair of tomboys going – all the way through the juniors the two of them had plagued the living daylights out of everybody. Annie had always kept up with the lads, roaming the brows on conker hunts, trekking all the way down to Trinity Street to stand on a soot-covered bridge getting train numbers, usually ready for a fight too. Now she talked . . . well . . . posh like, made you feel as if she knew things, as if she was better than everybody else. He'd heard that she still capered on at school and was popular for her sense of humour but at home – well, she seemed as miserable as bloody sin. And it had taken him two flaming years to pluck up the courage to talk to her now she'd gone posh. Oh heck! But there was something about her, something special that made his stomach churn, made him angry and happy at the same time. Was he, Martin Cullen, famous hard case of this parish, smitten with a lass?

'Boys do different things,' he muttered. 'Our Josie and our Ellen help me Mam, do the house and that.'

'And what do you do?'

'I mended the washing line this morning.'

She looked towards heaven before stepping back through the library door and he called after her, 'I fetched the coal in!'

Annie walked past the startled librarian who probably wondered why she had returned so soon. She slammed the door of the reading room and threw herself into a chair. So he'd brought the coal in, mended the bit of rope where

Bertha Cullen, on rare occasions, hung her dripping grey wash. Not that Annie wasn't fond of Mrs Cullen – oh she was, she really was, but Martin was becoming a real pain these days, a pain Annie could well do without. He was forever hanging about outside the house with his motley group of Teddy Boy friends, always casting the odd glance up towards her bedroom window where she would sit reading or scribbling.

Yes, perhaps she should go out sometimes for a walk over the Jolly Brows or the top field, get some fresh air and a bit of sun. But Annie only went out in the evenings. During the day she stayed in, emerging only when her mother left for the mill, then walking miles to visit aunts, friends, acquaintances from school. And if she were to come out in the afternoons, Martin would no doubt find her, follow her and regale her with tales of dances at the Palais where he could 'pass himself off as eighteen', or, worse still, he would fill her ears with nonsense about the fights down Folds Road, clashes with rival Teddies. Still, he wasn't all bad, she knew that. Somehow, she realised that his heart was not really in it, that he was out to impress, that he was not truly aggressive like some of the others.

She turned to glance through the window at the little garden at the back of the library where rhododendron leaves gleamed rich and dark while overblown roses tossed their weighty heads in the morning breeze. Because there was no school, Annie had been up since six o'clock as usual, raking out ashes and setting a new fire in the range. By 7.30, she had beaten the rugs, washed, rinsed and mangled the overnight soak and had hung the clothes to dry in the back street. The wash had to be out early so that it might be brought in before the lamp man came or the ragman's pony ploughed through the sheets while his master called 'rag-a-bone, donkey-rubbing-stone . . .'. By eight she was finished for the day, floors swept, steps scrubbed and stoned, kitchenette cupboard wiped out, sink bleached, table laid, kettle bubbling on the range. The next two hours had been spent in the attic studying until library opening time. Yes, Annie helped her mother alright. She did what little she could in that deadly atmosphere to help the poor benighted soul who had brought her into the world. But for how much longer would she be able to carry on? He had recovered now; he was watching, waiting, planning . . .

She jumped up from the table, opened the door and walked past the wide-eyed librarian, then after checking that the coast was clear, she left the library and went down past the doctor's to the milk bar where she ordered a coffee. The place was empty, the juke-box mercifully silent. Annie took her book to a corner table and began to read.

Across the road, Nancy Higson carried her husband's breakfast dishes through to the kitchen. She felt tired, bone-weary, worn out after twenty years slaving in a cotton mill and the same number of years worrying about money. But she carried on, filling the bowl, washing and drying the pots, carried on just as always for the sake of peace and for Annie. At least the rows between her daughter and her husband had virtually stopped now. Funny how he'd given over cursing and screaming at Annie since the accident. Something to be thankful for, she supposed. And there were people a lot worse off, weren't there? But oh, she wished things could be . . . different. Annie couldn't bear to be in a room with him for more than two minutes and it was such an uncomfortable way to live, trying to please everybody and finishing up pleasing nobody, least of all herself. But she was a good girl, was Annie – the house fair sparkled of a morning when she was off school. 'Course, she'd be over at the library now, picking a book to read.

Eddie Higson sighed, looked out of the window to assess the weather and took a Woody from a paper packet of five. The room was stuffy and overheated because of the range, but he said nothing. Nancy wanted a better cooker for the kitchen, a safer one, she said – one that wouldn't fight back and spit at her. The range had been good enough till now, so she could sod off for her new cooker. Anyroad, it was likely all down to that daughter of hers putting fancy ideas about because of all that education. Bloody education. The girl should be setting off for the mill any day now and if he'd had his way, he'd have driven her down there with a whip if necessary.

'It's half past ten, Eddie,' Nancy was reminding him now. 'Best of the day'll be gone if you don't get going.'

'Don't start your mithering, woman. I'm on my way.'

He nipped his cigarette and placed the stub behind his ear then shuffled through to the yard for his bucket and leathers. As he steered the newly acquired ladder cart through the gate, he grinned to himself, dragging the feet of the ladder across the bottom of a snow-white sheet. 'That'll show the young bitch,' he muttered, pausing to feel for the cigarette-end behind his ear. He'd have his day with that one as sure as eggs were eggs.

As he walked away, he didn't notice Nancy standing in the gateway shaking her head. After he had disappeared, she painstakingly removed the large double sheet from the line. It would have to go in the dolly for another soak – oh, if only she could afford one of those washing machines! Well, the cold war between Eddie and Annie was far from over – the thick black lines on the sheet were proof enough of that.

'How did that happen, Mother?'

'Ooh Annie, you made me jump!' Nancy clutched the sheet to her chest. 'Eddie caught his ladder on it . . .'

'Again?'

'It was likely an accident, love . . .'

'An accident? He did the same thing last week because he knows I'm doing the washing.'

'I'm sure he didn't mean it.'

'That's a load of rubbish, Mam and you know it. He's mean and spiteful – oh God, how I hate him!'

'Now you just stop that kind of talk, Annie. He puts food in your mouth, doesn't he? Do you think you'd be at St Mary's if he'd never worked to keep us all going? He took you on, I've told you before. He took us both on . . .'

'And killed your baby!'

They stared at one another across the small yard, then Nancy, her voice low, said, 'I think we'd better go inside, don't you?'

After closing the outside door carefully, Nancy rounded on her daughter. 'What do you expect, eh? You treat him with nothing but contempt – oh yes, I've seen the way you look at him. He helps us pay our way and don't you ever forget that!'

Annie's laugh, which was not really a laugh at all, made Nancy shiver. 'And you're grateful? Grateful to a lazy lump who should have been out cleaning windows for two hours at least? Grateful because you're forced to scrimp and save while he pours shillings down his throat in the Star? Oh, Mam.' As usual, in her anger, Annie fell back into her old way of speaking, vowels flattened, ends of words missing or distorted. 'You took him on, just you remember that. You took on a murdering bastard! He was fit for nowt when you married him and he hasn't improved over-much.'

'Annie!'

'I'm sorry, Mam. Sorry you have to bear the brunt of it. I'll go upstairs now before I say any more.'

Nancy Higson stood alone in the kitchen, her knuckles as white as the sheet she twisted between her fingers. Yes, she'd taken him on out of pity. Or was it out of fear? Had it been panic that forced her hand, panic because Billy had died and left her with a child to support? Would she have got another chance if she hadn't leapt at Eddie Higson's offer so readily? Or could she and Annie have managed alone? They'd have been re-housed, possibly somewhere nice – and she could have got a grant for Annie's needs. Dear God, why had she married him? He was a cruel man, of that she was sure. His victim had needed no grave, but he had murdered and in cold blood too. Nevertheless, Nancy felt duty-bound to defend her husband no matter what he had done. Marriage, like death, was inescapable and a thing to be endured.

Annie climbed to her room at the top of the house. From her window she watched Martin Cullen leaning on his gate. He took a comb from a top pocket and smoothed his fashionable quiff. A strange lad, that one, she thought as she took her seat and opened the Seton novel. He was brainy but stupid. Briefly, she wondered how somebody could be clever yet daft at the same time, but then she did know others of the same ilk: nuns, priests, teachers who were all clever but as thick as two short planks when it came to common sense.

The angry exchange with her mother had been upsetting, was yet another thing to forget. So she opened the book and immersed herself in the tale of wild romance. The room, the road, the moors didn't exist any more.

Annie had escaped.

She wouldn't look down, he knew that. He was beneath her in more ways than one, her sitting up there like a bloody princess in an ivory-tower, him standing in the street thinking about her as usual. She didn't even care whether he thought about her or not, didn't notice his existence most of the time. Whenever he did manage to engineer a meeting she always treated him as if he was only tenpence to the shilling, a few bricks short of a load, as if he needed another brain cell to qualify as a plant.

If only he'd tried harder. If only he'd passed that flaming scholarship instead of arsing about as if he didn't care or worse still, as if he didn't have enough chairs at home to do the soft test. Well, he wasn't thick – he'd show her that, right enough. Anyway, what difference would it have made if he had got a place? They would still have been separated, her with the nuns and him with the brothers. But she might have looked at him different if he'd passed. 'Naw,' he muttered, kicking a stone into the road. His Mam would never have let him go to the grammar anyway; she wanted him working pretty damn quick with all those mouths to feed.

Martin hated being in their house now. It had been alright when they were kids, it had even been fun living in a midden then, but now he was sick to the back teeth with it. Better out here on the road than in there, nowhere to sit, dirty pots and mucky clothes heaped everywhere, his Mam sitting either pondering or laughing in a corner, kids crawling out of every crack in the walls, muck and stench all around them. He wanted more than that, better than that. He wanted order, quiet, cleanliness and above all, success.

Ah, what the hell – she wasn't going to come out again today; he knew her pattern better than he knew his own. Even if she did come out, he'd likely open his big gob and put both feet in it again, start going on about girls and gangs and fights. And he did know about other stuff, he did! She wasn't the only one who read books and things. They did have common ground, he knew it. But what if the lads ever found out he could discuss Samuel Taylor Coleridge instead of just carrying on about James Dean and Bill Haley? But he wanted . . . oh, he didn't know what! Yes, he did. He wanted to say things. To her. Words he thought of while he lay in that stuffy, overcrowded back bedroom, things his mates would never understand in a million years. How the hell could he approach her? You couldn't walk up to a girl in the cold light of morning and say 'your hair's nice' or 'fancy a walk over the top?' Not with this girl, anyway. She was different and that was why he needed her.

He took a deep breath then gritted his teeth and looked up at her. She was like a statue, never moved except to turn a page or to push a strand of hair from her face. She didn't wear her hair in a pony tail like the other girls did. It hung loose like a silken waterfall down her back and shone in the sun, a mixture of gold and platinum threads – but he could never tell her that. And her eyes, cast down on the book now, were clear and green with long gold-tipped lashes. She was a tall girl, taller than him by an inch or more, but his thick crepe soles helped a bit. Still, she wasn't the type for a Teddy Boy, was she? He couldn't imagine her bopping at the Palais on a Friday or having a bit of fun in a doorway on the way home. He'd never gone all the way yet, but he'd had one or two of them breathing hard, panting for something he still felt too inept to try. He couldn't imagine her like that, giggling and groping in the dark, giving you a feel for the price of a lemonade and a couple of Woodies in the dance hall. One day, he would marry a girl like her, a girl beyond price.

The Hall i' th' Wood bus rattled past and she looked up from her book. Embarrassed beyond measure, Martin jumped up on to the garden wall and, holding an imaginary pole for balance, he executed an impromptu tightrope walk up and down, falling off at the gate and rolling on the ground as if mortally wounded. He picked himself up and began to walk with an exaggerated stiff-legged limp, then, turning to look up at her once more, he made a deep bow. She was standing at the window now, clapping her applause and half doubled over with laughter. He had made her laugh!

He pushed a hand through his hair, waved to her, then walked off grinning like an ape. She liked him, she was laughing at him. And anyway, he was one of the lads, wasn't he? He couldn't be 'in love' like they said in the pictures. But his heart was racing and he couldn't wipe this stupid smile off his face.

Never mind, time was on his side. He was not quite sixteen, only months older than her. But he'd be starting work soon, he'd have a few bob in his pocket. Maybe then, she'd like him more and . . . well . . . go out with him properly, be his girl. He met Lofty going into the Milk Bar. The gang was there, the jukebox was blaring. It was going to be a good day, this was.

'Your dinner's here, Annie,' yelled Nancy from the foot of the stairs. She walked to the range and lifted off the soot-blackened pan of pea and ham soup, setting it down on the metal side-shelf where it could keep warm. She had to get Annie's over with before Eddie came in, otherwise there'd be all that sighing and shuffling at the table again. She ladled a portion of soup into an earthenware dish as Annie came into the kitchen. 'There's fresh bread and marg if you want it.'

'Thanks, Mother.' Annie sat at the square table in the centre of the room and took a spoonful of the thick, scalding liquid. Winter and summer alike, Nancy Higson served at least one hot meal a day, soups, broths, stews, hotpots – 'to line your ribs against the winter,' she would say.

'Have you done all your homework?' asked Nancy anxiously. 'You shouldn't be reading all them stories if you haven't done your work for school.'

'I'm doing a couple of hours study every morning and I finished the essays in the first week.' The school work was no real problem to her. Even the long holiday assignments came with comparative ease – it was just a matter of organisation, get the right material, read it, answer the questions . . .

'Just don't be getting too cocky, that's all. Remember you're a scholarship girl and the town's paying for you.'

'I don't need reminding of that.' The nuns reminded them often enough that they were charity cases, financed by the ratepayers and supported by the Church. Yet the scholarship girls were usually the clever ones, the achievers, while fee-paying students tended to lag behind, spoiled brats most of them, pushed along by doting parents with more money than sense.

Nancy stared hard at the girl who had suddenly begun to call her 'Mother' instead of 'Mam', who now washed her hair twice a week and took more baths than Nancy considered necessary or even healthy. And she wouldn't have a bath at night like everybody else did, oh no, she had to be different, had to have her bath in the middle of the day and that often meant two sets of clean clothes instead of one. 'Just don't get past yourself, that's all, Annie . . .'

The loud click of the rusted gate latch, which reached even Nancy's mill-damaged ears, made her stiffen noticeably. He was back and Annie hadn't finished. And anyway, how many windows could he have cleaned in that short space of time? 'Don't start,' she warned her daughter.

'Don't worry, I'm not staying here to listen to him eating. It's like hearing the tide going in and out . . .'

A knocking at the back door prompted Nancy to look out through the side window overlooking the yard. 'It's Dr Pritchard's lad – what's he doing here? I'll bet his mam doesn't know . . .'

'I'll get it, Mother.' Annie ran into the kitchen to open the door. Simon stood in the yard, a school satchel under his arm, his face red with nervousness.

'Is . . . er . . . something the matter?' asked Nancy, peering over the shoulder of her daughter who was now the taller by several inches.

'I just . . . wanted a word with Annie, if that's alright, Mrs Higson.' As always, Simon was the essence of politeness.

Feeling rather snubbed and not quite understanding why, Nancy retreated to the living room. What was he doing here, the doctor's son of all people? Not that he wasn't a nice enough lad, though. And Nancy had never forgotten that great day out with his dad in that daft car – but they'd been kids then, Annie and Simon. Now they were . . . well . . . growing up, like. She was a dark horse, was their Annie, if she was knocking about with Simon on the sly. Apart from anything else, he was a Protestant, wasn't he? That was right, he'd got into Bolton School, but not without a lot of string-pulling. She remembered how proud she'd been when Annie had strolled through the scholarship exams while Edna Pritchard's lad could only squeeze in by the skin of his teeth and because of his parents' standing in the town.

Annie looked into the thin worried face of Simon Pritchard. She hadn't seen him for quite a while and he looked awful, worried half to death.

'You've got to help me, Anne. I'm in a hell of a mess.'

'Why, whatever's the matter? And why didn't you come to the front door?'

His deeper blush was the only answer she needed. His mother wouldn't like it. Of course, that was it. Edna Pritchard with her fur coats and her permed hair wouldn't like to think that Simon was becoming over-familiar with patients and other natives. Having to live in the area was probably bad enough for Mrs Pritchard, though the large corner building that housed both surgery and living quarters was by far the most imposing residence on the road.

Simon pushed a lock of dark hair out of his eyes. 'It's the French and the biology – I'm a bit behind,' he muttered.

'Come in.' She stepped aside and held the door wide.

'Are you sure your mother won't mind . . .?'

For answer she pulled him into the kitchen and slammed the back door behind him.

'We're going into the front room, Mother. Simon needs to borrow some school books – he forgot to bring them home and we use the same text-books, more or less.'

Nancy's hand slowed in its stirring of the soup as the boy and Annie moved through to the front room. By, she'd get her comeuppance would that lady if she had her eye on the doctor's son! Edna Pritchard wouldn't stand for anybody taking a pair of scissors to the apron strings – anybody at all. And she'd been barely civil to Nancy in the shops these past few years since Annie got into the convent right off while Simon had to struggle for Bolton School. Without being aware of what she was doing, Nancy patted her hair, preening herself almost. She would make something, would Annie. She wouldn't finish up with fluff in her hair, noises in her ears and shoulders bent from doffing four machines day in and day out.

Eddie Higson's bucket clattered loudly in the yard and Nancy filled his bowl while he washed his hands at the kitchen sink. She sat in silence as he ate his soup slowly and noisily. Apart from his eating habits, Eddie was a quiet man. Likely something to do with being a prisoner of war, sitting still for all those years, waiting, watching other men wither away. He never really mentioned it. The only thing he'd ever told her, after eight or nine pints in the Star, was of the day they'd woken up to find that all their German guards had fled. 'Some of the lads started walking towards England,' he had said. 'Daft buggers didn't even know which way to go. Then again, some couldn't walk, but they were all for being carried off home there and then. I crawled to the gate and waited for the Yanks. Two days we sat there, but then we were used to it.' Yes, he'd got so used to it, he couldn't break the habit even now. For hours he'd sit on top of the fire, even in this heat, smoking his Woodies or his roll-ups, thinking his own thoughts.

'Cup of tea, Eddie?'

'Aye. I'll have it up to the fire.'

She poured his drink. Like as not he'd sit here now till two o'clock, thinking. Then he might just bestir himself, get up off his bottom and do a few more windows.

'What do you think about, Eddie?' she almost startled herself by saying.

'What do you mean, what do I think about? What sort of a bloody daft question do you call that?'

She stacked the dishes, wishing she'd never spoken. But other people, other married people, surely they had conversations? Surely it wasn't always like this, with one stacking soup dishes while the other stared into the fire?

'I was just trying to . . . well . . . I was just wondering, like, what you think about when you sit there staring into the fire. When I was a little girl, I used to see pictures in the fire and in the clouds too . . .' Her voice tailed away. She expected no reply, got no reply.

Sighing, she carried the pots through to the kitchen and turned on the tap. There was no talking to him, was there? She'd have been just as well off having a word with the coalman's horse. Better shut up, anyroad. She was luckier than most, running hot water, nice bathroom with a flushing toilet and him talking about getting a television set. When he did speak – on rare occasions, like. She leaned against the sink, her hands gripping the cold porcelain sides. She'd give it all up tomorrow for a sight of that baby, the one that never was. Oh yes and she'd tell him where to shove his television set sideways if Billy would just walk in and say, 'I'm back, Nancy. It were all a mix-up . . .' A solitary tear escaped down her cheek and she brushed it away angrily. It was right what they said – no use crying over spilt milk. Or blood, come to that.

Eddie Higson lit his third Woodbine. What did he think about? Stupid cow, what did she know about anything? All she cared about was having a nice clean house and trying to get a new cooker. What did he think about? Because he did think alright, by Christ he did. Sometimes he lost track of time sitting here, remembering the so-called best years of his life spent in a long hut with narrow planks for beds, sitting, waiting, listening to the sounds of people pretending to be alive. 'Course, some soft buggers had to start digging their way out, but he never joined in their stupid games even when he had his strength. What did they want to get out for? To go tear-arsing round Europe till they found a bullet with their name on it? Oh no, he'd kept himself to himself. Then the bloody rations got cut because the guards had to punish the prisoners for trying to escape. It didn't take the Gerries long to find out that men with no food in their bellies and no flesh on their bones didn't have the strength to escape.

What did he think about? He thought about that one upstairs with her high-falutin talk and her fancy ways. He thought about the weeks he'd spent in hospital, about the agony the young bitch had put him through. He never worried about the others, the little girls he'd given pennies to in the past – they were off his patch, he never saw them twice. But that she-devil was always there, always a temptation. And somehow, he didn't fancy the very young ones any more. No, he was growing out of that. Now, all he could think of most of the time was Annie Byrne and her fresh young body, a tigress to be tamed. Could anybody blame him? Look at the shrivelled woman he'd married – she'd never even given him a kid, had she? Oh aye, there'd very near been a kid that time, but not his, never his. He wasn't really sterile – that was a mistake, he knew that now. But she'd gone with another man and he'd never forgive her for it. And look at her now – like a woman of fifty, she was. Not that she'd been like that when he married her. Oh no, she was a fine-looking piece then with good legs and a great figure. And she'd had no trouble getting that daughter off the first one, had she? Ten months married and she'd dropped one, but not for him, never for him. He still blamed her for that. After the operation two years ago, he'd had more tests, hadn't he? And they'd said he could have a kid if he tried hard enough. Tried hard enough? Christ, chance would be a fine thing. She didn't like 'that side' as she put it. It was a quick in and out at the best of times, enough to put anybody off. Had she liked it with him, the bloody war hero? Or with Ernie Bradshaw who was lucky to be alive after that going over Eddie and his brothers had given him?

He cleared his throat and spat into the fire, then grinned to himself. She didn't like him spitting in the fire, though she never said much. Except for her stupid questions and there hadn't been many of them just lately.

Yes, life was one long bloody think, come to that. Up a ladder, down a ladder, window after window, shut the gate, mind the dog . . . Aye, it got boring at times, though he'd copped some sights, by heck he had! Folk still in bed going hell for leather with the curtains open, nice young women half-dressed, one or two having a rinse in the scullery. Happen he could get a good time if he played his cards right, every woman had her price, didn't she? But it wouldn't be the same, wouldn't be her, the one he really had to have. Mind, there might be some sense in taking a look round till he could get her. Because he would in the end, by the hell he would!

Oh no, he could never tell Nancy what he thought about because what he thought about wasn't right. What he thought about had to be hidden away, out of sight, out of hearing.

But he'd have his own back on that young madam, no danger. He threw his fag-end into the fire and settled back for forty winks. It was hard work, cleaning windows.

'I'm just not going to pass my GCEs Anne, I know it. I'm so far behind now – it's getting to the stage where it's absolutely hopeless.'

'It's never hopeless. Look at the time I've had with the Latin, staying behind for extra lessons because I'm so thick at it. Even if you have to re-sit a few of them in the November, you'll get them in the end if you put your mind to it.' She looked down at the exercise book, wondering how he could have got it all so wrong. None of the adjectives agreed with the nouns, the verbs were barely recognisable . . . 'I think the first thing you must do is to learn the construction of a French sentence. It's not like English, you see . . .' And she heard herself repeating her teacher's words, lessons she'd been taught two or even three years earlier. Bolton School, undoubtedly the best for miles around, could only work with the raw material with which it was presented. Simon was not of the right calibre for such a high-flying establishment. Yes, he was behind. She corrected his work, explaining each step as best she could, unnerved by the look of blank incomprehension on the small worried face.

'Thanks, Anne,' he said after she had outlined the exercise in biology. 'I'll never make a doctor, will I? I think my father always hoped I'd take over after he's retired.' He laughed shakily. 'But he's a sensible chap. He probably realises that I have neither the ability nor the inclination.'

'And your mother?'

'My mother?' He sighed. 'She just flutters around with her bridge parties and her afternoon teas. She still hasn't recovered from the end of the war, hasn't forgiven the war for finishing. The war gave her something to hang on to, socks to knit, women's groups to organise. It allowed her to be Lady of the Manor, you see, gave her a sense of importance. Now she simply fills in time, bakes fancy cakes for her friends and tells everybody how well her dear boy is doing at Bolton School.' He walked to the window and stared, unseeing, out on to the road.

'I'm sure you could cope if you tried harder, Simon . . .'

He rounded on her. 'Tried harder? For God's sake, Anne – do you think I haven't tried? It's just not for me, I'm not an academic, that's all. But if one more person tells me to try, I'll . . . I'll . . .'

To Annie's surprise and horror, he began to weep noiselessly, a river of tears pouring down his narrow, sad face. Instinctively, she reached and put her arms around him. 'Don't cry – please, don't cry . . .'

The door opened and Eddie Higson eyed the scene coldly. They didn't see him. Simon's face was buried in Annie's shoulder and she, facing the window, had her back to the door. But Higson could tell that the boy was crying because his body was shaking with sobs. Silently, the intruder withdrew from the room. So that was the way the land lay, was it? She was ripe, ripe and ready and he must not think of it for it was driving him to madness.

He swept past a startled Nancy and slammed out of the back door. She didn't know what the world was coming to, really she didn't. The doctor's son in the house and Eddie slamming doors like that. She hadn't told him about Simon, of course. And he never went near the front room, he wouldn't know they were in there unless they'd made a noise and there'd been no noise, had there?

But Eddie Higson had heard what Nancy's damaged ears could not catch from the kitchen, those slightly raised voices, that catch in the lad's tone just before he broke down. The boy was crying, likely begging that one to let him have her. Why else would a big lad like that cry? And Eddie knew what it was like, how it felt to be deprived to the point where you felt you'd burst if you didn't get a woman, preferably a ripe, young one who needed the only education a woman was fit for.

He banged his ladder against a window sill and began to climb. The boy wouldn't get her easily. Eddie Higson knew that better than he knew anything.

Martin Cullen and Dennis Maher, the latter usually known as Lofty because of his height, which had never increased from the age of twelve, made their way along the cobbled entry at the back of Long Moor Lane. They had left the rest of the gang in the Milk Bar listening to a new record. Martin wanted to talk and they wouldn't understand. He could trust only Lofty not to laugh at him, but then Lofty had not the brain to laugh at anybody and Martin, who recognised Lofty's severe limitations, knew that he was using the lad as a sounding board rather than as a comprehending companion. This little weasel-faced lad had always treated Martin as something of a hero, mostly because Martin had watched over him and protected him from bullies throughout the secondary school.

They stopped across from Annie Byrne's back gate and leaned on a garden wall. The houses opposite Annie's, both front and back, were corporation and had gardens. Not that the Cullens' was a proper garden, mused Martin as he cast his eye over Mrs Chadwick's neat square of green. Their own garden was like a jungle, full of waist-high weeds and rusty prams, empty tins, punctured footballs and bits of broken furniture from his mother's famous clear-outs.

The washing had been taken in now, so they had an uninterrupted view of Annie's house, though she would likely be in the front as usual.

Martin glanced down at the small lad beside him. He didn't look more than ten or eleven at the most, a poor thin soul with huge eyes and a forest of curly black hair.

'What's up, Martin?' asked Lofty. 'I knew somethin' were up right off, as soon as you walked into the bar.'

Martin shrugged. 'I just . . . oh, I know this'll sound daft, but I've been thinking, like and . . . and I'm not going in for weaving.'

'You what? You mean you're not comin' with us on Monday an' after we got took on an' all?'

'No. I'm not going.'

Lofty's mouth dropped open as he stared at his best friend. Not going? After an apprentice weaver's job? It was a good job, was that. Lofty himself was going into the spinning rooms, doing odd jobs, a bit of work in the carding shop if he was lucky, running errands more like. But Martin had got took on proper, he'd get learned how to weave, how to make cloth, get set up for life. He was clever, was Martin.

'The mills are finished, Lofty. Oh aye, it'll take a few more years for it to peter out altogether, but they've already started on that rayon and nylon – there's not always going to be cotton mills, you know.'

Lofty thought about this. If there was no cotton, then there'd be no Bolton. Martin must be wrong for once. 'How come you found all that out then?' he asked.

'Something I read in a paper, Lofty. They reckon that foreigners can turn out cotton a lot cheaper than what we can. They'll be importing it by the mile in five or ten years. Then there's all these cheap new materials – I'm telling you now, the mills will close.'

Lofty had never given the future a lot of thought. All he wanted was a couple of bob a week to spend and a few more inches in height then he could get into the pub with his mates on a Saturday night. But he knew one thing – he wanted Martin with him. They'd been together since the nursery and Martin had always been his best mate. Lofty shuffled about uncomfortably. He hadn't the vocabulary to tell his friend how he really felt.

'What are you goin' to do instead, then?'

'I'm going down the *Evening News*, see if they'll take me on as teaboy, sweeper-up, dogsbody or whatever.'

'You what? Your mam'll bleedin' kill you! They only get shillin's fer that!'

'I'm not thinking about my Mam. Oh, I know she's a good laugh, but she doesn't really bother about me, you know. All she wants is a few more bob in her purse, but I'm thinking about the future, Lofty, planning my future. And the future's a long time to think about. The thing is, you and I have had no education, like.' He looked at his small friend who could scarcely read and write, though he could work out his dad's betting slips as quick as a flash. 'I want a start in life, Lofty and it has to be now. Seventeen or eighteen will be too late.'

Lofty felt lost. He couldn't, for the life of him, work out how Martin could turn down a good job just like that, a weaver's job with a bit of brass and proper learning for a trade. Then a thought struck him and he brightened visibly. 'But runnin' errands is not a good job, Martin. That's the sort o' thing I'll be doin' fer t' ring-spinners. Any bloody fool can run messages, even me. But you could be a weaver, a real weaver. Best I can 'ope for is the cardin' shop. I'll bet I never even get up to doffin'. And they'll always want weavers, won't they? Better a weaver than runnin' errands fer t' paper.'

This was one of the longest speeches Lofty had ever made and Martin smiled at him before saying, 'Even if they do want weavers, they're not having me. And running errands is just a start. They'll likely let me do a bit of office work after a few months, then I could learn how to take snaps and that, go to weddings and christenings.' He couldn't tell even Lofty what he really hoped, that he'd find a story, a story so good that they'd stop the presses and hold the front page while Martin Cullen typed his piece. That was another thing he'd have to learn – typing. 'We can still get together, Lofty. I can meet you after work and at the weekends.'

'It won't be the same.'

'I know it won't be the same, but it'll have to do.'

Lofty brightened once more. 'They might not take you on.'

'Makes no difference. I'm not going in the mill and that's the end of it.'

Annie's back gate swung open and she stepped out into the street. Martin felt the colour rising in his cheeks and, to cover his embarrassment, he threw back his head and laughed loudly, as if he had just heard a good joke. The laughter died abruptly as Simon Pritchard followed Annie out on to the narrow pavement, a school satchel clutched under his arm.

The street was narrow – just wide enough for the ragman's cart and Lamp Eel's new van, so Martin could hear every word that passed between the two near the gate.

'I'll see you tomorrow then, Simon – if you can get away. In the library at ten o'clock – that should give us plenty of time.'

'Good. I'll look forward to that. Cheerio . . . oh, hello Martin.'

Martin made no reply to the friendly greeting and Simon walked a few paces then set off at a run towards the corner, turning left for the main road.

'Been doing a bit of homework, then?' Martin's voice was mocking and cold. 'I see his mam's letting him out these days – happen she's got him weaned up to Farley's rusks now.'

'I wish you'd mind your own business, Martin Cullen. I'm tired of falling over you every time I step out of the house.'

'Ooh, pardon me, your royalness. Tell you what, get the corporation to shift me next time they do the middens and the bins.'

'There's a thought now.' Her eyes darted towards Lofty. 'I'll tell them to scrape your shadow up at the same time.'

'Hecky thump, Lofty. Let's get the riff-raff off the streets, eh lad? Let's keep them under lock and key or chuck 'em in with the pig-swill.'

Annie sighed. 'You know I don't mean it, Martin. I'm just a bit tired, that's all.' She turned towards the house.

'Hang on a minute!' called Martin. He fished a three-penny bit from his pocket and threw it at Lofty. 'Here. Get yourself a comic and a penny lolly.' Lofty caught the coin deftly and made off in the direction of Bryant's shop.

Martin sauntered with studied carelessness over to Annie and, trying to keep his tone casual, he asked, 'Are you . . . going with him?' He stared at his shoes.

'Am I going with whom?'

He suddenly felt choked and reached to undo the top button of his shirt. 'Him. The doctor's lad, Salmon bloody Pilchard, otherwise known as Ole Fish Face. Are you going with him?'

'Going where?'

'Any bloody where.'

'No.'

'Then why was he in your house?' He felt stupid. His voice was high-pitched like it used to be before it broke.

'We were studying together, Martin.'

He took a few paces and leaned against the wall, not

looking at her but oh, he could smell her. Like flowers, she smelled, like rain on a summer's day up on the moors . . . oh God, he couldn't look at her.

'I . . . don't want you going with nobody, Annie.' He could feel his cheeks burning.

'That's not right.'

'I know it's not right, but it's how I bloody feel!' He turned away and almost shouted this last part down the street.

'It's "I don't want you going with anybody", Martin.'

For a split second, his hopes soared, then he realised that she was just being superior again, was just pulling him to bits and correcting his English.

'I do know how to talk,' he said quietly. 'It's just that all the lads talk Bolton and they'd think I was a right girl's blouse if I started talking proper, like. I mean properly.'

'I know what you mean. And I'm sorry for teasing you.'

He managed to look at her now, but he could not quite meet her eyes, so he fixed his gaze somewhere in the region of her nose – he was close enough to count the freckles. 'I'm . . . er . . . I'm not going in t' mill.' He gritted his teeth. The mill, not t' mill. 'I'm going to try and make something of meself. It'll take a few years, but . . .'

'Martin! I'm so pleased. What are you going to do?'

He weighed his words. If he said 'I'm going to be a reporter', she might laugh. And what if he didn't make it? 'Office work – to start off with, like.' Oh why did he keep saying 'like' at the end of a sentence?

'Where?' She seemed genuinely interested now.

'Well, I've a few ideas – interviews and that – lined up.'

'Good.' She paused. 'Martin?'

'What?'

'Don't go dressed like that, will you?'

There she was, taking the mickey again. Briefly, he glanced at her eyes and found no mockery in them, only friendliness and what looked like genuine concern.

'I hadn't thought about that,' he said lamely.

'Hasn't Gerard any clothes that aren't . . . well . . . modern?'

She knew! She knew he was wearing his cousin's cast-offs! Christ, Bertha Cullen and her big mouth. Just wait till he got home, he'd tell his Mam off for letting Annie know. 'No, he hasn't,' he answered now.

'What about your uniform? The navy trousers – if you got hold of a decent tie, you might be able to get away without a jacket in this weather.'

'I'll think of something, ta.'

'Good luck then.' She turned towards the house.

'Annie!' She faced him again. It was now or never. He had to say something now. 'Your hair . . . it suits you that way.'

'Thanks.'

'You're . . .' He couldn't say it. Not beautiful, it would sound daft. 'You're a nice-looking girl . . .'

She held the gate wide. 'Look, Martin – I know what you're asking and the answer's yes. But I'm . . . not ready yet. I've a lot to do, you see. But I promise you I won't "go" with anyone else.'

'But you'll . . . go with me?'

'Sometime, yes. When I'm ready. Alright?'

'Yes . . . yes!' He knew he was grinning like a gorilla again.

'Bye, Martin.' She closed the gate.

He ran to the corner. Lofty was leaning in the shop doorway leafing through the *Beano*. Martin picked him up in a fireman's lift and whirled round until they were both dizzy. They flopped on to the pavement.

'Come on, Lofty. I'll read your comic with you.' And he led a puzzled Lofty up to the top field. It was turning out to be a great day, this was.

Chapter Two: Edna and Simon

Life, for Edna Pritchard, was a constant battle with soot and grime. She would never understand why David insisted that they live here, right on the corner of Long Moor Lane and Enfield Avenue, with all the buses rattling past and the dirt from mill chimneys floating up from the town when the wind was in the right direction. They could have got a nice bungalow up in Bradshaw or Affetside, somewhere pleasant yet not too far from the surgery. But oh no, David had to be on the spot for his precious patients. Mrs Clancy, their housekeeper, did her best, but the rooms were always filled with dust even though they were cleaned every day.

Edna examined the lace curtains at a front bedroom window. Her sharp eyes picked out some small black specks nestling between crocheted roses and, with an impatient tutting sound, she released the curtain wire from its end hook. Twice in a month she had washed these. It was hopeless, absolutely hopeless.

She looked round the room at the rich mahogany furniture which gleamed with many applications of beeswax and hard polishing. She wasn't going to lower her standards just because she was forced to live here. Though what poor Mother and Father would say if they could see her now – well, she shuddered to think. They had been so pleased and thrilled when Edna had taken up with young Dr Pritchard; after all, he was a professional man and the Hulmes, in spite of their wealth, were only too happy to gain a doctor as son-in-law. Their money had been acquired through trade and Edna's alliance with an educated man had been a feather in their caps. Would they still be pleased if they could see that their grandson was being raised in a working-class area?

Edna was the only daughter of the late Richard Hulme, owner of two ropeworks – or ropewalks as the locals called them – and a highly respected Conservative alderman in his time. His wife, Elizabeth, a shy and retiring creature, had been horrified when Alderman Hulme had been elected Mayor, but Edna had revelled in it, enjoying the few functions she had been allowed to attend in her dresses of lace and velvet, waving cheerfully but in a ladylike fashion from her seat in the Mayor's coach as they rode through the town. After all, she'd been educated by a governess, taught the arts that would equip her to be a lady, like embroidery, tapestry, needlepoint and flower-pressing. Her father, a hardened tradesman with two sons to take the reins after him, had doted on Edna, sheltered her from the grim realities of the world, treated her like some rare hot-house plant, educated her to feel and act like a lady. But now, Mummy and Daddy were dead and Edna was left to the mercies of her husband's whims, must survive as best she could in an environment for which she had never been prepared.

'Don't worry now,' her father had whispered on his deathbed. 'That man of yours has his head screwed on. I've left you enough for a proper practice. Get him to Rodney Street in Liverpool – that's where the pickings are for doctors and the like.'

But Edna's inheritance had remained in the bank. David was stubborn. He didn't want a private practice, he had fought for, voted for and was glad of the National Health Service and he cared deeply, too deeply for the snivelling creatures that filled his waiting room three times a day Monday to Friday and twice on a Saturday.

It might be more bearable if they had some sort of social life, she thought as she carried the curtains downstairs. But no, if he hadn't a surgery, then he was out on calls. On Sundays, he tinkered with his car and on the rare occasions when he did take a rest, he would read and snooze in his chair until he was needed yet again by one of his beloved patients. Sundays in particular were dreadful. He was always under his car in the avenue at the side of the house, acting like a common working man, up to his elbows in oil and grease, usually surrounded by interested onlookers who would stop for a chat and stay on to offer advice and opinions about the vagaries of the internal combustion engine.

She could not say that she had married beneath her. Her husband was, after all, a qualified practitioner. But the domestic environment was not what she would have chosen and David had turned out to be rather more . . . enthusiastic and down-to-earth than Edna would have preferred. Their interests did not match. David was not keen on bridge or gin rummy and when he did get a holiday by employing a locum, he would not attend the theatre, refused point-blank to accompany her to concerts in Manchester – could scarcely stir himself to go up to the school and discuss Simon's progress.

And that was proving to be yet another worry. Simon was not doing well. The teachers were all concerned as, indeed, was she. David simply was not being realistic. He believed that Simon was a late starter because of being a premature baby, that he would come on in a year or two, find his own level in time. Edna knew differently. Simon was a dreamer. He had inherited what she considered to be David's weaker traits and showed no signs of repeating his father's academic achievements. The trouble she had had with that boy! Trouble David chose to ignore or not to worry about. She remembered the time a few years ago when Simon had taken up with that Anne Byrne from across the road, a seemingly streetwise and waif-like creature with long plaits and darned socks. That would never have happened if they had lived at the better end of town, Chorley New Road perhaps, where Simon had attended his expensive preparatory school. Simon would have been able to mix with others of his own kind, the sons of doctors and lawyers instead of being stuck here in the midst of slums.

She slammed down the lid of her new washing machine. To be fair, she thought grudgingly, these were not really slums. The terraces on Long Moor Lane were mostly clean and well cared for, though one or two of the council houses, particularly that one of the Cullens', looked unkempt to say the least. And there were worse areas. She should be grateful that David had not, in one of his more pronounced fits of missionary zeal, dragged them all off to the back of Daubhill or Deane Road where the houses were small and poor.

And at least Simon seemed to have stopped associating with the locals. He had used to come in so dirty and unkempt after running amok with Anne Byrne and that drove of Cullens. David had tried to put his foot down, of course, had insisted that their son should be allowed to play outside with the others. But Edna had stopped it, indeed she had. She didn't want Simon getting mixed up with street children, urchins with runny noses and God knew what kind of diseases clinging to their filthy clothes. He might have picked up their habits too and she hadn't wanted her son playing 'knock at the door and run' or chalking hopscotches on the library path. No. Simon was going to be a gentleman if nothing else. And he'd never make a gentleman if he went about with creatures like Anne Byrne.

An infuriating girl, that. She used to be so thin and fragile, yet she always ran wild, always played with the boys. But the most annoying thing about her was that not-quite-politeness, the way she would always greet her betters in the street with a knowing smile that made one's flesh crawl, the way she offered to carry a bag or open a door. It was almost as if the child deliberately set out to mock and deride with her fixed grin that always remained in evidence after the offers of assistance had been refused.

She was too clever for her own good. Edna sniffed. By all accounts, Anne Byrne had turned out to be a great scholar, top of her class in most subjects according to David, who seemed to take an unnecessary interest in the girl. Edna had often noticed her going into the library, which building stood on the opposite corner of Long Moor Lane and Enfield Avenue and was, therefore, virtually next door to Edna's house. The girl was beautiful, one had to admit that. And she carried herself with such grace and poise, too much of these for one of her class, in Edna's opinion. Yes, she was glad she had managed to separate Simon from that young madam.

As Edna ran the thick lace curtains through the rubber rollers of the automatic mangle, Simon opened the back door and stepped inside.

'Where on earth have you been, Simon? Fortunately, it's a cold lunch – I've left it on the table in the dining room.'

'I've been to the library, Mum. Just trying to catch up on a bit of studying.'

'Good boy.' She leaned across to kiss him and Simon tried not to notice the face-powder setting in deep grim lines around her painted mouth.

He placed his books on the table. 'Is Dad in?'

'Of course your father is not in, Simon. He's gone to see one of Mrs Cullen's horde – measles again, I expect.' She shuddered. That family seemed to come down with just about everything, each member in turn going through every conceivable disease and taking up a lot of David's time into the bargain. Still, what could one expect of such people when they lived in filth and squalor – the place was probably overrun by mice and cockroaches. Oh dear, she hoped that David wouldn't smell when he came in.

'I saw . . . Anne Byrne in the library,' said Simon, having decided that it would be best to inform his mother rather than have her discover the truth 'accidentally' when peering through the windows. 'We've decided to study together during the holidays – help one another out.'

Edna worked hard to suppress her instinctive anger. Help one another out, indeed! She knew full well who would be teacher and who would be pupil in such a situation and she didn't want Simon learning anything from that girl, anything at all.

'Do you think that's a good idea, Simon?' she asked carefully.

'Why not? Why shouldn't we study together? We're the same age, we're doing the same subjects.'

Edna groped for words, trying to think of a feasible excuse. 'It's not a good idea, Simon, to associate too closely with patients.' She spoke slowly, attempting to keep control of her voice which had a tendency to rise in pitch when she became angry or excited. 'Her family will begin to assume a prior claim on your father, they'll take up more of his time if the girl starts helping . . . I mean, if you and she start studying together.'

'They're not like that, Mum – and you know it. I don't think Mr Higson has ever been to see Dad, and Mrs Higson doesn't come very often.'

Edna took up the curtains and started towards the door. They'd probably get sooty again if she hung them out, but what could she do? 'I just don't think it's right, Simon. The girl is not . . . well, you know what I mean.'

'Not one of us?'

'Exactly.'

'Then who is one of us?'

She turned at the door. 'Your school friends – why don't you telephone one of them? You could meet in the town centre, work in the big library – I'm sure you'd find more reference books there.'

Simon shook his head slowly. As if he could tell any of that crowd that he needed help. Not that they weren't already aware that Simon Pritchard was the class dunce, lagging behind all the way. It was because Anne was different that she did understand. She was succeeding in spite of her background while he was failing in spite of his.

Briefly, he found himself worrying whether or not he was as great a snob as his mother. Was he using a member of the working class in the same way as Edna used Mrs Clancy? Was Anne easy to talk to, easy to beg help from because she came from a lower order and therefore didn't matter? He suddenly felt angry. If he was a snob, then who had made him so despicable? He looked at his mother and decided that he would not be like her, he would be strong, defiant if necessary. From somewhere he found the courage to announce, 'No. That would not be convenient. Half of the boys are away on holiday anyway. I shall be working with Anne.' Without waiting for a reply, he left the room.

Edna stood in the doorway, aware that her mouth was hanging open. Simon had never answered back before. Her blood ran cold as she thought of her son consorting with Anne Byrne, learning from her, begging for help, feeling grateful too if her own judgement of Simon's predicament was correct.

In spite of the heat, Edna Pritchard shivered. There was something about that girl, something that had given Edna a strong sense of foreboding ever since she had first met her years ago, on the night when Mrs Higson lost her baby. Hadn't Anne Byrne run away after that, run off to live in an air-raid shelter? She was wild and yet too self-possessed for Edna's liking. No good would come of this, she told herself as she hung the curtains on the line. No good at all.

Chapter Three: With Premeditation

Eddie Higson had taken the day off. Bugger the windows, a man needed a bit of relaxation now and then. He staggered past the cooling tower and on to the playing field, making his way as steadily as he could manage along the cinder path towards the allotments. There he had left his bucket and ladder with an old gardener who often did him the favour of hanging on to these tools of trade while Eddie took the odd holiday. By, he should never have had that whisky though, not on top of the ale. He reached the small sports pavilion and decided to go in for a rest while the caretaker wasn't about. The green leather-padded form looked welcoming and he sank on to it gratefully, stretching out for a brief snooze to help him sober up. But he didn't get the chance to sleep for long, because it seemed that no sooner had he nodded off than somebody arrived on the open verandah and voices, one of them very familiar, began to drift through the window.

Martin and Annie sat outside on the bench, unaware that every word of their conversation was being overheard.

'What would you have done if you'd never passed for St Mary's?'

Annie looked into the unusually serious face. He'd made such an effort for this, their first walk together. His hair was free of grease and apart from the thick-soled shoes, he was not dressed in his Teddy Boy uniform. She hadn't meant to go out with him so soon, but he'd begged her to come, said he needed somebody to talk to and that if she could help Simon Pritchard with his flaming homework . . .

'I'd probably do something similar to what you're

planning. My mother wouldn't let me go in the mill anyway, so I'd have to find some sort of office job.'

'What about your Dad?'

There was a brief pause while she studied her hands. 'My own father's dead, Martin. I take no notice of Eddie Higson if that's who you mean. No doubt he'd push me in the mill alongside my mother if he could. So I do know what you're up against. Haven't you told your mother yet?'

He shook his head slowly.

'I wouldn't tell her if I were you, not till you've got a job. When you've actually been taken on . . .'

'But I have been taken on, Annie – in the weaving sheds.'

'I know that. But if you can get some prospects, surely she'll see sense?'

'Naw. She'll blow her bloody top.'

'Let her.'

'What?' He stared hard at her. 'By, I never thought I'd hear you telling me to defy my mother, Annie. These last few years, you've seemed to be such a . . .'

'A goody-goody?' She smiled. 'Far from it, Martin. I look at it this way – for a long time we've done what we were told, right? I've had to put up with a rotten stepfather and you haven't had it easy, have you? Well, just glance around you, Martin. Everything's changing. I've never been much of a one for history, but I've picked up enough to realise that for the first time ever, we can do as we like. I've probably known it for a while, because I refused to let them confirm me, if you remember. We're all rebels in our own way, you see. Now listen. My mother, although she's very intelligent, was thrown into the cotton trade when she was younger than I am now. She'd have given her eye-teeth for a chance to do otherwise, but there were no chances then. So. Move with the times and go for it, Martin.'

'And bugger the consequences?'

'Exactly. It's your future, nobody else's.'

He reached out and took her hand. 'You've got guts, haven't you? That's what I always liked about you, Annie, when we were kids.'

'We had some fun then, didn't we?'

'We did that!' He threw back his head and laughed. 'Hey, do you remember that time when you fell in Mrs Stirling's midden trying to get the ball?'

'Would I ever forget? And you pushed me right inside and shut the doors because my mother was coming up the back and you knew she'd kill me for playing in the middens . . .'

'And I'm leaning on the door all casual like – "nice weather, Mrs Higson. No I haven't seen your Annie just lately, Mrs Higson" . . .'

'Then when you finally let me out . . .'

'What a sight! Tea leaves in your hair and a sardine tin stuck to your frock. My, you fair clobbered me that day. I've still got the bruises.'

'You deserved them. You threw the ball in there.'

'You mean you missed it, butterfingers.'

She eyed him with as much coolness as she could muster. 'Rubbish!'

'Aye. That's what I said when you came out covered in it.'

He caught her to him and kissed her gently, first on the forehead and then on her slightly parted lips. 'You're good for me, Annie,' he whispered. 'Still as daft as a brush, aren't you?'

'Yes . . . yes, I suppose I am.' That a first real kiss could be so sweet and undemanding was both a shock and a relief to her. She found herself liking this nuisance of a boy, liking him a lot. Fervently she prayed that he would find what he wanted, that he wouldn't end up following in the footsteps of his forebears.

They wandered home hand in hand, a comfortable silence between them. As he left her at the gate, she laid a hand on his arm. 'Do it, Martin.'

'Oh I will. Now, I definitely bloody will.'

* * *

So that was the way the land lay, was it? Eddie Higson swore under his breath as he struggled to his feet. She'd the doctor's lad and Martin Cullen after her now. He stumbled out of the pavilion and into the bright sunlight, his eyes screwed up against its brilliance. His blood was boiling to fever pitch by the time he grabbed the ladder cart from a bemused allotment keeper. He steered it shakily under the railway bridge and past the school, his mind filled by the sight of her kissing that boy. And the things she'd told him too, about her rotten stepfather – he'd show her what rotten meant, by the hell he would.

Nancy had left by the time he got home, but he made no move to get his meal from the range oven. Instead, he ran up both flights of stairs and into the attic bedroom. She wasn't there, of course. He flopped on to the bed and lay there for a while, pondering the situation as best he could through the alcoholic haze which was slowly beginning to lift. Aye, she'd likely be out for the night now, messing about with lads until her mother got home. Then an idea filtered into his befuddled brain and he got up, grabbed a pencil and paper from the table and printed carefully, 'Nancy I've gone up to our Albert's will be back late. Eddie.' He walked down the stairs and pinned the paper to the front door. If the bitch was in the neighbourhood, she'd see it, read it and come inside thinking she was safe. Smiling at his cleverness, he went back up to her room to wait.

When the library closed at seven-thirty, Annie and Simon packed away their books and went their separate ways. Knowing that her mother would not be back for at least two hours, Annie decided to go to the Cullens' for a while – it was too late to start out for Auntie Jessie's now and she didn't want to be carting her satchel all over Bolton. Would Martin be in? Would he think she was chasing him if she visited their house after already seeing him this afternoon? Oh never mind, she told herself. She could not go home yet and there was nothing unusual about her visiting the Cullens once a week.

As she reached Martin's gateway, she looked across and caught sight of the note pinned to her own front door. Quickly, she crossed the road to read it, then, having gathered that Higson intended to be out until late, she went in, glad of the luxury of being able to spend an evening at home. Swiftly she ran up the two flights to her own room, tossing her school bag through the door as she entered.

'Hadn't you best get back down for the poker then?'

She stiffened as a hand came from behind the door and grabbed her hair.

'Scream and I'll bloody strangle you,' he said quietly. He twisted her round then hurled her on to the bed.

'Take your clothes off,' he growled.

She lay frozen and still as he approached her. He pulled her to the edge of the bed and began to fumble with her clothes, his hands tearing at the waistband of her skirt. 'Thought you'd got away with it, didn't you? But I've seen you with the lads, oh aye, I have that. And you didn't finish me with that bloody poker, not by a long chalk. If anybody's having you, it's going to be me, right?' He began to chuckle and she knew then that she dared not fight or scream; if she provoked him, he would surely kill her.

'And you'll tell nobody about this,' he went on. 'Because guess what? I'm going to say you've been after me for years, flaunting yourself, showing me your titties and giving me feels. I'm going to say as how I resisted you for a long time, but you finally got the better of me. Oh, it does happen, you know. Now get your things off before I rip them off.'

Like somebody in a dream, Annie removed her clothes then lay flat and terrified as he threw away his own garments. He eased himself on to the bed. 'You'll like it,' he whispered lewdly, the stench of stale beer and whisky pouring from between his grinning lips. 'I'll get you ready – see. . .' And he began to stroke her body, crooning almost as he lingered over her full, supple breasts.

Annie moved over towards the wall, her hand groping for the edge of her mattress. For how long had she been prepared for this? And wasn't this premeditation? Her fingers closed around the handle of a knife, the weapon that had been concealed beneath her mattress for two years now. He mounted her, his bony knees forcing her thighs to part. Just as she felt his ugly hardness against her body, just before he could pierce her flesh, she managed to pull out the knife.

He grunted his pleasure into her ear. He was there. After all these years, he was there. He found the virgin entrance and began to push gently against her. She hadn't screamed, hadn't given him a bad time, so if she was going to cooperate, then he may as well go at a proper pace, no use ripping her open when he could have her again and again if he treated her right and gave her a bit of fun. A split second before he could ease himself into her, a pain shot through his shoulder and down his left arm. This was quickly followed by another and another and his mouth gaped wide as he watched blood pouring from somewhere, all over the bed and all over her. He drew back as the red river continued to spurt, then he realised that she was stabbing him with a large carving knife, tearing at him wildly and repeatedly.

He rolled on to the floor taking a sheet with him and he used this to try to staunch the flow as he stumbled away from her. She was crouching now like a wild thing on the bed, her teeth bared, the dripping knife pointed towards him as she crept slowly forwards.

'You bastard!' she breathed between gritted teeth. 'You dirty, filthy, smelly bastard. Get out! Get out now or I'll stick this thing in your belly! You die slowly – very slowly – with a knife in your belly. Did you know that?' She walked round him in a slow wide circle. 'No, you wouldn't know that, would you? You don't know anything, because you're so bloody stupid. Did you really think I'd just lie there and let you? Did you?'

He writhed on the floor in agony. The sheet was soaked through and a large pool of crimson was spreading over the lino. But he would have to move – she was coming for him! He crawled out of the room on to the small landing, then fell headlong down the attic stairs, coming to rest on the larger landing below where he blacked out completely, mercifully released.

Annie opened her hand and let the knife slide to the floor. What now? What had she done and what must she do? The haunted face of Ruth Ellis entered her mind and she fled from this image, tearing around the room, stopping only when walls or pieces of furniture impeded her quick, aimless movements. Clothes. She would need clothes. After grabbing the nearest items, she left the room, climbing over his inert body at the foot of the stairs as she entered the bathroom. He looked dead. She was a murderess because she had planned this for years, hadn't she?

As quickly as she could, she rinsed the blood from her face and hands, then stepped into her clothes. She must think. Who would help her now? Where must she go? The doctor, she must get the doctor.

She flew from the house and ran blindly across the road, not caring about the traffic, not hearing when horns sounded. Dr Pritchard, slippers on his feet, newspaper rolled under his arm, answered the door.

'You've got to come,' she shouted. 'He's dead – I know he's dead!'

David Pritchard grabbed his bag from the hallstand and raced after Annie. When he reached the house, she was already waiting for him at the front door.

'He's at the top of the stairs,' she said, her voice filled with fear and panic.

David took the stairs two at a time and found Eddie Higson stretched out on the landing, stark naked and with a sheet wrapped around a badly gashed arm. He wasn't dead, of course. The bleeding had slowed, David thought, judging from the amount on the sheet and the rate at which the cuts were now bleeding.

Higson groaned and opened his eyes, then let out a faint cry as a needle entered his arm. The bugger was sewing him up and not giving him anything for the pain! He blacked out again as another stitch was inserted.

David Pritchard was a man of strong instincts. He drove the needle viciously into the patient's skin, not caring whether or not he hit another vein, not worrying about the pain he might be inflicting. The lacerations were not really deep anyway and there seemed to be no damage to muscle tissue. Whoever had done this had been defending rather than attacking. Anne, poor Anne. That fine healthy girl could have finished him off if she'd wanted to. For a few minutes he felt heartily weary of being a doctor, sick of the way he was forced to heal the injured no matter what the situation. For David understood this particular situation only too well at this moment. Somehow, he knew what had happened – the girl spattered in blood, the man lying naked at the top of the stairs.

When he was finished, he went down to attend to his real patient, the one who truly needed him. She was sitting by the fireplace as still as a statue, her face frozen with shock.

He cleared his throat. 'I've put him to bed.'

Without moving, she whispered, 'He isn't dead then?'

'No.' There followed a long silence.

'I planned it, you know. Just like Ruth Ellis, I planned it. That knife was under my bed . . . he will be dead next time. There's no way I can stop it happening.' She was staring at the floor as she spoke, obviously to herself, as if she were alone in the room.

He knelt beside her and reached for her hands, trying to rub some life into the icy fingers, but she recoiled from his touch.

'It's alright, Anne – it's me – David. David Pritchard. I'm your friend. Do you understand?'

She nodded mutely.

'Did he . . . hurt you?'

'Yes. Yes he did.' She was talking like someone in a hypnotic trance.

'How long has it been happening – this sort of thing?'

She looked at him now with great sadness, returning from wherever she had been in her nightmare. 'All my life, Doctor. All my life . . .'

Hot anger surged through his veins as he looked at this poor child, because she was a child, in spite of her womanly shape and her adult way of talking. He had never liked the man, had not cared for the shiftless, mean-looking creature. But he would never have believed that something of this magnitude had been going on right under his nose without him, the family doctor, being aware of it. Yet he had known in a sense, known that something terrible was troubling this girl. Why, dear God, oh why had he not forced it out of her?

'Anne. Look at me – that's it. Now. Did he push himself inside you? Do you understand what I mean?'

'I haven't been raped.'

'Has he ever raped you?'

'No.' She folded her hands in her lap and began to twist them about as if wringing out a dishcloth. 'The last time – a few years ago – I hit him with the poker. He had to go in hospital.'

David began to pace about the room, striding back and forth as he tried to organise his thoughts. 'Have you told anyone else about this?'

'Just a priest. He tried to help me, but he couldn't Nobody can help me. Nobody.'

He brought a chair and set it down beside hers. 'We have to tell the police about this, Anne.'

She stared at him. 'Because I'm nearly a murderer? It was premeditated, wasn't it? I read that in the paper about the woman they hanged . . .'

'It's not that!' he cried. 'We have to tell the police because he's a child-molester. He's the one in trouble, not you!'

'No!' The ferocity of this response startled him. 'If I've done nothing wrong, then there's no need for the police – don't you see? We can't tell anyone.'

'But he must be punished – he can't carry on – you can't carry on . . .'

'Doctor, for years I've been told what I can and can't do. People think we've no sense because we're young, but I can make decisions . . .'

'This is the wrong decision, Anne.'

'Will you listen to me please? I have to protect my mother . . .'

'No. Your mother must protect you, my dear.'

'Please, Doctor?'

'Alright, I'm listening.'

She leaned back in the chair before continuing and he watched the small beads of sweat pouring down her face as she struggled against shock, fought to find the words with which she might explain herself.

'Dr Pritchard, if people knew – the police, the newspapers and all that – then my mother would suffer unbearably.'

'These cases are not reported and anyway, that's hardly the point . . .'

'That's just a part of the point, Doctor. I would suffer too. I would be removed to a place of safety and the few rights I have as a mere child would be taken from me. I'd probably have to leave St Mary's in order to avoid explanations as to why I had been moved to a council home . . . don't you see? I'd be living in a home with orphans?'

'But that would not happen if he were imprisoned, Anne.'

She half-smiled patiently and with the air of one trying to explain a complicated fact to an infant. 'If he were imprisoned, then my mother would lose the chief breadwinner. She might even lose her home. Do you think I could live with her, look at her every day, knowing I've put her income in jail? And there's another thing too. He swore to tell her that I've encouraged him. What if she believed him?'

David sat very still as he took in the implications of what she had just said. By God, this one had a head on her alright. To think that she'd worked all this out and so accurately too. It was true enough, what she'd said. He wondered how many other intelligent and abused children had reached the same conclusion. How many such children were there, children who endured rape and molestation because they had not the courage or the strength to protect themselves as this one had?

She cut into his thoughts. 'I can't stop you doing what you think is right, Doctor. But please, I beg you – don't ruin what's left of my life.'

He took both her hands in his. 'I'll talk to him upstairs first. Look – I haven't decided what to do yet. Just try to keep calm and I'll bear in mind all that you've said.'

He rose and began to pace about once more. He should report this, he knew he should. But could he really go out now and destroy this child's future? On the other hand, did he dare to leave her to the mercies of a potential rapist?

They heard the front door opening and Annie shot a worried look in David's direction. 'Don't tell her . . . please don't tell her . . .'

Nancy Higson stopped in the doorway, her husband's note in her hand. 'What's going on? Is she ill – is she hurt?'

'Sit down, Mrs Higson.' He looked quickly at Annie, noticing the pleading in her eyes. 'There's been an accident,' he went on. 'Your husband fell over and cut himself . . .'

'But he left a note to say he was at his brother's . . .'

'Yes . . . well.' He coughed to give himself time. 'Before going out he . . er . . . went up into the roofspace and did a lot of damage to his arm on a rough beam.'

'Whatever was he doing up there?' asked Nancy.

'Looking for somewhere to put an indoor aerial for a television,' said Annie quietly.

'My God!' Nancy sank into a chair. 'Talk about accident-prone. How bad is he? Does he need the hospital again?'

'No, I've seen to him,' said David quickly. The man probably did need hospitalisation – possibly even a transfusion. But no. A hospital would recognise knife wounds, would ask questions, too many questions. He glanced at Annie. There, it was done. Rightly or wrongly, Dr David Pritchard was now part of the conspiracy. And he knew only too well that Eddie Higson would be glad to go along with the story.

'I'd better go up to him.' Nancy rose and took a step towards the door.

'No! No, you stay here with Anne. Make her some sweet tea – she's had a terrible shock. There's a lot of blood in her room and on the stairs – Mr Higson used one of Anne's sheets to stop the bleeding, you see. It hasn't been a pleasant experience for her. I've given him the treatment he needed, but I must go up and check on his progress before I go. You put the kettle on, Nancy. I'll be down in a few minutes.'

In the bedroom, David Pritchard shook the patient roughly until he woke, swearing because of the agony in his arm and shoulder.

'Right. You listen to me, you no-good skunk. Stay away from Anne – do you hear me?'

Higson nodded, his face contorted with pain.

'I know all about it, Higson. I know that you almost raped a minor tonight and that this is not the first time you've tried it. But it will be the last, you can be sure of that. If the poor child was not in such a bad state, I'd examine her just to make sure you haven't damaged her. Now.' He took from his pocket an empty envelope which he waved under Higson's nose. 'See this? Anne has made and signed a statement which I have witnessed, so it is now a legal document. Tomorrow, my solicitor will take a fuller account of what has happened and that will be lodged in his safe. If anything, anything at all happens to that child, my lawyer and I will bear witness against you. I'll see you go down if you so much as breathe on her again.'

'She knifed me! You've seen my arm,' mumbled the cowering figure on the bed.

'Yes, but she didn't do a good enough job, did she? She should have stuck you through your filthy black heart – vermin like you should be put down. I'll be back tomorrow to give you an injection and if you're very lucky, I may leave out the strychnine. And don't forget, Higson, you sustained your injuries in the loft while looking for a suitable location for a television aerial. That lie is for Anne's sake, not yours. Understand?'

Higson nodded, then groaned as he rolled to face the wall.

The doctor turned on his heel and left the room, a cold sweat breaking out on his brow. He felt as if he had been in the presence of something truly unnatural, something evil almost. Before going downstairs, he ran as quickly and as quietly as he could up to Anne's bedroom, picked up the bloody knife and shut it in his bag. He shivered as he passed Higson's closed door on his way back to the ground floor. Nancy met him on the bottom step. 'Is he alright, Doctor?'

'He'll survive. Give him rest and plenty of fluid.'

Annie had not moved from her seat by the fire. He walked over to her. 'Remember – he did it in the loft, Anne. Fell over, cut himself, then came into your room for help.'

'Thankyou, Doctor. I owe you a lot.'

'Yes, you do. And to pay me back, you will come to see me tomorrow. We have to make certain legal arrangements – take out an insurance if you like, to make sure that this never happens again.'

'My mother won't know?'

'No. No, she won't.'

He gave her a sleeping draught then stayed with her until she slipped into unconsciousness on the sofa. Gently, he brushed the hair from her face and sighed as he noticed dark shadows under her eyes.

On his way out, he stopped at the bottom of the stairs and called, 'Nancy? Fetch a blanket, will you? She's on the couch and I shouldn't move her if I were you – just let her sleep it off.'

He picked up his bag and left the house, noticing for the first time that he was still wearing carpet slippers. Oh dear, whatever would Edna say about that, he wondered irrelevantly as he entered his house. Suddenly exhausted, he leaned against the front door feeling as if he had aged ten years in this one night. He shook his head wearily. Had he done the right thing?

He sat up well into the night, his mind in turmoil. By two o'clock in the morning he had reached no conclusion. But he knew, as he had always known, that right and wrong were hard to define, sometimes impossible to separate. The child would be protected and that was all that mattered.

Chapter Four: Tensions

On a cold February afternoon in 1956, Nancy Higson sat in the doctor's waiting room, hands clasped tightly on her lap. The last few months had been hard and no mistake, what with Eddie coming off work for a while over his arm and Annie mithering off and on to leave school and get a job to help out. Now this. She let out a deep shuddering sigh. It couldn't be true, dear God no, not lung cancer. She'd watched her Dad die of that a couple of years back and it wasn't an easy death, not by a long chalk. And it had started the same way too, with a bad cough and then, later on, the spitting of blood into handkerchiefs and towels. Her fingers began to tremble again and she gripped her hands together more tightly until knuckles showed white through work-worn flesh. If only the doctor would hurry up. She had to get it over with now, while Annie was at school, she didn't want Annie worrying over illness in the house, not with her exams coming up this year.

Anyroad, it might not be cancer. Surely you could spit up a bit of blood without it being cancer? She tried to look on the bright side, but no, it had been going on for too long – it must be something serious.

The bell rang for her to go through and for a moment she remained riveted to the spot. This might be her last minute of near-sanity. If it was cancer or something like that, she felt she'd go straight out of her mind, they'd have to lock her up in a loony ward.

She dragged herself to her feet and knocked timidly on the surgery door before entering.

'Hello, Nancy – how are you?' Christ, he was so bloody

cheerful she could have hit him. She sank into the chair at the side of his desk.

'It's him,' she finally managed.

'Your husband?'

'Yes.'

He tapped a pencil on the desk. 'Come on, Nancy. Out with it.'

'He's . . . not right.'

David looked kindly at the poor tired soul beside him. Eddie Higson wasn't right? That was the understatement of the century. But what had happened now? Did Nancy know, had she found out? And had that bad bugger touched Anne again? He trod carefully. 'In what way is he not right?'

Nancy tugged at the top button of her coat and cleared her throat before going on, 'He's spitting blood, specially in the morning and sometimes of a night. He's got a bad cough, you see.'

Moments passed, the silence broken only by the tapping of his pencil and the rumble of a 45 as it clattered its way towards town.

'How long has he been seeing blood?'

'I'm not sure, Doctor – a good few weeks at least. He's one as keeps himself to himself, not a great talker. I haven't asked him. He likely thinks I know nothing about it.'

David nodded. Oh yes, Eddie Higson kept himself to himself alright. Too much to hide to ever open up to anybody. Perhaps he'd be answering to his Maker soon enough.

'What do you want me to do, Nancy?'

She shrugged thin shoulders. 'I don't know. He'll not come here to see you. If he thought I'd been across he'd blow his top, tell me off for interfering and mithering again. Oh, I don't know what we must do.'

'Well, I can't make a diagnosis without seeing him. Even then, I'd have to refer him to a specialist at the hospital.'

She suddenly brightened. 'If he's got anything serious, then it's not started overnight, has it? And he was in the Infirmary a couple of years back over his accident – they'd have noticed then, wouldn't they?'

'Not necessarily. Things take time to flare up and anyway, they might not find something they weren't looking for.' He rose and walked to the window, hands deep in his pockets, brow furrowed as he wondered what the hell to do.

'He was in a prison camp, wasn't he?' he asked without turning.

'Yes, he was.'

'For how long?'

'About three years, I think. They put him in hospital when he got home.'

'Was he very thin?' He looked at Nancy now, noticing for the first time that her hair was slightly streaked with silver although she was not yet forty.

'He weighed about seven stone. They couldn't keep anything down him except milk and suchlike. Even now, he doesn't like food with lumps in, rather have soup and rice pudding.'

Or alcohol, thought David, remembering the times he'd watched Eddie Higson struggling home from the Star using garden walls and lamp posts as guidelines.

'Nancy, I can't be sure, but I rather think it's tuberculosis of the lungs.'

'TB?' She was horrified. Only the poorest and dirtiest of people got TB. 'There's none of that in my house, Doctor.'

He sat down and patted her hand. 'It's everywhere – especially in a big town like this,' he said. 'And his resistance was probably lowered because of poor diet during the war – it's no reflection on you if your husband has tuberculosis.'

Mollified slightly, Nancy relaxed a little. At least there was a chance of it not being cancer. 'What are we going to do then, Doctor?'

'You'll have to talk to him, won't you?'

'Talk to him? He'd go straight through the bloody roof if I mentioned this. He won't come near you, I do know that. He reckons as you treated him bad over that arm of his, says you're a butcher – I think he's terrified of doctors and hospitals.'

David drew in a sharp breath. Here he was, getting enmeshed in a second conspiracy involving the Higson family. 'Then you'll just have to do your best. It's a notifiable disease, but I can't inform the Department until I'm sure. And I can't be sure till we've had it confirmed.' He paused. 'And we can't confirm what we can't examine. Look. Go home and boil the towels – keep yours and Anne's separate from his. It might be a good idea to give him his own set of crockery and cutlery, though boiling water should keep your utensils sterilised. Meanwhile, I'll try to work out a way around this, but it will take time and frankly, I don't know how much time we've got. After all, I'm just assuming that it's TB – but I'll do my best to find a way of getting him looked at. Alright?'

A sudden thought struck Nancy and, with her hand to her collar she said, 'What about my daughter? What if she's caught it?'

'Even if it is TB, I'm very sure that Anne doesn't have it. She's a fine strong girl – a credit to you, Nancy – she'd make a full recovery anyway.'

Nancy reached into her bag and brought out a greaseproof package which she unwrapped carefully. Inside was a man's handkerchief stained brown with dried blood. 'That's from this morning – he hid it in the dustbin. But I fetched it with me to give you an idea of how much he's bringing up.' Her face brightened once more. 'Hey – can't you send this to one of them laboratory places? Happen they can work out what he's got.'

David smiled grimly. This little woman was not behind the door, was she? With a bit of education, she might have gone far. 'No,' he replied. 'We need X-rays, fresh blood and sputum tests – not to mention a little cooperation from your husband.'

'I doubt you'll get that.' So did he, though he couldn't tell Nancy the real reason why.

'Come on,' he said now. 'Cheer up – things are seldom as bad as they seem.'

'You're a good man, Doctor. You've been a right comfort to me today and I'll not forget it. Ta.' She rose to leave.

'Send Anne to surgery tomorrow evening, will you?'

'What have I to tell her?'

'Tell her she's a guinea-pig – she'll like that. Say I'm running Mantoux tests for TB on a cross-section of the population and that she is to be my example of a typical sixteen-year-old female. And you'll need a test too, Nancy.' The plot, he thought, was thickening by the minute.

'Right. I'll send her in then.'

'Goodbye, Nancy.'

She left the surgery looking, David thought, a sight happier than when she had come in. Now, all he had to do was to persuade a man he hated and who hated him to come and seek treatment. He suddenly knew that he would not, could not do this. As long as the rest of the family was protected, then Eddie Higson could go to hell his own way. He shook his head slowly. Anne's 'insurance policy' was now in the hands of a lawyer, the child was safe at last. But was there a caring God after all? And was this His way of making Higson pay? Unless the man got immediate treatment, his death certificate was virtually signed – nobody who brought up that amount of blood each morning could survive for long without help. But he, David Pritchard, would not interfere in God's plan. Even a doctor could not intrude on divine retribution.

He walked to the window and watched Nancy scuttling across the road to boil her towels. Sighing deeply, he took his watch from the pocket of his waistcoat. Half past four – time for tea. Ah well, it was all part of a day's work, all part of life's complicated tapestry. He walked towards the living quarters, his mind occupied by just one thought. That girl had better be alright. If the brute had given her TB on top of everything else . . . He stood still in the hall for a few seconds. There should be no place in a doctor's heart for such murderous thoughts.

In the dining room, Edna was fussing with the tea as usual, arranging her china in exactly the correct order, milk, sugar and lemon to the left of her, teapot and hot water jug to the right. It was like watching a general planning a military campaign, everything present, in order and accounted for. Simon was sitting bolt-upright in a straight-backed chair, waiting for his mother to pour.

'Was that Nancy Higson?' asked Edna as she passed buttered scones first to her husband, then to her son, in accordance with her concept of doing things right.

'Yes,' David replied curtly, wondering how much longer he would be able to tolerate Edna without resorting to drink – or worse.

'Is she ill?' She stirred her tea slowly, delicately and, as always, in an anti-clockwise direction.

With exaggerated patience, David placed his cup in the centre of his saucer and unfolded a snow-white stiffly starched napkin, spreading it carefully on his lap. 'Could I have some jam please, Edna?'

Pouting in a way that might have been attractive in a woman half her age, she passed the crystal and silver jam pot to Simon, who handed it down the table to his father.

'I was only taking an interest,' she whined in that silly girlish voice.

'Edna.' David spoke with all the forbearance he could muster. 'Most of the people who visit my surgery suffer from some ailment or other. I cannot discuss the condition of patients – I should have thought you would understand that by now.'

Simon shifted miserably in his chair. He could feel the tension in the room and it made him prickly and uncomfortable.

'Stop wriggling at the table,' snapped Edna. 'And remember your manners – use the napkin.'

David looked at his unhappy son and was filled with pity for him. 'Had a good day, Simon?'

'Not bad. I'm getting somewhere with the biology, but the French is a bit much, I'm afraid.'

'He still studies with that Anne Byrne in the evenings.' There was strong disapproval in Edna's tone.

'Good. Glad to hear it – she'll make a good teacher one day,' said David.

'She may not become a teacher, Dad.' Simon glanced quickly at his mother.

'Oh really? What is she going to be then?' asked Edna with unconcealed sarcasm.

'She thinks she might be a doctor, Dad.'

'Really?' David's face beamed a wide smile.

'She'll be lucky,' muttered Edna almost under her breath.

'Then if she's lucky, it won't be before time,' said David, still grinning. 'And if and when she does make up her mind to be a doctor, then she'll be one, just mark my words.'

'What makes you so sure?' Edna's question was fired across the table like a bullet from a gun.

David leaned back expansively. 'Oh, several things. She has patience, humour, kindness – oh and a fine brain too. The latter does come in handy on the odd occasion.' He held out his cup. 'More tea please, dear.'

Chapter Five: Disruptions

Eddie Higson had spent three months in comparative heaven, so when the trouble started, it hit him doubly hard. It was as if everything was being taken at once – his health, his stamina and most of all, his Dolly.

He had found satisfaction in an unexpected quarter, the last place on earth he would have looked for it. Dolly Nelson was short and fat, had a plain face and frizzled brown hair – to say that she was not attractive would have been a kindness, because Dolly, even on her best days, was little short of downright ugly. He had collected her window money for years and never passed the time of day, never given her a second glance. It was common knowledge that her husband had left her with four kids and that she worked as an usherette at the Odeon, but until the day she called him in and asked him to mend a tap, he'd never had much to do with her.

'Your pipe needs fixing.' He turned to look at her – God, she was fat and all, stood there in her dressing gown with great blobs of white flesh bulging out at the top, nearly meeting her double chin.

'I'll pay you if you can mend it.' There was a knowing look in her eyes. 'Would you like a brew?'

'Aye, go on then.' He walked to the scullery door and she turned sideways to allow him through to the kitchen, giggling and exclaiming 'oops!' as he brushed against her. She made a great fuss of him, gave him a thick wedge of toast which he didn't eat, brewed him a second mug and all the time she leaned over him so that he could look into the deep valley between her breasts.

It was plain what she wanted and he had her there and

then on the peg rug in front of the range. She'd no shame, hadn't Dolly, didn't bother when he ripped at the gown to get at her, didn't seem to care about being such a big 'un. She wasn't good-looking by a long stretch, but by hell she knew how to go about pleasing a man. It was like sinking into a feather mattress or drowning in warm cream. Her breasts, too big for his hands, were huge soft pillows and the enormous brown nipples excited him to fever pitch, made him forget her face. And she liked it. He'd never had a woman before that liked it.

As time went on, he visited her two, sometimes three times a day, amazed at his own staying power. Not that she was hard work, oh no. Sometimes he'd just lie there while she did the lot and not always in the usual way. She had imagination, did Dolly and she was always ready for it. She could be up to the elbows in washing or baking and he could just go up to her, open her frock and take what he wanted.

He felt smug, wore the air of a man who has made a voyage of discovery and has stumbled on a secret too precious to impart to any other living soul. Nobody looked at fat women – he'd never have looked at one himself at one time, but now he knew different, didn't he? And the more time he spent with Dolly, the less ugly she looked, partly because he got used to her appearance, but mostly because she seemed to improve, as if she needed a lot of loving. Aye, they were two of a kind, him and Dolly.

But no matter how many times he visited Dolly, it was never enough. Even when he'd seen her twice in one day, he'd wake up at two or three in the morning, ready for more, urging Nancy on to her back so that he could get at her. It wasn't right and he knew it. It was like a fever driving him on, pushing him beyond all endurance.

There was only one thing for it – he'd have to leave Nancy and move in with Dolly, bugger what the neighbours thought. 'Course, the priest would be on him quick as a flash, but Eddie had never been more than a paper

Catholic, so he'd tell that lot where to go and all. It would be worth it just to know that Dolly would be there all the time, in the same house, the same bed, ready for him whenever he wanted her.

He'd say nothing to Nancy. He'd just pack his bag and bugger off, wouldn't even leave a note. As for that young cow who'd nearly cut his arm off, well he'd show her good and proper. They'd never manage on Nancy's money. Oh aye, that one would have to leave her posh school and get in the mill like the rest.

Then, just when his plans were laid, the bother started. He'd always had a cough, especially in winter, but this was different. The blood frightened him, but he told nobody – it would likely clear up in a week or two anyroad. But it didn't and the night sweats were getting worse, leaving him drained and useless, so he cut down his visits to Dolly because he was terrified of not coming up to scratch when it mattered. At times, he was back to what he considered normal and he would see her more often, pleased when she complained about missing him so badly. He had to save his strength for the one who would appreciate it.

Just one regret lingered in his sweltering brain and that was that he'd never given it to her upstairs. There was something about her – she needed showing that she was no different to the others. And however good Dolly was, he still hankered after some young stuff, a bit of uncharted territory to explore. Mind, he'd shown flaming Annie what was what, hadn't he? Oh aye, he'd given her some time and attention over the years, got her ready for the one thing a woman was fit for. Now some other bloody sod would be the first to dip his wick. No, he'd no chance now with that bastard Pritchard knowing so much. He should go and see him about this sweating, but he wouldn't, couldn't give him the satisfaction.

Still, he'd get better, wouldn't he? He had to for his Dolly. Christ, you could get lost in a woman like that, sink into her and not care whether you lived or died.

He looked at the dark shape beside him in the bed. Thin mean stick, she was, bothered more about her daughter than she ever did about him. She'd been going on for days now about some tests and X-rays the girl had been for and wasn't it great to know that Annie hadn't got TB. As if he bloody cared. He turned on to his side to try to sleep, but the heat was coming over him in waves, he was drenched with sweat – even the sheets were wet through.

The cough rumbled like a threatening storm deep in his chest, gathering force then rising up suddenly to explode wetly onto the pillow. He knew his eyes were bulging from his head as he fought to breathe. Blood spurted from his nose and mouth, shooting with great force across the bed and splashing on to the floor. Wildly, he kicked out at her until she woke, then, as light flooded the room, he sank into his own merciful darkness.

Whatever was wrong, it couldn't be her fault, thought Edna Pritchard, self-righteousness outweighing the misery she carried like a solid mass inside her body. She'd always done her best, kept a beautiful home, served meals that were nourishing and well-presented, taken good care of her appearance, brought Simon up carefully and properly.

Her bridge party had just finished and, as always, she felt a degree of dissatisfaction after her friends had left. Olive Mallinson with a complexion to suit her name and more diamonds on her hands than they had in Preston's window. Alice Barton-Bates who, after casting a last scathing glance at Edna's pathetically small front garden, had stepped into the brand new chauffeur-driven Rolls to be whisked back to her country mansion with its semi-circular driveway and acres of formal garden. Lastly, Sarah Pennington, a war widow whose husband had left half a million pounds to help her endure the heart-breaking loss.

Edna whisked lace doyleys from china plates while she

nibbled at the last of the cheese straws. She had been eating too much of late, especially when nervous or worried. She would have to cut down, or she might become as fat as that Dolly Nelson woman who had been at surgery this morning.

If only she could put her finger on whatever was wrong; if only Daddy were here to smooth things over like he used to. She sat gloomily at the window, watching the world go by through the lace barrier that separated her from the situation she despised so much. Perhaps David had another woman, someone more earthy and worldly-wise, someone with whom he might discuss politics and medicine, a partner who enjoyed his virility. But no, he had no time for that sort of thing – the practice kept him far too busy. Of course, they hadn't been really close since Simon was born. It wasn't her fault that she was frail. Hadn't she almost died giving birth and hadn't the specialist warned against further pregnancies? David must appreciate that – after all, he was a medical man.

Her pride had been hurt, though, when he had moved into another bedroom. Although she didn't want to be touched she felt, perversely, that he should still find her desirable, should want her even though her condition prevented it. And now, he treated her . . . how did he treat her? Not like a housekeeper, because he always had a smile and a kind word for the woman who came in daily. Not even like one of his patients, that silly flock of sheep who seemed to idolise him and hang on his every word. Oh no. His own wife might as well not be here at all, might be just another piece of furniture for all the notice he took of her. They talked at the table sometimes, but, more often than not of late, he would switch on the Home Service or worse still, read his paper during the meal, a habit Edna considered to be working-class and out of place in a doctor's home.

It was plain enough that Simon was on his father's side. He never said much, but when he did offer a few words, they were usually for David, seldom for her. Yes, Simon would probably turn out like his father, would copy his low-life habits and careless speech. It would happen, she was sure of it. Three times now she'd seen her son walking down the road to that dreadful Milk Bar with Anne Byrne and Martin Cullen. And there was another thing that hurt, though she could scarcely admit it. Martin Cullen and Anne Byrne hand in hand while Simon tagged along like a grateful puppy. Not that she wanted Simon to associate with the girl, but to think that she had the effrontery to prefer that awful boy, that the young madam could pick and choose between the two of them . . .

She gathered the dishes on to a trolley and wheeled it towards the door. She knew how Simon felt about the girl, his face lighting up whenever David mentioned her name. It was humiliating, it really was, she thought as she rinsed translucent china cups and Waterford sherry glasses.

As she was finishing the task, David entered by the back door, a bulky parcel under his arm.

'What's that?' she asked.

'It's a Dansette – a portable gramophone for Simon and his friends.'

She stiffened. 'Which friends in particular?'

'Oh, Martin, Anne, one or two others from the Milk Bar. They've nowhere to go when the bar closes, so I thought I'd give them that large bedroom at the back.'

'No, David.' Her voice was quiet but firm. 'I will not have people of that type in my house.'

He banged the parcel on to the table. 'People of what type? God, woman – we're all the same type. We all have blood in our veins, guts in our bellies, bones in our backs – at least, most of us do. What makes you so different, eh? Come on, you tell me, Edna. I'm sure the answer will be fascinating and very educational.'

She flinched. He had never shouted like this before. She found herself almost whispering in the face of such rage. 'I only want what's best for Simon. He should mix with the right class, boys from his own school. I don't want him wasting his life, David. And yes, I am different from these people.' She began to feel braver, more sure of her ground. 'My father educated me to be a lady. I am not used to . . .' she waved her hand towards the outer door, 'this kind of thing and have no desire to become a part of it.'

'Have you finished?' His voice was quieter now.

'Yes.'

He sat at the table, fingertips pressed together in an attitude of patience that thoroughly infuriated her. 'Simon has much to learn. Your attempts to shelter him from the world – yes, I know your intentions were good – have resulted in him developing into a shy and possibly emotionally retarded boy with a very poor self-image. You are not alone in your guilt. I too have tried to influence him, hoping he would follow in my footsteps. But why the hell should he? I would be indulging my pride were I to push him towards a profession for which he is not suited. You, Edna, are indulging your conceit by trying to turn our son into what you have become – a snob.'

She suddenly realised that he hated her. No, perhaps hatred was too strong a word for what he felt, perhaps contempt or even indifference would be more accurate. In her frustration, she began to weep. 'I'm not having them here. This is my house . . .'

'You can turn off the tap, Edna. And no, this is not your house – it is mine.'

The crying ceased immediately and a look of shock invaded her face.

'It's your home, but not your house. My name is on the deeds and your money is in the bank. Now, if you wish to continue living here, please feel free. If, on the other hand, you would prefer to find another house, one with a better address, I shall not stand in your way. However, I must warn you that in such circumstances Simon would doubtless opt to remain here with me. Meanwhile, I shall have whoever I like, whenever I please, in whichever room is available. After all, you have your bridge parties on my premises – why shouldn't Simon have friends in his own home?'

She was lost for words, yet more angry than she had ever been in her life. She picked up a glass and smashed it into the wall behind his head, then a cup, a saucer, a plate, another cup. When she found her voice, she heard herself using words she'd never uttered before, words she had never had occasion to use. And he was laughing, the bloody man was laughing! Enraged and out of ammunition, she ran to him, pounding her fists against his chest, screaming names, filthy names at him.

He grabbed her wrists and held her easily. 'So the old man did teach you something after all? Do you know what he was, Edna? A snotty-nosed kid with the arse hanging out of his trousers who had the wit and cunning to get out and make good. He broke backs in this town, walked over decent working folk and flogged them till they dropped. And he got rich, very rich. But you must never forget your roots, Edna. That's a terrible mistake. Because your roots will find you in the end and either let you down or pull you up. You can never pull them up, so don't try. You are working-class just like Anne Byrne, Bertha Cullen and the rest. The only difference is a few thousand in the bank. Remember that.'

He pushed her away, picked up his package and made for the door to the hall. 'You know, Edna – I rather enjoyed that. Your vocabulary could be quite . . . extensive if you worked on it.' He walked out grinning widely.

Edna surveyed the wreckage, forty or fifty pounds' worth of crystal and bone china scattered across the floor. Weeping hot silent tears she swept up the fragments, feeling as if she were throwing away her life as she dropped them into the bin. She felt shame and a bitter humiliation when she recalled some of the things she'd said, those dreadful words she'd used.

Well, it was all out in the open now. She wasn't going,

oh no, she wouldn't leave Simon with him and that girl. She was sick of the Higson family, sick to the core. All that frantic rushing about the night Eddie Higson had his haemorrhage – you'd have thought the world was ending. And now David and Simon were both running back and forth each day to see how poor Nancy was coping. To make matters worse, David was even driving the woman to the sanatorium once a week to visit her husband, leaving Anne Byrne to get up to no good in the house with that Martin Cullen – and possibly Simon too. Oh yes, she'd seen the Cullen boy going in at the front door bold as brass – and no doubt Simon would be sneaking in at the back. The girl was probably serving the whole neighbourhood, thought Edna viciously as she slammed a cupboard door.

There was nothing she could do. David had put his foot down hard and she'd just have to make herself scarce in the evenings if he was going to allow those creatures into the house.

But she was sure of one fact. Things would never be the same again. Edna Pritchard knew that as well as she'd ever known anything in her life before.

Chapter Six: Laughter and Worry

In the beginning, when he'd first gone into the sanatorium, Nancy had been beside herself with worry. Now, she was beginning to look happier and healthier than she had for years, though she was working longer hours. It was obvious that the manager at Millhouse didn't want to lose her, because he'd allowed her to work three full days so that she could visit Eddie in the evenings. He'd even hinted that Nancy might be foreman in time and the knowledge that she was so well thought of gave her confidence a boost. A woman as foreman? That would make a few heads turn if it ever came about. As well as doing her shifts, she had taken on the weekend cleaning at the Star, yet she didn't feel tired at all, just . . . well, guilty because half of her was relieved to have Eddie out of the road.

For Annie, it was a blessed reassurance to see him go, though she could never tell her mother that. When she had once more suggested taking a job to help out with money, Nancy had been horrified again. 'No! You'll not end up like me, that you won't! You're at school till eighteen, then college after that. Why do you think we've gone without all these years? For you to end up serving tea and toast in a café? For you to chuck it all away and be a doffer or a shopgirl?'

'I could go to the *Evening News* like Martin did. He's doing well now.'

'Aye. Brewing up and checking the Lost and Found. I know. He's talked to me and all.'

'But it's a start – I wouldn't mind . . .'

'Well I would.' Nancy grinned. 'And so does Bertha.

Eeh Annie, I must tell you. She was in the Co-op this after, creating over they'd got her divvy cheque wrong from last week – you know, the big one as goes at the top of your new sheet. Anyroad, she turns round and sees me standing in the next queue. "'Ey Nancy," she shouts. "Come over 'ere an' tell this soft bugger fer t' get a pair o' glasses, will yer?" So we gets it sorted – it was only pennies out – and then she starts in about their Martin. "Eeh Nancy," she says to me, dead serious. "It's awful. I should never 'ave let 'im do that paper round fer Bryant's – it's put ideas in 'is 'ead an' there was 'im down fer t' weavin'," she says.'

They both burst into gales of laughter. 'Oh Mother, you don't mean . . . she thinks the paper round was his downfall?'

'She does that. Happen she's got the idea as the newsprint rubbed off on his hands and got into his bloodstream.' Nancy wiped her eyes. 'She's bloody thick at times, is Bertha. Amazing how she managed to have a clever lad like Martin. Still, I had you, didn't I? But then your Dad was very clever.'

'Was he?'

'Passed all his subjects with flying colours in the army. Map-reading was his speciality – working out routes and roads round things, which bridges to blow up and all that.'

'You never talk about him. I often wonder what he was like.'

'Aye well. It doesn't seem right somehow, living with one man and talking about another. But I've not forgot him, Annie. Not a day goes by but I think of your Dad.'

'You loved him.'

'Yes, I did. Now, shift yourself and get them pots done. I'm going to see Eddie tonight, so I'd best spruce myself up a bit.'

Annie smiled. Although her mother was concerned about Higson, the atmosphere in the house was lighter, happier than it had ever been. A dark cloud had moved and let the sunshine in. And they weren't doing too badly financially either – Nancy's extra hours seemed to be almost replacing the small change that Eddie Higson used to hand over at the end of each week. Nancy even looked different when she came down ready to go out in her new clothes which she'd bought with a Providence cheque. The navy two-piece and spotted organdie blouse with the tiny bow at the neck made her look fresh and young – she didn't seem shrivelled any more. Her face had filled out a little and she had taken to wearing a dab of powder and a touch of lipstick 'to cheer Eddie up'.

'You look nice, Mother.'

'Well, I've got to do my best to lift his spirits. It's awful up there. Do you know, they've only got three walls? The fourth one's all big windows what they keep slid open all day – it's like blinking Siberia. Hey, shall I ask Edna Pritchard for a lend of one of her fur coats?'

'You could try.'

'She'd likely drop dead with shock. Even if she did lend it, I reckon she'd root through the bin so's she could stick the price tag back on.' Nancy pulled on her raincoat and picked up a scarf from the sideboard.

'Listen, Mother – why don't I get a Saturday job? They're always wanting people in the shops in town.'

'No. We're alright. We can manage if we just go careful. Look, leave them pots a minute and sit yourself down.'

They sat at the square table with its green and white check cloth and Nancy studied her hands for a few moments before speaking.

'Now, Annie. You know I'm not one for speechifying, but I'm going to have my say. Look at these hands – go on, look at them.' She held them out so that Annie could study the reddened skin, broken nails, enlarged joints.

'I never, ever want to see a daughter of mine with hands like these. I was but fourteen when I got set on, Annie, fourteen and frightened to death of the noise – I fainted twice in my first week on account of the heat. But there was nothing else, no chance of an education. That was just for the gentry, them as owned the mills.' She paused, her eyes bright with . . . was it anger?

'It's not that long since we got the vote, you know. Women were fastening themselves to railings, chucking themselves under horses' feet, getting force-fed in the jails when they tried to make a stand by starving. Did they do all that so's you'd end up with hands like mine? Oh I know somebody's got to do the factory work, but why can't women have chances to get on in life the same as men? Suffrage wasn't just to do with voting, Annie. It was about women being slaves – slaves to their husbands, slaves to the bosses who paid them in buttons for being female. Vote's not all we want, love. What we want is education. I'm telling you now, this has been a man's world since Adam was a lad and it's up to us women to change it. Your generation can do that. And the first thing you've got to do is educate the bloody men so's they'll recognise you for what you are – people first, women second.' Her eyes blazed with some inner light as she spoke.

'You've got a chance to fight on two fronts. You can lift yourself up out of the bottom drawer, get proper training and stand up with the gentry. And just as important – if not more so – you can get out there and prove yourself as good as any man. It's time for a woman's world. I decided that when you were born, decided to stop feeling sorry for you because you were a girl. Your Dad was a fighter and there's a lot of him in you. So get out, lass and kill them dead.'

Tears pricked Annie's lids and she blinked hard to stop them flowing down her face. Was this her mother, her quiet little mother who had gone along, a blind and uncomplaining servant to husband and employers all these years? How had she hidden all that anger, all that knowledge while she doffed tubes and made dinners? It was for me, thought Annie, she did it all for me . . . Then the tears defeated her and she covered her face with her hands.

'Nay, I didn't mean to upset you, lass . . .'

'But why didn't you fight for yourself, Mother?'

Nancy smiled reassuringly. 'Because it wasn't time, love. But it's time now. I can't let you leave school and if you took a Saturday job, you'd either neglect your books or miss out on your fun. And I want you to have some fun.'

'You didn't . . . you've never . . . had fun . . . oh, Mother, Mam . . .'

'What me? Me have no fun? I've near started a world war, never mind a riot in my time. Dry your eyes and I'll tell you the sort of thing I get up to.'

Annie rubbed her face with the sleeve of her cardigan and once the sobs had subsided, Nancy continued.

'It was Christmas. Foreman, a big daft lad called Tommy Sullivan, was as tiddly as a newt in the office. For once, I was glad of the noise of the machines, 'cos Tommy had been singing "Oh Little Town of Bethlehem" into an empty whisky bottle – he was using it as a microphone – for about three hours all out of tune. I was in charge of both rooms and I kept letting the girls go one at a time to listen at the office door – they were all paralysed laughing. We were getting nothing done – most of the bobbins were so overwound that they looked like giant beehives.

'So I decided we'd all sneak out early and we gets the shoes changed, grabs the bags and the coats and I'm there at the front leading all the girls out on their hands and knees past Tommy Sullivan's glass door. By now, he'd swapped his song – he was going in for "Silent Night" and it was that noisy, I'll swear they could have heard him under the Town Hall clock.

'Now you've got to picture this in your mind, Annie. We're all creeping down the stairs in a line with me at the front. All of a sudden, we come to a dead stop. Now the reason for this was quite simple really – the stair rail had gone up my sleeve – I was wearing that wide-sleeved green coat I used to have. And when this here stair rail reaches my elbow, I grind to a halt with a couple of dozen women behind me all whispering "What's up, Nancy?" Well, I could have told them what was up – the rail was up, right up. But I couldn't say it for laughing.

'Anyway, they all start laughing and all, but they've no idea what they're laughing at – and that makes me laugh even more. Then, to top it all, Tommy Sullivan arrives with his microphone and a couple of spare brown ales. "What's up?" says Tommy. Honest, I thought I was dying. I couldn't breathe for laughing and nobody had guessed what was wrong. I kept pointing to my arm, but with me being at the front, nobody could tell what I was on about.

'Then we got what the French call the piece de resistance. Soft Tommy shouts "Merry Christmas, girls," falls over the back of the queue and right down the stairs, finishes up in the Infirmary with concussion and alcohol poisoning, misses Christmas altogether. He's always blamed me for that, Annie. Mind you, he did give up the drink soon after . . .'

The two of them were helpless with mirth, screaming their laughter into a room that had not heard this sound for many a year. When their giggles began to subside, Nancy reached for Annie's hand and said, 'Never pity me, love. Don't go thinking as my life has been without purpose. I might not be a churchgoer, but I know everything's here for a reason, right down to worms and sparrows. Nay, don't feel sorry for me, lass.'

'It's Tommy Sullivan I feel sorry for . . .'

'Aye well, he had it coming. But I laughed all the way home that night on the bus. 'Course, the conductor had to say "What's up?" and that set me off again, I near went hysterical. He looked at me dead funny and I was beginning to think as how they'd send for a black van any minute and a couple of blokes in white coats.'

When David Pritchard walked into the house – because nobody had heard him knocking at the door – he found the pair of them doubled up in pain at the kitchen table.

Annie looked up at him. 'Have you . . . have you got your white coat handy? Only it's my mother, she's . . . she's gone . . .' Renewed gales of laughter followed the unfinished sentence and he joined in their mirth, unable to remain unaffected.

'He doesn't . . . he doesn't even know what he's laughing at! Just like. . . oh God . . . just like . . .' Nancy hid her face in her hands, incapable of continuing.

'But Mother, this isn't fair. If anybody ever asks me what's up, I'll never cope.'

'I know. I've been like that myself for years . . .'

Nancy composed herself with difficulty. When David asked her what the joke was, she said, 'I'll tell you in the car. Good job your driving's improved a bit.'

Annie waved as the car moved off. She'd had happy days before, days when she'd invented a new game, found a good book, days when parcels of goodies from Tom in America had arrived. But this was special. She felt really close to her mother at last. Any barrier had now been removed and even if Higson did ever return, surely this new closeness could not be destroyed.

'Oh, you're wrong, Mother,' she whispered to herself as she walked up the path. 'I didn't get all my little talents from my father.' And Nancy was just one among millions. There must be others, clever women all worn down by hard work and tedious marriages. And yes, it would be up to Annie's generation to redress the balance. She had to make it, must get to the top of one tree or another and take Nancy with her. Only then would the sacrifice be justified. As for him – well, she simply refused to consider him. He had just better not be around, that was all.

As she was about to close the door, she noticed Dolly Nelson hovering on the pavement, obviously in a state of indecision. 'Have you lost something, Mrs Nelson?' she asked.

'You might say that, lass.'

'Can I help?'

'Nay, I don't think so. Were that yer mam goin' off to see Eddie?'

'Yes. The buses to the sanatorium don't run too often, so the doctor gave her a lift.'

''Ow is 'e? Only 'e's cleaned me winders fer years an' I 'eard as 'ow 'e weren't so well.'

'He's got TB, Mrs Nelson. We don't know how long he'll be away, but somebody's going to rent the round, so your windows should get done soon.'

'Aye. Ta then, luv. Tell yer mam ter give 'im me best then.'

'Yes. Yes, I will. Goodnight, Mrs Nelson.'

'Ta-ra, luv.'

A feeling of unease came over Annie as she closed the door. The woman had never been near before – why the sudden interest in an absent window cleaner? She deliberately shrugged the thought away and got on with the dishes. Life was suddenly so easy, so relaxed, why spoil it by worrying about Dolly Nelson? It was great having the freedom of the house, no-one to avoid, no shadows to fear. She stopped suddenly, tea-towel in one hand, cup in the other. Her mother hadn't suddenly developed all this wit and intelligence – it must have been there all the time, hidden, weighted down by the silence that usually swamped this house. Was it possible that a woman of such obvious insight could live here and not realise, or at least suspect what was going on?

She walked into the living room and stood on the rug. Everything remained the same, sofa against the staircase, table in the centre, sideboard along the wall between kitchen and stairway doors. Had Nancy ever suspected?

Minutes passed, filled only by the loud ticking of the mantel clock. During those minutes, Annie, knowing that her mother's life had been dictated rather than chosen, concluded that some things simply cannot be dealt with by the human mind, that sensibility and reason can and sometimes must be poles apart. And during those minutes, Annie matured. She realised that even if Nancy had suspected, then her conscious mind could not have allowed such thoughts to filter through.

If anyone should ever ask Annie where she grew up, she would say 'In a living room in front of a range listening to a noisy clock.' It would be the truth.

Well, this was a pretty kettle and no mistake. Dolly Nelson opened her legs to the fire, heedless of the dark purple mottling on her shins, marks she had acquired over years by sitting too close to the heat. She couldn't even tell him! Three months gone and not a penny to her name – oh aye, he'd told her it was a chance in a million, him fathering a kid. But it was his alright. No use saying it was Eric's – she'd seen neither hide nor hair of him for nigh on a year, he was in a steelworks in Sheffield, never even wrote, just stuck a few quid in an envelope now and again for the kids. Eeh God, what a pickle.

She shifted her bulk and leaned over to roll her stockings down. And she missed Eddie, she really did. He'd never had a lot to say, but he'd kept her company and given her plenty of the other. But he'd given her something else, something she hadn't bargained for. Oh she was regular enough, but she never thought she'd catch, not now when she was but eighteen months short of forty. Mind you, given that she could still have a kid and that Eddie had a chance in a million, was it any wonder? Hammer and tongs they'd been at it, months on end, couldn't leave it alone.

Well, he'd have to be told and that was for sure. He was going to leave Nancy anyroad, so what difference? He could move in here when he got better, same as he would have if he'd stayed well. But it was going to take guts, going up to that place and telling him. If she was any good at writing and such, she could do a letter. Oh heck. She'd have to go up to the hospital, there was nowt else for it.

You couldn't say it right in a letter. Face to face, she could tell him she wanted him – and his kid and all. Not that that was strictly true – four was enough for anybody. But he'd never had a kid, not one of his own. It might cheer him up if he knew she had one in the oven.

Aye, she'd kept a watch on Nancy so she could work out visiting times. Nancy had been going of a Monday on the bus and a Thursday with the doctor in his car. Right. She'd go tomorrow, Friday night. He'd get right enough once he knew he'd something to get better for, something a bit more lively than that dried-up stick he'd married. What Eddie needed now was a real woman, one who knew how to go about catering for his needs proper, somebody who enjoyed a glass of stout and a bit of slap and tickle.

She dozed, her slack mouth twitching while she dreamed of herself and Eddie down the registry all dressed up for the occasion. Her eyes flew open as something quickened in her belly. No. She settled back. It was likely wind after that pork pie. Aye, she'd tell him tomorrow. It would all come out right in the end.

Chapter Seven: The Rape

He was going round the bend, he knew that for sure. There were four of them in the room, if you could call it a room – one wall missing half the bloody day and most of the night too. It reminded him of the other place where he'd gone crazy the first time, only then he'd been too weak from lack of nourishment to shout about it. This time he was getting fed and he sometimes had the strength to scream if he had a mind to.

Nights were the worst, because then he would dream about that prison camp, could smell the stink of vomit and dysentery all around him. He would wake moaning and shouting and nurses would run to his bed, rub him down, change the sheets, trying all the while to comfort him with their stupid talk. What the hell did bloody nurses know anyway? They'd somewhere to go after the shift, this was just a job to them. What did they know about being a prisoner? Because that was what he was, oh aye, he was in prison alright – even if there was a wall missing. They might just as well take his photo and stamp a number over it for all the chance he had of getting out of here – and there'd be no time off for good behaviour. He knew whose fault it was. The flaming Gerries had done this to him, hadn't they? God, and he used to think he'd had an easy war sitting it out and waiting for the end.

The other three patients had given up on him. Oh they'd tried the first few days, tipping him off about which nurses would sneak your fags in, where to hide them, how to grab a crafty smoke in the bog or by the window while the nurses were changing shifts. But they'd got the message in the end. They left him alone now and that was how he wanted it.

Nancy came in twice a week to cheer him up. And she did look cheerful and all, better than she'd looked for years, the bitch. It suited her alright, having him locked up with TB. Dolly had faded into the distance, it seemed years since he'd seen her. She wouldn't want him now anyway, not with this rotten disease. And he had his eye elsewhere, didn't he? Not all the nurses were male and that little blonde on nights would do for him if he could just get her on her own. Aye, she reminded him of somebody, did that one. She'd be due on about now, happen he'd have a wander down to the kitchen for his cocoa in a bit. He looked at the other three, all chatting about their families and swapping magazines that their visitors had brought in.

He got up, slipped into his dressing gown and went out into the corridor. Light streamed from the kitchen at the far end – aye, she'd be in there now with the drinks on a trolley. He'd go and have a look at her – looking cost nothing, did it?

She turned from the sink as he entered the kitchen. By the hell, she was a bonny piece, blonde hair, blue eyes, good legs. The buttons fair strained over the top half of her body where the uniform clung so tightly that little imagination was needed to visualise what was underneath. And nurses were supposed to be fair game, weren't they?

'Hello, Mr Higson. Has your wife been in to see you tonight?'

'Aye, she came in for an hour.'

'Good. Here's your cocoa.'

He sat on the edge of the table, his eyes fixed on her round ripeness. He itched to touch her, felt his body stirring in readiness. She handed him the drink and he reached out past the mug, his fingers closing over a warm soft breast.

'Now stop that, Mr Higson.' She sounded cool, as if she was used to it, not a bit put out or frightened.

'I just want a little feel, that's all.'

She slapped his hand away with the air of one brushing

off a troublesome bluebottle. 'Come on now. Drink your cocoa and pop back into bed like a good boy.'

Suddenly he was filled with a blinding rage. Be a good boy, do as you're told – who did she think she was? She reminded him of . . . yes, that snooty she-devil at home, that runt with the high-falutin voice and the big ideas. He felt strange and dizzy. The room began to recede, everything seemed to be turning dark red around the edges. He grabbed her, turned her round so that her back was towards him and clamped a hand tightly over her mouth. He didn't hear the cup as it clattered to the floor, because by then he was in another time, another place and there was no knife under the mattress. He would show her now. She'd have to be punished for the knife and the poker too. Oh yes, now was his chance to teach her, to use her for the one thing women were fit for.

She was beginning to struggle, but they usually did, didn't they? They were good at that, pretending they didn't want it, didn't enjoy it. Well, she was going to get it at last. He'd give it to her good and proper, make her pay, make them all pay.

He dragged her down and straddled her, punching her hard on the jaw when she opened her mouth to scream. Grinning lewdly into Annie's face, he fastened his fingers round the throat and squeezed until the girl went limp. Quickly, he did what he had to do, ripping into her swiftly, his excitement mounting as she regained consciousness. 'Aye, I've got you,' he whispered hoarsely. 'Where's your knife now, eh? I told you it would be me, I told you I'd get you first.' He slowed his frantic movements and tore open the top of her uniform, pulling away the underwear to expose her upper body.

He was panting hard, ailing lungs struggling for the oxygen he needed to complete his task. He clawed at her trembling flesh, then sank his teeth into a nipple until he tasted blood. There was no end to it, no end. He could go on all night, he knew he could. Feverishly, he thrust deeper, his body slapping against her thighs. Annie Byrne was his, finally his. No matter who had her in the future, she'd never forget this, never, never. He felt power, real power rising in him, driving him on to hurt, hurt this girl, the one he'd prepared, the one who was a woman now. It was so good, just a hair's-breadth from pain when he finally exploded in an orgasm that went on and on until he had emptied himself into this female vessel. When at last he slumped over her, his tortured lungs rasping, he felt a momentary satisfaction he had never known before, as if he had won a prize or killed an enemy.

Then they came in looking for their cocoa, another nurse with them. For a second or two he felt confused as he looked at the girl on the floor. The face was wrong. It was bloody and bruised, but he could still tell that it wasn't . . . Before he could begin to think straight, he was dragged to his feet and out of the room. A man was crying, the stupid bastard, crying like a kid. What for? He'd only had a woman – she'd live, wouldn't she? He'd only done what every man wanted to do.

They carried him up the corridor and threw him into a bathroom. Four of them came in with him, bolted the door, then laid into him. They weren't supposed to be strong, TB patients, but they found the energy from somewhere.

The beating was so brutal that when the staff eventually broke down the door, it took them a while to work out which was the victim. The five of them lay on the floor covered in blood. Eddie Higson's blood. Four stood up and stumbled away. The fifth didn't move.

They sat at the table with the green check cloth, Annie, Nancy and Dr Pritchard. Nancy was numb with shock while Annie sat pale and still, whitened fingertips gripping the edge of the table. David Pritchard felt as if his heart would break for these two women. Yes, she was a woman now, was little Annie. What he'd just told the pair of them was enough to make her grow up.

'What will happen now?' she was asking.

'Well – he's heavily sedated and he's being given some fairly intensive care. He won't be charged until he recovers consciousness. When he did come round last night after the . . . er . . . fight with the other patients, he was obviously unaware of where he was.'

Nancy lifted a shaking hand to her brow. 'But why would he attack a nurse? He's not a violent man . . .' She looked quickly at her daughter. 'He used to hit Annie, but he hasn't for a long time – has he, love?'

'No. No, he hasn't.'

'I think you should leave the room for a few minutes, Anne,' said David quietly. 'I have to talk to your mother in private.'

After a glance at each of them, Annie left the room without question.

'She's a good girl, Nancy.'

'Aye, I know, I know.'

David reached two cups from the sideboard then, after taking a bottle from his bag, poured a hefty measure of brandy into each one. She was going to need it once she'd heard what he must say. And he'd need it too, because he was about to break every rule in his book. He drank deeply while Nancy sipped at the burning liquid, coughing as it caught her throat.

'Drink a bit more, Nancy. It'll take the edge off things.'

She obeyed, welcoming the warmth as it flooded into her, soothing jagged nerves, taking the stiffness out of her hands.

He refilled the cups. 'Right.' He breathed deeply. 'Eddie was found by four patients in the kitchen of the sanatorium. The nurse – a female – was unconscious on the floor. They took him away and gave him a beating – he's lucky to be alive.' He watched Nancy's eyes as questions began to arrive in their grey depths. 'She'd been raped,' he finished, almost in a whisper.

'Raped?' Her jaw dropped. 'Raped?'

'Yes.'

'By . . . by Eddie?'

'He was the only other person in the room, Nancy. And . . . well . . . his pyjama trousers were disarranged. There's no doubt in my mind that he did it.'

She remained very still, eyes fixed on him, mouth still slightly agape.

'There are witnesses, Nancy – people who will testify . . .'

'No! No, I don't believe it! I won't believe it!'

He could make her believe it, he knew he could. But how would she take the rest of it? Would she even choose to disbelieve the awful truth which he must, he felt sure, tell her now on this night before it was too late, before she started to become defensive of Eddie Higson, before she could consider ever allowing him back into her life? And into Anne's life too.

'He's a very sick man, Nancy. Some experts in tuberculosis believe that many sufferers display certain symptoms and that one of these can be a heightened libido. That means they want – they need – a lot of sex.'

'But that's not normal. Rape, I mean. It's not normal.'

'No.'

'Then why did he do it?'

'I honestly don't know. He must be very ill indeed – and not just physically ill.'

With trembling fingers she picked up the cup and helped herself to some more brandy. 'Doctor – you mean he's mental, don't you?'

'Possibly.'

She gulped the drink in two swallows, catching her breath as it seared past her throat.

'You're going to have to be very strong now, Nancy. What you said before – about rape not being normal – you were right, of course. Your husband's behaviour has been . . . odd for some time.'

The brandy was beginning to take effect and Nancy stared at the wall behind the doctor's head, speaking, it seemed, to herself.

'She never liked him. My little Annie – she used to say "He's a bad man, he's a bad man."'

'Children are quick to spot oddities. You know the saying – out of the mouths of babes – well, Nancy, Anne was right. And she should know better than anybody else.'

'She was so funny.' Nancy sighed. 'Begged me not to marry him, she did, but you do what you think's best, don't you? I'll never forget the day we . . .'

'Nancy! Listen to me now, my dear.' He moved his chair closer to the table and took her hands in his. 'You know I care a great deal for your daughter. Well, I may hurt her very deeply by what I am about to do, but it must be done, I'm afraid. You see, it's up to you now – you must protect her.'

'Protect her? What from?'

'From him, Nancy. I promised that I would never mention this to you. I'm even violating a patient's confidence – breaking an oath, I suppose. But I care more for you and for that girl out there than I do for my job. A lot more.'

Nancy stared at him for a long time before speaking. What was he saying? What did he know about Eddie and why did Annie need protection? Somewhere at the back of her mind, a warning bell sounded, dull, far away, yet menacing. No, it couldn't be! None of this was true, none of it real. He'd had a reputation at one time, had Eddie. It was likely something from his army days, kept on file, passed down from one doctor to another. He couldn't be a rapist. Annie was safe – she'd always been safe . . .

David read her confusion and tightened his grip on her hands. 'He didn't manage it the last time, Nancy. She coped extremely well. He has the scars on his arm to prove that.'

He watched her face closely, waiting for the impact. At

first, she simply looked puzzled, then a dim light invaded her eyes and her cheeks showed twin spots of colour as she suddenly sat bolt upright in her chair. 'You mean . . . oh no . . . it can't be, it mustn't be . . .' She nodded her head towards the door.

'Yes. Yes, Nancy.'

The noise that came from her then was unearthly, something between a howl and a scream, a sound that David had certainly never heard before. She began to rock back and forth, her face nearly hitting the table, the chair almost tumbling backwards each time as she pulled at his hands. 'No! Aw no, Doctor. Not that – tell me it's not true!' It couldn't be, it couldn't be. 'Not my Annie! No, no, please – not my little girl . . .'

He gritted his teeth and hung grimly onto her hands. She continued to rock violently, putting him in mind of certified cases he'd witnessed long ago during his training. Dear God, had he gone too far? Oh he didn't care about himself and some outdated bloody oath – they could shove the practice, but what had he done to this little woman? He should have waited. If only she would cry, she had to cry.

The tears came at last in floods, torrents pouring from her eyes and nose, while from her wide open mouth she howled her primeval misery.

When Annie ran into the room she found them both standing by the sideboard clinging to one another. Seeing Dr Pritchard crying was a terrible thing. He didn't make a sound, his face was still as a stone; the only movement on it was made by tears as they ran down, dripping unheeded into Nancy's hair. Annie didn't need telling – she knew what had brought this on. Her eyes met David's and found confirmation there.

Nancy turned and opened her arms to her daughter. The three of them wept together, clung together for comfort, each feeling glad that the others were there, that something was over and finished with forever. Annie, her face buried in David's rough tweed jacket, breathed in the medicine and peppermint smell of her saviour, her heart almost bursting with gratitude. Her mother would not, could not grieve forever. As if chains were being tossed aside, she felt her first sense of imminent freedom. Soon, very soon, when Nancy could come to terms with this new shock, mother and daughter could begin, at last, to live.

They were alone now. Nancy had managed to stir herself sufficiently to make a pot of tea and they sat, one each side of the grate, cups balanced on the full-width fireguard. Inch by inch, she had dragged most of the story out of her daughter, her lips tightening into a hard straight line as she listened to the horror of Ensign Street, the nightmare of her present home, the indignities Annie had suffered in this very house, in the bathroom so treasured till now, till all this . . .

She looked at her beautiful child, this precious girl who had endured so much. 'So you never told me because he said he'd kill us?'

'That's right.'

'Did you never tell anybody, love?'

'A priest. He came up and thumped him.'

'And I'll finish him off, by Christ, I will! I'll go up to that bloody hospital and I'll wring his neck! Holy Mother of God . . .'

'Don't, Mam. Nothing's changed, has it? We're still the same. This went on for eight or nine years – I don't see why you want to do something now, when it's all over.'

'I want him to pay, Annie.'

'It's too late, Mother. Anyway, he has paid.'

'Paid? Has he bloody hell paid!'

'I clouted him with the poker and put him in the infirmary, didn't I? I half-drowned him, I knifed him – there's been enough violence.'

'He's not dead yet. I want him dead so's I can dance on his grave.'

'Mother . . .!'

'Anyway, why didn't you tell me when you got older, eh? I can understand about when you were little and he threatened to kill you . . .'

'He said he'd swear I'd encouraged him. I was afraid he might just be believed.'

'I'd never have believed him, Annie.'

'The court might have! Don't you see – it was the only way. I was so confused – I knew you'd kill him if you ever found out. And where would that get you? Prison – or worse. Dr Pritchard wanted to get the police, but I told him I didn't want to end up in a children's home and I didn't want you to lose the breadwinner.'

'Breadwinner? He's not given me enough for a scrape of marg during the last two years . . .'

'That's not the point! I just did what I thought best and Dr Pritchard backed me up. We got a lawyer to draw up a paper about what Eddie Higson had done to me over the years. We used that to blackmail him and he's never touched me since. Only now, he's done it to somebody else instead.'

Nancy walked across the room, placing her hands on her daughter's shoulders. 'My good brave lass,' she whispered before pulling Annie into her arms. 'We shall never set eyes on him again, I promise you that. The law'll see to him now.'

'Thanks, Mother.'

'What for?'

'Just for being my mother.'

'Nay, lass. If I'd been a good mother . . .'

'You didn't know . . .'

'I knew you hated him. I should have found out why.'

'Never mind, Mam. You know what you always say about spilt milk.'

'Aye, but you're not milk, Annie. You, my girl, are the cream. And never forget that.'

* * *

Dolly was puzzled. Frightened too, if she could but admit it. It had cost her one and six and all to get up there, then they wouldn't let her see him, said he was in isolation or summat.

She eased herself on to the bus seat which, though intended for two, managed to accommodate just Dolly and her bag, leaving little room for anyone else. So. It looked as if it were going to be a long job. If he were that bad as he had to be put on his own, then this one in her belly would likely be at school before its dad got out. Still, right was only right at the end of the day. He'd had his fun and she wasn't going to pay his whack as well as her own. Bad enough going through birthing a child, without having him as fathered it out of the road and not tipping up a few bob. Aye, there were nowt else for it, she'd have to call and see his missus, get the cards on the table and demand her rights. Mind, that Nancy were a dark horse. Quiet like, but Dolly reckoned she might turn nasty if pressed. And what about the flaming neighbours? Oh, she'd have to say as how Eric had been back for just the one night, sneaked out in the early hours and left her up the spout.

But she'd best get through to Eddie some road and if it had to happen through his missus, well it was just too bad. She could stick up for herself, could Dolly.

She took a bunch of grapes intended for Eddie and pushed them one by one into her mouth, heedless of the juice dripping down her chin. She'd been partial to a bit of fruit lately, probably summat to do with the kid on the way.

The bus stopped right outside the Higsons' house, so she got off, might as well get it over and done with and she could always catch another for the last two stops. The girl opened the door.

'Is yer Mam in?'

She looked as if she'd been crying. 'She's not well, Mrs Nelson.'

'Oh. Well, I'm right sorry to 'ear that. Nothin' serious, I 'ope?'

'Just a bad cold.'

Dolly felt as if the wind had been taken from her sails. 'Tell 'er as 'ow I want to see 'er – when she's better, like. Ask 'er will she call round one afternoon – I'm off matinees, so I'll be in all week.' Yes, that might be better. Better on her own patch than in Nancy Higson's kitchen.

'I'll tell her,' the girl said.

'Right then, luv. Ta-ra now.'

It was a fine night. She'd walk home, it wasn't that far and she'd a couple of nice green apples to keep her company.

'Who was it, Annie?' Nancy stirred the fire, then set the old blackened kettle on the grid to boil yet again.

'It was Mrs Nelson.'

'Dolly Nelson? What did she want?'

'I don't know.'

'Didn't she say?'

'No.'

They were both bone-weary; this evening had gone on forever. Nancy, after hearing all that from Annie, was almost too tired to care about what Dolly Nelson might want. The initial shock was over, but now the guilt had started to move in, creeping over her like icy fingers as she asked herself why she'd left Annie with him all these years, why she'd never listened, never noticed. She beat her closed fists against the wall. Jesus, Mary and Joseph, if she had him here now, right now . . .

'Don't, Mam.'

Nancy straightened. 'Did she leave a message?'

'She wants you to go and visit her.'

'Visit her? I don't know her. Last time I saw her she was buying tripe in the Jubilee Stores – months ago. We say hello, but we never pass the time. Whatever can she want?'

Annie, whose senses in spite of tiredness were still alert to the point of pain, said, as casually as she could, 'Don't go, Mother.'

'Why not?'

'I'm not sure. I just know you shouldn't go, that's all.'

Chapter Eight: Repercussions

It was a long upstairs room at the back of the house with two mock-Georgian windows, each covered by the lace curtains Mother seemed so taken with. Dad had made it really comfortable, with a carpet square that could be rolled back for dancing, a couple of tables with folding canvas chairs, a dartboard on the wall and a larger table for records and the Dansette.

Simon opened a bottle of lemonade and took a swig, aware of how horrified his mother would be if she realised he had sunk to such depths. She was furious about all this, he could tell, though little had been said. There was an atmosphere in the house, not the usual coldness, but a crackling silence, as if a thunderstorm would shortly break.

He stacked the records, looked at his watch, then went on to the landing. It would be better if he met them out on the road. Mother would consider the felony thoroughly compounded if they were to ring the bell like normal visitors. Her bedroom door was open and he could see right into the flowery girlish room with its frills and rose-pink lighting. She sat by the window in a chintz-covered nursing chair, peering out, waiting for them to arrive. He felt pity for her, so much that he almost ran in and said, 'It will be alright.' But he couldn't. Something in the way she sat, motionless and ramrod-stiff, precluded any such approach – as indeed did reason – he knew she would never approve of Anne and Martin, let alone Lofty and the rest.

He ran down the stairs at speed, opened the front door and waited under a white light illuminating the brass plate that announced his father's profession. They advanced, a tangle of stick-thin legs in drainpipe trousers, bopping and jiving along the road while the girls, in rustling skirts with layers of net just showing at the hem, followed in a manner only slightly more sedate. Dad was out on call, so his main line of defence was temporarily down. And he wanted it to go well this first time, especially after Dad had said to take care of Anne as there'd been a bit of trouble which must not be mentioned.

They burst in, bringing life and colour into the tastefully drab hall, some of the boys running partway up the stairs to slide down the highly polished banister several times. Anne and Martin were the last to arrive, separate from the rest, hand in hand as always. And yet although they were outwardly a pair, Simon felt they were incomplete without him. A strange trio, this, he thought. Himself, cherished son of a self-appointed lady of the manor, then Martin Cullen, product of a poverty-stricken home containing no less than seven children . . . and lastly, but never least, Anne Byrne. How to describe her? Daughter of a dead soldier, child of Nancy Higson, doffer and ring-spinner of this parish?

'Hiya, kid.' Martin clapped a hand on to Simon's shoulder.

'Hello, Simon.' She stood under the square chandelier, her hand still in Martin's. No, he couldn't describe her, apart from how she looked, that sad-happy smile, the fall of yellow hair left loose to cover her long back right down to the waist, clear green eyes set wide under a smooth white forehead, the small straight nose with its sprinkling of freckles. Nonconformist might be the word for Anne, who seemed unaware of, or at least unaffected by, the fashion of the day, rarely tying her hair back into a typical pony-tail, never to be seen in a skirt held impossibly wide by layers of crackle-nylon. As usual, she wore rolled-up jeans, white socks and sandals and an over-large sweater with a plain crew neck. But she stood out, for her brightness came from within and she needed no garish feathers to enhance her beauty. Because for Simon, she was beauty – not beautiful, but the very essence of all that was soul-touching. Was empathy, he wondered, akin to love? Yet he felt no jealousy, no resentment towards Martin. He liked him, loved him even, in the way one might love a brother, an older and more worldly-wise blood relation who offered comradeship and demanded little in return.

She placed a hand on Simon's arm. 'I can't stay long. My mother isn't too well – Auntie Jessie's with her just now, but I'll have to get back before she leaves.'

'I'm only glad you came. War could break out at any minute – I may need troops.'

Martin stepped forward. 'Listen, Sime. If she doesn't want us, we'll go – I'll get them all out if this means trouble for you.' The noise from upstairs was deafening, music blaring, laughter and the stamping of feet echoing throughout the house.

David let himself in at the front door and Simon, relieved beyond measure, stepped aside to allow his father into the hall.

'Noisy, eh?' grinned David, his eyes flicking towards the ceiling. He followed them upstairs and into the room, his smile broadening while he watched a pair of rock 'n' rollers whose dancing displayed a degree of athleticism that had to be admired. When the performance had ended, Lofty offered him a lemonade and David sat on a canvas chair sipping at the mug of fizzing liquid. One of the girls, brightly painted and in a dress of multi-coloured glazed cotton, came over to him. 'We want to say ta, Doc, for lettin' us come in your 'ouse.'

'Hello, Margaret – I hardly recognised you! You're welcome, all of you. Now listen.' They waited, respect plain on their faces, for David to continue. 'I'm laying down no rules, but don't go wild. Know what I mean?' They nodded, murmuring their agreement. 'This is a big house, plenty of room for everyone, but please remember that it is fastened to the house next door, that glass is thin and that if you get too loud, you'll disturb the whole neighbourhood.'

Margaret smiled. 'We don't dance all t' time, Doc. Sometimes we just sit talkin' – or listenin' to Annie more like it. Once she gets on 'er 'igh 'orse over summat, she can start a right good thing goin' – interestin' – you know?'

'Oh shut up, Maggie,' said Annie, blushing. 'You give your sixpennyworth and you know it.'

'Aye. But t' difference atween thee an' me is I allers wants fivepence change!'

They all laughed and Lofty broke away to put another record on the Dansette. David slipped out quietly, only to find that Margaret had followed him on to the landing.

''Ey, Doc. Can I 'ave a quick word?'

'Certainly. Here or in the surgery?'

'Oh 'ere'll do. It's nowt really, just me Mam – she's gone a bit funny, like. She sits there for hours, starin' into t' fire, there's never no tea when we come in from school. She's like . . . sad, if you know what I mean.'

Poor Margaret, thought David. Not yet fifteen and with the body and mind of a woman already. He thought about Dolly Nelson, knowing only too well the reason for her depression. A fifth child on the way, her husband gone, no sign of the baby's father putting in an appearance or offering support. 'I've seen your mother. She'll get better in time, I'm sure. But you're a sensible girl – there is something you can do to help.'

'Consider it done, Doc.'

Yes, she was a bright girl, this oldest of Dolly Nelson's children. Young people these days had a certain resilience, pondered David, wondering obliquely whether all that cod-liver oil had done some good after all. These war-babies were a tough breed, stronger in mind and body than any previous generation. 'Try to get her to eat the right foods, Margaret. She's overweight . . .'

'I know, she's fat, I've told 'er that.'

'Fish, green vegetables, fruit – those are the kind of foods she should be eating.'

'Aye. She's taken to fruit lately.'

'Well, that's a good sign, isn't it?'

As she went off to join the others, David remained on the landing, his head moving slowly from side to side. Yes, it was a sign. But not necessarily a good one.

Jessie Gallagher sat in the rocker by the living-room range, staring at her sister who occupied the straight-backed chair opposite hers. Jessie's mouth hung open, her jaw slack yet immovable as she tried to take in what their Nancy had just said. And the way she'd told it too, like she was reading it out of a book, like it had happened to somebody else.

'I don't want it spreading, Jessie. I've told you because I trust you and . . . well, I needed to talk to somebody round my own age and it had to be family.'

'Does our Annie know?' Jessie finally managed.

'She knows he went for a nurse – she doesn't need any pictures drawing.' Of course, she hadn't told Jessie about the other thing, about him and Annie . . . Unable to sit still with the thoughts, she jumped up to pour tea.

'Well,' said Jessie. 'Well, I'll go to the foot of our stairs – who'd have thought it, eh? And him such a quiet man.'

'Happen it's the quiet ones that need watching, Jess. Them as makes a noise gets things out of their system. He was a brooder.' Yes, she was talking about him in the past tense and that was right, because he'd gone, gone forever, just as if he were dead and buried.

'Will it get in the papers, Nancy?'

A spoon clattered to the floor as Nancy steadied herself against the table's edge. 'Eeh no – I never thought. Oh my God, how could I forget the papers? Oh no, no . . .'

'Now calm yourself. See, sit down while I make the

brew. What's done's done and there's nowt to make it different.'

Nancy sat by the fire while Jessie took over the tea-making, stirring a little extra sugar into her sister's cup. 'I wish I'd kept my gob shut now, I do. I'd no intentions of upsetting you, not with what's already on your plate . . .'

'Nay, you're right, lass. It's a consideration, by God it is.'

'Give over. It might never get in the *Evening News* anyroad.'

'*Evening News*? This could make the front page of the *News of the World*, this could. After all, if that poor nurse was hurt bad . . .' For the first time, Nancy found herself really thinking, caring about his victim. She must be in a terrible state. Aye, Nancy knew what he could be like. She felt sick to the core as she remembered the black silent shape hovering over her in the night, his body slick and vile-smelling with all that sweat. Oh, she'd had to put up with it – he was her husband. Even a paper Catholic couldn't refuse. But the other things he'd tried to make her do, unnatural things, nothing to do with making babies, then the anger when she'd refused to allow . . . She fled to the kitchen and retched fruitlessly over the sink while Jessie patted her back and murmured words of comfort.

'Oh Jessie – that poor girl . . .'

'Come on. Have you finished? See, have a glass of water – sip it slow now.'

But she couldn't swallow, her stomach still heaved. 'To think I lived for years with a creature like that . . . oh Jessie, Jessie . . .'

'That's right, love. You have a good cry, it's only natural.'

When Nancy was calmer, they returned to their seats by the fire. Jessie knew she would have to be going soon. Where was that girl? Fancy her leaving her Mam at a time like this. 'Where's Annie?' she asked now.

'With her friends – oh I made her go. If you'd seen the

state she was in the other night, you'd have done the same. She's never left my side till now – I had to kick her out. Even then I saw her standing at the corner waiting till she saw you get off the bus. This isn't something she can tell her mates, Jessie. She'll have to put a brave face on and the sooner she starts, the better. Don't you worry. She'll look after me alright. We'll look after one another.'

'Well, I'll have to get the ten past. Eugene wants the last half hour in the Feathers and I'll have to see to the kids.'

'I'll be alright. Anyway, it's only twenty to.'

A sharp rapping at the front door brought them both to their feet.

'I'll go,' said Jessie.

'No.' Nancy rubbed her face with the corner of her apron. 'I'd better do it. It might be to do with what's happened. I've got to face these things, it's my problem, not yours.'

She was somehow not surprised to find Dolly Nelson on the doorstep.

'Can I come in, Mrs 'Igson? Only I've sat in waitin' fer you ter drop by, like . . .'

Nancy stepped aside to let her pass, noticing how the woman's vast bulk seemed to fill the narrow vestibule.

As they entered the living room, Dolly exclaimed, 'Ooh, I never realised as 'ow you 'ad a visitor.'

'It's alright.' Nancy spoke from behind the woman. 'You can go in.'

The two sisters stood side by side with their backs to the fireplace as Dolly eased herself into a chair at the table. Moments passed while they waited for her to speak.

'It's . . . well . . . private, like.'

Nancy glanced at Jessie. 'It doesn't matter. Whatever you've come to say can be said in front of my sister.'

'I'll go if you want.' Jessie made for the sofa where her coat lay, but Nancy took hold of her arm and pulled her back.

They both continued to stare at the massive female

whose flesh seemed to overflow into every corner of the room.

'It's about your Eddie,' she eventually began. ''E's in the 'ospital, isn't 'e?'

'Yes. The TB sanatorium,' replied Nancy.

'Only I've gorra message for 'im. Summat as won't keep.'

Nancy walked to the table and sat down opposite Dolly, wondering what was coming next and how much more she could take. This woman was trouble, she knew it in her bones. And Annie had said as much in her own way, hadn't she?

'What message?'

Dolly studied Nancy carefully for several seconds before announcing, 'I'm carryin'.'

'What?'

'You 'eard – I'm carryin'.'

'A . . . a baby?'

'Aye.'

Nancy's fists curled themselves tight on the green check cloth. A million to one chance, a million to one, thank God it was Dolly and not . . .

'Are you sure it's his?' Jessie was asking now.

'It's Eddie's right enough.' The answer came loud and definite.

A million to one and a million thoughts in her brain. It might have been his own baby he'd kicked to death that time . . . he killed babies . . . he raped nurses . . . a million to one . . . he nearly raped Annie . . . a baby was coming, the nurse was having a baby, Annie was having his . . .

Nancy slumped across the table in a dead faint. The two women leapt up and lifted her, dragging her across the rug towards the sofa.

'Eeh nay,' puffed Dolly. 'I never expected 'er to take on this road. Good God, it's not th' end o' t' world now, is it?'

'She's a lot on her mind,' said Jessie curtly. 'Just lift her legs up then get that tot of brandy off the sideboard – fetch a teaspoon while you're at it.'

Jessie poured drops of brandy between her sister's lips while Dolly patted Nancy's cheeks gently. 'Come on now, lass. Buck up. It's me what's in t' family way, not thee.'

Nancy coughed as the alcohol hit her throat and her eyes flew open, fixing themselves on Dolly's anxious round face.

'Mrs Nelson . . .' Nancy struggled to sit up.

'Call me Dolly. And lie down, fer God's sake.'

'Mrs Nelson.' She gripped Dolly's wrist. 'Were you willing?'

'Willin'? Oh aye, I see what you mean. Yes, I were willin'.' She cast a puzzled look in Jessie's direction. 'Why should she ask that?' she mouthed in a whisper.

Jessie drew Dolly away from the sofa. 'She's confused, I reckon. Not been well, you see, not eating enough. She's gone and got herself lightheaded, that'll be why she fainted. Anyroad, she looks to have dozed off now, so come and sit by the fire for a bit.'

'Ooh, I'd never 'ave come if I'd 'ave knowed she were like that,' said Dolly, smacking her thick lips over a cup of sweet stewed tea. 'I mean, it were a case of not knowin' where to turn. You see, I'm up t' spout – t' doctor says so, so it must be reet. I've no man. I've got four kids already an' now Eddie's landed me wi' another bellyful.'

'How long was it going on, you and him?'

'Oh, months. I 'ad 'opes of 'im comin' ter live wi' me. We was proper fond o' one another, me an' Eddie. Got on a treat, we did.'

'Does he know about this baby?'

'Nay, why d' you think I'm 'ere? I didn't come just to make trouble, tha knows. I've been up the 'ospital an' they said no visitors, said as 'ow 'e were in isolation or summat. So I couldn't tell 'im, could I? Is 'e bad?'

'Oh, he's bad alright.' The irony in Jessie's tone passed unnoticed.

'I see. Will 'e not be comin' out then?'

Jessie shrugged her shoulders. 'I've no idea. But if he does come out, it won't be for a long time.'

Dolly balanced her cup on the fireguard. 'Oh 'eck. What the 'ell am I goin' ter do?'

'How far gone are you?'

'Too far fer a bottle o' gin ter do any good, I can tell yer.'

'Well, in that case, I'm as flummoxed as you are. He's not likely to be earning, so if it's money you're after, you've come to the wrong shop. Our Nancy's got nothing to spare and anyroad, she can't be paying for his mistakes – aye, and yours too.'

Dolly stared miserably into the fire. 'I just want 'im told, that's all.'

Jessie measured her next statement carefully. 'Then you'll have to tell him yourself. Nancy won't go near him now she knows he's been getting off with you. She's a proud lass, is our Nancy. The marriage was going sour anyroad. No,' she sighed. 'I don't reckon his chances of seeing her again after this.'

'Oh well. I can't say as 'ow I blame 'er. I just don't know what ter do.' She paused, deep in thought. 'I reckon there's nowt for it but to sell me 'ouse. That's if Eric'll let me – 'e pays t' mortgage. But if I could get a few 'undred together it would see me through till our Maggie's workin' an' till I can get back ter me job.'

Jessie glanced at the clock. 'I think you'd best be off now. Our Annie'll be in soon and the less she knows about this the better.'

Dolly heaved herself up and made for the door. 'Are you sure she's alreet?' She pointed to the motionless figure on the sofa.

'She'll be fine. Go on now, you've enough of your own without worrying over our Nancy. And I'm sorry if I was a bit sharpish earlier on – it was the shock, you see.'

'Don't worry. I'll see meself out. Ta-ra then.'

Jessie walked over to the sofa and stared down into Nancy's wide eyes.

'Thanks, Jess. You did well there, you're a fast thinker. Has she gone?'

'Aye, she's gone.'

'But for how long?'

'For good, love. She's gone for good.'

Nancy walked along the green-tiled floor towards large double doors. Why did they always have to paint these places dark cream? The stench of disinfectant pricked her nose and she sniffed to stop herself sneezing. A porter rattled by with a trolley full of bowls and bedpans, the noise of his progress bouncing off close walls.

She wasn't really sure why she was here – impulse, she supposed. But it wasn't something she was looking forward to, she knew that. And she ought to be putting all this behind her for her own sake and for Annie's, but well – you couldn't just leave somebody stuck on their own in hospital now, could you? Especially somebody with nobody else in the world as cared a damn whether they lived or died. No, it was only right and proper, Nancy Higson, she told herself. Get in there and do your duty like you've always preached.

She pushed the doors open. It was a large ward with a row of beds at each side, every bed with a neatly mitred white cover. Some were occupied, but other patients, those almost ready to go home, sat in small easy chairs in the centre of the ward, reading or chatting quietly. A Sister in dark blue came up behind Nancy. 'Mrs Higson?'

'That's right.'

'You are expected. Go to the end of the ward and through that door.' She pointed. 'It's a side ward – a single, for obvious reasons.'

'Yes. I'm sorry you've been caused so much bother.'

'It's not your fault, Mrs Higson. You must never blame yourself for what happened.'

Nancy took the last few steps with hesitation, then

braced herself before knocking timidly on the door.

'Just go in,' called the Sister. 'Go on – you'll be alright.'

After taking a deep breath, Nancy opened the door and stepped into the room. Tall windows were shaded by slatted blinds and all the paraphernalia was there, dripstand, tubes, bottles, but no longer connected to the patient, thank God.

'Are you awake?'

'Yes.' The voice was little more than a whisper.

Nancy crept to the bed. The girl's face was purple with bruising on the left side and in spite of the dimness, clear marks of strangulation were visible on her throat.

'It was good of you to let me come, lass.'

'It was good of you to want to come.' The voice was low and hoarse with damage.

'I've brought you some flowers – see?' She held them up.

'Thankyou. They're lovely.'

Nancy pulled the one chair over to the bed and looked down into the girl's face. Dear God, she couldn't be much more than twenty – twenty-two at the most. And she looked so much like Annie, even with the bruises the resemblance was plain to see. Hatred for him flooded through her veins yet again, a blind nauseating hatred that made her take in air as she sat down suddenly.

'Don't upset yourself, Mrs Higson – please.'

'You're telling me not to be upset? Good God, after what that bugger did to you! How could any man in his right mind . . .?'

'He's not. He's not in his right mind.'

Nancy picked up her bag. 'I'd best go, lass. I can tell it's hard for you to talk and it's only a few days since he . . . since it happened. Nay, I don't want to be making you go all through it again in your thoughts.'

'Please don't go. See – you can get me a glass of water.'

Nancy helped the girl to sit up and handed her the glass. It was obvious that she had difficulty in swallowing the liquid.

'You see – I'm alright – just bruised and shocked.' She sank back into her pillows. 'Come closer. I have to whisper because my larynx is damaged – not permanently, so don't start worrying.'

Nancy moved her chair to the top of the bed and leaned over, directing her better ear towards the girl's mouth. 'Hey, we're a pair between us, aren't we? Me with a pair of useless lugholes and you with your croaky voice. Nay, I'm not making light of it, lovey, it's just my way.'

The girl was trying to smile. 'He won't be charged,' she whispered.

'You what? No, you're letting him get away with a crime as near bad as murder as you can get! And it very near was murder – am I right?'

She shook her head. 'He just blacked me out. I don't think he meant to kill me.'

'Aye, I suppose you're right there. I can't see even that bloody swine wanting a dead one – eeh, I'm sorry, lass . . .'

'Don't keep apologising.' She paused. 'They're going to start tests on him, Mrs Higson. Special tests – on his mind.'

'Is he crackers?'

'They don't know yet. But there are signs of paranoia – he could be schizoid.'

'What does that mean?'

'It means there's a chance that he may be crackers. At the moment, he doesn't know where he is half the time.'

Nancy shook her head slowly. 'No. I've lived with him long enough to know he's not soft in the head. He'll be acting daft on purpose so he won't get judge and bloody jury. Still, I suppose if he acts mad for long enough, he might even finish up that way. Anyroad, what if they say he is fit to go on trial? Surely you'll press a charge then?'

'I can't,' whispered the girl. 'I can't do it.'

'Why not? Hey, I don't want you worrying over me and mine. If the papers got hold of it, we'd likely survive.'

'It's not that.' She looked directly at Nancy now. 'It's me – I can't do it. Oh, I know they'd keep my name out of the papers, but it would get about, I know it would. And if Pete ever found out, he'd kill him, sane or not.'

'Pete?'

'My boyfriend. He's in the army, stationed in Germany. And . . .' She paused, a hand to her throat as she swallowed. 'He might not want to marry me if he knew I'd . . . well, you know . . . '

'Been raped?'

'Yes.'

'But . . . but it wasn't your fault, was it?' Nancy stood and began to pace the room angrily. 'By God, it is a man's world, isn't it? One of them might not want you because another's had you against your will. They all want sex – well, most of them do at any road – wherever they can get it. But they expect a woman to come pure and lily-white to her marriage bed. What I'd like to know is this. If all the men are wandering about having sex and all the women are keeping themselves to themselves, then what the hell's going on? It's double bloody standards all the way, isn't it? I'll tell you what – it's a damn crazy world we're living in.' She waved her arms wildly to emphasise the words.

'Some of them think we want to be raped anyway.'

'How convenient for them! Aye well, they have to say that because a lot of them are not up to much and that's their excuse for not coping proper. Yes, I get your drift, lass. My hearing might not be up to much, but I'm all there with me lemon drops. Huh, talk about a man's world? What sort of a world have they made, eh? Full of war and rape and flaming arguments. Oh, I'm not saying they're all bad. Nay, I'm not that daft. But most of them are . . . oh, what's the word? Arrogant, that's it. Arrogant because they've got an extra bit stuck on between their legs. Pity they don't keep their brains in their trousers and all – we might be better off.'

She returned to sit beside the bed. 'Listen to me, Mary Greenhalgh. I got your name off your mate at the sanatorium – dark-haired girl – Brenda, isn't she?' Mary nodded. 'And she told me your Mam's dead and your Dad's gone off to Canada. Aye, she told me a lot about you and I hope she doesn't get into trouble, because I'm right glad I came, I'm pleased to know you, Mary Greenhalgh. If there's anything I can do for you, then phone our Dr Pritchard – see, here's his number and my name and address on this envelope. If you've no voice, get the Sister to ring. Just you get the word to me and I'll come. Aye, I will that.'

Mary smiled wanly through her tears.

'Now, Brenda said as how you're not well fixed with your digs. If you want a bed, there'll be one at our house. And don't worry about him coming back – I put the deposit down and I've paid the mortgage out of my own wages. Anyroad, after what he's done, there's nobody'll force me to take him back. And there'll be nothing of his left. His stuff's going on the ragman's cart tomorrow. So if he wants anything, he can whistle for it, see if it'll come.'

The girl gripped Nancy's hand tightly.

'Eeh lass, you do look bad. I'm sorry it was my . . . ex-husband as caused it.'

'I hardly knew what was happening,' whispered Mary. 'It was mostly afterwards I felt the pain.'

'Aye. But you felt the fear just before, didn't you?'

'I was a fool. I thought I could manage him. You get a fair amount of that sort of thing from men in hospitals.'

'Then it must be put a stop to.'

'Well, it won't happen to me again – I'm not going back.'

'Just you come to me when you get out of here. You can sort your future out when you're in a better frame. Will you come?'

'I don't know. I'll have to see . . .'

'You'll be safe. He'll not be back, I promise.'

Mary raised herself on to the pillows. 'No, he won't be coming back, Mrs Higson. The disease is rampant and he's allergic to both penicillin and streptomycin.' She paused. 'He'll be dead within the year.'

There followed a short silence, then Nancy picked up her shopping bag and smiled. 'Well then, that's alright now, isn't it?'

Chapter Nine: Confrontations

By the summer of 1956, Martin felt as miserable as sin, sick to the back teeth of his mother forever moaning about him not getting a proper wage, fed up with Annie and her studying, tired of his workmates' taunts about his dashing off to meet a schoolgirl in his lunch break. After Colin Marlowe spotted them together in Tognarelli's, life became almost unbearable.

'Can't you get a proper woman then, Cullen?'

'Best not have it off with her – we'll be seeing you on the front page.'

'When's her birthday, then? Is it fourteen or fifteen next?'

He'd show them, he would that. He wasn't going to be a junior forever – oh no, not bloody likely. With a couple of little ideas up his sleeve, Martin stormed out of the office one June afternoon, deliberately ignoring wolf-whistles and an enthusiastic chorus of 'Rock-a-bye Baby' as he stamped through the main news room. Aye, his twin sister Josie had had the right idea, clearing off to Manchester, getting digs then a job in a big shop, taking typing lessons at night so she could train for a secretary. At least their Josie had got away from home. And what was he hanging around for? To live in a mucky midden, to get laughed at, to let Annie Byrne drive him mad by keeping him at arm's length?

He jumped on a bus outside Gregory and Porritt's and sat glowering all the way to Breightmet. Yes, he'd show them down the office alright. He'd contacts of his own now, was on his way to meet a ringer from the big Corpy estate and he'd be giving them a story once he'd got to the bottom of these football ticket forgeries.

After his business was completed, Martin stood waiting

for the bus back to town, a smile of self-satisfaction on his face. He was ten bob lighter, but with a pocket full of shorthand notes and a printer's plate that should never have seen the light of day, he felt very pleased with his afternoon's work.

'Hiya, Martin!' It was Maggie Nelson in a tight button-up cardigan worn back to front, her large breasts straining against thin nylon.

'What are you doing up here, Maggie?'

'We moved, didn't we?' She turned sideways, hands on hips, to give him a better view of her magnificent hour-glass figure. 'That's our 'ouse over there.' She pointed. 'Come on – they're all out. 'Appen you might fancy a cup o' tea?' Her hands moved slowly up then down over the broad black elastic waspie belt. Martin loosened his tie. God, she must be about 40–22–36, this one. In time, she'd likely run to fat like her Ma, but right now, she was a prize and no mistake.

'Are you working?' he asked as they walked towards the house.

'Off and on, like,' she grinned, tossing peroxide curls.

They had got no further than the hall when she pressed herself against him. 'I've allers fancied you, Martin. Still goin' wi' Annie? Nay, yer want to forget 'er, lad. I can give yer a good time, a bit o' proper lovin'.' She pulled him into the living room. 'Well, are yer goin' fer t' stand there like 'im outside o' Bowes?'

Martin remained riveted to the spot. Yes, he probably did look like the dummy that used to occupy the pavement outside a tailor's shop in the town centre. But what the hell was he going to do? He loved Annie, he was going to marry Annie one day, wasn't he? But when? If she was going in for a doctor, it could be bloody years. And he'd be a fool to pass this chance up. Slowly, he removed his jacket and tie. If only the damn fools at the office could see him now! Panic and excitement joined forces in his chest, the former winning by a knockout when Maggie stood naked beside him. He'd never done it before! And here was this gorgeous and obviously experienced specimen pushing him on to the wide sofa, tearing off his shoes and socks, pulling at his trousers, fondling, stroking, kissing every straining part of his frustrated body.

In the end, it didn't matter that he was new to it, because she mounted him, guided his flesh until it melted into hers, lifted his head on to cushions so that their mouths might meet each time she rose in her slow, languorous ritual. Then, when he knew that he could not last for one more second, she pulled them both off the low couch and on to the floor so that their positions were reversed. This sudden move broke the rhythm and he found himself able to continue, his pleasure and confidence increasing as he watched her travelling towards climax. Deliberately, he closed his eyes against the sight of those beautiful rose-tipped breasts, determined now to stay the course. When she screamed her final throes of joy, he opened his eyes and, caught up in his first ever sight of female ecstasy, he echoed the sound and gave in to his own urgent need for release.

For a few breathless moments, he lay on top of the girl, his head against the wonderful softness of her, his hand slowly caressing creamy curves. Then he looked up into her face and saw the hard, streetwise expression, noticed the layers of pink foundation and powder, the matted eyelashes with their thick coating of black mascara. His heart lurched, his mind cried out to Annie – oh God, what had he done?

'What's t' matter, Martin? Didn't yer like it?'

He struggled to his feet and grabbed his clothes.

'What's t' matter?' she asked again.

'Nothing. I've got to get back to the *News*, that's all.'

She raised herself to a sitting position. 'I'll bet Annie Byrne never gives yer a good time like that, eh?'

'Annie's different. Leave her out of it.'

''Appen I might. 'Appen I might not.'

He rounded on her. 'What do you mean by that?'

'She'd be right interested ter know about this, wouldn't she?'

Swiftly, he pulled on his trousers. When he was fully dressed, he turned to look at the naked girl at his feet. 'Don't tell her.'

'Okay, I won't. As long as you come back, like. We could meet up regular, 'ave our fun an' nobody 'll be the wiser. Get me drift?'

He nodded, ready to agree to anything in his desperation to escape.

'Tuesday then? Jolly Brows, near that little 'ill over t' top. Seven o'clock?'

'Right.'

'You'd best be there, Martin. I don't like bein' stood up. I can get right nasty if I get stood up.'

Disgusted with her and with himself, he walked quickly out of the house, slamming the door behind him. How would he ever look Annie in the face again?

But when night came and he lay in his lonely bed, Martin remembered only the pleasure. When he slept, he was tortured by dreams of Maggie and her voluptuous body. When he woke, he knew that he was hooked. No matter how hard he fought the urge, he would be meeting Maggie Nelson, taking what she offered so freely. But his pillow was wet with tears.

It was strange having an emancipated mother, one who did the washing when she felt like it, who loudly declared her conversion to the Labour Party, often going round distributing leaflets for the Socialist cause. Nancy Higson, now a fully-fledged foreman with a decent wage, was no longer up and coming. She had arrived, had launched herself on an unsuspecting world with a bang rather than with a whimper. There was talk, of course, what with her poor husband being stuck in hospital for God knew how long and her never visiting him. But Nancy rose above it all, got her hair permed in soft waves, bought a Coty compact of Fair Beauty and took to wearing soft coral lipstick. She also had her ears pierced, an event that led to some discomfort and several interesting expletives until the pain died down.

On Thursday evenings, she attended the Amy Walker School of Dance, for which purpose she acquired two strapless frocks, one in sequined black tulle over taffeta, the other in a figured emerald brocade with a matching stole. At last, Nancy had her green dress.

Annie, her feelings mixed as she watched the butterfly emerging from its grey chrysalis, held her breath, hoping that the wings would dry quickly and that nothing sharp would inflict pain on this reborn creature. It seemed that Nancy's youth had not been missed out, but had simply been postponed until circumstances allowed it to occur.

Mother and daughter stood now in the doorway of the Bodega coffee bar, the older woman still complaining about what they had just consumed in the café's darkened depths. 'I'm sure they make it with Lux flakes. Given a kiddy's clay pipe, I could have blown a fair bubble with that mess.'

'Frothy coffee's all the rage, Mother.'

'Aye well, they should have given us straws – I finished up with a moustache after dipping myself into that cup. And it was cracked.'

They began to walk through the town, pausing occasionally to gaze into shop windows.

'How do you think I'd look in that hat, Annie?'

'Drowned.'

'Shall we go in and try it?'

'Oh, not on a Saturday – it'll be packed in there.'

They stopped on the corner by Timothy White's and Taylor's. 'I'm glad you've got the exams over,' said Nancy. 'But you still seem bothered over something or other. Is it to do with Martin?'

Annie shrugged her shoulders.

'What's up, lass?'

'He's got . . . I think he's got somebody else. Oh, let's go home.'

Nancy trotted beside her long-legged daughter, then grabbed her by the arm. 'Slow down, for goodness sake! Do you think I'm a flaming racehorse? Tell me what's up before I give you a clout. You're not too big for a thump, you know.' She could see that Annie's temper was roused – the two spots of colour on her face were always a dead give-away.

'Margaret Nelson, Mother. That's what's up.'

Nancy stiffened. 'Dolly Nelson's lass?'

'Yes. And she's not a lass, she's a bloody whore!'

'Annie! Will I wash your mouth out with a block of carbolic? What's got into you at all? Oh, bloody hell – talk of the devil!'

Annie was just about to make a remark about the pot calling the kettle black, when she noticed the frozen expression on Nancy's face. She turned from her mother to see Dolly Nelson, pram in front of her massive body, waddling along the pavement towards them. It was too late to take evasive action – the woman was upon them before they could move.

''Ow are you then, Mrs 'Igson?'

'Fair to middling,' Nancy managed.

Annie peeped into the pram. 'Is it a boy or a girl?' she asked as politely as she could, wishing Maggie Nelson's mother would disappear in a puff of smoke.

'It's a boy,' answered Dolly proudly. She turned to Nancy. ''Ow's my little lad's dad, then?'

'The less said about that, the better.' Nancy made to move away.

''Ang on!' screamed Dolly. 'Kept quiet long enough, I 'ave. An' I've 'eard as 'ow yer never even visit the poor sod.'

'He's not fit to visit. He's in a secure wing at the mental

hospital. They can't have him in the TB place because of his state of mind. He's isolated on account of the infection and because he takes bad turns.'

'No wonder, if nobody visits 'im!'

Annie had recoiled from the pram as if bitten by a snake. 'Is this . . . his child?'

'Aye,' said Dolly. 'Your little brother in a way.'

Annie drew herself to full height. 'Eddie Higson is no relation of mine, Mrs Nelson.'

'Or mine,' added Nancy firmly.

'You bloody bitch! No wonder 'e turned ter me! Aye, an' it's me 'e'll come to when 'e's reet!'

Annie, her face ablaze with temper now, stepped forward to stand between her mother and this awful woman. 'He won't be coming out,' she said, fighting to control her voice. 'He's allergic to all the antibiotics and he'll die soon of tuberculosis. I think they're surprised he's lasted this long. He's incurable.'

Dolly sagged against the pram. 'Dyin'?'

'Yes,' replied Annie.

'And you never even go ter see 'im?'

Nancy stepped forward to her daughter's side. 'We would as soon visit Old Nick himself.'

'Well . . . well . . . you right pair of bitches, you. 'E's better off without you!'

Annie grabbed Nancy's arm and dragged her away, marching her off, picking up speed until they were both running.

'Don't look back, Mother.'

'Don't worry, I won't.'

They reached the bus station and sat on a bench to wait for the 45, Nancy panting slightly after her run.

'Why didn't you tell me, Mam?' asked Annie after a while. 'Why?'

'There was no need.'

Annie sifted through her thoughts for a few minutes. 'Yes, I suppose you're right.' She noticed that Nancy looked downcast to the point of heartbreak, so placing her arm about her mother's shoulders, she whispered, 'Hey, you know what annoys me most about you?'

'No – what?'

'You're always flaming well right!'

Nancy shook her head slowly. 'Nay, lass. I'm right when I'm not wrong, same as everybody else.'

Annie's temper still simmered beneath an outwardly cool facade. She stepped on to the bus, her mouth set in a grim determined line. No wonder Maggie Nelson was a whore – she'd followed in her mother's footsteps, hadn't she? And now Annie and Nancy were both suffering, each affected by one generation of that dreadful family. Martin, the damned fool – she would sort him out tonight. It was time now, time to wipe the whole Nelson family out of the picture forever.

Martin rolled away from Maggie, sick to the core for the umpteenth time. And now she was coming on with all the love stuff and about her mate getting wed next year – oh God. That was the trouble with sex, he mused as he fastened his trousers. It was a bit like beer – the more you got, the more you wanted. But he didn't want her, oh no, not a lifetime with Maggie flaming Nelson. He watched her as she pulled down her skirt and fastened the grass-stained blouse. Sometimes, he hated her. And because he hated her, he was beginning to dislike himself as well.

'Lovely evening, isn't it?' The voice came from the top of the mound behind which he and Maggie were supposedly hidden. He didn't need to look. It was her alright. She wore a blue and white striped dress and her hair was coiled into a perfect chignon, making her long neck appear more slender than ever. She stepped down the slope as if she were entering a drawing room or attending a gathering of debutantes.

Maggie hastily finished fastening her buttons while Annie knelt on the grass beside her.

'Tell me, Maggie,' she went on, her tone conversational, 'how long have you been a prostitute?'

'You what?' A look of amazement came over Maggie's painted features.

'Is this something that's passed on from one generation to another – like a legacy? Because your mother's quite generous with her favours, isn't she? Though why anybody should want to touch such an ugly heap of blubber . . .'

'Shut yer gob, Annie Byrne! Just 'cos I've took your lad . . .'

'You've taken nothing of mine, Maggie Nelson. If I really wanted something, there's no way a cheap little slut like you would get her hands on it.' She turned to Martin now. 'How much does she charge, by the way?'

'What do yer mean, 'ow much do I charge? An' mind what yer say about me Mam.'

Annie continued to stare at Martin until he flinched under the coldness of her hard gaze, then she slowly moved her head towards Maggie. 'Your mother had a bastard recently – a boy, I believe. Some man must have a strong stomach. I can smell your mother from forty paces.'

'You bloody cow . . . !' Clawing hands reached out for Annie's hair, but they never attained their target. With a blow that might have felled a sapling, Annie sent Maggie reeling back. The girl lay still and silent, terror plain on her face as Annie rose gracefully to her feet.

Now she turned the full force of her anger on Martin. 'Has it never occurred to you that you might catch something from her? Stay away from me, Cullen. I never want to set eyes on your silly face again. I never did like red hair anyway – not on a man. It's alright for little boys, but you can never be a man, not with a carrot head.'

Then she turned on her heel and walked away.

Martin, heedless of Maggie's pitiful cries, ran after Annie. When he caught up with her on the cinder path, she turned and spat into his face. 'Scum!' she shouted as he wiped his cheek. 'I love you, Annie,' she mimicked.

'Don't leave me, Annie. There'll never be another girl, Annie. And there you are, copulating with a dirty piece of rubbish . . .'

'But you wouldn't let me near you!'

'That's because I don't want you near me! I don't want anybody near me! And even if I told you the reason why, you'd never understand because you're thick. Did you know she was advertising your business with her all over Bolton? Perhaps she's hoping you'll give her a reference.'

'Annie . . . Annie . . .'

'Don't "Annie" me! I'm finished with you. Go away, stay away, don't come back. I'm using simple words for your bloody simple mind, then I can be sure you understand.'

He stood uselessly and watched her walk away. He hadn't seen this side of her before, didn't realise till now what a temper she had. What could he do anyway? She'd told him plain enough to bugger off – aye, that's what he'd do! To hell with her and all of them.

Martin left home that night, taking with him just his clothes, a battered typewriter and one small framed photograph. In his poky back room in Mayfield Street, he placed the picture in the bottom of his suitcase, then pushed the case under the bed. He could manage without her. He had to.

Susan Birchall was a suitable friend for Simon. Her parents were Methodist, but that was a small fly in the ointment and Edna's church wasn't very high, merely moderate in her estimation. Not that Simon was old enough to be considering a permanent liaison, but it was nice to see how carefully he was choosing these days. Those awful people still came on Wednesdays, but, she thought magnanimously, that might be looked upon as charity work. And at least Martin Cullen and Anne Byrne were conspicuously absent of late. Yes, one had to be thankful for small mercies.

Susan was a sweet child, not as mature in appearance as that awful crowd and she didn't have the 'knowing' look that was always so obvious in Anne Byrne's expression. Of course, the Birchalls were quite eminent, the father a solicitor, the mother related to the Partingtons who owned land near Preston. Susan possessed all the ladylike virtues, was a competent pianist, an excellent horsewoman – and her embroidery had to be seen to be believed.

Edna smiled as she arranged some yellow flowers in a rosebowl. It was a lovely day. The muted strains of Vivaldi's *Four Seasons* floated gently down the stairway, so much more appropriate than the raucous sounds that often came from what Edna had decided to call the recreation room. She could picture the scene – Simon at a table with his books, Susan sitting demurely in a chair working on that lovely tapestry she always seemed to bring.

Edna picked up her basket and walked to the foot of the stairs. 'I'm just popping out to the shops – shan't be long,' she called.

'Bye, Mrs Pritchard,' Susan's high girlish voice called in reply. Such a polite girl, such a lady.

The lady in question thrust her small hand down the front of Simon's trousers, eager fingers manipulating his clothing until they found their goal. As her own undergarment had been reposing for some time in her capacious sewing bag, there was no such obstruction for Simon's hand as she guided it along her thighs. After a few moments of frantic activity, she pulled away and swiftly removed the rest of her clothes, beckoning him to follow as she went out on to the landing.

In his mother's room, she re-positioned the long mirror so that it would reflect the bed, then she threw herself on to the pink flowered counterpane, small hard breasts thrust upwards like twin cones, one hand working between her thighs while the other reached out for him.

For a split second, he wanted to run, but he knew he'd never face the mocking laughter that would result from such action, so he joined her on the bed. With practised ease, she peeled the clothing from his body, stimulated him to adequate hardness, then pulled him fiercely into her flesh, her head turned all the time towards the mirror so that she could watch their movements. She reached her peak as soon as he entered, the thin body rising from the bed to meet his loins. He followed quickly, shuddering as he spent himself without pleasure inside her hot moistness.

There was no tenderness, no word of affection. She pushed him away, leapt from the bed and began to restore the room to its original order. Methodically, she straightened the bedcover, shook the pillows, moved the mirror while Simon stood, feeling foolish and very naked, at the side of the bed.

'Not much of a gentleman, are you?' she asked coldly.

'Sorry?'

'You didn't pull out. A gentleman always pulls out.' She laughed at the expression on his face. 'Don't worry, dear boy. My fault too – should have brought a towel for Mummy's counterpane. Anyway, it's fine – wrong time of the month for it to be a problem. But you should pull out. Everybody does.'

Miserable and shamefaced, Simon dressed then returned to the recreation room. She followed, pulling on her clothes quickly, attacking her tapestry with renewed vigour as soon as she sat down.

Simon stared at her. This had been his first encounter with sex and he had hated it. Seconds ticked by as a light began to dawn in his clouded mind. He didn't like women, not in that way. He looked back over the last few months, knowing now why he had never been jealous of Martin and Anne. He was different. Yes, he knew what he was and the knowledge made him shiver.

When Edna put her head round the door ten minutes later, he was at the table with his books. Susan looked up from her needlework. 'Shall I help you put the shopping away, Mrs Pritchard?'

Yes, she was a lovely girl, thought Edna as she went downstairs to make tea. Such a nice little friend for Simon.

Chapter Ten: Dénouements

Annie opened the front door and steadied herself against the jamb as she stared into her own face. No, not quite, she reassured herself. The eyes were blue and she had to look down an inch or two to meet them. But in spite of the shorter hair and some slight differences in colouring, she might almost have been staring at her own twin sister. The girl looked as if she had been weeping too, just as Annie herself had wept these last few days.

'Is . . . is this Nancy's house?' The voice wavered.

'Yes. But she's out, I'm afraid. Can I help? I'm Annie.'

'Will she be long?'

'Only a few minutes, I think. Come in, please.'

They walked through to the living room where the girl perched anxiously on the edge of the fireside rocker. She stared at Annie, her hands picking nervously at a small clutch-bag in her lap. 'We . . . we look alike, don't we? I noticed that as soon as you opened the door. I'm a bit older than you, mind. But I felt funny then, when I first saw you.'

'So did I.' Annie smiled in what she hoped was a comforting way. 'We're all supposed to have a double, aren't we? I read that once in a newspaper . . .' She forced herself to sit down, determined not to prattle on.

'I'm a friend of your mother's. We sometimes had a drink in Barton's tea-rooms when she was part-time. Only I've not seen her for a while, not since she went back to five full days. We write – she's foreman now, isn't she?'

'Yes.' Annie glanced at the clock. 'She's often a bit late with all the paperwork. And she does take the job seriously – if one of her girls is ill, she goes and visits – does what she can for the family.'

'Yes, she would. She's a great lady, your mother . . .' The girl turned towards the range and rubbed a hand across her eyes.

'I know that.' Annie cleared her throat. 'It's alright, you can cry if you want to.' She felt the need to draw this visitor out, to find out who she was and why she was here. 'I've been doing a lot of that myself lately.'

The girl blew her nose into a small white handkerchief then turned to look at Annie. 'Have you, love? Why, what's the matter?'

Yes, she could confide, she sensed that. And such confidences would help this obviously sad young woman to open up. 'Oh, I've let myself down in a big way, lost my temper, lost my boyfriend, clouted a big horrible girl across the mouth. I've got a problem with my temper, you see. I try to carry on like a young lady, the way the nuns have trained me – but you know what they say about silk purses and sows' ears? Well, that's me. You see – what's your name, by the way . . .?'

'Mary.'

'You see, Mary, I told him to get lost and he did. My boyfriend – he just disappeared. Of course, my mother treats it all as a big joke, probably to cheer me up. She keeps telling me to get the Irwell dragged, then not to bother because if he's chucked himself in there, she says, he'll likely have melted with all the rubbish they pour in. I mean, it wasn't serious, not really, between Martin and me. But he was my best friend and I got rid of him just because he was . . . well, seeing another girl. Have you ever done anything as daft as that?'

'Many a time, Annie. There's plenty more fish in the sea, especially at your age.' She smiled wanly. 'Don't worry, he won't be in the river.'

'No, he isn't. He's at the *Evening News* making a name for himself. But I should never have spat in his face. There I was, all done up in my best dress trying to look like Princess Margaret and what did I go and do? I've never been so ashamed of myself! So don't bother about crying in front of me. I'll probably join in and keep you company.'

They heard the front door opening. 'Annie? Get that kettle on, I'm as dry as a new sock. That Elsie Tunstall took one of her turns in the lav again – she'll have to go in hospital and get it all taken away, she will. Are you there, Annie?'

Annie smiled at Mary. 'Here comes trouble now,' she whispered.

Nancy burst into the room. 'Weeks ago I told her – fibroids, I said . . . oh, hello Mary. Well.' She glanced quickly at Annie. 'What a nice surprise. You've met my daughter, then?'

'Hello, Nancy. Perhaps I shouldn't have come . . .'

'Don't talk so daft. Get that coat off this minute, Mary Greenhalgh. I've told you before and I'll tell you again – my door's always open.'

Annie jumped to her feet. 'Mary? That Mary? The one who . . .'

'That's right, lass. Now do your job and get that kettle on. I've told you – my throat feels like it's hand-knitted.'

Annie fled to the kitchen and filled the new electric kettle. Moving automatically, she redistributed the ham salad so that it filled three plates, then, while she cut and buttered bread, she listened to the heartbreak as it poured from the next room.

'I couldn't, Nancy. I couldn't. Every time he came home I made excuses. So he's gone and married a German girl . . . I'll never be able to . . . never get married . . . have babies . . . all I wanted, Nancy.'

Nancy's voice cracked as she answered, 'You will. Give it time, Mary. Rome wasn't built in a day, love . . .'

'Terrified of men, I am. Even though I've left the sanatorium and gone over to geriatrics, I go to jelly if some old chap looks at me sideways . . .'

'It'll pass, it will . . .'

'No! Look at me! Look at my hands – I can hardly change a dressing now, let alone handle a hypodermic. I can't talk to anybody about it. Nobody knows except you and the people at the sanatorium – most of my friends have left now, got married and moved away. It's as if I've done wrong, like I'm a criminal or something . . .' Her voice tailed away as she saw Annie in the doorway.

'The only crime you committed, Mary, was that you were born looking very like me.' Annie held back her own tears determinedly. 'It was me he was after, not you.'

'That's right,' whispered Nancy. 'I've know all along, ever since I first set eyes on you, Mary. But it was Annie's secret, hers to tell or keep. He'd been setting about my Annie for years, only I didn't know till the night after he hurt you.'

Mary stared across the room at this taller, younger version of herself. In that moment, a link was forged that would last a lifetime, a friendship born of pain, nurtured by total empathy, bonded through the tiny woman who joined them together now by welcoming them both into her open arms.

'Mary will be living here from now on,' Nancy announced. 'We're going to adopt her, Annie.'

Annie nodded, incapable of speech.

Using her native wisdom, Nancy left the girls together while she finished preparing the meal, wiping yet another tear from her face when she noticed how Annie had divided the food. Aye, this was a blessing alright. Now, Annie and Mary could talk, talk like she'd done with their Jessie. They'd say things to one another that they could never speak about to somebody Nancy's age. It would hurt, aye it would that, she thought as she scalded the teapot. But once they'd got through the hurting, then the mending could begin.

'I'm not condoning anything, Edna! I'm merely encouraging Simon to bring his friends home – would you rather he met them in the street?'

'I'd rather he didn't meet them at all. Especially that one. Her previous . . . arrangement seems to have been dissolved, so now she turns to Simon. And you are allowing them to use a room – an upstairs room – for goodness knows what purpose!'

David flung his newspaper across the room. 'What do you think they're up to in that room? Would you care to elaborate on your statement – or rather your accusation – so that I might assess it, even comment on it?'

Edna stiffened. 'Don't act stupid with me! You know exactly what I mean. There's no need for me to produce maps and diagrams.'

David stared up at the ceiling, shoulders raised in a gesture of frustration as he sighed deeply. He really didn't understand this woman, hardly knew who she was. She certainly bore little resemblance to the person he'd married, the girl whose freshness and naivety had so enchanted him. Those qualities and not a little coercion from both families had led to this . . . misalliance.

He turned on her now, his body rigid and poker-straight on the edge of the sofa. 'Thank God for this generation!' He waved a hand towards the upper floor. 'Independent, strong-minded, adaptable. I can't see them being forced by family into careers or marriages just because such plans are deemed by their elders to be suitable.'

She looked down at her flawlessly painted nails. 'I suppose this implies regret that you married me?'

He took a deep breath. 'Yes, I'm sorry that we married.'

'Nobody forced you!' There was a small catch in her voice and a raising in its pitch as she lifted a lace-trimmed handkerchief to her lips.

'There were pressures.'

'I wasn't aware of them.'

'Really? Then allow me to produce the maps and diagrams. Firstly, your parents set out their stall with you as centrepiece. Secondly, my family came along and bought their pitch, hook, line and sinker. Excuse any mixed metaphor, but this is hardly the time for perfect grammar. Thirdly, you were sent out to ensnare me. Fourthly, I got caught – the bait you used was your virginity.'

Edna's jaw dropped. 'Would you rather I hadn't been a . . . a virgin?'

'I'd have been more pleased had you not used your intact status as a bargaining point.'

He rose now and stood before the fireplace, legs apart, hands clasped behind his back. 'Some women are honest whores. They go on to the streets, use their bodies to make a living. Other . . . prostitutes, for want of a better word, are more astute. They make a man pay for his whole life and with his whole life.' He gazed around the room with the air of a man addressing a large audience.

'These two categories of female have one thing in common – they don't enjoy the sexual act. Streetwomen regard it as a mere commodity, something to be bartered for the price of a meal. Those in the latter and more respectable division tolerate it as part of a bargain, a thing they must endure, a price to pay for a roof, for a life of security and ease.'

She stood, her eyes ablaze with fury. 'And I am one of the latter group, I suppose?'

He nodded, his face expressionless.

'How can you say that to me? You know I've never been strong since Simon was born. If I've seemed . . . distant, it was because I was terrified of pregnancy!'

'You need not have become pregnant again. I could have guaranteed that you wouldn't. As it happened, I was not sufficiently interested in regaining your favours, therefore it mattered not at all that you shut yourself away from me.'

She took a step towards him. 'You moved out of the bedroom!'

'That's true. I saw no point in staying, you see.'

Edna's mouth quivered for a second, then her teeth were suddenly bared into a snarl as she spoke. 'So you've satisfied your lust elsewhere with the other kind of whore?'

'Come come, my dear – don't be crude. Let's just say I've been discreet. After all, my baser instincts – as you no doubt call them – have needed to be appeased occasionally.'

'Oh, my God!' She flung herself into a chair, fingers

clawing at the handkerchief. 'What have you done? Suppose my friends were to find out – these things are always found out in the end – how shall I hold up my head?'

'That reaction is exactly what one might expect of you, Edna. You cling to your good name as fiercely as you once shielded your precious virginity! You are a complete and utter sham! Did you imagine that I'd gone without the comfort of a woman for more than fifteen years? How gullible are you, for heaven's sake? But you won't discover who she is, nor will your friends. That is, if you have any friends. I imagined that they were mere callers or bridge partners.'

She wept silently into her hands, her whole body shaking with shock and humiliation.

'And another thing,' David continued. 'I want Simon to choose his own friends, his own career and eventually, his own wife. History must not repeat itself. If I were you, I'd be more selective about the people you encourage to call here.'

She dried her eyes. 'What do you mean?'

'Susan Birchall.'

'Susan? She's a friend of Simon's.'

'Yes. A suitable friend in your book, I'd imagine. Well, her father is trying to marry her off. In fact, she's being put up for auction by all accounts.'

'She's only a child . . .'

'Ah yes, but a child with a problem. The first was the postman, or was it the gardener? No matter. She was discovered with one or the other in what is usually called a compromising situation. There was no question of prosecution – family name and so on – I'm sure you'll understand that aspect, Edna.' He paused to light a cigar.

'I'm certain none of that is true,' wailed Edna. 'It's gossip – idle gossip. Susan is a lovely girl.' She waited, teeth gritted, while he threw a spent match into the grate.

David looked her squarely in the face. 'More recently, she was found in the summerhouse with four boys. She was entertaining them in a variety of imaginative ways. I understand that the parents are virtually keeping her under lock and key until they can marry her off. So, if she's being allowed to see Simon, he's obviously on the shortlist. And we don't want a nymphomaniac in the family. What would friends and neighbours say then?'

Her mouth opened and closed, trying to frame words that her dry throat could not produce.

'What's the matter, Edna? You look like a goldfish out of water. Surprised, are you? Surprised that a girl of good breeding can be so disposed? I'll surprise you even further. That girl upstairs, in spite of her "unsuitable background", will not be the one to introduce Simon to the pleasures of the flesh. She has a higher moral standard than you could ever imagine or achieve, because she won't barter her virginity or go under the hammer to the highest bidder for the sake of a wedding ring. And I'd be delighted if she married my son in a few years. Because Anne Byrne will arrive clean – not necessarily virgin, but definitely clean.'

Her eyes, round with shock as she took in the news about Susan, narrowed now at the mention of Anne's name. She rose from the chair and stood stiffly beside it, her hand straying to the edge of a table as if needing the encouragement of its inanimate stability. 'I have several things to say to you.' Her voice shook as she spoke. 'I don't believe all that about Susan. Furthermore, I will not have my standards – moral or otherwise – compared to those of that creature upstairs. And I demand to know the name of your . . . paramour.'

'Why? Would you like a divorce? I'll gladly get you some evidence. Certain women are happy to earn the odd hundred for the use of their names – and a little photography.'

'I will not have a divorce! But I want her name!'

'Really? Will you break all her windows? No, that's too honest a response for you. You might send an anonymous letter – yes, I can imagine you pouring venom on to paper and not having the courage to sign.'

She suddenly felt afraid and powerless. He had shattered her long-term hopes for Simon and Susan. Whether or not he spoke the truth, she could not risk having the girl in the house again. And he was positively nurturing Simon's association with Nancy Higson's daughter. Now, finally, he was admitting that he had another woman, someone he intended to protect.

With unsteady hands she poured a small sherry, swallowing her pride as she gulped down the liquid. She had to ask. 'Do you . . . love this woman?'

The grandfather clock at the far end of the room sang the hour in gentle Westminster chime.

'No,' he said at last. 'I have never loved a woman, never had that rare privilege. I like and respect her, but love – according to what I've read and heard – has always eluded me completely. She is not in love with me either; we simply comfort one another. Now, I've finally found the courage to be as honest with my wife as I've always been with her.'

'Do I know her?'

His eyes travelled from the top of her head right down to her feet. 'You don't know anybody. You measure people, judge them, use them . . .'

'Very well then,' she interrupted. 'Is she among my circle?'

He shook his head slowly then stalked out of the room, slamming the door as he left. In the hallway, he leaned on the banister, his heart racing. She was going insane and she would take him with her. But there had been no need for him to lash out so viciously. It was like kicking a dumb defenceless animal with neither wit nor wisdom to protect itself. Why, after all these years, had he turned on her like that?

He stared up at the chandelier, his eyes narrowing against a thousand shards of reflected light as if he might find a solution in these insubstantial splinters. Dear God, if she ever found out that his source of comfort was part of her bridge four, then her world would collapse. Yet he knew that Edna had not the courage to pursue the issue, that she would nurse it within herself where it would fester like a gangrenous sore.

His friendship with Sarah Pennington had always been easy and necessary to both of them. She, a widow with a young family and a vast inheritance to protect from fortune-hunters, he, with a dead marriage and a son who would surely have suffered had his father found a permanent new mate. For a brief moment, David saw Clive's young face, watched the train pulling out of Trinity Street, heard his dead friend calling 'Look after Sarah.' Clive had become one of the few to whom so much would be forever owed, shot down over Germany. Of course, Edna had soon tired of caring for Sarah and her children. He smiled to himself, knowing somehow that Clive would have approved of his way of 'looking after Sarah'.

But David would never forgive himself for what he had done to Edna this evening. He had behaved stupidly, irrationally, like a spoiled brat. But whichever quality might be required to make him return to the drawing room and apologise, explain, negotiate – whatever he needed to find within himself to put things on a better footing, smooth things over, make some kind of order – eluded him completely. Life, from now on, promised to be completely unbearable.

Meanwhile, Edna sat in a stupor, her second sherry already consumed, a third in her glass. She would, she concluded, do nothing – simply because she could do nothing. She didn't want divorce, abhorred the concept of scandal, was not equipped for 'scenes' of any kind. The name of the woman was not important. Things could continue the same on the surface – nothing would change. And she was far too busy for such trivia. Tomorrow was bridge day, she had baking to do, standards to uphold. She drained the glass. David could find his own way to the devil.

Chapter Eleven: Dolly's Lot

The house was situated on a new council estate in Breightmet, on the hem of Bolton's ever-spreading outskirts. It was one of many such concrete and pebble-dashed buildings that were springing up to replace decaying or bombed-out row houses and to accommodate the post-war explosion of population.

Dolly Nelson's was an end house, edged on two sides by open fields, the front facing the blind end of another corner house across the way. Dolly hated it. For a kick-off, it was back to front. Whoever heard of a back kitchen at the front of a house? If she stood at the sink all day and looked out of the small window, she could stare, if she chose, at a blank wall or if she craned her neck to the point of pain, she could just about see up the avenue. There was nothing worth looking at, few buses, no cars, no late-night revellers rolling home from the pub. The flaming bus came only twice an hour and what with the pram to push, she'd managed the six-mile round trip to town just once since she moved in. Aye, and she'd not forget that in a hurry, meeting Nancy Higson and her stuck-up kid.

The 'front room' was at the back of the house, running its full width with two large windows looking out on to a garden. Beyond the garden were fallow fields and the only passers-by she'd seen so far were a stray cow and a couple of dogs from the estate. She was bored out of her mind.

Dolly stubbed out her Woodbine in a cracked saucer and lifted Johnny from his pram. He never cried, didn't Johnny, not like the other four little buggers who'd woken up screaming every day and gone to bed in the same state. Their Johnny was an angel, the only thing left to brighten her days since Maggie went off. 'If she thinks t' middle o' Bolton's paved wi' gold, she's another think comin', she 'as,' announced Dolly to the placid child while she fiddled with her buttons. Obediently, the baby accepted the breast, his unwavering deep-set stare fixed on Dolly's face.

He was a bonny lad and no mistake, with peach-tinted cheeks and eyes of a blue so dark that it bordered on violet. Like Eddie's, thought Dolly to herself. Yes, he was very like his dad, quiet and still most of the time. She wondered if Eddie had got the letter she'd finally scraped together on a bit of paper out of their Stevie's homework book. Aye, she'd tried to let him know about his lad. She hoped they'd sent it on from the sanatorium to Prestwich Mental Hospital. Funny, that. She'd never heard of anybody being treated for TB in a loony bin before. Still, that sanatorium had likely driven him daft. Aye, and the bloody Higson woman was having a right good time now by all accounts, going dancing, buying new frocks, taking in lodgers now Eddie was out of the road. Alright for some, it was, made up to foreman, going about with nice-looking fellers, putting shows on with the formation team.

Dolly was in trouble. Any money from the sale of her old house had disappeared now, squandered on cheap sticks of splay-legged furniture, a television set, some gilt-framed convex mirrors, contemporary paper on her fireplace wall and a load of that nice Skaters' Trails carpet that was all the rage. 'Course, things for the baby had cost a bob or two and all.

She shifted the child to the other milk-swollen breast. Aye, there was plenty for him, but what about herself and the other three? Eric's money still came regular, but it was hardly enough to pay for rent and electric and she couldn't do without her fags and her stout, what with her bad nerves and needing fluids to keep the milk coming in. She looked at the dozing infant. Them new doctors down the clinic were on about his development, talked as if there were summat up with him. And she was sick of folk looking in the pram and saying about his unusual eyes. He was beautiful, their Johnny. Nowt up with him – they could all say what they liked.

Still, it wasn't right, none of it. Except for Eddie Higson, she'd still be up Long Moor with her job at the pictures and folk to talk to. Aye and their Maggie would likely have stopped at home instead of legging it hell for leather. She'd been a good help, had Maggie, what with her wages and giving a hand in the house. The oldest of the three boys was but thirteen and lads weren't the same, you couldn't expect them to wash pots and sweep carpets, could you? And the way Maggie had left too, never a note nor nothing, just a postcard a few days after with a photo of the Town Hall clock and a line to say she was alright.

Dolly placed the sleeping child over her shoulder and reached to flick through the pages of an old *Reveille*, the wrapping from last night's chips. Aye, that was a laugh and all, the chip shop ten minutes away and having to warm them up when you got them home stone cold and stuck to the paper.

A car drew up outside, but Dolly remained where she was. It would be nowt to do with her. Then the front door opened and a familiar voice cried, 'Dolly? Dolly Nelson? You in there?'

Dolly hastily dropped the paper, fastened her frock and was just placing Johnny in his pram when Bertha Cullen walked in.

'Tha'd best sit thisen down, Dolly. It's not good news I've fetched.'

'Why? What's up?'

'Come on, lass. We'll sit at t' table.'

The two women lowered their not insubstantial bodies on to frail metal-framed dining chairs.

Bertha leaned forward. As was the custom with most of her generation when speaking of something unsavoury, she mouthed half her words as if the whole world might be listening. 'I've knowed all along as it were summat ter do wi' your Maggie, our Martin leavin' 'ome an' splittin' up wi' Annie. Common knowledge it is now, as your Maggie were givin' our Martin a good time – if yer get me drift?'

'So?' Dolly bristled.

'Well, it weren't just our Martin. An' it weren't just fer free, like.'

'Stop messin' about in t' bushes, Bertha Cullen. Get it spit out!'

'It's not me what's been messin' about in t' bushes, Dolly. It's tha daughter what's been up ter no good.'

'Oh aye? An' what bloody business is it o' yourn?'

'I don't like seein' a young girl puttin' 'erself about. 'Er 'll end up in t' courts afore she's much older.'

Dolly leaned back on to the chair's yellow plastic cover. 'Like I said, spit it out afore I lose me patience!'

'T' doctor's fetched us – Dr Pritchard. Yer see, Dolly, I caught sight o' your Maggie a few times toutin' fer business outside o' t' wine lodge. I knew I'd never manage 'er on me own, so I got t' doctor fer t' come down in 'is car ter pick 'er up. I 'ad fer t' drag Maggie by the 'air into t' car. It were all done fer t' best, Dolly.'

'Where the bloody 'ell is she?'

'Outside wi' Dr Pritchard.'

'Then tha'd best give over wastin' time an' fetch 'em in!'

Dolly waited in the hallway, arms folded as far as they would reach across her huge chest. As soon as Maggie appeared between the two escorts, Dolly pulled her inside the house. 'Get up them dancers this minute, Maggie Nelson! I'll deal with thee after.'

As soon as the girl had reached the landing, the three adults made their way into the kitchen.

'I'm sorry about all this, Mrs Nelson,' began the doctor. 'Margaret has taken a room in Sherwood Avenue where I have several elderly patients. Of course, I visit regularly and I knew that your daughter was having . . . men calling on her quite frequently. But Mrs Cullen brought things to a head this lunchtime and . . . well, here we are.'

Dolly's eyes narrowed. 'Is she still at Woolworth's?'

'Aye,' replied Bertha.

'Then 'ow come she's toutin' in 'er dinner hour? 'Ow would she get up Sherwood an' back in time fer work?'

David Pritchard glanced at Bertha. 'She uses her friend's flat near the Lido on Bradshawgate, we believe. Between the pair of them, they've quite a business going. I'm sorry to be the carrier of such bad tidings, Mrs Nelson, but we thought it best to bring your daughter home straight away.'

'Aye. Well you did right. 'Appen you'd best be off now and tend your own business. I suppose yer'll 'ave plenty fer t' talk about now, Bertha Cullen? Yer'll be able ter tell yer mate Nancy 'Igson all about it, eh?'

Bertha breathed in sharply. 'You ungrateful bugger, you! As if I would! There's not a word'll cross my lips. Me and Nancy 'as better things fer t' talk over.'

'Oh aye? Like 'er leavin' a chap ter die on 'is own? Like 'er goin' about dancin' an' takin' boarders in?'

'Now, ladies . . .' began David.

'This is no bloody lady, Doctor,' said Bertha. She turned and stamped out of the room.

'I'll . . . I'll leave you to it then, Mrs Nelson.'

'I reckon you'd better.'

She waited until the car pulled away, then shouted from the foot of the stairs, 'Get thisen down 'ere!'

A shamefaced Maggie entered the kitchen where her mother was arranging mugs and plates on the table.

'We'll 'ave a cup, lass. Sit down, I'll not bite thee.'

'I'm sorry, Mam . . .'

'Nay, never bother. We'll soon be to rights, tha'll see.'

They sat at the table drinking tea, Dolly studying her daughter closely.

'So. Yer on t' game, are you?'

'It was fer the rent, Mam. I couldn't manage on me wages. I won't do it no more – honest.'

''Ow much was you gettin'?'

'About a quid a go.' Maggie, her cheeks blazing, stared down at the stained tablecloth.

''Ow many a week?'

'Ten, maybe more.'

'That's a fair amount o' brass. 'Ave yer spent it all?'

'I've a bit in t' Post Office.'

Dolly stood up and walked to the window. It was dead quiet round here, so quiet that she reckoned the house could burn down without anybody noticing. 'Yer've got to stop off the streets, Maggie.'

'I will, Mam. I will. But I can't live 'ere – there's nowt goes on, nowhere ter go . . .'

'Then we mun make a life, eh?' She turned to look at her daughter. 'Listen ter me, our Maggie. I'm stoney – never been so broke in me life. We could . . . well . . . set up shop, like.'

''Ow do yer mean, Mam?'

Dolly sidled towards the table. 'Get yer gentleman callers ter come up 'ere! I can keep t' lads upstairs, yer can use t' best room – that couch makes to a bed, tha knows. An' if there's any bother, yer'll 'ave yer old Mam ter look after yer.' She smoothed her tangled hair. 'Fact is, one or two of 'em might fancy a bit of older stuff – I could maybe 'elp out.'

Maggie's jaw dropped. 'We'd . . . we'd be runnin' a brothel, Mam!'

'Nay, lass. We'd be stayin' alive best way we can. It's money fer old rope, isn't it? I mean, we could buy a few bottles in, sell drinks on t' side . . . it'd be like 'avin' a party a couple o' nights a week. Come 'ome, Maggie. I'll look after thee. Yer never know what yer might pick up on yer own – yer could get a flamin' murderer or summat. What do yer say?'

Maggie stared at her mother for several seconds. 'Alright, Mam. We'll give it a try. But . . .'

'But what?'

'Well, it seems right funny, does this. I thought yer'd kill me an' 'ere we are talkin' about . . . well . . .'

'About settin' up in business is what, Maggie. Look at it this road – we're 'elpin' out, aren't we? Some women doesn't like doin' it. So their poor 'usbands 'as ter go wi'out. If we give t' men what they want, then they'll likely give over mitherin' their wives.'

'Eeh Mam, you're a bugger!'

'Aye well, 'appen yer've took after me, eh?'

The baby whimpered and Maggie leaned over to look into the pram. 'Is 'e alright, Mam?'

''Course 'e is. 'E's not complainin', is 'e?'

'No . . . no. I just wondered . . .'

But Dolly's mind was too full of plans to give heed to Maggie's wonderings. Yes, they had the answer now, a bit of life with money thrown in as a bonus. She took the last Woodbine from the packet and grinned. There'd be plenty more, plenty to go round for everybody.

Chapter Twelve: Departures

Eddie Higson, after surviving well beyond the expected span, died in June 1958, just as Annie was completing her advanced level examinations. Nancy, on receiving the news from local police, decided not to tell her daughter yet, then, after making arrangements with the undertaker, she sent word to his brothers. The older man, Bob Higson, arrived at the house and demanded to know why Nancy had never visited Eddie and why she now refused to attend his funeral. So she told him straight, with Mary at her side, both women hoping that any trouble would be over before Annie got back from school.

'He was a rapist and a child-molester,' said Nancy, not prepared at this stage to pull any punches.

'I don't believe it!' came the reply. 'That was all rubbish about him and that kiddy down Emmanuel Street. They proved nowt at all! The child was lying!'

Nancy folded her arms and stood squarely before him. 'That girl and her mother were both killed, weren't they? After your Eddie had gone off to the war. I remember old Florrie Hyatt trying to tell me about that, only I wouldn't listen – just like you, I didn't want to hear bad of him. Well hear me now, Bob Higson. That brother of yours interfered with my daughter, likely affected her for life, he did.' Without glancing at Mary, she went on, 'Then he raped a nurse up at the TB place. Oh yes, he was very generous with his attentions, was your brother. Even got one of his customers pregnant. But above all, he was a . . . a . . . what's that fancy word, Mary?'

'A paedophile.' Mary's voice was quiet.

'That's right. He liked little girls. And you expect me to

go to his funeral?' Nancy's tone was bitter and sarcastic.

Bob shuffled about uncomfortably, his face reddened by embarrassment. 'To be honest with you, Nancy, we did know as how he was a queer fish – kept to himself most of the time, then given to odd fits of temper. But we never thought he was one for children and suchlike. Oh heck.' He sank into a chair and sat twisting his cap between his fingers. 'In spite of that business in '39, we never cottoned on, never knew he was that bad.'

'Well he was,' snapped Nancy.

'Anyroad, he suffered for it. Like an animal in a cage, he was . . .'

'We don't need to know all that,' said Nancy firmly. 'I'm convinced he got himself in there so he wouldn't be tried. Then he likely went mad at the finish knowing he'd never get out. You just see him buried decent with his father. I've got my own plot – my bones could never rest easy with his.'

Bob rose from the chair. 'Nancy, lass. I feel awful coming up here on the bounce like, especially after what you've just said. Let us chip in for the burial, give you some money back for Annie . . .'

Nancy held up her hand. 'I'll say this for you – you're a decent sort, Bob Higson and I appreciate your offer. But no, I owe the man one debt and that's to get him safely buried, thanks all the same.'

He left bowed and round-shouldered, Nancy closing the door securely in his wake.

'Right. That's that then, Mary. Pour us both a drop of brandy. Thank God I took a couple of days off – you'd have had his brother to deal with and you on the flaming night shift.' She sipped her drink. 'Daft, isn't it? I get three days' compassionate leave because I've lost a husband I didn't want anyway. Never mind. Cheers – here's to us and our Annie.'

As they raised their glasses, the subject of the toast burst in like a whirlwind, books and papers scattering about her person as she entered the room. 'I've finished!' she cried, tossing a handful of notes into the air.

'Then you shall have a brandy too,' said Nancy. 'After all, you're eighteen – time you got introduced to the booze.'

'Oh give over, Mam,' laughed Annie, lapsing into her old mode of speech. 'I've been pinching the odd drop since I was about fourteen – it would be no novelty.'

Nancy clipped her playfully round the ear. 'Sit down, Annie.'

'What is it, Mother?' Annie placed herself in the fireside rocker.

'He's dead.'

Mary came and squatted on her haunches in front of Annie, this new grown-up little sister whom she had learned to love. 'Yes, he's gone, Annie.'

'Eddie Higson?'

'Yes.' Mary gripped Annie's hands. 'He died two days ago, only we never told you on account of that big exam today.'

Annie's eyes filled with tears.

'Nay,' said Nancy. 'You're not weeping for him, are you?'

'No.' She sniffed hard. 'I'm crying for what he was and what he did. We don't know – perhaps he couldn't help it. He might have been born bad and now he's died all on his own.'

'Honest! She'd see good in Jack the Ripper, she would!'

'Please, Nancy,' whispered Mary. 'He was looked after, Annie. Don't go upsetting everybody, especially yourself. And I'm not waltzing off on nights leaving you in tears.'

Nancy and Mary went to the table and carried on setting places for the meal. Annie sat very still, staring into the grate as she spoke in a voice that was barely audible. 'I read that any man's death is diminishing to the rest of us. It's forever. Death's forever. The only thing we can be really sure of is that we'll die. That's why people write poetry, try to tell us to look at things now while there's still time. I don't like the thought of people dying, no matter what they've done. But I feel so awful, because I'm glad he's gone. Does that mean I'm a bad person too?'

'It means you're bloody human, Annie,' said Nancy.

'Did he die peacefully, Mother?'

Nancy would never tell her daughter the truth, that he had gone out raving and bathed in his own final haemorrhage. 'Yes, he went quiet enough.'

'Good.' Annie rose, deliberately pulling herself together. 'I'll just go and change into some human clothes.'

'Hang on!' called Mary from the sideboard. 'Two letters for you – one's from America, I think.'

Annie took the envelopes and sped to her room, opening Tom's first. His letters and parcels had arrived frequently over the years, providing great pleasure for Annie and her friends with whom she'd often shared Life-Savers, coloured bubble-gums, bright American comic papers and lots of other carefully chosen mementos. Sometimes, he even sent clothing and items of jewellery, things that were not available in England, so that Nancy and Annie often wore things that attracted attention and comment. Always, always, Tom sent his love.

She smiled, noticing yet again how American her Tom had become.

1517 Forest View
Philadelphia, Pa.
U.S.A.

June 1st 1958

Hi Annie,

How are you doing? I've got a good job now in the steelworks, promoted to supervisor just last month. This means I'm in charge of the two P's – paint and people. I don't know which is worse! I wish you would get out here and see this beautiful country. Philly itself is really busy, but there's some cute places around and you would surely love Pennsylvania.

I am busy most days. Everything needs repainting the minute you've done it. We paint everything that don't move and a few things that do! Paint sure spreads easy!

I've saved nearly enough to visit back home and the guys upstairs are letting me save vacations too so I'll have six weeks in England once I've enough dough. I guess England will seem small. This one state is enormous compared to Lancashire.

I've travelled a bit, went to Niagara a few weeks ago – boy, you should see that water, it kind of makes you want to cry. All that natural power is frightening.

Also I've been to Fort Ligonier, Pennsylvania-Dutch territory. You would love them forests, Annie. This place is full of trees – I guess that's how it came by its name. I'm sending you some souvenirs, Penn-Dutch aprons, tea-towels and the like so you can get the flavor. America has everybody's history rolled into one heap, that's why it's so interesting.

Well, I'm 32 and still not married. Did you wait for me or are you about to marry some college professor?

I'll be seeing you. Best regards to your Ma and hooray for her getting to be foreman.

Lots of love,

Tom.

Annie placed the letter with the others in a drawer of the tallboy. She held on to the second envelope for some time, turning it over slowly in her hand. It bore a London mark and the address was handwritten. She had applied to no colleges in the south and anyway, with her new career decision, she did not expect to hear anything for a while, her late change of mind having made the applications tardy. Slowly, she opened the letter.

113, Sandfield Road,
London EC4

14th June 58

My Dear Annie,

Yes, I'm in London – for the time being. I've gone freelance and already have two assignments lined up. My interest in photography paid off, because I now do the journalism and the pictures, so I don't have to cart a photographer around with me. I'm calling myself a photo-journalist, which sounds a bit posher than tea-boy! I leave for Africa in a day or two, raring to set off on safari.

It seems stupid now, the way we quarrelled. I hope you are happy and that your career will be a success. I write to my mother occasionally, I think she's glad of the pound or two I manage to send at last. She tells me you still visit and keep them smiling like you always did.

Don't you dare forget me, Annie Byrne. You can't write, because I don't know where I'll be, but I'll send postcards and photos from wherever I happen to get to. Look after yourself, kid. I'm coming back one day to see you. I expect you have a boyfriend (or several?) but I'm sure we can get together for old times' sake.

Hope your Mam is well – I hear that your stepdad is not in good health and I'm sorry, though you never did like him, did you?

Will write again and hope to see you sometime soon.

My love to you,

Martin. X

Annie stared for a long time at the single sheet. This was the first time he'd contacted her. Did he want that old flame – never more than a flicker – rekindled? What had she felt for this boy so long ago? Not love. Love was surely something bigger, greater than the childish feeling they had shared. But there had been tenderness, affection, care – and she missed those now.

She walked to the window and found herself smiling as she watched Dr Pritchard struggling to start Genevieve. That car must be as old as the hills. He stood on the pavement, his mouth moving as he spoke to this beloved object, coaxing, stroking the bonnet as if the thing could hear and feel him. She shook her head. Such a marvellous doctor, such a wonderful, lovable and sweet man.

Sighing, she turned away. Tomorrow would be another big day, another hurdle to leap, her final interview with Mother St Vincent. And these letters had unsettled her, had reminded her that there was a great big world out there ready for the taking. But first, she had to get past this tiny but commanding woman who was fighting her every inch of the way. And Annie was going to fight back. After all, life could be short – Eddie Higson's span had covered a mere forty-three years. Again, she wept briefly, praying that she would not waste the rest of her own years hating a dead man.

Then she heard Genevieve leaping to life and she grinned through her tears. 'Hatred is a waste of energy,' she heard David Pritchard saying. He was right, of course. Human, lovable, but right.

They sat in their usual places, the small nun to the left and the tall girl to the right of the window, a tea-tray occupying the table between them. Mother St Vincent, elbows resting on chair arms, fingers tapping together in front of her Cross and Passion badge, stared hard at Annie. Annie played with the fringed end of her prefect's sash, a long red strap that went over one shoulder, tied just below the waist on the opposite side, then dangled down towards the hem of her tunic.

'Annie Byrne! Will you for once listen and pay attention? I have always hoped – no, that's the beginning of an untruth – I have always known that you are Oxford material. Many is the day I have said to myself, "There goes a girl of high academic calibre."'

Annie's mouth twitched. She would miss this woman, really she would. Only Mother St Vincent could put a capital 'I' in the middle of 'calibre' and get away with it in a dignified fashion.

The nun coughed as if irritated by Annie's faint smile. 'And you arrive here now, at the eleventh hour, to tell me that you have the vocation?'

'That depends what you mean, Mother. I'm going to hang on to my legs, that's for sure.'

'Legs? Legs? What have legs to do with it at all, at all? You see? You have me so dismayed I'm sounding as if I just now stepped off the boat with my apron full of potatoes! We are talking about your future, girl. And sit up straight would you, or you'll be getting a curvature!'

Annie straightened her spine, wondering at the power of this frail creature who now rose from her chair, the great wooden rosary with its metal crucifix clanking and clattering as she paced the small area. After muttering and mumbling to herself for a short time, the nun stopped and faced Annie. 'So there you sit, with the world as your oyster, telling me that you're away to get a diploma. Not a degree, mind. A teaching diploma.' She spat this last word as if it were acid. 'And when I give you my opinion, you begin a conversation about legs.' She turned away impatiently and Annie, catching a glimpse of a highly-polished black shoe, found herself assessing the size of Mother's feet. Smaller than a ten-year-old's, they were. Probably a size two – even a one . . . 'I used to think nuns didn't have legs,' she heard herself stating absently.

'Pardon?'

'Sorry, I was thinking aloud. I had the idea, when I was a child, that there were two kinds of teachers, those with and those without.'

'Legs?'

Annie nodded, not daring to meet Mother's eyes.

'And how did you imagine that the Sisters moved about?'

'I'm not sure. Perhaps I thought they floated on a cloud, or had wheels . . .' Her voice tailed away.

'That was a foolish concept, was it not?'

Annie sighed. 'And a sobering one. If you'd known some of them, you would not have expected them to have simple human parts.'

'I know all of them, Anne. And I can assure you that they are in no way different from the rest of you.'

'I know, I know – I'm sorry . . .'

Mother returned to her seat, pushing away the small table so that cups and saucers rattled, the sound seeming to reflect her impatience and displeasure. She smoothed the heavy black skirt. 'I do not know what to say to you, Madam Byrne. But then I have seldom known what to say, for haven't you always been the difficult one, giving me desperate trouble half the time, then affection and respect for the rest of it? Your teachers here have all convinced themselves that you would be doing the medicine. That's a fine analytical brain you've been blessed with, a mind that could get you into the business of helping the sick, of healing bodies . . .'

'I see, Mother.' Annie's eyes flashed, showing an odd mixture of amusement and anger. 'You'd rather I dealt with bodies and left the minds alone? I've been accused in the past of being a – what was it now? – ah yes, a disruptive influence. Are you afraid that I might cause children to think for themselves, that I won't let them be a herd of sheep guided and forced along against a will they're not allowed to have? Was it St Francis who said

"Give me a child until he is seven and I will show you the man"?'

Mother bristled visibly and Annie studied the three perfectly placed round-headed pins which kept a waist-length black square fastened to the miniature head.

'I am not telling you not to teach! Don't be trying to twist the words before they're ever out of my mouth! Get a good Honours, teach a subject . . .'

'No. I don't want to work with older children, those who've already had their indoctrination one way or another.'

'You are impertinent, child!'

'I am eighteen years old, Mother!'

'And I'd surely put you over my knee this very minute, only I'd need a crane to lift the size you are!'

Both women were now perched on the edge of the chairs, each breathing heavily and staring hard at the other. Annie leaned back slowly and deliberately, stretching out her long legs and crossing her ankles. 'We must agree to differ, I'm afraid. I'm going to Manchester. In two years I'll be supporting my mother. I shall be attending college, learning the principles and practice of education with Scripture and Comparative Religion as part of the course.'

'Defiant to the last! You'll need a dispensation from the Bishop to attend a non-Catholic college.'

'No. I am not a confirmed Catholic.'

'And if I refuse you a reference?'

Annie shrugged her shoulders lightly. 'Then I'll have to write and explain such bigotry to the college principal. And you and I would not part the best of friends.'

The ensuing silence was short, because next door in the practice room, someone began to play the piano very badly, like a mouse running up and down the keys. From time to time, the music teacher bawled loudly at the poor sufferer at the keyboard. Unable to contain herself, Annie began to giggle while Mother's shoulders shook with ill-contained mirth. 'Sure, that's nothing,' the nun finally managed. 'You should hear Katie Maher at the violin. I always do school inspection during her lessons, for I cannot bear the agony of hearing a cat being strangulated.'

'Haven't you . . . oh what a din . . . haven't you any earplugs?'

'Indeed I have not. Do as I do, endure it and offer up your suffering for the souls in Purgatory . . .'

'Except for Katie Maher. You don't offer up Katie Maher . . .'

'Anne, there is a limit to every mortal's endurance. Katie Maher's fiddle is my personal limit.'

'Oh, Mother, Mother . . .' Annie cried, reaching for a handkerchief, her face suddenly sober. 'I shouldn't be laughing.'

'Why not? Laughter never did harm.'

'Well, it's just that my . . . stepfather died a few days ago. Laughing seems wrong.' She paused and glanced at Mother St Vincent. 'You see, Mother, I hated him. He was cruel and hurtful – once, he kicked my mother so hard that she lost her baby. I have been . . . filled with hatred for years and years.'

Mother St Vincent stared hard at Annie. 'I thought I detected a note of hysteria. And yes, yes, this explains a great deal about you.' She fingered the edge of her stiff white collar as she pondered, repeating slowly, 'This explains a great deal, Anne Byrne. So. Perhaps you're relieved that he's gone?'

'Yes, I am.'

'No doubt God will forgive you for that. But I'm disappointed that you never told me these troubles. I might have helped.'

'Some things are too bad to talk about.'

The nun sighed deeply. 'I suppose you're right. It's not all of us can do the dirty washing in the street now, is it?' She paused and studied Annie for several seconds. 'Alright then. You can have your reference. I wish though . . .

still, no matter. Perhaps you'll come back to the Faith in your own time. I'll . . . I'll miss you, child.'

'And I'll miss you too.'

'Like you'd miss the toothache? Go on with you. Write to me sometimes, Anne Byrne.'

'I shall. Goodbye, Mother.' Annie rose to leave.

'God go with you.'

Annie left school by the front door that afternoon, marching out through the teachers' entrance in a last silly act of defiance. She took the horrible brown hat and flung it into a bush as she walked towards the bus stop. By the time she reached home, her brown and yellow tie was adorning a lamp post in the town centre, while the ribbon with which she had been forced, for seven years, to tie back her hair, was fastened to a used ticket box on the bus. It was over. Over and just beginning.

Simon had scraped by sufficiently to gain a place at the art college in Manchester where he intended to qualify as an illustrator. Annie received one distinction and two credits, thereby ensuring her entrance to teachers' training college in September.

They sat now in Simon's recreation room, talking about their respective futures, though Annie was doing most of the talking. Simon seemed distant, often making inappropriate responses to Annie's questions.

She waved a hand in front of his face. 'Hello! Anybody in?'

He stared at her for several moments.

'What's the matter, Simon?'

He shrugged his shoulders. 'Can't talk about it,' he muttered.

'Oh. Would you like me to go?'

'No! No, don't go – look, I'm sorry. I'm just a bit . . . preoccupied . . .'

'Preoccupied? You're absent without leave, Simon. I've been talking to myself for the last ten minutes.'

'Sorry.'

'Stop saying that! Look, either you tell me what's wrong or I go.'

He jumped up quickly, the flimsy canvas chair falling back as he rose.

'Oh God!' He put a hand to his face. 'She knows!'

'Who knows?' Annie stood and placed a hand on his arm. 'Who knows what?'

'My mother! She saw us . . . in here . . . she saw . . .'

Annie picked up the chair and forced him to sit down again. 'Start at the beginning, Simon.'

'I don't know how. But I can trust you, can't I? It's not really a secret any more, but at least you won't spread it around. How though, how do I tell you?'

'With words, Simon. You can tell me anything – I won't be shocked.'

'Promise?'

'Promise.'

He swallowed audibly. 'Do you know . . . what a homosexual is?'

'Yes, I do.'

Seconds passed. 'I'm one,' he declared finally, his voice deliberately steady. 'I used to wonder why I was never jealous of you and Martin. One time, I saw you kissing and half of me wished I was in Martin's place, but the other half . . . I was so confused.'

She took his hand. 'Oh Simon, Simon . . .'

'I had one experience with a girl – Susan Birchall. It was horrible.'

'But . . . but you may be ordinary after all! This could be a phase because of that bad experience . . .'

He shook his head vehemently. 'No. I have a friend, someone from school. I am fond of him and I believe he cares for me too.'

'But is it so terrible?'

'Yes! Yes, it is! Everyone will expect me to marry and have children – especially my parents. Though my mother . . .'

'What about your mother?'

'Last night,' he said, almost in a whisper, 'she found us in here. She is the last person in the world who might accept. What we were doing must have seemed so awful to her . . .' He broke off, his voice cracking with tears.

'She'd have to know sometime . . .'

'Yes! I suppose she would have to find out that her son is a pervert!'

Annie thought briefly about the real pervert she had known, the one who had been buried some weeks ago. Between Eddie Higson and Simon, there was no comparison. 'You're not a pervert! You'd never inflict pain or force your attentions. You're just . . . different, that's all.'

'Yes – different. I'll be an outcast unless I live some sort of pretended life, force myself to marry and have a family.'

'That wouldn't be honest, especially for your wife.'

'I know! I know I can never be normal.'

'You're still the same old Simon.'

'Yes. Salmon Pilchard, Old Fish Face.'

'I never called you Fish Face.'

He smiled sadly through his tears then went to stand, hands in pockets and with his back towards her as he stared through a window.

'Has she told your father what she saw?'

'I doubt it. They don't communicate. On the other hand, with a thing of this magnitude . . .'

'Don't you think you should talk to him first?'

'I can't. Except for Paul – he's my friend – you're the only one I've spoken to.'

They remained in the room for an hour or more, sometimes sitting silently, often pacing together as they tried to talk their way through to a solution.

Later on, Simon became even more agitated. His father had been out for some time, but was expected back shortly for evening surgery. There had been no sound in the house, no sign of his mother going through her customary tea-making ritual.

'Knock on her bedroom door, Simon.'
'I daren't go near after what's happened . . .'
'Then I'll do it!'
'No!'
'I'm not afraid of her, Simon.'
'That's why she doesn't like you. She calls it lack of respect . . .'
'Well, one of us has to find her.'
'Okay, okay, I'll go.' He made for the door.
Annie heard him crossing the landing and tapping gently, then suddenly he was screaming, 'Anne! Anne!' Annie sped across the landing and into Edna Pritchard's bedroom.
The woman on the bed had arranged everything beautifully. She lay flat, her hands clasping a posy of flowers against her breast. The cream-coloured peignoir was of pure silk, her face was perfectly made up and she had even tied a chiffon scarf under her chin and around the top of her head so that she would not die open-mouthed. The pink of painted nails showed fiery red against the whitening flesh of her hands. Beside her, in a perfect copper-plate hand, lay a note.

To Whom it May Concern,

I wish to be interred in Heaton Cemetery with my parents. No undertaker is to interfere with my body which is to be buried exactly as you find it. Please remove the scarf once you have ensured that my mouth will remained closed.

The will is with my solicitor whose details are known to my husband. I have no reason to live. I therefore choose my own time, place and method of dying.

Edna Marguerite Pritchard

The two young people stared in frozen shock at the figure on the bed, then Annie leapt forward to feel the wrist, seeking a pulse. But the icy stiffness of the arm told its story and Annie dragged Simon out of the room. She felt a strong urge to run – somewhere, anywhere – to find help, but she dared not leave Simon who was leaning heavily on the banister, fighting for breath.

Then the front door opened and Annie leaned over the rail screaming, 'Doctor! Come quickly!'

The man raced up the stairs. 'What is it?' he asked, his eyes riveted to Simon whose stomach now heaved. Simon turned, pointed to his mother's room, then fled to the bathroom.

David entered his wife's bedroom. There was no need for him to touch Edna; the signs of rigor were plain to his practised eye. He turned from the bed and felt Annie's arms around his shaking body. But he saw nothing, heard nothing except his own voice. 'My fault. I killed her . . . I killed her.'

'Come away, Doctor – come away.' He seemed not to hear, so she pulled him gently from the room.

'Why couldn't I just . . . what have I done? She didn't need to know . . . I should have . . .'

Annie quickly worked out the geography of the house and led the doctor to his room. Like an obedient child, he allowed himself to be pushed on to the narrow bed.

'Doctor? Dr Pritchard?' She shook his shoulders.

'What? Anne – where's Simon?'

'In the bathroom being sick.'

'She's dead.'

'I know.'

'I told her . . . things. I shouldn't have done it . . .'

'I'm going downstairs to put up a note cancelling the surgery. If anybody's ill, they'll have to go to hospital. Stay there – don't you dare move.'

She ran down the stairs and found a notepad on which she printed a very shaky announcement. After fixing this to the front door, she sat for several minutes in the dining room, trying hard to hang on to what was left of her composure. But her eyes wandered unbidden over Mrs Pritchard's precious things, china in glass-fronted cabinets, crystal decanters encased in a polished tantalus, the framed tapestry hanging proudly over the fireplace. Simon's mum had stitched that with her own hand, a hand that would never lift another needle, pour a drink, dish out a dinner.

So hard, Mrs Pritchard had seemed, so steely and indestructible. But everyone had a breaking point – even this soul of iron had been worn down, corroded past mending . . .

Reaching out to steady herself on the arm rest, Annie rose from the carver and placed herself in front of the tapestry. 'I'm sorry, Mrs Pritchard,' she whispered. 'Sorry we never tried to understand.'

But there were two still living, two who needed her now. So she turned from what was left of Edna and steeled herself to return to the upper floor. From the landing, she saw Simon sitting at the foot of his father's bed.

'It was my fault,' Simon was saying.

So he had just now told his father! But what a terrible time to have to do it.

Annie could see that even in his state of double shock, David was fighting for control, fighting to shield his son. 'No, Simon. Your mother found out that I'd been unfaithful – in fact, I told her. She might even have discovered that my mistress was a friend of hers. That's why she killed herself.'

'An affair's normal, Dad. But yesterday, she found out . . .'

'No! She would not kill herself because of your preferences! Believe me – she has threatened this for years, but I thought she was being over-dramatic. You must not blame yourself!'

Annie knocked on the open door. 'Shall I get an ambulance or something?'

David nodded. 'Please. Arrangements will have to be made.'

'Mrs Pritchard left very precise instructions, Doctor . . .'

'She would. Oh yes, she would.'

Annie stayed with David and Simon for the whole evening, leaving just once to tell Nancy what had happened. Mary and Nancy brought food which nobody ate, then Annie remained to answer any telephone calls. Edna's body was removed and taken to the morgue. The cause of death would have to be established, so whatever the poor woman's wishes might have been, that final message would be ignored.

At ten o'clock, Annie unlocked the medicine cabinet and took out four sleeping pills, forcing the men to swallow two each. When they finally drifted off into restless sleep, she took the phone off the hook and went home.

'Eeh, Annie,' cried Nancy. 'Why?'

'Because she couldn't face life any more.' Annie allowed her tears of shock to flow now. 'Oh Mam, it was awful . . . awful . . .'

They gave her a hot toddy and put her to bed. Mary sat the whole night in Annie's chair by the window, watching the lights going on and off in the doctor's house. Each time Annie moaned in her sleep, Mary leapt up to stroke her head and soothe away the nightmare.

This child, this eighteen-year-old girl, had experienced more in her short life than most people did in a full three score and ten. Sighing, Mary resumed her seat and watched the dawn break over Bolton. Edna Pritchard would never see another dawn. Others had been left to face many such mornings.

Part Three
Anne

1960

I escaped from college in late June with a cartload of useless books, distinctions in some final exams and a marked dislike for certain educationalists. The system was changing and loud voices were proclaiming the benefits of 'learning by discovery' which, roughly interpreted, meant let the little beggars do as they like. I tried these methods once during a teaching practice in Stockport, found myself reading a story to three children while the other forty-six did interesting things like throwing paint, eating jigsaw puzzles and getting up to no good in the boys' toilets. I therefore gained one of my distinctions by writing a thesis on this load of progressive rubbish and emerged with an undeniable suspicion that the three Rs still had a place in our schools.

I threw off the student garb which included shocking-pink stockings, bright tartan skirts and two college scarves sewn together to make one long enough to go round Manchester Town Hall. It was like getting rid of another uniform.

The courses had proved disappointing, though scripture fascinated me because I discovered that the Old Testament was so crammed with anomalies and improbabilities that it was either a pack of lies or a collection of interesting errors. Comparative religion sessions were another eye-opener; Islam was too weird and wonderful for me, while Buddhism proved unacceptable as I had no desire to return as a spider or, worse still, as another human seeking Nirvana. This, apparently, was on offer to those who did nothing at all apart from following some odd eight-point plan in their minds – I never did get to grips with it. So I left poor Buddha sitting under his tree and decided to be a Christian after all.

As the college was in Manchester, I was able to come home each weekend. I received the full grant of £25 a term, a total of £150 throughout the two years. This laughable amount forced me to take a Saturday job in Marks and Spencer on Deansgate where I thoroughly enjoyed selling stockings from ten till six, for which service I earned a guinea a day, a wage that compared favourably with the pittance I would eventually receive as a qualified teacher.

During what was left of my weekends, I spent time with Simon, who also came home each Friday and with his father who taught me to play a mean backgammon and a passable game of chess. Simon saddened me. He remained quiet and withdrawn; I knew that he would always blame himself for his mother's suicide.

I had just two boyfriends during my time in college. The first, Mike Stewart, hailed from Bradford and I soon learned to imitate his fascinating accent. We were never close – merely part of a group – and we drifted apart when he met a stunning girl from the university who enticed him to her lair from whence he would emerge dazed and unshaven to take in the odd lecture.

My second encounter, with John Beresford, was slightly more intense. For a whole term we mooned over one another, passing love-notes and poems across lecture halls while the Philistines around us sniggered at our pure and beautiful romance. When John suggested that our relationship should become less than pure and more than beautiful, I lost him too because of my blunt refusal. John went off in a huff to comfort himself with a florist's assistant from Wythenshawe. I retired to a corner and licked my shallow wounds which healed after a fortnight because I was invited to write the lyrics for our revue, an exciting honour given only to the favoured few.

And now it was over. For all my pains, I would soon be receiving the princely reward of £32 each calendar month, for which sum I must take charge of and educate a class of no less than forty-five infants.

My mother was very proud. 'You'll be able to save up.'

'For what?'

'For the future, for holidays and nice clothes.'

'I'll pay my keep like Mary does.'

'We'll see. I'm alright now, you mustn't worry over money.'

She didn't need my salary, probably didn't really need me any longer. She loved me, I was still her favourite girl, but Mary was there now to keep her company and although I felt no jealousy, I sometimes had a sense of being surplus to requirements. This was all a part of my mother's plan for me. She had given me the wings and now she wanted to see me fly.

Then, during the long break between college and my first term as a teacher, life suddenly went completely mad. Tom and Martin returned almost simultaneously to colour and disrupt my existence to the point of exhaustion. I was not surprised when Martin pursued me relentlessly – after all, we had had some kind of relationship in the past. But when Tom began to press his suit, I was amazed.

Tom was the kind of man who might sweep any girl off her feet – tall, bronzed, muscular and with a slight American accent that lent him a film-starrish air. But it was plain from the start that he had come home with the intention of taking me back with him.

'You'd love it, Annie. Remember how you begged me all those years ago to take you with me? Well – now's the time! You could have a real good look around, then if things worked out – who knows? We might even get married once you know me better.'

I sat in the passenger seat of the large hired car, squirming because I didn't know what to say. The Tom I knew from his letters was not the same as this powerful person who sat by my side.

'What d' you say, Annie?'

'I . . . don't know. I have to get through my probationary year . . .'

'You can do that back home!'

'This is home, Tom.'

'Yeah. Well I guess I have two homes now. Think about it, Annie. I've saved all the photographs and letters over the years – I knew my Annie was growing up to be a real beauty. And when the guys hassled me about not being married – well, I'd tell them straight – "I'm going home and get my English rose", I'd say.'

His arm crept along the back of the seat and he pulled me as near as the gear lever would allow. The kisses were sweet and tender at first, then, as his tongue began to probe, I pushed at his chest. I liked him, really I did. But there was something missing, something I knew about. Whatever this something was, I had met it before and let it pass me by. But I couldn't remember where or when.

Martin was a different matter altogether. His confidence was unshakeable from the start, that very first day when he walked into our house and swept me off my feet, not caring who was watching.

'Eeh, Martin!' cried my mother. 'Put that woman down this minute!'

Then I stood and watched as he kissed my mother and introduced himself to Mary. He was taller than I remembered and his voice was cultured and controlled.

He turned to me now. 'Am I welcome, Annie Byrne?'

'Of course you are.'

'Then I shall be escorting your daughter this evening, Mrs Higson.'

'Nay, don't tell me, lad. She's her own mistress now – not that she's ever been any different, come to think . . .'

'Will you come?' he asked me.

'Yes.' Perhaps he was whatever I'd been missing. So I went and listened to him talking over dinner, spinning tales about his exciting life and how many pages of his passport were full. No, I wasn't bored, I told myself firmly. I was tired, that was all.

Fighting him off was not easy. He was strong and determined to have his way. Not that there was room in his little two-seater sports car, but he had parked right out in the country and escape would not be easy.

'Come on, Annie. You know I've always loved you . . .'

'For goodness sake – grow up, Martin! I wasn't born yesterday and neither were you! I haven't seen you for years – what do you expect? I'm not going to give in just like that! So, if you're determined to carry on with this, you can do it alone.' I reached for the door handle.

'I'm sorry – look, I'll slow down, I promise.'

'You will grind to a complete halt, Martin Cullen! But the car will move! Now – this minute!'

He started the engine.

'Move!' I shouted.

The car leapt forward. 'I didn't mean to upset you, Annie. Your picture has been in my wallet right next to my heart for a long, long time. I just got carried away. You're more beautiful than ever – it's not easy for me. In a few weeks I'll be gone. Come with me, Annie.'

I gritted my teeth. Not again, not another one. Everybody suddenly wanted to take me away!

'I'm not going anywhere, Martin. I'm a Bolton girl and Bolton's where I'll stay.'

'And marry a boring Bolton man and have boring Bolton kids?'

'Probably.'

'Think about it, Annie.' He pulled up outside our house. 'And by the way, who's this American I'm hearing about?'

'He is an old neighbour from the other side of town. He emigrated and has come back to visit family.'

'Spends a lot of time with you, doesn't he?'

'That is my business!'

He grinned in that boyish way I remembered so well. 'You're going to marry me one day, Annie.'

'Really? Then drop me a line so I'll remember to go to the church!'

I stamped into the house and banged the door.

These two situations continued for weeks. I juggled with them, divided the hours and days as fairly as I could between the two of them, hung on grimly to my virtue as I tried to decide which, if either, was the right one for me. I was pulled this way and that, persuaded, cajoled, bribed almost . . . then, finally, I had had enough. Arrangements had somehow become muddled, I knew that the two of them would arrive this evening – dear God! I couldn't even live in my own house any more! Every time I opened the door, one or the other would be there complete with chocolates, flowers and an inane grin. But both together? That I could not face.

So I simply walked out and went across to see Simon. He would listen. He would understand. But David opened the door to my frantic bell-pushing.

'What the hell's happened to you, Anne? You look . . . rather flustered to say the least.'

'Just hide me! Put me in a cupboard, lock me in the lavatory – where's Simon? He'll help me.'

'He's out for the evening.'

I glanced over my shoulder. 'Then . . . give me an injection, send me to hospital, say I'm in a coma . . . anything! I'll even play backgammon. Please?'

He took my arm and led me through to the drawing room. The minute he touched me I knew what had passed me by, knew all about that missing something. It was terrifying, like an electric current running up my arm and right through my body. All I was aware of was him, that peppermint and medicine smell, the tweed jacket, a hint of cigar smoke. We stood in the doorway of the room, an untidy room now with no wife to care for it. And I looked at my darling scruffy saviour from the past, with his over-long hair and not quite clean shirt.

'David!' I heard the second syllable as it rose like an alarm, a warning to myself.

'Anne?'

I stood to one side then and watched this girl, this terrible wanton creature as she put her arms around the man and kissed him. But I did not remain an observer for long. He was shaking just as he had on that awful night two years ago when his wife had died. We had to lean against a wall because I too was trembling violently.

So, having come to this place to seek refuge and protection from virile suitors, I found myself in the hands of a truly experienced man, one I had loved forever without quite realising the fact. It was so natural, so perfect and beautiful. He wiped out all the pain and confusion, eliminated every fear, treated my body with a reverence that shook and delighted me. I didn't care in those moments whether or not this would be forever. Now mattered. Now was all that mattered.

'Oh my darling girl. I am so sorry . . .' he murmured afterwards.

'Don't be. Can't you see what you've done? Don't you realise how terrified I was of all this? I didn't know it could be so wonderful.'

'Yes, it was. But it shouldn't have happened – apart from anything else, I'm your doctor.'

'Then I'll get another – I've been thrown out of better surgeries than yours. Please don't be sad . . . please?' I stroked the head that nestled between my breasts. 'I love you, David. I think I've loved you since I was fifteen.'

'That was gratitude,' he answered, his fingers gently tracing the contours of my upper body. 'Never confuse gratitude with love.'

'Then what do you feel for me, Dr Pritchard? Is this lust?'

'No,' he said quietly. 'I have the temerity to love you, though God knows I'm too old for you. But I've been a member of the Total Idiots' group for some time now.'

'Tell me how you qualified.'

He lifted his tousled head and looked into my eyes. 'I've wished you were older. I've imagined how it would be if I were twenty years younger . . .'

'But you're not. What does age matter anyway?'

'It matters. I think you should get dressed and go home, my dear.'

I moved away from him and began to pull on my clothes with furious haste. 'Get dressed and go home, my dear,' I mimicked viciously. I dragged my fingers through my hair in an attempt to restore it to some kind of order. 'I don't suppose there's a comb in this dump, Dr Pritchard?'

'On the hallstand.'

I stamped through into the hall and stared at the mirror. I didn't look any different, no matter how many angles I tried and this disappointed me beyond measure. That he would follow me I did not doubt for a moment. Where had I got the wisdom, the certainty that this was what magazines called 'real love'? From him, I supposed, from this thing between us that was a fact, a thing that belonged to neither and yet to both of us. He came up behind me and our eyes met in the glass.

'You're angry,' he said flatly.

'Angry? Why the hell should I be angry? Nothing's happened, nothing real. It obviously meant little to you when I said I love you. No, I'm not angry, Doctor. I'm bloody furious!'

Then he started to laugh, that awful infectious guffaw that made you either join in or thump him, so I thumped him good and hard, swinging round from the mirror and delivering the full force of my clenched fist, which was not inconsiderable, on to his chest. He coughed, stepped backwards, then grinned broadly.

'Right,' he said quietly. 'I suppose you're going to insist on making an honest man of me. Because you hold all the trumps and you know it, Anne. But it won't be easy. I had to give you the chance to walk away from it. What we're going into will take some explaining.'

I tapped my foot. 'What would you have done if I had walked away?'

'I'd have come after you.'

'It's a good job you said that, David Pritchard!' I reached for him and we clung together saying all the silly things that come with new-found love. And all the time part of my mind was wondering what might or might not have happened if Simon had been at home, if I hadn't got into that dreadful mess with Tom and Martin, if . . . But no, this would have found us sooner or later.

So it was all arranged, mapped out within the hour, at the end of which time we made love again. I had never imagined such happiness, not for myself. For years I had kept my distance, denied my sexuality, indulged my fears. This was not just compensation, it was liberation too. There must be a God, there must be a plan.

We dressed, then hand in hand for all the world to see, we walked across the road to tell my mother. Just as we reached our gate, he began to chuckle again.

'What's the matter now?' I dug him in the ribs. 'Pull yourself together – this is a very solemn occasion!'

'Remember Blackpool?' he asked. 'She's no easy opponent!'

'She's only little.'

'Yes, so is a bottle of poison. Do you realise – I'll be the same age as my mother-in-law? She'll never buy this.'

'David!' We stood on the pathway facing each other. 'You'll just have to trust my salesmanship.'

My mother was seated at the table with Mary and Bertha Cullen when we entered. They all looked startled when they saw David, but I quickly beckoned to my mother to follow us into the kitchen. I closed the door, took David's arm, then faced her.

She stared at us for some moments. 'What the hell's all this?' she asked eventually.

'Nancy . . . I want to ask for your daughter's hand . . .'

Her jaw dropped. 'You what? You bloody what?'

'We're getting married, Mother.'

'You're . . . you're . . .? No such flaming thing! Still a kid and wanting to chuck your life away – not likely!'

'I love him, Mother.' I squeezed his hand. 'And he loves me.'

There followed a deafening silence during which I could almost feel the straining ears in the next room. Then in she waded – at the deep end as always. 'When you're forty, he'll be sixty bloody odd! Are you daft, lass?'

'No and I'm not a kid. I'll be twenty-one in five months.'

'Don't you come the clever lip with me, our Annie!'

David coughed. 'She'll be well looked after, Nancy.'

'Aye. So will you, eh? Specially when she's shoving you round in the wheelchair.' She turned her venom on me again. 'Years we went without. Now you've got the training and a good job – what the hell do you want to go getting wed for? I've fetched you up to know you don't need a man. But if you've got to have one, why can't you pick somebody your own age? There's Martin – and Tom's only in his thirties.'

David's tone was quiet but firm. 'She doesn't want them, Nancy. She wants me.'

I straightened my spine and looked down on my angry mother. 'Either you accept this or I leave home. That way, I'll be able to do as I please. You can't boss me around forever! I thought it was bad enough when I was a child, you, the nuns,the priest – but we've reached the end of that particular line now. Would you rather David and I lived over the brush as they call it? Because I'm going to live across the road whether I marry him or not.'

She glowered and opened her mouth to speak, but a tapping at the door to the living room put a stop to whatever she was about to pronounce.

Mary opened the door an inch or two. 'Tom and Martin have both come back,' she whispered. 'They're sitting in the front room looking daggers at one another. And we can all hear what's going on in here.'

My mother followed Mary into the living room.

David drew me into his arms. 'Perhaps she's right, darling.'

'No!' I mouthed fiercely. 'She can't take away what's happened between us. I won't let her spoil it, I won't!'

We walked into the living room just as Tom and Martin arrived through the other door. My mother stood at the far side of the table, arms folded, one foot tapping on the floor.

'Well, Tom. Well, Martin. Lady Annie's led you both a dance, I'm afraid.'

'Now, Nancy,' said Bertha. 'Don't go so 'ard on t' lass. She's nobbut doin' what she thinks is reet. Just leave 'er be.'

'Please, Nancy,' begged Mary. 'Let's not have a scene.'

Tom stepped forward. 'What's going on here?'

Martin tried to push his way into the crowded room. 'Yes – what's all this about?'

David placed himself in front of the sideboard, leaving me to stand by the kitchen door. He was obviously preparing to fight alone for the cause. He cleared his throat. 'Anne and I want to be married. Obviously, Nancy is under the impression that I'm taking out some kind of insurance policy, getting myself a young wife who will see me through my dotage. This is not the case. Anne and I belong together.' He reached out an arm and I ran to him gladly. 'We didn't plan to fall in love, Nancy. And please, please don't turn away from your daughter now. She loves you. In the past, she has proved how much.' My mother flinched slightly as she took in the meaning behind his words.

Tom shook David's hand vigorously. 'I won't pretend I'm not disappointed, but you sure got a great girl there. Congratulations.'

Martin turned and left the house, slamming doors as he went.

'Tek no notice to 'im,' said Bertha. ''E'll likely get over it.'

My mother, her face white with fury, stormed out of the room and up the stairs.

'Well,' Bertha struggled to her feet. 'I'll . . . er . . . I'll just go an' see ter me . . . me ironin'.' She waddled out, leaving Mary, Tom, David and me standing uncomfortably about the room.

Tom looked at Mary. 'We could . . . go for a drink, you and I. . .'

'Yes . . . yes, I'll just get my coat.' She fled from the scene.

'I'll . . . I'll wait in the car.' The door closed behind Tom.

David shook his head. 'We've upset everybody's apple-cart, Anne.'

'I don't care! We've got one another and that's all we need.'

The next morning I lay in my bed and waited for the inevitable. She hadn't come downstairs again after that dreadful scene the previous evening, but I knew she hadn't finished with me, not by a long chalk. Somewhere inside myself, I felt torn in two, yet I realised that my love and need for David would win hands down if it came to actual warfare. And the opening salvo was about to be fired, for I could hear her coming up the attic stairs.

She entered my room quietly, which was an ominous sign, walked past the bed and opened the curtains at my three-sided window. With her back towards me, she began to speak, her voice almost a whisper.

'You're not asleep, Annie. I'd know if you were asleep. Likely you've been awake for hours.' She paused as if deep in thought. 'Twenty years I've watched you grow, cared what happened. I've not done it all right. If I'd done it all right, things would never have got so bad for you.'

'Please, Mother . . .'

'No, lass. I'm up on the horse now and it's taken a fair climb. I shall get off when I'm ready.' She cleared her throat as if embarrassed. 'Before I start, I've got to say I'm sorry over what happened last night, me kicking off like that in front of everybody and showing you up . . .'

'That was my fault. David and I should have waited until . . .'

'Shut up, Annie, will you? Let me say my piece, because I've been up all night practising.'

She lowered herself into my chair at the window and shook her head wearily. I couldn't see her face, but I could read its cxpression from her tone. At first, it was almost as if she were talking to herself.

'When they came with that telegram, I thought my world was over and finished with. I loved him. We fought like cat and dog, but that was part of it, you see. It was like we enjoyed the fighting for the sake of making up. Eeh, when I think back . . .' She disappeared for a while inside her own precious memories and I lay motionless, waiting for her return.

'He was a daft lad, was Billy Byrne. First off, when I said I wouldn't have him, he sent me a note to say he was going up Dawson's chimney with four butties and a bottle of tea. It said "If you don't come and shout yes, I'll starve to death." So I went and there he was, top of the mill stack and all I could think was he'd either fall off or get covered in soot. It was Sunday, so he never did get dirty, because I shouted and he came down fast as a monkey. I married that lad and I thought it was forever. Only it wasn't. Nothing ever is.' She bent her head for a few minutes and I longed to run to her, but something about the way she sat, so stiff and still, made me stay where I was.

'After Billy had died, I put his things – letters, the wedding ring and all that – in an old biscuit tin. I gave it our Jessie to hold for you – I couldn't keep it in the house while . . . while the other one was here.' She sniffed audibly. 'Ever since the day we got the news and you ran to the lions, you've been looking for Billy. I don't mean you've walked round expecting to find him, but inside, in here,' I heard her strike her breast with a clenched fist, 'you've been searching. So now you've found him. But a husband can't be a father, Annie. You're making a terrible mistake that can't be undone easy. So there. I've had my say. Now it's your turn.'

She dried her eyes and faced me and I saw the depth of her sadness and confusion.

'It's not like that, Mother – I promise! I love David. I want him like . . . like a woman wants a man.'

'Aye well. You can want a lot of men in that way. It doesn't mean you love them.'

'I know, I do know that!' Oh what could I say to make her understand? 'It has to be him, Mam.'

'Well, I shan't agree to it.'

'I don't want to hurt you, Mother. If only you knew how much I don't want that. But if I have to, then I must. He's mine. I already belong to him and there's nothing I can do to change it.'

'You don't want to change it, do you?'

'No, I don't. And I won't allow anyone else to spoil it either.'

She walked unsteadily across the room and sat on the edge of my bed. 'We're going to fight, Annie, you and I. And there's neither of us will fight clean.'

'Then that's too bad, Mother! If two grown women can't talk this thing out properly and sensibly . . .'

'What's it got to do with bloody sense?' Colour rose in her cheeks and her voice grew louder. 'What's the sense in getting wed to a man twice your age? And he's a Protestant too . . .'

I heard myself chuckling grimly. 'You can jump off that wagon, Mam. I'm hardly a Catholic and you've not seen the inside of a church for years.'

'That doesn't matter,' she shouted. 'A Catholic is always a Catholic!'

'And that's what you call a sensible argument? If you can't think of anything better . . .'

'Ah, but I can, I bloody can that! His first wife poisoned herself, didn't she? Took a load of pills and a gallon of sherry by all accounts . . .'

'Yes, but . . .'

'Never mind but! Never mind all the flaming buts, Annie! Something drove her to that. Do you want to end up the same road as her? Well . . . do you?'

I sat bolt upright in the bed. 'That is unfair, Mother!'

'Aye, lass. I warned you it wouldn't be fair boxing, didn't I? A man whose wife does herself in has a few questions to answer. Maybe I can answer for him, eh? He's out on his blinking rounds all the time or sitting in that surgery of his. Them two never had more than half a marriage. Poor woman didn't have a husband!'

'Poor woman? Oh Mother, what a hypocrite you are! You'd no time for her when she was alive, we were always cracking jokes about her . . .'

'That's as may be. Only the joke's over now, specially for her! How do you know what he's like to live with, eh?'

'I don't. But I know him, he's a good man.'

'A good doctor, I'll grant that. But how can you be sure he won't push you into doing what she did?'

'That, Mother, is mean, spiteful, despicable . . .' I groped for words then leapt angrily from the bed, grabbing my folded clothes from the top of the tallboy.

'Aye, but you've no answer to it, have you?' she screamed.

'I don't owe you or anybody any answers! How dare you – you of all people? Did you know what Eddie Higson would be like to live with? And even if we leave your mistakes out of this, Mother – and I'm quite sure that we should leave them out – who are you to judge David, to undermine him? And isn't it time you credited me with a bit of intelligence? Do you think I'd go off and marry a dangerous man? Can't you get it into your head that I, Annie Byrne, have seen danger at close quarters and can now recognise its stench from a mile away? Are you implying that I'm so bloody stupid?'

She stood up and glared hard at me. 'Right then, Annie. On your head be it.'

'Mother . . .' But she was already out of the room.

I ran to the top of the stairs and called after her. 'Mam, you are hopeless! You talk about liberation and freedom of choice, about it being time for a woman's world – then you say I can't choose. I am just about sick and fed up with you! You're like a book that's been written back to bloody front!'

She turned at the foot of the attic stairs. 'Don't you take that tone with me, lady. I'm not having you losing your temper just because I stick to my guns in my own house! Anyroad, I'm off to our Jessie's for a week or two, give you time to come to your senses.'

I heard myself gasp. 'You . . . you won't be at my wedding then?'

She stuck out her chin. 'Bolton Wanderers could be at home. Happen I might call in at the match instead.'

I sank on to the top step. 'But . . . you've always hated football.'

'Exactly.'

'You are so stubborn!' I jumped up and threw my handful of clothes at her head and she sidestepped quickly to avoid these flying items.

'I'm not as stubborn as you are, lass,' she said quietly.

Then she was gone. She took her packed suitcase to work and did not return home that night. When she had been gone for a week, we had a meeting, Mary, Simon, David and I, all sitting round the table with the green and white check cloth.

Simon scratched his ear thoughtfully. 'I suppose we have to look at it from her point of view.'

'Fire away,' I said. 'If you can work out her point of view, you deserve a medal.'

'Well,' Simon went on slowly. 'Say I came home with a forty-year-old woman – I know it's not likely, but say I did – what would you think, Dad?'

David gazed steadily at his son. 'I can't answer that. It would depend who she was.'

Mary sighed loudly. 'There's nothing to be gained from this, Simon. We've tried just about everything now. I went up to Jessie's and tried to make Nancy listen . . .'

'You were lucky,' I snapped. 'At least she opened the door. When David and I went . . . oh, I'm sorry, Mary. I didn't mean to bite your head off.'

'Perhaps you should go alone, Anne,' said David.

'I will not! That's exactly what she wants me to do!'

'Then you're just as bad as she is!'

I shook my head slowly. 'You don't understand, any of you. She's made up her mind and so have I. Talking won't do any good. I think we'll just have to go ahead without her.'

David looked quickly at Simon and Mary. 'Would you two mind? I'd like to talk with Anne for a little while.'

After they had gone, he reached for my hand. 'Look, I don't want you to regret this. In years to come, you may well blame me – or worse still, blame yourself for this rift. I'm lucky, I suppose. If Simon had been opposed, I would have had a similar problem. Are you sure you want to go on without her?'

'Absolutely. She'll come to terms with things after the wedding.'

'How do you know?'

'Because she's my mother and we're very alike. She won't punish me for long, David. You don't know her – it's hard to explain. But we'll have to get married without either her blessing or her presence. She'll come back, believe me . . .'

Mary came. And Bertha and Tom, though the latter was due to fly back to the States the same evening. We had chosen a tiny chapel on the northern edge of the town, so many centuries old that I had to stoop to get through doorways, bending my head to match the height of those who had built it of huge stones and solid dark oak.

Tom was to give me away and I felt that this was appropriate because he'd helped me to survive twenty long years earlier – I owed my life to him.

We stood at the altar while the vicar intoned the service, David holding my hand throughout. When it came to the words 'Who gives this woman?' and Tom stepped forward to do the honours, there was a sudden pushing and shoving aside and there she stood, resplendent but breathless in a pale green suit with white trimmings.

'Hang on a bit,' she said to the disconcerted vicar. 'Only I want a word.'

David hid a smile behind his hand, but I was used to this. Hadn't she always been there in the right place though not necessarily at the right time? Only my mother would dare to cause such a commotion during a marriage ceremony. She pulled me into her strong little arms then reached across to pat David on the shoulder. 'I had to make sure she was sure. If she'd taken any notice of me, I'd have known you were wrong for her. You have to test her at times. You'll find that out once you're wed,' she said, paying no heed at all to the small congregation who gasped at this interruption.

Then she turned her attention to the poor clergyman. 'No disrespect to Tom,' she announced, 'but this here is my only daughter. I gave her life and she owns herself, always has and always will. So nobody gives this woman. My daughter gives herself.'

The vicar, a man of about six feet in height, stared open-mouthed at this tiny intruder.

She looked him up and down. 'It's alright,' she said. 'I've finished now. You can carry on when you're ready.'

She stood by my side throughout the rest of the service, her little head held high and proud while I married David Pritchard. After the service, she pursued us into the registry then out into a bright August sun.

'I'm a daft old bat,' she said, her hat askew after hugging me and David. 'But I'll never be any different, will I?'

'No Nancy,' answered my husband. 'You're incurable, thank God.'

She took me aside. 'Nay lass. I couldn't let you get married without me here, could I? There's no show without Punch.'

'Or Judy, Mother.'

She smiled broadly. 'That's right. Let's never forget Judy.'

Author's Note

A very special thankyou to those men and women who, in spite of some distress, managed to share their experiences with me. The help they gave was invaluable. In all these new friends, I found an unquenchable thirst for living, an unusual tenderness of heart and actual proof that meaningful life can and does continue after damage.

None of us can condone my Annie's way of coping, but, taking into account the era in which this author placed her, we should at least understand her great dilemma. Even in these more enlightened times, situations like hers do exist, cries for help are not always heard.

My prayer is that all our Annies will find the courage to speak out, the strength to persevere and, eventually, the ability to forgive a society which often fails to notice. If this novel helps to save just one child, then it will have done its job.

Ruth Hamilton.